THE FLAME KING'S BRIDE

FIRE AND DESIRE 2

CHLOE CHASTAINE

THE FLAME KING'S BRIDE

Chloe Chastaine

His desire for me burns hotter than flames, but unseen forces threaten to tear us apart.

I was the Flame King's reluctant mate, a bride he snatched from another man's funeral pyre. Zabriel was chosen for me by fate, and I fought my craving for him every step of the way.

At seven feet tall and riding the biggest, meanest dragon in the flare, Zabriel is an Alpha who can take whatever he wants and burn those who stand in his way. Yet he healed my wounded heart with coaxing words and fiery kisses until I craved no one but him.

In the midst of war, I found love in the arms of the Flame King.

My first heat is drawing closer and soon Zabriel will finally claim me and make me his. I'm his Omega and his bride, but I'm also a witch. There are many in Maledin who would rather see me burn than become Zabriel's bride, or even kill their king before he can marry me.

Friends wear masks that conceal their blood-soaked intentions. Enemies past and present are sharpening their knives. Dragons hunt for prey, and protecting the man I love could leave my heart bleeding on ashes.

Author's note: The Flame King's Bride is a steamy, non-shifter MF romance set in a fantasy world of magic and dragonriders. Zabriel is a possessive hero, and Isavelle is a strong but sweet heroine. This is the second book in the Fire and Desire trilogy and ends on a cliffhanger.

AUTHOR'S NOTE

This book has a size difference, knotting, slicks, nesting, and scenting (but no shifting). Zabriel is a batshit obsessed hero, and Isavelle is innocent and sweet but clever enough to wrangle this king. On a serious note, this book has swearing, blood, mentions of sexual assault, violence, death, and detailed sex scenes on page. It is not suitable for those under eighteen.

1

———

Zabriel

Burning, blistering pain. It drags across my flesh with talons of pure fire. Blisters bubble up and burst open, each one a fresh surge of agony that makes me writhe upon the ground. I grit my jaw so hard that my teeth might shatter.

Scourge looms over me in the canyon, his red eyes narrowed in disgust.

"Like you never did anything foolish in a rut," I pant. Sweat runs down my face and drips onto the dust. I'm stark naked, my elbows braced against the ground with my fists clenched, and despite all the pain, my cock is stubbornly hard.

My knot is *aching*.

Even ablaze with agony, I want my Omega. Isavelle ran to

fetch help after I was showered in fiery sparks inside the burning eyrie. Though my back has been completely burned, I kept my word. Not one ember touched her skin.

Scourge snorts through his nostrils and slams his taloned forelegs against the ground. It's his rut as well as mine, and I just ruined it for both of us. Esmeral has run off as well. Scourge and I chased Isavelle and Esmeral through the skies over the castle before catching up to them at the old wyvern eyrie atop the cliffs. Scourge set the tower of the building afire when our Omegas fled inside, and instead of chasing them out, I decided that was the ideal moment to tear off my Omega's clothes and finally make her mine.

And make her mine I did. My knot throbs at the memory. I saw her beautiful body for the first time and squeezed every lush handful of her. I tasted her. Isavelle's slick was gushing between her thighs. My Omega let me fuck her. The memory alone causes heat and pain to surge through me so strongly that I nearly pass out. I barely got anywhere. She's not in a heat. She was too tight, but she was so eager for me.

Previously, Isavelle has been so afraid of me. My scent meant nothing to her, and she didn't recognize me as her mate or her Alpha. There have been times when I've wondered if she would ever allow me to bestow a kiss on her lips, let alone push my tongue and my cock inside her sex.

But every week, day, month, or second that I waited for her was worth it to hear Isavelle beg me to thrust into her. Isavelle wanted me, not her heat. I earned Isavelle's trust and desire slowly, and our bond is all the sweeter for it.

Everything was going beautifully until a burning building collapsed on top of us.

My back is a lake of agony. Burns aren't life-threatening

for Maledinni, though they are painful, and healing from them this rapidly? Excruciating. My reddened flesh seethes and boils. Sweat beads on my forehead and drips down my nose.

This isn't the first time I've had to suffer through the debilitating pain of a healing burn. When I was seventeen, I flew with Stesha and a group of young dragonriders into the mountains to hunt down an enemy spellcaster. It was a lich. A powerful, undead mage possessing destructive magic and the ability to dominate and control living beings that had fled its home in neighboring Grendu and was terrorizing mountain villages.

It should have been an easy mission. Nilak, Stesha's dragon, followed the lich's scent and led us to its lair in a mountain cave. There were six of us, including the dragonmaster: myself; my brother, Emmeric; my sister, Mirelle; Stesha's ward, Zenevieve; and my best friend, Onderz. I was the eldest, and Mirelle was the youngest at just fourteen. My father was against Mirelle going because of her age and the fact that she was an Omega, but Mother wished her timid daughter to learn some self-confidence before she was mated. Father appealed to the dragonmaster, expecting him to forbid a weak and useless Omega from being in his hunting party.

Stesha folded his arms and thought about this for a long time. It wasn't a comfortable place to be, trapped between the king and queen. He was going to disappoint one of them with his answer, and everyone knew it was dangerous to disappoint the king.

To everyone's surprise, Stesha sided with the queen, stating that every dragonrider has the right and responsibility to make themselves useful to Maledin, including Omegas. So Mirelle came with us.

Up on the wintry mountain, Mirelle's face was white from terror as she and her dragon, Dianthe, stood at the mouth of the lich's lair. None of the bigger dragons could enter the long, narrow cave to help their riders search for the lich's phylactery—the magical vessel that held the evil mage's soul tethered to this earth.

Stesha stood with his arms folded and his brows drawn tightly together as Mirelle and Dianthe slowly and cautiously moved into the cave.

Onderz darted forward. "I'll go with you, Mirelle."

Stesha put out a hand and held him back. "She's an Omega, not a snowball on a summer's day. Stay where you are."

As my sister and her dragon disappeared into the darkness, Emmeric called after them, "Be careful not to touch anything. You never know what might rip your soul painfully from your body in a lich's lair."

Mirelle's whimper echoed back to us, but she and Dianthe kept moving. The tip of Dianthe's tail disappeared, and then there was silence from within the tunnel.

Onderz paced back and forth, and it was only the fact that Stesha was bigger and stronger than he was that prevented him from running after his mate. I was feeling uneasy that my sister was in a lich's lair. She had Dianthe to protect her, but still.

What felt like an eon later, there were sounds in the tunnel, and then Mirelle and Dianthe appeared, the dragon carrying something in her jaws. Mirelle beamed at us, flushed with accomplishment. "The cavern at the end was big enough for Dianthe to turn around in, and look what we found."

The dragon carefully laid the object onto the snow, and we all clustered around to look at it. The phylactery resembled a silver lantern with greenish flames flickering within.

Stesha glanced at Mirelle. "It must be destroyed. Will you and Dianthe do the honors?"

My sister turned toward her dragon and spoke with her silently. The dragon focused on the object and a rumbling emanated from deep within her chest. She opened her jaws, and we all jumped back as a stream of yellow dragonfire shot toward the phylactery, completely engulfing it. Snow melted away in a ten-foot radius. We felt the scorching heat of the fire and heard something unnatural shrieking in anger and pain.

Dianthe closed her jaws, but the fire burned on for several more minutes. When it died down, Stesha crouched and carefully inspected the melted and twisted object. There wasn't a flicker of green left. The phylactery was blackened and empty.

He got to his feet and nodded sharply at Mirelle. "Good."

An avalanche of praise from the dragonmaster.

Mirelle was so relieved and happy it was all over that she hugged her dragon's slender neck and nearly burst into tears. Emmeric opened his mouth to say something snide, but Onderz elbowed him in the stomach. My brother bent double, gasping for breath, while Onderz wrapped Mirelle tightly in his arms with a huge smile on his face.

Onderz and Mirelle were a fated pair, something they'd known for just a handful of weeks at that time. Seeing Onderz with my sister was...strange. My goofy, reckless friend seemed to change overnight. He wasn't just an Alpha anymore. He was Mirelle's Alpha. Everything he did now, he thought about her first. He might not say her name, but I could always see my sister reflected in his eyes. I was three months older than Onderz, and I was the crown prince. Where was *my* Omega? It didn't work like that, and I had no right to expect an Omega just because I would rule Maledin one day. Hundreds of Alphas who believed they were deserving were passed over by the gods. Look at Stesha. He held the second highest position in the country after my father, and he won every tournament and fight against the other Alphas. He might be a surly, demanding bastard, but he was tough as dragonhide and you would think the gods would want a dozen little Steshas running around Lenhale. Yet he didn't have an Omega, and he never would. It was too late for him, but there was still time for me.

My chest ached as I looked around at the barren mountainscape. I felt sure that I was supposed to mate an Omega.

So where *was* she?

Stesha mounted Nilak and yelled at us to get a move on, reminding us that the destroyed phylactery would draw the lich back to his lair. We all scrambled back onto our dragons and flew into the sky. Wingrunners and experienced dragonriders would hunt down the lich, which was a far more dangerous task.

The first sign that we'd lingered too long and the lich had returned was an enormous ball of green magic hurtling right toward me. I heard Stesha shout a warning, but Scourge and I were already banking hard, and the magic skimmed past his black, scaly body.

The lich was beneath us on the mountainside somewhere.

I craned around to see what Nilak was doing. If the dragonmaster wanted us to flee, we would follow. The pristine white dragon dived and unleashed a great torrent of dragonfire. My heart leaped, and a moment later, every other dragon joined in. Zenevieve on Minta. Emmeric on Shar. Onderz on Zeith. Shortly after, the mountainside was ablaze. There was so much fire and smoke that it was difficult to see, but Scourge spied the dark shape of the mage fleeing down the mountain and gave chase. My dragon caught up with him easily, his scales glowing with heat, and he unleashed the biggest torrent of dragonfire that I'd ever seen from him. The lich disappeared beneath the molten heat with a scream.

We circled over the spot, hunting for any sign that the lich had shielded himself. When the flames died down, we landed.

I dismounted and drew my sword, but I could already see that there wasn't much left of the lich apart from a smear of ashes and bones. He could probably do with another blast of dragonfire, just to be sure, but as far as I could see, the lich was defeated. By us, trainee dragonriders. By the crown prince and his dragon. I was anxious to prove myself as the future ruler of Maledin, and I was suddenly awash with overconfidence and foolish pride.

I raised my sword in victory, not realizing that Scourge had already heeded my mental wish for more dragonfire and had opened his jaws. Liquid fire engulfed my hand and sword. I dropped the burning metal and grasped my elbow with a scream. My whole hand and forearm were ablaze, and

I could feel the dragonfire eating away at my flesh. The pain was so severe that I nearly blacked out.

There was the sound of dragons landing, people shouting, and running feet. Two people that I thought were Onderz and Stesha grabbed hold of me from either side, hauled me over to a snowdrift, and then forced me to shove my arm into it. Instantly the snow evaporated with a hiss into gouts of steam. Everyone heaped more snow onto my arm. More and more, on and on, until finally the glow of fire died away.

Stesha was standing over me with his hands on his hips, glacial blue eyes lit with fury. "Zabriel, I have never seen anything so manifestly senseless in all my life. What the hell do you think you're doing?"

I wanted to shout at the dragonmaster, *Isn't it obvious what I'm doing? I'm in fucking agony.* "My hand, by the gods, my hand."

"Whose fault is it that you're burned?" Stesha demands.

Even as I was writhing about in pain, the dragonmaster was going to lecture me. "I know, I *know*."

"I said, whose fault is it?" He glares around at the others to check that they're listening to this important lesson.

"Mine, dragonmaster," I say through clenched teeth. It's always the rider's fault and never the dragon's. Stesha drummed that into us before we were even allowed to mount up. If someone is trampled, burned, gnawed, or slashed by a dragon, it's the rider who must take responsibility. *Dragons aren't stupid*, Stesha told us. *People are.*

Zenevieve shot me a sympathetic look as she helped Mirelle pack the snow tighter around me. Onderz dumped so much snow onto my arm that I nearly disappeared beneath it.

Only Emmeric stood back, and there was laughter in his eyes as he grinned at me.

Shar, my brother's beautiful midnight blue dragon with golden flourishes, sensed his rider's good mood and lowered his head companionably onto Emmeric's shoulder, resting it there.

Emmeric immediately shoved him away with a muttered, "Get off."

Shar retreated a few paces and hunched low to the ground with his head bowed, the posture of an unhappy dragon.

The snow finally stopped melting, and I drew my arm out. My leather armor had burned away, and so had a great deal of my flesh. My arm was an angry red mess of blackened tissue, and some of the bones of my hand were visible. I grimaced at the gruesome sight. This was going to be painful as hell while it healed. I would be stuck in the Flame Temple for weeks.

Scourge snorted and pressed the smooth, flat part of his head against my back. He was sorry. He was so sorry. He hadn't meant to hurt me.

I only had one thought for Scourge, and I sent it to him over and over again. *You're the best and bravest dragon in all of Maledin.*

"Blood and wyvern piss, Zabriel," Stesha muttered, pinching his eyes and sighing. For a foolish second, I believed I was about to receive some sympathy. Stesha threw up his hand. "I will have to waste your father's time with this."

Oh, dear, I thought sarcastically. The crown prince was

injured on one of Stesha's missions. My flesh and skin will regrow, and this injury will barely leave a mark, but what about the dragonmaster's precious reputation? Did I not spare a thought for his good name when I injured myself so selfishly?

Stesha gave me one last glare, turned on his heel, and strode back to Nilak.

"How do you live with him?" I snarled to Zenevieve under my breath.

"Oh, he's fine. The dragonmaster isn't nearly as fierce as he seems," she said with a shrug and then smiled mischievously at me. "But I don't get on his nerves like you do."

"I didn't get burned to annoy Stesha," I snapped at her.

Everyone knew that Zenevieve was Stesha's favorite, which was even more apparent fifteen minutes later when Zenevieve went to remount her dragon and accidentally sliced her palm on a half-shed scale. Stesha heard her cry of pain and went over to see what the problem was. There was the tiniest trickle of blood on the Beta's palm, which she hid behind her back. She only offered it up to the dragonmaster after he demanded to see it.

If anyone but Zenevieve made a peep about such a little cut, they would have been blasted with the full force of the dragonmaster's ire for wasting his time. Stesha examined Zenevieve's hand like it was critically injured, then he licked the pad of his thumb and tenderly drew it over her cut. Alpha saliva is healing. There were three Alphas in the party, not including myself, but no one had offered to lick *my* wounds.

I turned the blackened, twisted mess of my hand and forearm back and forth in the pale sunlight. Maybe I couldn't blame them. Even I didn't want to put something so gross in my mouth.

Emmeric was watching Stesha and Zenevieve with a nasty smirk on his lips as if he was amused by some private joke.

"What's so funny?" I asked.

"So many things that are far, far over your head," my brother responded with a nasty laugh.

Whatever that meant.

At the time, I dismissed the things Emmeric said due to his contrary nature. I didn't believe he felt one-tenth of the contempt that he showed for me, our family, his dragon. I've learned that painful lesson in the years since. When someone shows you who they are, doubt them at your peril.

As soon as Stesha headed back to Nilak and was out of earshot, I called to Zenevieve in mock concern, "Are you sure you'll survive?"

Zenevieve was smiling as she gazed after Stesha, and she turned red from embarrassment. "Don't tease me. You know Stesha gave my dying father his oath that he'd keep me safe. He takes his promises seriously."

I wanted to rile her up even more by calling her the dragonmaster's pet. My arm throbbed, but as annoyed as I was with Stesha, I was glad that Zenevieve was smiling and so meticulously protected after her parents were killed. Besides, if I upset her, Stesha would tell Nilak to belt me with her tail down the mountainside.

After we all returned to Lenhale, I spent a painful week in the Flame Temple's infirmary regrowing all the burned flesh on my arm.

I stare at my right hand as pain flickers over my back. Six

years later, there's barely a sign that I ever bore such a severe injury. I could do with someone heaping snow on me now, but there's been a thaw recently.

Smoke is pouring from Scourge's nostrils, and he's pulsating with frustration.

"Stop glaring at me. I want to be up to my knot in Omega as well. As soon as I can stand up, we'll go find them."

I got carried away with the *I am the fire* thing, but every Alpha goes halfway crazy during their ruts, and how could I not lose grip on reality the first time I had my Omega beneath me, wet and panting and so eager for me to make her mine? I waited months for Isavelle to finally accept me, and while I don't begrudge her even one of those days, it's also not in an Alpha's nature to be patient. I had to fight my instincts to claim her for weeks on end. With the sparks drifting down around us, all I could think of was how perfect it was to be spending my first rut with her amid ash and flame. Isavelle wasn't even close to taking all of me, but my sweet girl was trying. When I get her in a false heat, she'll likely be able to take me all the way to my knot. Then when she's finally in heat...gods.

The cavern is shadowy, rocky, and empty except for me and Scourge's bulk filling the narrow space. The scent of honeysuckle and sticky sweet apple fritters is all over me. My Omega's slick.

I groan and push a hand through my hair, a fresh wave of desire surging through me, and I sit up with a growl. My rut is nowhere near over. My knot is aching. Where the fuck is my Omega? I never explained to her about Maledinni and fire. If I were human, I would have been killed just now, it's very hard to harm a fully grown adult with flames. A single limb or even two limbs engulfed by dragonfire? Survivable. More than that? Possibly.

If only Isavelle had lingered for another moment, she would have seen my flesh begin to heal on its own. I struggle to my feet and limp along the canyon, my knot bumping against my thighs with every step. Scourge follows behind me, hungry to sink his teeth into Esmeral's neck. She and her rider have likely headed for the Flame Temple to beg the *Hratha'len* to come help me. I picture how the Temple Mothers' lips will twitch as they gently reassure my Omega that her mate is perfectly all right and she should hurry back to him. She's probably on her way back to me right this second. I straighten my back and pick up the pace. I'm still in pain, but my strength is returning.

A piercing scream emanates from the far end of the canyon toward the dragongrounds. Esmeral's scream, and it's filled with terror and fury.

A wave of alarm passes through me. "*Isavelle.*"

Scourge thunders along behind me, and as soon as he has space to spread his wings, he leaps into the sky and soars overhead. I reach the dragongrounds to discover the flare clustered together, their necks craning as the dragons hunt for something. I skid to a halt and breathe in deeply, trying to find Isavelle. The scent of my Omega lingers in the air, but she's not here.

The small turquoise and gold dragon is turning on the spot, frantically searching for her rider. Scourge roars overhead, and all the dragons scatter. Still no sight of Isavelle. My dragon lands beside Esmeral and presses the top of his head to the smaller dragon's flank, urging her to communicate to him what happened.

I break into a run, my heart in my mouth. Scourge rounds on me with a roar, and the mental pulse he sends me nearly knocks me off my feet. In images and sensations, he tells me what Esmeral has seen.

Isavelle disappearing, pulled through some strange, flickering doorway.

Isavelle is gone.

2

————

Isavelle

"I said, get on your knees, girl." The High Priest seizes me by the hair and pushes me to the floor. I cry out in pain and try to pull away from him, but he's stronger than he looks.

"You reek of a man. You reek of sex," he snarls. Loose robes adorn his body, and a cowl covers his head. From beneath the shadowy hood, his gray eyes burn with hatred, and his silvery bearded jaw is clenched tight. "You touched him, and you let him paw at you. Hold out your disgusting hands."

My hands have caressed Zabriel's handsome face. Clung to him in fear and in love. Touched his body to give him pleasure. Delighted in my mate's strength and size. There's nothing disgusting about any of that, and no one will ever make me believe that again.

"I won't," I say in a voice that shakes with anger and fear. "I've done nothing—"

He grasps my wrist, pulls my arm out, and cracks a birch rod across my palm, causing a violent red welt. I cry out, and tears spring into my eyes. My flesh burns and starts to bleed. The High Priest strikes me again and again until blood runs freely over my fingers and tears down my cheeks.

Finally, he lets me go, and I crumple to the floor, clutching my bleeding hand to my heart and shaking with sobs.

The High Priest stands over me, breathing hard. "Filthy. Unclean. Blood and pain can only begin to cleanse you of your sins. You must be made penitent." I can feel his eyes scouring me with revulsion and sadistic delight. "Where else did he touch you? Did he tend to the wounds we so righteously scored into your flesh? Did he grope your body and do foul things to it?"

Sweet memories flood my mind. Zabriel, holding me in his arms, both of us submerged in blissfully heated water while he uncovered all the bruises and cuts on my body. Zabriel touching me so tenderly. Zabriel filled with rage at the sight of all my injuries. I wasn't even aware of his scent then, but I was still drunk on it. Even more intoxicating was the fact that he cared I was hurting. He was filled with blistering rage and swore vengeance on my torturers.

I take a deep, calming breath and wipe the tears from my cheeks. I've survived the High Priest before. I can do it again. "You can beat me as much as you like. You'll never change how I feel about Zabriel."

"We'll see about that. Hold out your other hand."

If I don't do as he says, he'll force me. If I submit, then I'll be admitting that I am unclean. Good Brethren girls should be ashamed to want a man to do so-called repulsive things to her. If I won't feel shame, then he will make me feel it.

I fought hard to rid myself of all the shame I felt when Zabriel wanted to kiss me and touch me. My body responded to his in ways that shocked me and delighted him. I made Zabriel suffer through weeks of rejection and self-doubt. He blamed himself for my tears and confusion. I won't do that to Zabriel again. I will hold out my hand to the High Priest, but not in defeat. He can beat me if he likes, but no amount of pain will change how I feel about my mate.

I raise both hands, palm up, but I also raise my chin and meet the priest's hateful eyes. "Do as you wish. It's nothing to me anymore."

Annoyance flickers over the High Priest's cruel features. I'm supposed to cower before him and sob for forgiveness, but instead, I'm making a mockery of my submission by daring to stare back at him.

He takes a firmer grip on the rod and brings it down across my palms. The pain makes me flinch, but I can bear it. I've been beaten so many times, in so many ways, by so many priests. Instead, I think of Zabriel.

Zabriel.

My Alpha. My mate. My king. He must be in so much pain from his burns. I refuse to believe he's dying because the Flame King can't possibly perish in a fire. I'll find my way back to my king and my dragon, Esmeral. Turquoise and gold flash in my heart. Bright, happy colors. In my mind, I hear her excited trill of greeting and the leathery rustle of her wings. My friend. My twin.

As the High Priest beats me, I look right at him, and he

doesn't like that. Finally, he screams in outrage and backhands me across the face. I fly to the side, and my cheek throbs, but I can't help but laugh. He really thought that I would submit to him.

Deep, masculine laughter fills the tower, echoing my own. With my cheek pressed against the flagstones, my body clenches in fear.

Emmeric strides forward. "Yes, it's funny, isn't it? I laughed just like this as I impaled your mother and brother on spikes."

It's a very different feeling when Emmeric looms over me. A chill sweeps down my spine. I push myself into a seated position and turn to him. Zabriel's brother wears long, dark robes with ornate decorations. His hair is long and brown, and his gray eyes are very cold. I study him minutely, the man I mistook for my mate.

Emmeric gives me a wintry smile and cups my jaw, caressing it with icy fingers. How is he so cold? "We look alike, Zabriel and me. There is only one year between us, and people often said we were so alike that we were more like twins. Still, you think an Omega would know her own Alpha."

There are differences that I should have noticed. Emmeric's face is narrower, and his body is leaner. Zabriel has an athletic, muscular body, but Emmeric doesn't look as if he's accustomed to lifting anything heavier than a book. His eyebrows are thin rather than thick, and his complexion is pale while Zabriel is tanned, and of course, he doesn't have Zabriel's black hair and red eyes. Zabriel's features changed to those dramatic colors after he bonded with Scourge.

"Have you bonded with him?" Emmeric sneers. "Oh, I

hope you have. It will be all the sweeter for me knowing that he fills your heart, and all it took were a few sad words from me to fool you. I never imagined I would meet another Omega, but it's amusing knowing they're still as brainless as they always were."

I jerk my chin out of this hateful man's grasp. "I never imagined I would meet the Shadow King only to discover he's a weakling cowering behind a magical barrier."

Emmeric's eyes narrow for a fraction of a second. Maybe he is scared of Zabriel and the might of his dragon army.

I push even harder on that tender spot. "How does it feel knowing that after he was freed, it took just one week for Zabriel and his dragons to kick you and your disgusting Brethren out of Maledin?"

"Shut your mouth, girl," the High Priest snarls. "You will not speak in this manner to your husband."

I stare between the two men in shock. "Husband? What are you talking about? I'm not marrying *him*."

The rod is twitching in the High Priest's hand like he's dying to use it again. "The false king will not make you his queen. You belong to the Shadow King. You were being brought here weeks ago when that traitor snatched you away."

Emmeric settles on the edge of a cluttered desk, folds his arms, and smirks at me.

"Zabriel is not a traitor to Maledin. Zabriel has liberated Maledin from the Brethren who treat us like we're nothing, and he didn't steal me from you. He saved me because he's my mate and I'm his." I didn't think of it as being saved at the time, but now I see things clearly. I know his scent, and it sings to me. I will be Zabriel's queen and no one else's.

"Mate," the High Priest seethes. "Like you're some kind of animal. The church does not recognize mates. You will be purified of that man's contamination, and then you will be presented to the Shadow King."

"Your wife?" I say to Emmeric. "I would rather die. You won't lay a finger on me."

Emmeric neither moves nor speaks. Suddenly, an invisible cord wraps around my wrists and throat. I'm yanked up into the air, my head thrown back as I struggle to breathe. The cord tightens maliciously. My legs flail in the air. Black dots swarm before my eyes, and my heart pounds in panic.

"Of course you would rather die," Emmeric says, sounding bored. "You'll take care of that yourself once I'm done with you, just like Mirelle did. Omegas are so predictable."

He doesn't want me, I realize. He wants me dead. This man raped his sister, and she was so distraught that she threw herself from her dragon and died. Her mate followed her into death, and Zabriel and his family were devastated. If I kill myself after this monster finishes with me, Zabriel won't want to live, and Emmeric will win.

Pain fills my heart as I picture my Alpha's grief-stricken face, his heart brimming with pain because I suffered the same fate as his sister. I can't allow that to happen to the man I love. Maledin needs him.

Emmeric moves in front of me. I feel the hem of my dress being lifted. I'm wearing nothing beneath it. A cold hand wraps around my inner thigh.

"No," I wheeze. "Don't."

I'm on the verge of passing out when the magical bonds release me, and I fall painfully onto the stone floor in a heap. I lean on my palms, dragging breath back into my lungs.

Emmeric leans down and whispers, "I will do whatever the fuck I want with you."

I squeeze my eyes shut in horror, still feeling the ghost of that corpse-like hand gripping my thigh. There will still be enough pieces of me for Zabriel to love after Emmeric is done with me, won't there? My mate's touch will still feel warm and loving?

As if he's proved his point, Emmeric strolls back to his desk and continues conversationally, "So you see, it won't be long until you're dead and my brother and his flying beasts are trapped beneath tons of rock once more. What a trying few weeks it's been. I've had hundreds of years of peace while the Brethren take care of all the little sheep in Maledin. I've been making such excellent progress with my work. Then up springs my brother again, and suddenly Maledin reeks of the Maledinni." He wrinkles his nose. "Humans are an annoyance but at least they don't stink. As you die, don't forget that this is all your fault for being a stupid little Omega who mistook me for your mate."

He's right. I should have known my own Alpha even though I was confused by my visions and impossible things were happening one after the next. I might have figured it out sooner, only in my vision Emmeric—

Emmeric acted like he knew me.

Didn't just know me. Longed for me. His disgust at the way I smell is an afterthought. He's pretending, and I want to know why. I think back to the first time I encountered Emmeric and the longing on his face. The way he reached for me.

Everything clicks into place, and suddenly I know a lot more about Emmeric than he undoubtedly wants me to know.

"After all this time, you still want one," I say, shaking my head in wonder. "You thought you deserved one. That you were being given one."

"What are you talking about?" Emmeric snaps.

He might not have his dragines. I have no interest at all in finding out whether he has a knot, but Emmeric is still an Alpha.

"When I appeared before you all those weeks ago, you knew what I was right away. An Omega."

"Of course."

"You thought I was yours."

Emmeric's eyes blaze, his nostrils whiten in fury, and he spits, "How dare you? I am dragonless. I am *pure*. I rid myself centuries ago of my designation. A mate would be less than useless to me."

I calmly meet his blistering gaze. "You're getting so angry because I'm right. If I die, it won't be by my hand or because of my stupidity. It will be because of your childish spite that Zabriel was granted something that you weren't."

Emmeric is torn between losing his temper and pretending he doesn't understand what I'm talking about. His eyes are filled with rage, but his face is fighting for control over his expression.

A stupid little Omega figured him out, and he hates it.

"Foul little witch," Emmeric seethes, shooting to his feet. "Witches always had lying tongues and disgusting, dirty minds. The witchfinders should have slaughtered you as a child, but none of them could do as they were told."

"It's not me, obviously, but perhaps you were granted an Omega," I say, and I marvel at how calm I sound. I'm about to die, but I'll go out knowing that I've given this hateful man a few moments of misery. "Do you think she's out there? Maybe you already killed her hundreds of years ago and you didn't even notice. Maybe she's alive in Maledin right now, her Omega nature awakening, longing for the Alpha that she'll never be able to love because he's completely lost his mind. But if she were alive, that would mean you have a chance to redeem yourself and be loved, and after everything you've done, I don't think you deserve it. No, you were never granted an Omega and you never will be."

"Only an Omega would be self-centered enough to believe that the reason I've devoted myself to my life's work is because I wasn't granted a stupid little doll to fuck."

I nod in mock sympathy. "You're right, it probably wasn't the only reason. Zabriel was your parents' favorite. That must have hurt too."

The tower room throbs with silence.

The High Priest lifts his arm and strikes me across the face with the birch rod. I tumble to one side, crying out in pain, and my eyes swim with tears. My cheek stings, but I barely have time to press my palm to my bleeding face before the High Priest lashes me all over my body. My arms. My chest. My bare legs. My back.

I scream in pain. How is this real? I was safe. Zabriel was my protector, the dragons and their riders overthrew the Brethren, and nothing like this was ever supposed to happen to me again.

Emmeric thinks Omegas are stupid and weak, and maybe he's going to destroy me, but I'm not going quietly. "Is it because Zabriel was born to be king that you hate him so much? Because everyone loves him? Because he possesses the biggest dragon? Or were you *surprised* when everyone turned on you for raping your sister?"

I keep it up as long as I can, but soon, my head aches and my ears ring. Blood stings my eyes. I regret not one word of what I've said, but the pain is unlike anything I've ever known. As I writhe in my own blood, Emmeric gloats at me from across the room, his smile growing wider and wider. *This is better,* his glowing eyes say. *The mouthy bitch is finally getting what she deserves.*

If I don't do something, Emmeric is going to watch me be beaten to death.

"Please," I gasp, entreating the High Priest. "Please stop, you'll kill my baby."

The High Priest stops with the rod raised over his head, and his gray eyes are filled with surprise and uncertainty. "You're with child?"

"She's not with child," Emmeric says.

"Please, your emissary must have told you of my condition," I pant, wincing in pain as I sit up. It was quite the performance that Zabriel and I gave for the priest who came to Lenhale. The priest demanded that I be handed over to the so-called true King of Maledin. Zabriel and I were wearing very little as if we'd just been called from his bed, and Zabriel informed the priest that we were as good as married in Maledinni tradition. We had already slept together, and I was pregnant.

"Priest, you're a fool if you believe a word out of this girl's mouth," Emmeric says with scorn. "I'm beginning to wonder if you're the best choice to rule over Maledin in my stead if you're so easily manipulated by a stupid little bitch."

I entreat the High Priest with my eyes, pouring every ounce of sincerity into my expression that I can. Maybe I'm only delaying the inevitable, but it's something. I might find a way out of here. Zabriel could rescue me.

"But what if she is with child? The Brethren's teachings tell us that every unborn life is—"

Emmeric strides forward and knocks the High Priest aside, muttering, "Idiotic religious zealots." He stands over me with a fuming expression.

I cup my hand over my belly and gaze up at him in supplication, performing my little heart out. "It's the truth. Surely you have a shred of mercy in your heart."

"Me?" Emmeric says with a gleam in his eyes that turns my blood cold. He tips back his head and laughs, and the mannerism reminds me so much of Zabriel, only it's all wrong. Zabriel would never laugh while I was suffering.

Emmeric leans closer and inhales, and he says in a strange, rasping voice, "You reek of my vilest enemies. The boy with the black dragon. The girl who has lost her mind. The man with the white beast."

I gaze at him, perplexed. "Do you mean Zabriel, Zenevieve, and Stesha? Why don't you just say their names?"

Emmeric's eyes flare with a green fire, and he looks so frightening that I jerk back.

He closes his eyes, and when he opens them again, they're gray, and he smiles lazily at me. In his usual tone of voice, he says, "You're not pregnant. From the smell of you, you haven't even been through a proper heat cycle yet. I might reject everything about my former self, but I haven't forgotten it.

You think an Alpha can't tell, even me?" He sneers the word Alpha as if it's just as repulsive as I am.

The High Priest raises his whip once more, but Emmeric is still looming over me. He watches me for a long time with an inscrutable expression on his face. "Did you beg him to knot you even though you weren't in heat? No doubt my pathetic brother wouldn't do that, and he's been following the *Hratha'len's* rules like a good boy. Those hags have no idea what they're talking about. If an Omega craves a knot, I say give them a knot." A smile spreads over his face that's as achingly beautiful as Zabriel's, but it's all wrong. Twisted. Malicious.

He takes the birch rod from the High Priest and lashes it viciously across my face. My head whips to one side, and I go sprawling across the ground.

"I'm better than you disgusting, rutting, slicking fools," Emmeric seethes. "I was here long before you were born, and I'll be here long after you're dead. I'll keep cleansing the country of Maledinni. How did you enjoy my work in Amriste?"

Not long ago, Emmeric used Zenevieve to trick me into flying to Amriste, where I found half the village dead and impaled on spikes. My mother and twelve-year-old brother were among them. I searched so hard to find them alive, and it was the worst pain I'd ever endured knowing I'd failed.

Emmeric wants me to beg him to tell me where my missing father and sister are and if they still live, and as much as I need the answer, I know he'll never tell me. I scramble for something else to say. "Zenevieve. What did you do to her? Why did she pretend to be a woman called Odanna? How did you keep her alive all this time? Where's her dragon?"

Emmeric casts a sly smile at me. "Zenevieve was useful for a while. I almost forgot that she had a dragon. It's dead. Centuries ago. I killed it for fun."

Her dragon is dead and her mind broken. Poor Zenevieve. "Where's your dragon?" You were one of the king's sons so you must have a dragon.

"I killed him, too. I don't want or need a dragon." He reaches down and grabs me by the hair, dragging me up onto my knees. "You're boring me. Let's get this over with. It's a shame there isn't an Alpha with a knot around here. Then we could make sure you didn't go to your death without fulfilling your only purpose in life."

"Your Majesty." The High Priest hurries to Emmeric's side. "I think I can be of service. You shouldn't sully yourself with her dirty blood and degrading body." He sounds breathless and excited, and somehow even creepier than Emmeric. "Let me have her."

"What?" Emmeric snaps. "Don't be ridiculous. What can you do?"

The High Priest inhales deeply while staring at me. "She never smelled like this before. She never looked like this before."

"All she reeks of to me is Omega," Emmeric says through his teeth. He hasn't caught on to what the High Priest is saying, but I have, and horror prickles down my spine.

"Yes. She's different. I'm different. My teeth are aching. I smell things that I never have before. My appendage has had a strange swelling these past few days."

"What?" Emmeric pinches his brow. "This can't be happening."

The High Priest's eyes are feverish, and he doesn't seem to

have heard Emmeric. "Let me have her, Your Majesty. You asked for an Alpha with a knot. I'll make sure this Omega knows her place."

Emmeric sighs and gazes at the ceiling as if his patience has worn so thin it's about to snap. "The Maledinni have always been a thorn in my ass. Humans are far easier to control. A little fear. A little pain. They *want* to obey. They don't start getting stupid fucking ideas and wanting to mate with everything that moves." He waves his hand at the High Priest as if shooing a fly. An enormous wave of power knocks the High Priest into a wall. He slides to the ground and falls into a heap. "Get out of my sight."

The High Priest gets painfully to his feet. "But you said you wanted her to suffer the ultimate humiliation. I can do that. For you," he adds quickly.

"I told you what your job was. You're to beat her, not fuck her."

"But you said she must be—"

"Cease telling me what I have or have not said," Emmeric shouts at the top of his lungs, "or I will hurl you from this tower and watch your body smash upon the rocks."

As Emmeric and the High Priest shout at one another, I crawl toward the door. The High Priest, an Alpha. How sickening that a man like him should be granted an Alpha's strength and instincts when he will never act as a true Alpha should.

I make it all the way to the door, and I'm unnoticed as I open it and slip out onto a landing with a descending spiral staircase. Then I get to my feet and run, fingers brushing the walls as I turn down and down and down. I don't know where

I'm going or what I'm going to do except find a way out of this place or at least somewhere to hide.

The staircase ends in a darkened corridor. I seem to be in a castle similar to Zabriel's home in Lenhale, but it's a lot older and crumblier. I can hear Brethren voices up ahead, droning in prayer. Behind me, two male voices are raised in anger. Emmeric and the High Priest have noticed that I'm gone.

I yank open a nearby door and glimpse some dusty stairs descending into darkness, and I hurry in and close the door behind me. I'm enveloped in suffocating darkness, and a stuffy, moldy scent fills my nose. I press my ear to the door and listen.

"Find her, or I will have your head."

"Oh, I'll find her."

There's an explosion, and I wonder if Emmeric has blasted the High Priest into a wall again. "If you do anything that I have not ordered you to do, I will rip the living flesh from your bones."

There's no response from the High Priest.

Heavy footsteps sound along the corridor. The droning prayers cease as Emmeric shrieks, "Find the girl, or I will execute every last one of you."

I can't go back into that corridor, so I'll have to go down into darkness. I keep one hand against the stone wall to steady myself, trying not to think about spiders or rats. There's not a single breath of fresh air or one ray of light, and I wonder if this is what Zabriel suffered for five hundred years beneath the mountain.

The stairs end at a door so dusty and stiff that I have to push hard against it for several minutes. Finally, it gives way and springs open, and I stumble into a large room. There is some moonlight coming through narrow windows. I close the door behind me and wait as my eyes adjust, hoping I haven't reached a dead end.

There's a dark shape on the ground that's so large that for a long time I think that it *is* the ground. As it slowly comes into focus, I gasp in shock at what I see before me.

3

____

Zabriel

I take the steps up to the Great Hall three at a time and grasp both handles on the massive double doors. They weigh a ton and normally take four men each to move them, but my panic and rut give me the strength to pull them both open at once.

Just a few hours ago, I sat on the throne at the head of the room, a hairsbreadth from sentencing Zenevieve, a former trusted and beloved dragonrider, to death for betraying the people of Maledin. The room was filled with people who listened as she admitted to all her crimes in a dull, lifeless voice. Only Isavelle reminded me that I was in a rut and of my wish to be merciful. The young woman is now locked in the dungeons.

The Great Hall is full of many of the same people. They stand in casual groups, no doubt discussing the day's calamitous events, which include the king and his dragon chasing their Omegas through the skies over the castle.

I stride forward, calling out, "Isavelle has been taken. Every dragonrider, every wingrunner, report to the dragongrounds or the eyrie and await orders."

Conversations cease. Heads turn toward me. Mouths fall open.

Godric, my second-in-command, a dour man in his forties with a hooked nose and fair hair raises his eyebrows. Ashton, captain of the wingrunners, a company of swift and fierce wyvernriders, has frozen with a crust of bread halfway to his lips. Dusan, one of Isavelle's wingrunner bodyguards, is pouring ale for Fiala, her other bodyguard, and it overflows while he gapes at me.

I'm accustomed to my orders being obeyed within a fraction of a second. Now, everyone gazes at me as if I've sprouted two heads.

"*Now*," I shout. I infuse my command with an Alpha's roar, and it reverberates off the walls, the ceiling, and every set of eardrums in the place. A roar can't force a person to do something they don't want to do, but it can strongly compel them, depending on their designation. An Omega is the most susceptible.

Everyone snaps out of their confusion and hurries to follow my orders.

Godric makes his way toward me through the crowd, his brows drawn tightly together. "When did this happen, *Ma'len*? How did this happen? Are there enemies within the castle at this moment? I will dispatch soldiers to any place you name."

I don't know how to answer him. It should have been

impossible for Isavelle to have been kidnapped. Our enemies should not have been able to infiltrate this place. "My mate was taken by magic from the dragongrounds just minutes ago. I believe it was the Shadow King, which means Isavelle has been taken behind the barrier to the south. We must fly there at once. I need dragonriders. I need the spellbreakers."

A voice speaks at my elbow. "May we inform the Temple Crone that the spellbreakers are required while we're on our way to the eyrie, *Ma'len*?"

I turn and see Fiala, a stocky woman with a habitual scowl, though at this moment, her eyes are filled with concern. Isavelle's bodyguards no doubt believed that she was safe while she was with me. "Yes. Go. And then report to the eyrie."

Captain Ashton passes us, and I call to him, "Captain, how many wingrunners are presently in Lenhale?"

He answers promptly. "Forty-three, *Ma'len*."

"Take three dozen to the barrier immediately. I will send a dragon to wait by the Proxen Road, and you are to inform the rider if you sight any Brethren or enemy mages."

Ashton nods sharply. "At once, *Ma'len*." He hurries out of the hall.

Everyone else is staring at me, soldier, maid, and worker alike. I feel the weight of their shock like an accusation I well deserve.

"They're all so disappointed in me," I mutter to Godric. "I can see it in their eyes. I've let them all down by not protecting their future queen."

Godric clears his throat. "Actually, *Ma'len*, I believe that people are staring because they are not accustomed to seeing...well, quite so much of their king."

I look down at myself. I'm stark naked. I've burst into the Great Hall in a rut, shouting my head off and wearing nothing but smears of ash. My knot is swollen and I'm hard.

"Ah. Right."

"Come with me, *Ma'len*. We shall dress you for battle."

Up in my rooms, Godric helps me put on clothes and plate armor. All the while Scourge swoops past my window, again and again, urging me to hurry. Beyond him at the dragongrounds, Esmeral is shrieking in panic and despair.

"I will take dragons with me to the barrier, but half the flare will remain in Lenhale to protect and patrol the skies."

"Yes, *Ma'len*. I will put every soldier in the castle and the capital on high alert," Godric replies.

I have no qualms about the castle guards as they were sealed under the mountain with me and are all well trained and loyal to the city itself, but the City Guard is made up of men who were born under the Brethren, and they're not familiar with our ways. Their loyalty has not yet been tested. "The City Guard—"

"They are a new unit, but they are all seasoned soldiers and residents of Lenhale who are loyal to the people who live here," Godric assures me. "Their families live here, and I believe they will stand and fight to protect it. Even the humans."

Do I detect reservation in his tone? My rut is making it difficult to focus. "I don't care about the blood in their veins, I care if they will fight our enemies."

"They will, *Ma'len*, and you will find Lady Isavelle and bring her home," he assures me.

It heartens me to hear him say that. Godric is as loyal as they come, though occasionally I've felt that he doesn't like or approve of Isavelle. She's always been very...human. She didn't believe she had a designation or Maledinni blood for a long time, and she was preoccupied with the fate of the human refugees instead of falling into an adoring heap at the king's feet. As frustrated as she made me, I admired her strength of character. A queen should hold her people in her heart.

But no one else was admiring her. Godric, Stesha, and undoubtedly other Maledinni took a dislike to the newest Omega who was refusing to act as was expected of her.

I finish buckling on my gauntlets. "I believe it, and it gladdens my heart that you believe it too. Now, go see to the soldiers. Make sure that we have a home to return to once I have found my mate."

When I reach the dragongrounds, Esmeral is flying back and forth, unleashing a high, keening wail. A well of despair opens up in my chest witnessing her distress. When the Shadow King came for Isavelle, I couldn't stop him from taking her.

A dozen dragonriders have assembled, and they stand at the center of the flare, but one dragon and rider are noticeably absent. Stesha and his icy white dragon, Nilak. A few hours ago, I locked Stesha's former ward in the dungeon, and no doubt he's furious with me. I had hoped he and Nilak would guard the spellbreakers. There are only two in all of Maledin, and they're too precious to lose.

I spy a tall woman standing beside her Alpha female dragon. Sundra, a formidable swordfighter, and the silver dragon, Merrex. I look around for Tish, as the two sisters are never far from one another, before remembering that Tish and her dragon are dead. Damla had her soul core torn out of her chest. I squeeze my eyes shut and pinch my brow. What they say about Alphas having a brain between their ears and another in their knot is feeling pretty accurate. Only the brain in my knot feels functional right now.

There's another dragonrider and her dragon standing nearby, a pair I trust to be levelheaded and watchful. A heavy crossbow expert named Calliope, and her pale green dragon, Verdun.

I signal to both the women. "Calliope and Sundra, fly your dragons in protective formation around Heloise and Elysant. You must protect the spellbreakers at all costs. Never let them out of your dragon's sight and keep to the center of the flare."

The two women nod sharply and say in unison, "Yes, *Ma'len*."

I call two dozen more names and signal them to mount up as I climb onto Scourge. My heart feels like it's encased in thorny vines. Spellbreakers perform counter-magic against individual mages, and I'm going to ask them to punch a hole through a barrier that's been impenetrable.

Beneath me, Scourge is restless, and sparks fly from his nostrils. All the dragons in the flare are shifting uneasily.

I speak slowly to prevent myself from falling into a rage. "The enemy that we have driven out of Maledin has snatched my mate and taken her beyond the barrier to the south. Tonight, we fly there to take her back. Those who remain behind, patrol the skies around the capital and keep everyone safe. We will return with your future queen."

The cry comes back from every dragonrider. "Yes, *Ma'len*."

We will succeed tonight.

We have to.

The wingrunners meet us in the sky over the castle, and I lead my fighting force south. After several hours, the moon and stars have moved through the heavens, and we finally arrive at the massive, dome-like barrier that keeps us out of the scrubland and mountains beyond. All is quiet and deserted as we circle down to land beside the barrier.

On my command, the dragons, wyverns, and riders spread out in a semicircle around the spellbreakers. The barrier is a crackling and malevolent sheer wall before us. My rut makes me want to punch it, but the brain between my ears tells me that would be suicidal.

"I need you both to weaken this barrier," I say, standing before Heloise and Elysant. "Create a hole large enough for a man to pass through, if not a dragon. I'm aware that I'm asking you to perform what might be an impossible task, but you are our best hope of rescuing the future queen."

Both women gaze up at me with serious, focused expressions and nod sharply. "We will do it, *Ma'len*."

I step back from them, making room so they can take up position side by side. The women glance at each other and then raise their hands in unison. Balls of fire grow in their hands, and they hurl them at the barrier, which crackles loudly and glows where it was struck. The glow dissipates, and the barrier still stands. The women try again, and again, the booming sound of their magic nearly deafening us with each strike.

Thud-thud. Thud-thud.

The dragonriders and wingrunners hold their weapons in their hands and gaze out into the darkness, prepared for an assault from the Shadow King.

Sometime later, the spellbreakers are covered in a sheen

of sweat, and their faces are ashen, but they keep trying. Asking them to break through this wall of energy seems like hoping one raindrop will wear away a mountain. Anger and dread break over me. Unable to keep still, I pace the length of the barrier, trying to think of another way through. Desperate to reach my mate. She's all alone and in danger, and there's nothing I can do to save her. What kind of Alpha am I? I think I can rule Maledin, and I can't even keep my mate safe?

My pacing has taken me beyond the protective semicircle of dragons and wyverns when the barrier just ahead of me ripples. A man half runs, half falls through it from the other side and then falls to one knee, panting. The man is dressed as a soldier, though he's older than most Brethren soldiers I've encountered. There are lines on his face and silver sprinkled through his short beard.

I gaze at him in shock, and then lunge forward and haul him to his feet.

"Who are you?" I snarl with both hands clenched on the front of his uniform. "How did you get through that barrier?"

The man's eyes widen in fear and widen even more when he sees the dragon army at my back. "I'm—I'm—" he stammers.

"I asked you your name and how you got through that barrier."

"I'm—I just—"

My threadbare patience snaps in two. "Do you see my eyes? Do you see that black dragon behind me? I'm the one your people call demon. You have likely heard that I am bloodthirsty and violent. I have cut down dozens of men in cold blood, and though tonight my blood is hot, your death will be slow and painful if you don't. Answer. My. Fucking.

Questions." I pull him closer until we're nose to nose and I'm roaring in his face.

The soldier swallows and gasps. "I'm a deserter. I surrender to you, Your Majesty. I was a foot soldier in the Brethren Guard. I don't believe what the priests tell us. I don't want to fight anyone." He points toward the barrier with a shaking finger. "Those people are insane."

He's rather old for a foot soldier. Perhaps the Shadow King is so desperate that he'll put a man past his prime in uniform. "How did you pass through this barrier?" I demand.

He hesitates for a fraction of a moment. "A blessing from the Shadow King. It's how all his soldiers traverse it."

I gaze at the rippling surface of the barrier. It has shredded those in my army, but his men are able to pass through it like it was made of air. I wonder what kind of blessing he means, but a far more pressing matter is at the forefront of my mind.

"Did you see a woman behind that barrier tonight? Golden hair, this tall?" I hold the edge of my palm to the middle of my chest.

The soldier shakes his head. "I didn't see anyone. I'm not important enough to personally speak with the Shadow King. I merely guarded the outer buildings."

He's telling lies, or half-truths at the very least. His speech is full of minor hesitations, and he's staring too intensely into my eyes, desperate for me to believe him. Is he afraid of me and all these dragons because he has fought and slain my people? Is there something more insidious that I'm missing? Or am I being distracted from the matter at hand?

I need to think but my thoughts are jagged and chaotic.

My hands slowly unclench, and I lower the man to the ground.

Behind me, one of the dragons stretches and flaps their wings, sending a gust of wind whipping around me and the enemy soldier. I breathe in, a trace of a scent reaches my nose, and my heart pounds.

I drag the man up into the air until his legs are dangling off the ground. He shouts and twists in my grip, but I don't let him go. Scourge pushes through the other dragons until he's at my side. He lowers his massive head and parts his jaws.

"You're lying to me."

"I'm—I'm telling the truth," the man gasps.

"Do you know what dragonfire does to a body? It eats away at flesh and bone like acid. Or should I feed you to my dragon? I never tire of the sight of him rending my enemies' heads from their worthless bodies."

"Y-your Majesty, I am but a soldier. I swear that there's nothing I can tell you about the Shadow King or any woman. I saw no woman."

Scourge has detected the same scent that I have, and he roars at the same time I shout, "*Liar*. You reek of my mate."

Isavelle's fragrance is on his skin. He hasn't touched her, but he's been close to her. Within feet of her.

"The woman your Shadow King has stolen from me would tell me to be merciful, but she's not here to curb my thirst for violence," I say through clenched teeth. "You have three heartbeats to start talking, or I'm going to start ripping off limbs. He has her. The Shadow King. Where?"

"All right," the man shrieks. "I'll tell you. He has her in his castle beyond the barrier. He was torturing her, and he wanted me to hurt her as well, but she's so small, and she wept in fear, and I just couldn't do it, so I ran away."

He could be telling me the truth, or he could be lying to my face. I'm too far gone in my rage to know. "Who is *he*?"

"He's the Shadow King."

"Not good enough," I say, and Scourge roars and snaps his teeth at the man.

Sweat runs down the soldier's face, and he cries, "I don't know anything about him. I don't know his name or where he came from. He just always *was*. Since before my time. Before anyone's time."

That makes not an ember of sense. "What does this man look like?"

The man studies my face. "Young. He looks a lot like you, only his hair is brown, and his eyes are gray. He speaks about the dragonriders as if he knows you all personally."

Apprehension slams down my spine. I pull the soldier closer to me and breathe in deeply, hoping I'm not about to catch Emmeric's scent.

The first thing I notice is this soldier is one of us. Not human, but Maledinni, and his designation is emerging. An Alpha, but a rather pathetic one. I hunt through his scents of sage and beeswax, oily vindictiveness, and the sickly scent of cruelty for someone else. Someone who shouldn't exist.

Someone who should have died five hundred years ago.

My eyes widen. There it is, in this man's hair. Burnt sugar and licorice. Overripe fruit and the sensation of the ground being yanked out from beneath me.

My fingers loosen in shock, and the soldier slithers to the ground at my feet. My brother, the betrayer, rapist, and murderer, killed the king and queen and fled into the Bodan

Mountains like the coward he is. We pursued him, every dragonrider, wingrunner, and *Hratha'len*, but we never found him, and we were suddenly and inexplicably sealed beneath the mountains. Isavelle broke the spell, and I liberated the people of Maledin from the cruel, power-hungry priests. I thought Emmeric was long dead. I didn't think for a moment that he could have been the one to trap us for five hundred years. He never had that kind of power. How is any of this possible?

Once, Emmeric was interested in dragon magic and he trained half-heartedly with the *Hratha'len*. He was gifted, but he found the lessons boring. I remember the Temple Crone telling my father that Emmeric had one of the quickest minds she'd ever encountered.

After he raped Mirelle, Emmeric disappeared for years. Perhaps he went in search of more powerful magic, but that's as far as I can take my suppositions. I have never studied magic or understood it in any detail. All I know is there is dark and powerful magic in the world, and someone as clever as Emmeric could learn to wield it if he wished. He hated our father. He hated me, though I don't know why. But to kill Mother? To doom every single one of our people? Our dragons? If he is the Shadow King, why did he do it?

And what does he want with Isavelle? Emmeric always laughed at my suffering, and now he holds the dearest one in my heart in his vile clutches.

I shove my fingers through my hair and growl. I want to shout and roar and give in to my fury, but it would accomplish nothing, and I would only feel worse when I saw fear and anxiety in my soldiers' eyes as they realized their king can't control his temper. I saw that look many times on the faces of the soldiers and advisors who worked with my father.

Scourge roars and launches himself into the air. I watch his massive body flying along the barrier, hungry to breach it and burn all our enemies to cinders. I envy him as he vanishes into the sky, for no one begrudges a dragon a burst of fiery temper.

I am not my rut. I won't give in to it now. My Omega would want me to be the best man I can be if she were here. I have to be strong for her.

The soldier has taken advantage of my moment of distraction and is crawling away from me on his hands and knees into the darkness. With two long steps, I cross the ground between us and haul him into the air.

"Where do you think you're going?" I seethe. "You're going to tell me everything you know about the Shadow King from start to finish, and if I suspect you're lying to me or holding anything back, dragons will start taking bites out of you, and you'll be still alive while they start to eat you."

4

———————

Isavelle

A dragon.

My heart pounds against my ribs. There's an enormous, dark-scaled dragon lying on the ground with its neck and tail curled around itself. It's so large and so dark that for a moment I think it's Scourge. As I hold my breath, I realize it's not quite so big as Zabriel's dragon, and its snout and head are narrower and less spiny than Scourge's. It lies perfectly still, as if in death. I might believe it's dead if not for two things; firstly, its body and scales are too lustrous and pristine for a dead creature; secondly, it's being held down by glowing green manacles around each of its legs and another around its neck.

Such a beautiful creature in chains. A dragon should be among its own kind, a proud and free dragon in a flare. I think of Esmeral, my small, beautiful dragon who clawed her determined way into my heart. How I miss her. How it would break my heart to see her locked up like this.

My fear dissipates, and I'm filled with sympathy for this dragon. Emmeric has done this; I have no doubt about it. I search the room for a way to free the dragon, like a key to open the iron locks or a hammer to break them, but there's very little here except for some old, broken furniture and a door in the far wall. Giving up my search, I take a closer look at the dragon and wonder what kind of magic is being used on the chains. They flicker and glow with eerie green light.

"Get away from that dragon."

I stand up quickly and turn around. Emmeric stands framed in the doorway where I entered, and I wonder how he found me until I see drops of my blood at his feet. I left a trail leading right to me.

Emmeric's smirking, taunting expression has vanished and he glares at me with narrowed-eyed hate. When I don't move, he growls, "I said, get away."

"What are you doing to this dragon? Whose is it?"

"Don't touch it," Emmeric says through his teeth. He glances from the dragon and back to me, and then at the door behind me. "It's been a delight meeting you, Isavelle, but now it's time to go." He lays sneering emphasis on the word *delight*.

I watch him warily. "Why is this dragon in chains? Why are you keeping it locked up? It belongs with the flare."

"Are you going to try my temper until I slit your throat?"

Something strange is happening, and I don't trust Emmeric one bit. "You'll let me go back to Maledin? Just like that?"

He shrugs, feigning nonchalance. "I've got what I wanted, and now I'm bored with you." Emmeric unfastens something from around his neck and shows it to me. It's some kind of amulet with a stone. He holds it aloft between his thumb and forefinger, and a soft yellow glow lights his face. "I'll even give you this. My personal gateway crystal. This will allow you to pass through the barrier, but not for long after it has left my presence, so you had better hurry."

The crystal beckons me like a beacon of hope. With it, I'll be able to run back to Zabriel and safety, but it feels wrong. It feels too easy. "Why would you let me go?"

A nasty grin spreads over his face. "Isn't it obvious? You're so stupid and easy to manipulate. Not only can I break into your visions, but I can step through a portal and drag you back here any time I like. Sending you back to my brother reeking of me, and him knowing that I could have done anything I wanted with you, understanding that I still could..." He savors this for a moment. "That's the kind of torment gold can't buy. Will you sleep soundly in his arms from now on, or will you fear me every time you close your eyes? When you open them again, you could be here, far from anyone who cares if they hear you scream."

I can sense Emmeric's putrid scent all over me, and Zabriel will recognize it the moment he holds me in his arms. "I'll be too busy fantasizing about all the ways we'll kill you," I throw back at him.

He holds the glowing crystal aloft. "Once this crystal leaves my hand, you'll have one notch of a prayer candle to pass through the barrier or stay sealed behind it forever."

Emmeric knows how long a Brethren prayer candle burns? Noticing the surprise on my face, he rolls his eyes.

"These fools continue to pray to their god to give Maledin back to them, day and night. This war is not about gods and heathens, but the pure, unadulterated power of mages versus dragons." He sneers the word *dragons*.

I glance at the crystal, and it beckons to me, promising freedom. "If I leave, I'm taking the villagers from western Maledin with me. If this is about mages versus dragons, then you don't need prisoners."

"You'll leave alone, or I will kill you where you stand. Don't test my mercy. It's only a matter of time before you and my worm of a brother and every other Maledinni are dead, so enjoy your mate while you can." His expression transforms with mock sympathy. "I almost feel sorry for you knowing that the weeks you have left to live will be filled with suffering. But it can't be helped."

I open my mouth but close it again. What I almost said was, *Don't pretend that you're letting me go for any reason other than that I've found a dragon that you wish I hadn't.* There's something strange about this dragon. This dragon is important, but I'm careful not to look at it again. A stupid Omega couldn't possibly have noticed how protective he is of this creature.

"Now, go. Or I'll kill you," Emmeric says in a flat voice, and he throws the amulet across the room.

I catch it and turn it over in my hands. The rock is cool to the touch and glows faintly. My heart aches at the thought of leaving all the villagers behind, but I'll be able to tell Zabriel everything that I've seen here, and it may help him and the *Hratha'len* bring down the barrier that protects this place.

I turn and hurry toward the other door and wrench it open. There's another long corridor and a door at the far end. Emmeric mutters a word, and the door springs open, revealing the night sky and the undulating barrier beyond.

"Oh, Isavelle? One last thing." The casual note in Emmeric's voice makes ice dance down my spine.

I glance over my shoulder. "Yes?"

A smirk tugs at the corner of his mouth like he can't contain his glee. "Name a village."

"Why?"

"It's a simple question. Name a village. Any village in western Maledin." His gray eyes sparkle with malice.

"Why do you..." My flesh crawls in horror. "You want me to name a village so you can kill all the people who are Maledinni?"

More families dead or torn apart like mine. Now I understand why the priests were always so cruel to everyone in Maledin. Emmeric was their master, and they learned heartlessness from him.

"Where are my father and sister?" I demand. "Where are the survivors from my village?"

Emmeric's face hardens. "Name a village, or I'll choose five."

The names of a dozen villages and towns in western Maledin flit through my mind. Some are small hamlets with half a dozen families. Others are bustling market towns with hundreds upon hundreds of people. I could choose the smallest village I can think of. I could choose a place I've never been before, so the blood on my hands is at least unknown to me.

The crystal is tight in my fist. Whether I name a village or not, people are going to die, and that's on Emmeric, not me.

Giving Emmeric a silent look of scorn, I turn and run up the stairs. I wonder if I've made the right decision or if I've just condemned five times as many people to death. As I push through the wooden door, I expect to feel something sharp drive itself between my shoulder blades and for Emmeric to taunt me for believing that he'd let me escape.

Nothing happens, but there's a prickling sensation in the back of my neck as I run through the darkness toward the barrier. It crackles before my eyes. A wyvern and its rider were torn to shreds when they accidentally flew through it. I glance at the yellow crystal nestled in the palm of my hand. Either I'm about to pass through it unscathed, or Emmeric has persuaded me into killing myself. Either I believe in this crystal, or I stay here. My mate must be frantic for me by now —if he's not gravely injured or dead. The yearning to be with him is overwhelming.

I reach the barrier and run straight through it.

Green lightning crackles over my skin and hair. There's no sound. No breath. No light.

Then I'm through it, and the moon and stars in the sky shine silvery white overhead.

I've made it. My chest heaves as I take deep, thankful gulps of air. My curls spill over my face, and as I push them back, I realize I'm not alone.

Farther along the barrier are massive shapes in the dark with long necks and powerful wings. My heart soars to see them.

Dragons.

Once they filled me with terror, but now they mean safety. They mean home. They mean my Alpha has come for me, and Esmeral must be close by as well. I long to throw my arms around Zabriel and Esmeral and be kissed by my mate and scolded in high, chittering tones by my frantic dragon.

A massive man is standing not far from me, holding a

struggling figure aloft in one hand. I recognize his strong, proud profile and billowing black hair and cloak. Zabriel, dressed in moon-silvered armor and standing as tall, proud, and strong as the first moment I laid eyes on him.

Not injured. Whole and well.

The most beautiful sight I've ever seen.

The man he's holding aloft sees me, and our eyes lock. My elation turns to shock as I recognize him. It's the High Priest. He must have run through the barrier and been caught by my mate.

"You," the High Priest says in a choked voice.

Zabriel turns his head. There's so much fury in his eyes, but it all melts away as he cries out, "Isavelle."

While Zabriel is distracted, the High Priest reaches beneath his cloak with a vindictive smile and draws a dagger. It glints into the moonlight, the point viciously sharp.

I open my mouth to cry out a warning, but it's too late. The High Priest stabs Zabriel beneath his raised arm. Zabriel is fully armored, but there's a gap between plates by his ribs. As the dagger sinks in, my mate cries out in pain and drops the priest, who rolls away in the dust.

Overhead, a dragon roars in pain and fury.

"*Zabriel,*" I scream, running to him just as he collapses onto one knee, his eyes wide and fixed.

I reach my mate, and the stench of blood washes over me. My fingers hover over the blade's hilt, wanting to yank it out but afraid of causing my mate more damage and pain. What if the blade has pierced his lungs? His heart? Blood is seeping out between the armor plates.

I look around for help and see the High Priest standing by the barrier. His gray eyes are filled with disdain.

Zabriel's pained, raspy breathing fills my ears. "Isavelle," he pants. "*Sha'len*. Is that really you?"

There's the sound of panicked shouts and running feet, and a moment later, I'm surrounded by dragonriders and wingrunners. They race toward the High Priest, weapons raised, but they're too late.

With a final, hateful glance at me, the High Priest steps through the barrier and disappears.

5

Zabriel

Tears drip down Isavelle's beautiful face as she kneels before me in the dirt. Fresh cuts lace her cheeks and throat, and bruises blacken her tender flesh. My soldiers swarm around us, and they're getting in the way of me focusing on my mate. I try to draw her against my chest, but people are gripping my armor. I throw everyone off me with a roar and get to my feet, pulling Isavelle up with me. She shan't sit in the dirt when she is my bride.

I wrap my arms around her and bury my face in her neck, seeking her sweet scent and the warmth of her flesh. "*Sha'len.* My Omega. Little dragon. You're alive. You came back to me."

"Alpha, you're hurt. Please, you must let us help you," she sobs.

Even a mountain falling on me couldn't make me let go of her. The dagger beneath my right arm may as well be the bite of a gnat. I rock Isavelle back and forth in my embrace, my body shuddering in relief. Her frantic pleas subside, and she wraps her arms around my neck and holds on, moaning softly as I use my scent to soothe her distress.

I pull back a little so I can gaze down at her, my thumbs wiping the tears and blood from her wounded cheeks. "I have never been so afraid in my life."

"I'm here," she assures me, her fingers winding through my hair. "You found me."

"You found *me*, my clever little mate." If she hadn't, I'd still be pacing up and down this hateful barrier, lost, afraid, and panicking. The stormy emotions in my rut reach a crescendo. "I'm never letting you out of my sight ever again," I snarl and slam my mouth over hers.

Isavelle melts in my arms, surrendering to the kiss, parting her lips for me so I can plunder her mouth with my tongue. I break the kiss, but it's agony not to feel her lips against mine, so I kiss her again and again. The ache that has consumed my soul these past few terrible hours begins to ebb away as Isavelle's scent fills my nostrils, my arms hold her wonderful body, and my lips devour hers.

"You escaped him, didn't you, my clever little dragon? You escaped the Shadow King and ran back into my arms. I was coming to get you. Nothing could have kept me from you, but you came back to me all by yourself."

"All I thought about was you," Isavelle cries tearfully. "He wanted to hurt me to make you suffer."

My blood rages. "My brother took you?"

Isavelle nods, her expression anguished. "Yes, it was him. I don't know how it's possible that he's alive after all this time. He's been the Shadow King for five hundred years."

My rut-addled brain can't make any sense of this, so I shove all thoughts of my brother aside and focus on my mate. There are cuts on Isavelle's face. Blood on her clothes. My heart crumples in despair. Seeing her like this is a hundred daggers in my side. "How badly are you injured? What did he do to you, *sha'len*?" My voice cracks and my throat fills with pain. "Did he hurt you like he hurt Mirelle?"

She is still my mate no matter what, and I won't let her leave me. I will hold her close and adore her even more than I ever did. I won't allow anyone or anything to make my mate feel like she is broken or used or tarnished.

Isavelle takes my face between my hands and speaks urgently. "He didn't, and neither did anyone else. What you can see is the worst of what happened to me. Cuts and bruises, that is all. No broken bones. No other pain. Nothing bad happened to me." She touches her face and her chest and shows me the bruises and cuts on her arms, legs, and back.

"Nothing *bad* happened?" I seethe, my relief that Emmeric didn't hurt her like he hurt Mirelle being swept aside by a fresh wave of fury.

"These small pains are nothing to me," she assures me. "I am with you and nothing else matters. I feel no pain, only happiness. I can tell from your scent and the way your eyes are burning that you are still deep in your rut. Will you let us help you? You're injured, and we must be gone from this place before Emmeric sends soldiers through the barrier to attack us."

I lift my arm in irritation, gazing at the dagger stuck in my flesh. That cowardly idiot of a deserter should never have been able to stab me. How infuriating. I reach across my body and grasp the hilt of the dagger.

Captain Ashton rushes toward me, calling urgently, "*Ma'len*, whatever you do, don't—"

I wrench the dagger from my flesh and hurl it aside. "Don't what?"

The captain's eyes widen in horror. "Someone help me with *Ma'len's* armor. We need to take it off him immediately."

Three people surround me, pulling at the fastenings on my plate armor and getting in the way of me holding my mate.

"I'm *fine*," I growl, shaking them off. "Get away from my Omega. She's hurt. I need to hold her."

Ashton turns to Isavelle, desperation in his brown eyes. "My lady. Please ask your mate to cooperate with us. We have to treat his injury."

Isavelle strokes my hair and plants soft kisses all over my face. "Zabriel, let them take your armor off. I'm not going anywhere, I promise."

I don't care about the blood flowing down my ribs inside my armor. My instincts are telling me to shove everyone away from my mate so I can protect her.

Isavelle whispers in my ear, "I won't leave your side, Alpha. Your rut is my favorite scent in the whole world."

My rut. That's right, I'm in a rut. I might not be thinking clearly judging by Isavelle's gentle insistence and the horrified expressions on the faces of all my soldiers. I allow my soldiers to guide me over to a rock, and I sit down with Isavelle held firmly on my thigh. Ashton doesn't have the easiest job of getting me out of my armor. Tough. I'm not letting go of Isavelle. I watch as several of my soldiers pull off my gauntlets and chest piece, and then I refocus suddenly on the welts on Isavelle's face.

I grasp Ashton's wrist. "Wait. Stop what you're doing. My Omega is hurt."

Ashton turns to Isavelle. "Are you in immediate danger, Lady Isavelle? How is your pain?"

She smiles up at him. "I'm perfectly well, Captain, thank you. Please tend to the king."

Ashton nods and goes back to what he was doing.

"I'm telling you, she's hurt," I shout, twisting away from these irritating people. There's a pinch in my side, but I ignore it. "Get your hands off me and attend to your future queen."

Ashton pleads with my mate in tones of despair. "Lady Isavelle, please can you distract him?"

"Distract me? I don't need to be distracted, I need you all to—"

Isavelle takes my face between her hands. "Alpha, do I smell different while you're in a rut?"

My face relaxes into a smile. How I love when she calls me Alpha. I haven't savored that nearly enough. "You smell even sweeter, little dragon. Your scent is telling me how much your pretty cunt aches for me to fill you up."

Isavelle makes a choking sound and covers my lips with her fingers. "Oh, my stars. Is he delirious? How much blood is he losing?"

I'm vaguely aware of buckles being undone and my under armor being stripped away. Ashton is doing something to my side while Isavelle strokes the back of my neck. Fuck, that feels good.

"There is blood, but not an alarming amount, my lady,"

the captain says. "*Ma'len's* rut, the stress of tonight, and the burns he suffered earlier seem to be, ah, lowering his inhibitions."

I press a woozy kiss to Isavelle's throat. My burns are a distant memory, and I can't even feel the wound in my side. I wish everyone would fuck off so I could get back to rutting my mate. She took me so beautifully just hours ago, almost all the way up to my knot. I groan as the sight of her stretched tight around me floods my mind.

Someone has their ear pressed against my back. "It doesn't sound as if there's blood in *Ma'len's* lungs."

I twist sharply, trying to see who's there and what they're doing. "What the fuck is going on?"

Cool fingers touch my cheek. Isavelle implores me with her green eyes. "My love, will you kiss me?"

I smile and slant my mouth over hers. She need only ask.

"Can you cough, *Ma'len*?"

I'm about to tell the man not to ask me idiotic questions when Isavelle implores me with her big green eyes.

"Will you cough for me, Alpha?"

"Anything for you, *sha'len*." I cough six times, and then a seventh for luck, and then glance at Isavelle, hoping she's impressed with her Alpha's strong-sounding lungs.

"That was a good sound, wasn't it?" she asks Ashton.

Ashton nods. "As far as I can tell. I don't think the king has a punctured lung, but that's all the field medicine I know. The Temple Mothers need to examine him as quickly as possible. Lady Isavelle, will you please keep talking to the king while we bandage him up?"

I scowl at Ashton for speaking like this to my Omega. "Ashton, stop harassing my mate."

Isavelle cups my cheek, holding her forearm close to my lips. "Your dragines must be aching, Alpha. Do you wish to bite my wrist?"

I close my eyes, take her arm in my hands, and sink my teeth into her like my mate is a soft peach. Not too hard. Not too deep. Just enough to feel her beautiful flesh between my teeth.

"Drink this, Alpha."

I'll do anything my mate asks. I release her, take a swig from a wooden cup, and taste bitter havina tea. It's a mild stimulant that soldiers drink in the mornings and before battle, and it clears my head.

The world suddenly comes into focus. I'm sitting on a rock with Isavelle perched on one knee while Ashton winds a bandage around my chest. A dozen Betas are gazing at me in mild shock, and two Alpha women have their hands over their mouths, smothering their laughter.

The past few minutes have been hazy. Have I been saying and doing some very stupid things? Surely not. I clear my throat, deciding to pretend as if nothing has happened. In a serious and kingly voice, I ask Ashton, "My wound. How bad is it?"

"The dagger missed your organs, *Ma'len*, but your muscle has been damaged and you're bleeding. I'm bandaging you as tightly as I can."

"Would you like to bite my wrist again, Alpha?" Isavelle offers.

Oh, fuck yes, bite her. My dragines throb, and I seize her arm—

I frown at the angry red dimples in her flesh. There are bite marks there already. When was I biting her? I take another uncertain glance around at my soldiers, wondering what I've been doing and saying to my mate in front of them. I love to hold Isavelle on my lap and kiss her, showing all my people that their king has found his beautiful Omega. Anything else that goes on between us is not for their eyes. I feel a throb of jealousy and dismay as I wonder if they now know how sweetly Isavelle gasps when I bite her. I wish I could knock that information out of their heads.

Isavelle doesn't seem offended. In fact, she's smiling at me as I hold her arm just inches from my lips. I clear my throat and, instead of biting, I slide my tongue over her flesh, soothing the marks.

"I think my rut and injury made me lose my head. You were trying to distract me from what Ashton was doing, weren't you?"

Isavelle smiles and shakes her head. "I'm just happy to be back in your arms."

"So I wasn't being completely stupid in my rut?"

Isavelle's bodyguards are standing close behind her, and they've heard our conversation.

"No, *Ma'len* wasn't being *completely* stupid," Dusan says with a grin. Fiala elbows him in the stomach, and he doubles over with a wheeze.

I glare at him. "I heard that, Beta."

But Isavelle is smiling, and Dusan's impertinence means nothing if Isavelle is smiling.

"I'm just happy that I can hold and adore my Alpha," she says, and my knot twitches. A parade of filthy words trots onto my tongue. I swallow them down before my best soldiers hear how my mate's tender cunt clenches so beautifully on my shaft as she comes.

It does, though.

Her tender cunt is everything.

I may have said and done some foolish things in the past several minutes that I can't remember, but Isavelle is cuddled close on my uninjured side and perched on my thigh, and if she still adores me, I don't give a damn about anything else.

There's an impatient scream to our right, and we all turn to look. Esmeral is clawing at the ground, frantic to reach Isavelle. Scourge, concerned that the overexcited Omega will make our injuries worse, has his teeth around her neck and appears to be holding her down.

"Scourge," Isavelle gasps in horror. "Let go of Esmeral."

I glance at my dragon's jaws. "*Sha'len*, he's not biting hard enough to restrain her. He's just cautioning her to curb her excitement so she doesn't trample us."

Isavelle relaxes a little, but I see how much longing there is on her face as she looks at Esmeral.

I kiss my mate's palm and release my hold on her. "Go to her," I say, but then clench my fingers on hers and add, "but do not leave my sight, or I will chase you down and bite you harder than Scourge is biting Esmeral, my injuries be damned."

Isavelle presses a swift kiss to my lips and then runs to her dragon. Scourge straightens up and stands protectively over the reuniting pair. Esmeral chitters madly at Isavelle, sparks erupting from her throat and flying around her head. Her long, flexible neck wraps around Isavelle's back, and she uses a powerful leather wing to clamp her against her side. Isavelle wraps her arms around her dragon, closes her eyes, and leans against her turquoise and golden scales.

"I'm so sorry. I didn't mean to vanish like that. You must have been so scared."

Esmeral shrieks and chitters again when she hears the word *vanish*.

Isavelle presses her cheek against her dragon's flank. "I know. It was horrible, wasn't it? We're going to have to do something about my visions so I know which ones to trust and which ones are dangerous. I don't want any of us to go through something like that again."

My mate turns and looks at me over her shoulder, her expression anguished and sorrowful. I shake my head, telling her that none of this is her fault.

Esmeral fusses over Isavelle, sniffing her everywhere and butting her gently with the top of her head before releasing her. Isavelle turns to Scourge and embraces his bulk, her arms spread wide as if to hug him. It would be easier to hug a mountain. Bending down his massive head, he snuffles at her clothes and then gives an angry snort and a shake of his head.

"Do I reek of Emmeric?" she asks. "You must know his scent just as Zabriel does."

She doesn't reek of my brother, but his scent is on her. The past feels dangerously close tonight. Scourge's red eyes meet mine, and I can feel his relief that we have her back but also how much he wants us all to be gone from this place and back within the safety of the flare.

Ashton finishes with my bandage, and I get to my feet and call to my soldiers, "Prepare for the flight back to the capital. We are leaving imminently."

There's a chorus of, "Yes, *Ma'len*," and everyone gathered around me returns to their dragons and wyverns.

"Can you fly?" Isavelle asks, returning to my side and helping me back into my torn and bloody under armor.

"Of course I can fly."

A turquoise head grasps Isavelle's skirts and tugs urgently with her teeth.

"Esmeral, I know you want your rider, but I want her too," I say. "Will you allow her to fly with me back to Lenhale?"

Esmeral bares her teeth at me in refusal, and I recall Stesha telling me that my mate is a brat and so is her dragon. Not the word that I'd choose, but Esmeral is certainly feisty for an Omega.

Isavelle places her hand on Esmeral's flank, and a moment later, Esmeral closes her jaws and steps back.

"What did you tell her?"

"I told her that someone has to go with you and make sure you don't faint and tumble from Scourge's back."

I laugh, which makes the wound in my side burn, and wrap my arm around Isavelle's waist as I climb with her up onto Scourge. Normally, I would bound up onto Scourge one-handed with Isavelle held securely against my side, but tonight, she grasps the leather straps with me and helps me climb.

When we have settled in the saddle, I take the extra precaution of lashing myself into it before settling my mate in front of me. While I wait for the others to finish mounting up, I douse Isavelle in my scent, soothing her for the flight to come and smothering the scent of my brother and the unknown, silver-haired Alpha. The prick who stabbed me. I don't know what happened to him after I dropped him, but I presume he escaped, for now. Because she smells of him, I know that he had a hand in hurting my mate as well. Whoever he is, he's a dead man.

As we take to the skies and head for Lenhale, I take one last look at the barrier dropping away beneath us. I will find a way through it, and once I do, Emmeric will be finished.

He's a coward, but he can't hide from me forever.

My mate nestles against me, her wounds lit silver by moonlight. I recall Stesha licking the pad of his thumb and soothing Zenevieve's cut palm all those years ago. It's not something I've done before as it has never occurred to me, but I can do it now. I take Isavelle's face in my hands and gently run my tongue over the cut on her cheek.

Isavelle's eyes widen in surprise. "What are you doing?"

"Healing you. Soothing you," I murmur and lick her again. "Alpha saliva is healing. Lovers and close friends do this for their special ones if they're Alphas. Alpha parents soothe their children's wounds like this." When her true heat comes and I rut her for days on end, I will do this for her, healing the bite marks I'll give her and soothing her pussy if she's sore.

"How does it feel now?" I ask, pressing a gentle kiss to the cut on her cheek.

Isavelle closes her eyes. "Better. So much better."

A moment ago, the cut was red and raised. Now there's a thin pink line and the swelling has gone down. I lick every cut I can find on her face, neck, and arms. "You'll heal quickly now."

By the time we land at the dragongrounds, the sun is coming up. Isavelle's bodyguards and several more wingrunners escort me to my bedchamber, no doubt concerned that I'll collapse before I get there.

The Temple Mothers arrive a few minutes later and stitch up and redress my wound, telling me how lucky I am that I was only stabbed in the muscle and not through my ribs to my lungs. One of the mothers tends to Isavelle as well, pressing cool compresses to her bruises, bathing the dust and blood from her body, and helping her dress in a clean shift.

Isavelle comes over to me and marvels at my back, running her fingers over my smooth skin. "Just hours ago, you were covered in burns, and I was terrified you were going to die."

"Fire rarely kills a dragon, my lady," one of the Temple Mothers tells her. "But *Ma'len* would have been in considerable pain as he healed. He has been through an ordeal this night, and so have you. You must be gentle with each other." But she says that with a pointed look at me, not at Isavelle.

Finally, the two of us are alone together, and I wrap my Omega in my embrace.

"Are you sure you want to touch me? Don't I still smell like him?" Isavelle asks with a worried look on her face.

"No," I lie. There are still lingering traces of Emmeric on her body, but I'm not going to force her to scrub herself down like she's unclean. I'm not going to make her hate her own skin as others have. "You're my beautiful little dragon and everything I crave."

I bury my face in her neck and breathe in deeply, and I'm rewarded with her rich, sweet scent.

"I'm so ashamed," Isavelle continues, her voice muffled in my chest. "The reason he was able to take me away was because I allowed him to fool me again with a vision. I'm meant to be a witch, yet all my abilities have done is hurt us and put your dragons and soldiers in peril."

"If anyone is to blame, it's me. You told me exactly who you saw in your vision, and I should have realized it was my brother."

Her hands clench on my shoulders and tears spring into her eyes. "I didn't know my own Alpha. I thought he was you."

Maybe he had her fooled for a moment, but that was my fault. I never told her how much Emmeric and I looked alike before we bonded with our dragons. In the vision that our dragons shared with me, Isavelle's face was filled with terror, and she was backing away from her kidnapper. "*Sha'len*, you knew he wasn't me. Something gave him away. What was it?"

She wipes the tears from her face and thinks. "The way he spoke about Scourge. He made it sound as if your dragon is manipulating you, but I know that you and Scourge love each other. When I hesitated to take his hand, impatience flashed in his eyes. That's when I knew for sure that whoever was standing in front of me wasn't you. You have never been impatient with me. You've always waited for me to be ready for you."

I groan and wrap my arms around her, holding her tight against me. "See? You do know me. You have nothing to blame yourself for."

Isavelle's arms coil tightly around my neck, and she whispers in my ear, "Zabriel, please kiss me. Make me forget it all happened."

I slant my mouth over hers in a hungry kiss. Her soft, warm weight in my lap causes a fresh wave of powerful desire to slam through me. I can do better than kiss her. With both hands, I cup her generous ass, squeezing and kneading as my tongue caresses hers. I pull her shift up over her head, and I see up close how her beautiful body has been inflicted with bruises.

Anger boils in my chest. "Look at what he's done to you. I curse the blood in my veins that I share with Emmeric."

"You have only been a blessing to me, never a curse. I'm all better now that I'm with you."

We touch each other with gentle fingers, careful of the other's injuries. I'm shirtless, and with her help, I get out of my breeches as well. I wrap my arm around my mate, preparing to lower her onto her back so I can feel the tight grip of her body on my cock.

Isavelle stops me with a touch. "Wait. Maybe we shouldn't do this. You have stitches on your ribs."

"Something so petty as a few stitches will never stop me from loving you. I'm in my rut. I need you."

Isavelle twines her fingers through my hair, gazing at the upward thrust of my cock and my swollen knot between us. "Then you lay on your back. If you promise to lie still, I will give my Alpha what he craves."

"How will you do that?" I ask as I slowly sink back on my elbows and then lay on my back.

Isavelle kisses down my chest and then my stomach. Her breasts feel wonderful pressed against my aching knot. "You used your mouth on me. Is that something you would enjoy as well?"

Both my fists clench on the sheets. I thrust against her, and gaze at her with lust-filled, narrowed eyes. "Your mouth? *Sha'len*, I will lose my mind if you suck me with your mouth."

She strokes me gently with her fingers, her green eyes gleaming. "I don't know what I'm doing, so be patient with me."

"Always," I say, smoothing back her hair. "I don't know how this works either, only that couples—" I break off with a groan as she runs her tongue up my length. I thought I'd never know anything sweeter than thrusting into my Omega, but feeling her soft, warm tongue caressing me is an even higher pleasure.

Isavelle opens wide and takes the head of my cock in her mouth, and my body explodes with pleasure. She lays down against me, sucking me up and down. There were so many times I craved to kiss my mate, taste her, fuck her, and now look at her, her naked body wrapped around my thigh, my cock filling her mouth.

"*Sha'len*, if I'd lost you, if he'd taken you away from me—"

"Shh, Alpha," Isavelle whispers, and draws her tongue up my length before taking me in her mouth once more.

"Lick my knot. Please. *Please*."

Isavelle smiles against my rock-hard flesh. "Is the mighty Flame King begging for something from his little Omega?"

I gather up all her heavy golden hair in my hands, holding it tightly as I breathe hard. "You'll do exactly what your Alpha asks. You love being a good little dragon for me, don't you?"

Isavelle squeezes her thighs together and says in a breathy whisper, "Always," before running her tongue over my knot. "You taste so good."

By all the fucking stars in the heavens. "I can't take this anymore. I have to fuck you."

I try to sit up, but she stops me with a hand on my stomach. "Zabriel, you can't."

"You're trying to kill me. Your Alpha is in a rut. He needs to fuck you."

"I am trying to keep you alive. The Temple Mothers told you to be careful of your wound, and when we do *that*, you are so vigorous." A pretty blush spreads over her cheeks as she talks about sex. "You will break open all your stitches."

"Then come up here and sit on me. I will do nothing but hold you and lie still."

I hold out my hand to her, and she accepts it, moving up to straddle my hips. Her thighs are wet with her slick, and I stroke her, getting the wonderful slipperiness all over my hands.

"That's my good fucking Omega," I whisper, grasping my cock and fitting it against her entrance. "I need you so much. I have to claim you even deeper than I did the first time."

"I need you, too," she whimpers, planting her hands on my chest and sinking down my length. We both cry out at the same time.

"My Omega. My woman. I'll never let you out of my sight again."

"I don't ever want to be parted from you," Isavelle cries as she moves up and down on my cock.

I force myself to lie still and allow her to control what's happening for as long as I can, but without meaning to, I find myself clenching the muscles of my thighs and ass and thrusting up to meet her.

"Zabriel, you're pulling on your bandage when you do that," she warns me.

Bandage? What bandage? I don't feel anything except for my Omega clamped tightly around my cock. "*Vru'mai desh.*" *Fuck me, please.* "Just a little deeper, *sha'len.* I need you closer to my knot. I know you can take more," I coax her in a low voice. I'm only half as deep inside her as I was in the wyvern eyrie.

Isavelle's head tips forward and her hair spills around her face as she watches herself fuck me. "You're so beautiful when you fill me up like this, Alpha."

I groan, and my eyes roll back in my head as I lose all self-control. With a growl, I take her hips in my hands and gather myself beneath her for a really good thrust.

"Zabriel, you'll hurt yourself."

"I'm fine. Be a good girl and let me fuck you."

But to my astonishment, Isavelle walks her knees together and draws me almost all the way out of her as she shakes her head. "When you're healed, you can have me as hard and deep as you crave, but for now, lie still."

I argue and cajole and threaten, but she only shakes her head stubbornly and tells me she'll get off me altogether if I won't listen. I let go of her hips and clench the sheets with both hands. This goes against every instinct that's churning through my body. Not rut my mate who's slicking all over my cock? This is unacceptable.

I manage to lie still for a few minutes as Isavelle rises up and sinks down my cock, but soon her cries of pleasure and the bounce of her breasts have me forgetting myself again, and I start to thrust upward.

Isavelle bursts out laughing. "You're doing it again."

I fall back with a growl. "I'm your Alpha. I'm supposed to be in charge."

"Keep still and let me move for both of us."

"I'm *trying*."

"I really am worried about your injury, but at the same time..." Isavelle runs a teasing finger down my chest. "It's pleasing being in charge of the Flame King for just a little while."

I give her a smoldering smile. "I knew it. You're tormenting me, *sha'len*. When the time comes for your heat and you're begging me for relief, I'll remember this and torment you right back."

6

Isavelle

My eyes open wide. "You won't give me what I crave when I'm next in my heat? But my Alpha loves to please me."

"Your Alpha is patient and loving and he adores you." Zabriel grins, showing off his pointed dragines. "And he has a long memory."

My body flushes with heat at the sight of his teeth. Perhaps he does have a long memory and this will come back to bite me. To distract him, I draw a finger over his stomach, up over his knot, and part my inner lips. "Look how well I'm taking you, Alpha. Stretched so tight around you. There's so much of you, and I just want more and more."

Zabriel's red eyes sharpen, and his grin fades as he refocuses his attention. He grasps my waist. "Fuck yes. So beautiful. You can have as much of me as you want."

I cover one of his hands with mine to remind him to keep still, then I sink even further down his length. The stretch deep inside me feels heavenly. As I move up and down, my thigh muscles burn and my palms against his strong chest are damp with perspiration, but I don't stop. I'm transfixed by the sight of my beautiful man, his silken black hair spread out around him on the pillow, and his red eyes burning into mine.

I reach down and caress Zabriel's knot with a twisting stroke of my fingers. His eyelashes flutter, and his massive chest expands with a deep breath.

I'm back by his side. We win. The Shadow King—more like Shadow *imposter*—told me that it was only a matter of time before we are dead, but it's going to be the other way around. It won't be long before Zabriel brings down that barrier and drives his cruel, murderous brother into the past where he belongs.

Zabriel squeezes my breasts with both hands and rocks up into me. My head tips back in pleasure.

"I'm going to come," I moan as I feel his hips thrust into me. "Be careful of your stitches," I whimper, but I'm too far gone to do anything to stop him now.

"I'm barely moving, Omega," he says with a breathless smile, pumping into me harder and harder. "Now, stay just like that and let me fuck you."

"But you...we have...to be careful..." All my protests become cries of pleasure as he bucks beneath me. It feels like I'm riding a wild dragon. His stomach muscles beneath my hands are hard and clenching rhythmically.

"You take my cock so well, *sha'len*. I'm going to fill you with so much cum until you're bursting."

His filthy words and sharp thrusts push me over the edge into my climax, and a moment later, Zabriel follows me with a roar and a final thrust.

Knowing how much pleasure it gives him, I reach down and squeeze his throbbing knot as I collapse forward on his chest.

"Yes. *Yes.* Squeeze me, *sha'len*," he whispers in my ear. "Wring every last drop of cum out of me and into you."

His mouth seeks mine, and as he kisses me, he sinks his dragines gently into my lower lip.

"I missed you so much," he whispers.

My eyes lock with his. "I missed you, too. You're all I thought about."

"Don't pull yourself off me. I want you right there."

I don't want that either. I feel so full of him and his cum, and I cup my belly as I sit up, certain that it looks more swollen than usual. Taking his hand, I place it against my stomach and ask him, "Can you feel yourself in there?"

Zabriel's red eyes blaze with delight. He tries to sit up, and he winces. "Yes, *sha*—ow."

"Are you all right? Have I hurt you?"

Zabriel grasps my shoulders and reassures me with strokes of his thumbs. "I'm all right. Lay down on your side with me."

We both move carefully onto our sides with his cock still deep inside me and rest our heads on the pillow.

His hand caresses my belly. "When I finally knot you, you're going to be so swollen with my cock and my cum."

I smile and trace my fingers over his lips. "I can't wait."

Zabriel presses slow kisses to my cooling brow. I can feel

his cum welling up and dripping out of me, but his cock stays rock hard. "If I'd lost you..." he says raggedly.

I lift my chin and press my lips to his. "Emmeric wanted to scare me, the High Priest tried to shame me anew, but they're both cowering behind the barrier, terrified of the Flame King."

"The High Priest was there?" Zabriel asks, a worried line appearing between his brows.

I hesitate and then tell him. "The High Priest was the one to stab you."

My mate breathes in sharply. "The one who shrieked *demon* at me when Scourge landed atop the old king's funeral pyre? The one who beat and starved you for a year? Who nearly had you burned alive? Who stole you from me? I had him in my grasp, and I didn't snap his pathetic neck? How did he beat you? Tell me everything. I need to know."

My heart hurts at the thought of inflicting every moment I spent with our enemies on my mate. Emmeric doesn't have to keep me hostage to torment us. We'll torment ourselves for him if we allow it.

"You can see it all with your own eyes," I tell him, and his face creases in pain as he studies my wounded flesh. "But what you can't see is the way I was able to turn Emmeric and the High Priest against each other. That was how I managed to escape. They fought, and I ran."

"I'm so proud of you," Zabriel breathes. His cock is still inside me, and he thrusts upward, sending pleasure shooting through me.

I stroke his chest. "I think the High Priest decided to flee from Emmeric as well, which is why you caught him dressed as a soldier and did not recognize him. If only I'd been able to stop him from stabbing you."

Zabriel frowns, trying to remember what happened at the barrier. "Where is he now? Do my soldiers have him captive or did he escape into Maledin?"

I shake my head. "He escaped back through the barrier. I wonder if he'll return to Emmeric and tell him that he stabbed the Flame King or if he's gone on the run." The High Priest is an Alpha. What a disgusting thought. I hope that he isn't gifted an Omega. Men like him don't deserve someone who is totally at their mercy.

"My brother. How did he look?" Zabriel asks.

"I don't know what's happened to him in the past five hundred years, but if he ever had your size and strength, he's much diminished. He claims that he hasn't got his knot or his dragines anymore. He said he doesn't want or need his dragon, yet when I ran, I found a dragon chained in the dungeons. In fact, I think the reason he let me go was to get me away from that dragon."

"What did the dragon look like?"

"A beautiful deep blue, almost black. Its talons were tipped with gold, and there was a blaze of gold along its snout. I couldn't see its eyes as they were closed. The poor creature was held down by magical chains and appeared to be unconscious."

I feel Zabriel's pulse thunder beneath my fingers and his expression fills with anguish. "Shar. You saw Shar? I didn't think he would be alive after all this time. To chain up a dragon, it's despicable."

"Who's Shar?"

"My brother's Beta dragon. So, he's anxious that no one gets near his dragon. That's an interesting piece of information." My mate lies quietly for several minutes, lost in thought. When he finally speaks, his voice has a faraway quality. "Shar was such a beautiful dragon. When he took to the skies, everyone coveted him. Such grace, and he was smart as well. Whip-smart. In that, he and my brother were alike. When I was fourteen, and Shar, Scourge, and a dozen other dragons were juveniles, I watched them all, hoping that one of them would choose me. Scourge most of all, but Shar as well. I loved him dearly." The memory of the midnight blue dragon shines in his eyes. "Poor Shar, locked up like that. Do you think it's strange that I feel so much for a dragon who isn't my own?"

I rub my cheek against his shoulder. "I love Scourge. I love the little hatchlings who fall asleep beside me while I meditate in the Flame Temple. I adore the sight of the proud dragons in the flare. I can believe you loved Shar."

Zabriel's smile is bittersweet. "Shar liked to play and romp around with the smaller dragons. Esmeral would have delighted him."

A playful dragon whom everyone loved, and now he's chained up in a dungeon. "If that was Shar I saw, then we must free him and return him to the flare where he belongs."

"We must," Zabriel agrees.

I twist Zabriel's long hair around my fingers, thinking. "Strange that a sweet-natured dragon such as him chose a rider with a black heart."

Zabriel sighs heavily. "Quite. I remember not long before he hurt our sister he ranted about his weak and stupid dragon. He made sure that Shar felt his displeasure because the dragon winced in pain whenever he lost his temper."

"He hit Shar?"

"Not with his fists. With his mind."

"That's despicable."

"Isn't it? All the dragonriders were angry with him, and the flare turned against him after that. Whenever Emmeric entered the dragongrounds, Scourge would follow him, wings unfurled, jaws parted in threat as he protected the other dragons. But Emmeric wasn't always so cruel. Before we understood what it meant that Father was king and I was the crown prince, he and I were just brothers who loved to watch the dragons. We would dream out loud of the day we'd be chosen by our own dragons. Later, Emmeric's playful nature gained an edge until it was honed as sharp as a knife. I think he learned to hate his family. Mirelle was Father's favorite. I was Mother's favorite. Emmeric was no one's." Zabriel turns bleak eyes toward me. "Do you think that's why all this happened?"

"That Emmeric tore Maledin apart and caused the suffering of tens of thousands of people because he wasn't your parents' favorite? It doesn't seem like a good enough reason, but what would be good enough for the things he's done?"

"Maybe he wanted to be king that badly. People have done terrible things for the throne."

"But Emmeric never even sat on the throne. He got rid of all the dragons and the Maledinni and put puppets on the throne so he could get on with his work."

Zabriel frowns in thought. "Which is?"

I search my memory for any clues. Something Emmeric said. Something he did. Some possession in that tower room. I shake my head. "I have no idea, but he's certainly a powerful mage these days. He's been hard at work at magic."

Zabriel strokes my hair, his expression rueful. "Maybe there was something I could have done to turn him away from the dark path he set out on. He was my brother. I could have made a difference."

"This is all Emmeric's fault and Emmeric's alone."

Zabriel is silent, and I can sense how much he blames himself despite my words. He presses a kiss to my throat. "You must be exhausted, *sha'len*. Sleep. I'll watch over you."

"You need sleep as well."

"I can't right now. My rut will keep me awake for hours yet."

The swelling of his knot has gone down, but his cock is still rock hard and deep inside me.

I remember how needy I get in my false heats. "If you want me, promise me you'll wake me up."

Zabriel's breath catches. He hesitates for a moment and then says, "I will try not to. You need your rest."

As I close my eyes, I wonder if I'll be able to sleep at all with Zabriel's cock lodged deep inside me, but with his arms around me and the comfort of him filling me, I drift off to sleep.

I DON'T KNOW if it's my Alpha's rutting scent surrounding me, his body against mine, or simply that I want him so much, but when I awaken, my core is aching for my mate.

Zabriel feels me stir and places his lips against my ear. "*Sha'len*, you've been slicking all over me in your sleep. I've been holding still for hours, desperately trying not to fuck you. Do you need me as much as I need you?"

"Please, Zabriel," I moan, arching my back to drive him deeper. I barely finish moaning his name before he pulls out, rolls me away from him onto my other side so my back is against his chest, and thrusts into me.

My eyes open wide as pleasure shoots through me. The drag and slide of his cock drives all sleepiness away, and I moan and clutch my arms over his that are holding my body.

I feel the scrape of his bandage against my back and remember his stab wound. "Wait, your injury. You must stop."

"What injury?"

"You know what—"

"Hold still, Omega," Zabriel growls, and his voice seethes with authority.

I stop struggling in his embrace. Something in his voice makes me melt against him. It's like the time we were sitting on his throne and he first commanded me to say, *Yes, Alpha*, and then I slicked myself all over his lap.

"Mm. I think my growl is getting stronger. It feels good to do what I say, doesn't it?"

I reply without thinking. "It always feels so good to do what my Alpha says," the needy Omega inside me agrees.

Zabriel moves his hand between my legs and strokes my clit, and my eyes close as pleasure overwhelms me.

Zabriel is lying on his uninjured side. He hooks one of my thighs up so he can slam into me deep and fast. As soon as his rut passes, I'm certain he's going to feel where he was stabbed, but right now, all my mate is interested in is ramming his cock as far into me as possible. It's all I'm able to think about as desire knocks all the sense out of my head.

"*Sha'len*, I'm all the way to my knot. Do you feel that? Fuck. *Fuck.*" His breathing has grown frantic.

Something hard and swollen pounds against my entrance with a wet slapping sound every time he thrusts. I reach down between my legs to feel his knot against me and moan in delight. All of my mate's cock inside me, and I'm not even in a false heat. Sleeping with him inside me must have helped me take all of him. Zabriel was probably sinking deeper and deeper as I slept, challenging himself not to wake me.

"Your mating gland smells so good, Omega. I want to bite you here so much." His teeth scrape over my sensitive nape, and my pussy spasms around him.

"Bite me, please," I moan.

"You have enough injuries on your body already. I'll only hurt you."

"Then hold me with your teeth," I beg him.

"By the fucking gods," he growls. His whole body tightens with his climax, and his thrusts make his knot slam against me over and over again. As he sinks his teeth into my mating gland, my body lights up in pleasure, and an orgasm rips through me. I'm locked in my Alpha's tight embrace, his cock deeper than it ever has been before, his teeth holding my nape securely. There's so much tension in his jaw.

Zabriel draws back and runs his tongue over the marks he's left on my neck. "You amaze me, Omega. You give me so much pleasure. I'm the luckiest Alpha in the world."

His praise twines through me. "I'm the luckiest Omega in the world, you mean. How long was I asleep?"

"For all of the afternoon. It will be sunset in an hour. Here, let me..." He loosens his embrace and draws his cock slowly out of me. "I must give you some rest from me, even if it makes me ache to let you go."

I turn toward Zabriel, wrap my arms around his neck, and kiss him.

"Are you sore?" he asks.

I shake my head and smile. "I feel wonderful." It's the truth. I might ache a little between my legs, but it's an ache that means I have my mate back. "I would like to go see Esmeral before it gets dark. Will you come with me?"

Zabriel glances toward the door, and I can sense how much he wants to, but he shakes his head. "It's considered poor behavior for Alphas to be too much among people during their ruts, and I have already made a spectacle of myself." Zabriel laughs and scrubs a hand over his face.

"What's so funny?"

"I could tell you, but I won't deny Dusan the pleasure of telling you himself, and you can all have a good laugh at my expense."

"You are my mate and my king. I won't allow anyone to laugh at you," I protest.

"I don't mind in this instance. I am too happy and relieved knowing that I have you back and that I can laugh at all."

We get out of bed, and while I clean myself up with a basin of cool water and a cloth, Zabriel dons a long silken robe and opens his bedroom door.

Calling to a guard I can't see, he says, "Will you please send word to Lady Isavelle's bodyguards that they are to come here at once? She wants to see her dragon."

I get dressed, and Zabriel and I wait by the door, holding each other, my cheek pressed against my mate's chest as I listen to the steady thump of his heart. His flesh burns hotter than usual because of his rut, and he can't stop squeezing me and breathing in my scent. His own scent grows stronger and stronger, and I sense that he's dousing me in it so I'll reek of him wherever I go in the castle.

"You mustn't linger at the dragongrounds or go anywhere else," he tells me with a growl in his voice. "The only reason I'm letting you out of my sight is because you're going straight to Scourge, and then coming straight back to me. Scourge will watch over you while you and Esmeral spend a little time together. I trust him always to protect you as fiercely as I would."

"I promise I will come straight back," I assure my mate as I plant a kiss on his muscular chest.

There's a knock on the door. I attempt to draw myself out of his arms, but Zabriel lets me go reluctantly. I press kisses to his wrists and palms as I step through the door, as reluctant to leave him as he is to leave me, but I must see my dragon.

"I will be right back, Alpha, I promise."

My bodyguards hold their halberds—tall pole weapons with a wicked blade on one end—with even more determination than usual. As they escort me down the corridor, they stand close as if I might be snatched from them at any moment.

"It is wonderful to see you safe and well and walking these halls again, my lady," Fiala says. The normally stoic woman's voice is husky with emotion.

"I wish I hadn't caused you all such worry," I tell her. "It's a relief to be back after such an ordeal. Zabriel hasn't slept yet, but I was able to get a little rest."

Dusan says with a glint in his eyes, "I'm surprised your mate has allowed you up for air, considering his condition."

I blush, but I shoot him a smile. "I was reluctant to leave him as well."

"Lady Isavelle is too kindhearted to tell you to shut up, but I will," Fiala tells her friend. "It's rude to speculate about an Alpha's rut or an Omega's heat."

Dusan laughs. "I didn't so much speculate as bear witness. We all did."

"Oh?" I ask. "Zabriel hinted that something happened while I was gone, and I should ask you about it. What was it?"

A huge grin spreads over Dusan's face. "*Ma'len* was quite a spectacle. A prodigious, swollen, upright spectacle that couldn't be missed even if you were standing at the summit of the Bodan Mountains."

Fiala squashes Dusan's fun by speaking over him and telling me matter-of-factly that Zabriel stormed into the Great Hall, naked and shouting orders, and conspicuously in his rut. "As soon as he knew you'd been taken, *Ma'len* wasted not a moment in his efforts to get you back. The king protects his bride. He didn't have time to think about how he was dressed."

"Now we know that *Ma'len* is kingly in all the ways," Dusan adds with a knowing smirk.

A proud smile spreads over my lips. "He is. In every way."

7

____

Isavelle

We reach the dragongrounds, and I glance around for my dragon. The flare is all gathered together, which makes it difficult to spot one dragon among all the gleaming, colored scales.

Scourge sees me and makes a whuffling sound in greeting. A moment later, a turquoise and golden dragon shoots into the air with a delighted scream. Esmeral streaks over to me and lands in a shower of dust and flapping leathery wings.

I throw my arms around her neck, beaming from ear to ear. Emotions flash between us as fast as lightning. Happiness. Relief. Excitement. Esmeral can smell my Alpha's scent all over me. She's delighted that he and I have been so intimate together, and she proudly lets me know that she and Scourge have been as well. To my surprise, it doesn't feel strange that Esmeral and I should know such things about each other. It feels like they were meant to be shared.

There's a steady *thump-thump* noise, and the sky overhead darkens. Scourge has stalked his way through the flare and is looming protectively over us. His massive bulk is a comforting presence, and his red eyes are warm and benevolent as Esmeral and I communicate and embrace between his massive front legs.

Those red eyes narrow and glow hotter as they wander over to Dusan, as if Scourge knows what we've just been discussing.

"Feel like making more quips about *Ma'len* being kingly?" Fiala asks dryly.

Dusan swallows as he stares up at Scourge's pointed teeth. "I'm good."

Esmeral sends me a mental picture of us taking to the skies together.

"Soon," I assure her. "I want that as much as you do." We have flown together, but I still don't know what I'm doing, and I hold on for dear life rather than effortlessly sit atop my dragon like Zabriel and the other riders. Some flying lessons would be a good idea.

Overhead, Scourge makes an approving rumbling noise.

Not long ago, I was adamant I didn't want a dragon or a mate, and I was going to return to my home in Amriste as soon as I could. Esmeral was wretched over my rejection of her, and her mate could feel her pain. Now he can see for himself how happy I am with Esmeral, and I'm covered in Zabriel's rutting scent with no intention of leaving. Everything is just how the Alpha dragon wants it to be.

His family is complete, but I feel a pang in my heart as I

remember what's left of my family is still missing. I wish I'd tried harder to find out where Dad, Anise, and the other missing villagers are, but Emmeric would probably have killed me if I'd tried.

I spend a little while longer with my dragon until Scourge lowers his head and nudges my side, telling me to go back to my mate. No doubt the dragon can feel how desperate his rider is for me to return through their mental connection.

I press a hand to Scourge's head, something I never could have imagined doing just a few weeks ago. "Thank you, Scourge. I'm going. Zabriel's injury has been tended to. He will go riding with you as soon as he can."

A thought occurs to me as Fiala, Dusan, and I cross the bridge back to the castle. I glance back at the dragongrounds, searching for Stesha or his white dragon, Nilak. They weren't among the dragons and riders who flew with Zabriel to the barrier, which strikes me as strange. Whenever Zabriel flies into battle, Stesha is his second-in-command.

"Where are the dragonmaster and Nilak?" I ask my body-guards, and they exchange worried looks. "Stesha didn't do anything foolish, did he? I hope he didn't go against Zabriel's orders and take Zenevieve from the dungeons."

"I bet he thought about it," Fiala mutters. "But no, my lady. The dragonmaster is...well, he seems to be..." She trails off, glancing at the darkening skies.

"He left," Dusan snaps, anger darkening his face. "He abandoned *Ma'len* in his hour of need."

Stesha left Lenhale? Dismay settles in my heart. Who's going to watch over the flare if we have no dragonmaster?

"Dusan and I never had much to do with the dragonmaster, but we know that he cared for Zenevieve and was very protective of her," Fiala tells me. "While she remains in Lenhale, he won't abandon her."

"Gods, I can't believe that Emmeric was the one who took you," Dusan mutters. "He was alive all this time, and Zenevieve was with him."

"And he was doing gods know what to the poor girl," Fiala replies. "I feel for *Ma'len*, and I even feel for Stesha. There's nothing more painful to an Alpha than knowing the person that they instinctively protect at all costs has been suffering."

"Do you believe that Zenevieve isn't at fault for deceiving me and passing on information about me to Emmeric?" I ask her.

"That's what I think," Dusan says. "Zenevieve was always good and kind and never had any reason to betray Maledin."

Fiala hesitates and says, "She had no reason to betray Zabriel or her country, but..."

"But what?" I ask.

"Emmeric may have preyed upon her hurt and anger. That's all I'll say. The Temple Mothers are tending to her, and we'll know more when she awakens and *Ma'len* is ready to question her."

"The prince was a master of manipulation," Dusan says.

"He's no prince. He's a dead man," Fiala mutters darkly.

Fiala and Dusan take me to Zabriel's chambers and see that I get safely inside. The room reeks of frustrated Alpha. I inhale deeply, savoring the delicious scent. Delicious to me, anyway.

Zabriel is pacing up and down the room, his silken robe falling off his muscular shoulders and a deep scowl on his handsome face. He has one hand pressed over the wound on his side.

"Are you in pain? I can send for the *Hratha'len* to bring you relief."

When he sees me, his brow softens and he holds his arms open so I can run into them, which I do, though I'm careful not to bump against the bandage or hold him too tightly.

"This stupid injury? It's not the pain that's bothering me," he growls. "I can't do what I would normally do in a rut, and it's making me crazy."

"What do you normally do?"

"Take to the skies and fly far away from people. Run up a mountain. Swim against a strong river current. Get myself off ten times in a row and then run down the mountain. Well, I've been doing the ten times part."

"I've only been gone a short time," I say with a grin.

"And every moment was an age," he says, pressing his mouth to mine. Zabriel wastes no time in stripping us both naked and carrying me to the bed, where he shows me just how much he ached for me to return to him with swift, hungry thrusts of his hips.

After, I lay gasping on the bed, held tight in Zabriel's arms.

"Sleep, now," he murmurs in my ear. "My Omega has been through an ordeal and her Alpha is too demanding of her."

"What about you?" I ask sleepily, rolling toward him so I can push my face into his big, comforting chest.

"I'll watch over you. You're safe, *sha'len*."

"I always feel safe when I'm with you," I whisper and then drift off into nothingness.

I sleep through the night and wake to sunlight streaming

through a chink in the window coverings. Zabriel brushes my hair back from my face with a smile and kisses me.

"Did you sleep?" I ask him between kisses.

He shakes his head, takes my face between my hands, and kisses me. Something thick and swollen presses against my thighs, and I wonder if he's been hard all night.

"My poor Alpha. Two nights without sleep. You must be exhausted."

"Don't feel sorry for me," he murmurs with a smile. "I'm the only Alpha in the kingdom who has been holding his Omega close all night."

There's a knock on the door, and we hear the voices of the Temple Mothers. Zabriel wraps me in a sheet and dons his robe before calling out that they may enter.

Two women are here to tend to my mate's wound. They take off the bandage to inspect the stitches, and they scold him gently when they notice how irritated the wound looks from moving too vigorously. They glance at me, clearly naked beneath the sheets, and I guiltily duck my head.

"It's not my mate's fault. She's been telling her Alpha to lie still and mind his stitches, but the king won't listen," Zabriel tells them. He doesn't look the least bit chastened by their severe looks while they rebandage his injury. In fact, his smoldering glances at me tell me that he's going to go right back to irritating his wound as soon as they leave the room.

No sooner than the door closes behind the Temple Mothers, Zabriel reaches out with his large hands and unravels the sheet from my body.

I press my hands against his chest and shake my head, laughing. "I have been humbled and reprimanded by the

Temple Mothers, and I must look after my king, even if he refuses to look after himself. Lie down, Alpha. Please."

Only with much imploring does Zabriel allow me to push him onto his back, and he watches me climb astride him.

"This time, you must lie still."

His hands squeeze my thighs as I position his cock at the tip of my slick entrance and slide down his length. We both moan at the same time.

"I will lie still, but I need to squeeze my knot while you fuck me," he says through his teeth, gripping himself with both hands.

"Does that feel good?" I ask, watching the muscles of his arms bunch and flex as he appears to strangle his own cock.

"Everything feels good, but I am aching for relief. My rut has never made me so desperate to shove my knot in..." He growls, the deep rumble making his chest vibrate beneath my fingers. "*You.*"

Zabriel comes with a roar, his head tipping back and the muscles of his throat working. Zabriel's strength is like nothing I have ever witnessed. He wields a heavy sword that's taller than I am, and he can lift and throw grown men as if they're balls of crumpled paper. Yet despite the power in his tightly clenched hands, his knot suddenly expands and throbs, forcing them apart.

I'm gazing at Zabriel's knot in shock when my Omega instincts suddenly kick in, and the sight, sound, and feel of my Alpha climaxing and pumping his seed into me makes heat and pleasure soar through me. I move even faster up and down his length until I climax as well.

Feeling dazed, I stare at his knot lodged between my thighs, thick veins standing out all over it. How he's going to get that monstrous thing inside me one day without splitting me in two, I have no idea.

Zabriel is panting with his eyes closed and his body goes limp on the bed. He licks his lips, but they remain dry. I wonder if he's been drinking any water or if he's too distracted by his rut. I get up and pour him a cupful and hold it to his lips, and after some murmurs of encouragement, he swallows the water down.

There's a large tray of food beneath a cloth, but not one morsel has been touched. I recognize a bowl of vegetables cooked in herb sauce. Zabriel likes to eat it at feasts, and so I take the bowl over to him.

"There is food here if you wish to eat." I stir the stew enticingly, but when he catches its scent, he wrinkles his nose and turns away, muttering that he's not hungry.

With a cool, damp cloth, I bathe the sweat from his brow and the sticky trails of my slick and his cum from his thighs and cock.

Zabriel reaches up and cups my cheek. "You're so beautiful."

He says that to me often, and my instinct is to silently reply, *No, I'm not.* Next to Zabriel with his strong body, his proud and handsome face, and long black hair, I'm exceedingly ordinary. But I'm beautiful to him. I wonder if he loves me. Actually, I'm not certain if couples even say *I love you* in Maledinni culture. I've heard him say he loves fire and flame. He loves to soak in the bathhouse beneath the castle.

My parents would tell each other *I love you* often and call one another *my love.* I'm falling in love with Zabriel, and that love has nothing to do with my designation or his scent and everything to do with the man Zabriel is. As I gently stroke the cool cloth down Zabriel's chest, I feel my human side more keenly than I have in some time. I open my mouth to ask, *Do you love me?* But what if he says, *No, what kind of question is that?* and turns over and falls asleep? If Alphas and Omegas are fated for each other and have no choice but to want each other, what need do they have for love?

My gentle attentions seem to relax Zabriel, and his eyes drift closed. It seems like my Alpha's rut is finally receding. I sweep the hair from my mate's forehead and kiss his cooling brow. "Sleep well."

"Stay with me," he mumbles as his eyes close. "Don't go. Can't...protect you...if you leave."

"I'll stay, I promise."

"Stay...forever," he mumbles sleepily. "Want you here. Move all your things but...keep your nest if that's...what you want."

I've been sleeping in Zabriel's rooms every night recently. I never moved my belongings, though I never had many. Sleeping every night with the king in his chambers while we're unwedded would have made me the subject of gossip and scorn under the Brethren, but the Maledinni are unfazed by mates having sex with each other before any kind of official ceremony. The most important part of our mating will be when he knots me and drives his dragines into my mating gland, leaving scars in my flesh. That's how he'll make me his bride. I feel hot just thinking about it.

I hold Zabriel in my arms and watch him sleep, and there's nowhere I want to be except by his side.

❧

My mate awakens with a dragon-sized hunger.

I fell asleep shortly after he did, and I open my eyes to him polishing off the last of the food from the tray and swallowing down a whole jugful of water, not bothering to pour it into a cup.

"*Sha'len*, let's go downstairs to the Great Hall for breakfast. I need to eat a meal and show everyone in the castle that I've spent my rut with my Omega."

"What do you call the food you've just...wait." I feel myself blush red to the roots of my hair. "You need to what?"

Zabriel smiles disarmingly. "I need to eat a meal. This was no more than a snack."

"No, the other thing."

His smile turns suggestive. "I just spent my first rut with my Omega. The whole castle needs to see you in my arms and know that you've chosen me. It's tradition."

I understand Maledinni custom well enough now that I don't wonder if he's making it up or if this is unimportant and I can refuse. He wouldn't say it if it wasn't important. Besides, Zabriel has been very generous to me with his customs. When I asked for the Maledinni villagers of Amriste to be given a dragon burial after Emmeric brutally murdered them, Zabriel agreed, even though none of those people knew they had been Maledinni or sworn allegiance to him.

But surely I've been well and truly claimed in everyone's eyes by now.

"Do you think that everyone got the idea that I'm yours when you chased me through the skies on your dragon, walked stark naked into the Great Hall in a full rut and shouted that I'd been taken from you, and then flew at the head of an army to steal me back from your brother?"

Zabriel leans down and rubs the tip of his nose against mine. "I'm sure they did, but it's tradition. Not a formal occasion and a feast like we will throw after I've knotted you, but this is still something to celebrate."

My eyes widen. "We will celebrate with a feast when you knot me?"

He laughs. "Of course. Don't you feast after happy unions in your culture as well?"

I relax a little hearing that. "We do, actually. In my village, we would share a meal and then drink a toast to a couple who declared their intention to marry, and then again when they did marry."

Zabriel kisses me softly. "It is very much like that, and it makes my heart feel lighter to know we have a reason to be happy this morning after so much terror."

I take his face in my hands and smile. "Then it will make me happy too."

As we enter the hall in fresh, clean clothes, dozens of soldiers and castle workers look up from breaking their fasts. First there are happy cries of greeting and congratulations, but as the dragonriders see their king hand in hand with his mate, the cavernous room erupts with wolf whistles. I hear lots of teasing comments about how flushed and healthy our cheeks look and how messy our hair is. I know for a fact that's not true because Zabriel brushed my hair before brushing his own, but I play along, pretending to smooth down my hair.

Amid all the shouting and stomping, Zabriel takes a seat at a trestle table and pats his thigh, a smoldering smile on his lips. "I'm hungry, *sha'len.*"

My mate looks as if he's more interested in eating me than

his breakfast, which leads to even more ribald comments and whistles. I play along, tapping my smiling lips and pretending to consider him, sidling closer but staying teasingly out of reach.

"But, Alpha, have you not eaten your fill yet?"

"Never," he declares, grinning so widely that he reveals his dragines and resembles a hungry dragon. He snatches my hand, tugs me to him, and settles me in his lap. My heart pounds as I wrap my arms around his neck. There are tingles low in my belly. Zabriel kisses my smiling mouth, and everyone in the Great Hall applauds and whoops.

A few minutes later, the table is groaning under the weight of food as people pile dishes before the king, insisting that he must be famished after his rut. I munch happily on an apple, enjoying the warm security of Zabriel's arm around my waist as he devours bread slathered in honey and butter.

A young trainee soldier who can't be more than fifteen says earnestly to Zabriel, "How brave you were to steal your bride back from the Shadow King, *Ma'len*."

Zabriel swallows, raises his voice, and speaks clearly so that his voice carries throughout the Great Hall. "My mate saved herself from the self-styled Shadow King. She walked through the barrier right into my arms and told me our enemy's name. This imposter is my brother, the former prince. Emmeric yet lives, and he is our true enemy, not the Brethren and their soldiers."

As soon as Zabriel utters his brother's name, silence falls in the Great Hall, and his final words ring in the air. Some people appear shocked. Others who were born in New Maledin appear puzzled, for the name Emmeric must mean nothing to them. Others appear crushed, as if they heard the rumor that Emmeric was alive, but they didn't want to believe it.

"Is the dragonrider Zenevieve in league with your brother Prince Emmeric, *Ma'len*?" someone calls.

"Former prince," Zabriel replies. "And former brother. I ceased to call that man brother after he hurt my sister. I will speak with Zenevieve and decide what is to be done with her. For now, good health to you all and clear skies to my dragonriders." He lifts a cup into the air.

Everyone lifts their cups in the air and replies with "good health" or "clear skies."

When they turn back to their meals, I chew thoughtfully on an oatcake for a moment and then say to Zabriel, "May I come with you when you speak with Zenevieve?"

Zabriel's brows draw together as he considers this. "As the future queen, that is your right, but I am warning you that I will be overprotective while you're in her presence."

Understandable, considering that it's because of her I was lured to my village and attacked by Brethren.

After we finish eating, Zabriel leads me into the dungeons. They're dark and damp and the walls drip, and there's no natural light or fresh air. Zenevieve is lying on a narrow pallet in a cell, attended by two Temple Mothers while armed guards keep watch outside.

Zabriel stands over her and speaks in a cold, severe voice. "Zenevieve. Are you awake?"

Her eyes are closed and sweat beads on her brow. She seems to stir at the sound of his voice.

"Wake up," he says sharply, and the cell reverberates with his Alpha growl.

Without meaning to, I stand up straighter and endeavor

to appear more alert, even though I'm not the one to whom he's talking.

Zenevieve's lashes flutter, and she slowly drags her eyes open. As soon as she takes one look at Zabriel, she starts screaming. "Emmeric. No—don't. *Please.*" She sits up and tries to scramble away from him, but her back is against the wall and she's trapped. My mate watches her as if trying to discern whether she's acting or if her confusion and fear are real.

I can't help but attempt to allay her fears. "This is Zabriel, Zenevieve. Look, he has red eyes. Emmeric doesn't have red eyes."

Zenevieve starts to sob. "Don't lie to me. Zabriel is dead. You killed him long ago. Everyone I know is dead."

Zabriel's jaw flexes, but there's pity in his eyes as he turns to the Temple Mothers. "Is she trying to trick us?"

One of the Temple Mothers steps forward. "I believe Zenevieve is too unwell for subterfuge. She's suffering from some unknown illness, and we are trying to keep her calm."

The young woman is whimpering and clawing at the walls, mindless with fear that Zabriel is Emmeric and he's come to hurt her.

"Perhaps if I speak with her alone," I suggest.

Zabriel clenches his jaw, and I can tell he doesn't like the idea. He turns to the two guards stationed outside. "You two. In here." They enter the cell, and we all have to shuffle up to make room in the tiny space. "I will leave Lady Isavelle here to speak with Zenevieve, and you two will see to it that she is safe. Not one hair on her head is to be touched."

The guards and the Temple Mothers incline their heads, and the woman in red robes who answered Zabriel's question says, "*Ma'len*, we swear on our lives that your Omega is safe with us."

Zabriel takes my shoulders in his hands and presses a kiss to my forehead. "I will be three steps away. No more than that. If you're sure you'll be all right, I'll wait there. Call out if you need me."

I nod and assure him that I'll be fine.

As soon as Zabriel is out of sight, Zenevieve's crying and shaking calms down. She lies down on the cot once more and closes her eyes.

I kneel by her bed. "Zenevieve, it's me." Can I even say *it's me* after everything that's happened? I wonder if the young woman who was my friend even exists. There were times when "Odanna" seemed to fade away, and I caught a glimpse of another woman, vulnerable and confused, before she was wiped away and the person Emmeric wanted her to be returned with a placid smile. There's no response from Zenevieve, so I try again, speaking her name louder and gently shaking her shoulder.

The young woman's eyelashes flutter. She opens her eyes, and though they're glazed with fever, they lock onto mine.

"It's Isavelle," I tell her.

Her brows draw together in confusion, and she asks in a dry, cracked voice, "Who are you?"

8

Zabriel

I stand with my back against a damp wall with my arms tightly folded, feeling the cold of the dungeons seeping through my clothes and into my flesh. I've never ordered anyone to be locked up before, and I don't relish that someone's down here in this dank place because of me. I never could have imagined that I would have to order that someone as close to me as Zenevieve be put behind bars.

I've known the dragonrider all her life, first as a toddler running around with a hobby dragon made from a stick and a stuffed stocking between her legs, laughing with delight. Her grandfather was the former dragonmaster until he passed away and Stesha took over. It was only natural that she always adored dragons. She and her family left Lenhale for a long time, only returning after her brothers were married. We met again as teenagers, equally determined to become the best dragonriders in Maledin, and we always had plenty to talk about and do together. Stesha paired her with Minta before I bonded with Scourge, and I was breathless with envy to see Zenevieve holding the green and black hatchling in her arms. A dragon and rider to be matched so early is unusual, but Stesha knew what he was doing, and no one could deny how perfect Zenevieve and Minta were for each other.

Mother once suggested that I consider Zenevieve for my future queen, and then laughed at the horrified face I pulled. Zenevieve is beautiful, but she was like a sister to me. Mother pointed out that she would make an excellent queen, but I wasn't going to marry for strategic reasons. I was going to marry for an all-consuming need for my mate, or I wouldn't marry at all.

When Zenevieve's parents were killed, I clumsily tried to comfort Zenevieve, but I don't think I was very good at it. She went to live with the dragonmaster, and from then on, she was either with him, with Minta, or with both of them. By then, we were both learning how to ride our dragons, along with some other young riders, and Stesha was our teacher. By the gods, that man was stingy with praise with all of us as he taught us to ride and various fighting methods while mounted on a dragon. Well, most of us. He bestowed Zenevieve with approving nods, and his tone was distinctly warmer as he told her, *That was better* or *You've improved since last time.* We would all roll our eyes and call her *dragonmaster's pet* while she basked in his attention with a sunny smile on her face. The thing was, we could grumble all we liked, but Stesha wasn't wrong. Zenevieve was a much better dragonrider than any of us.

At age sixteen, Zenevieve was stunningly beautiful, and every single one of my peers among the dragonriders and wingrunners would gaze longingly at her as she walked by or flew overhead on Minta. But of course, there was Stesha not far behind her, glowering at all the boys if they so much as breathed in her direction, as overprotective of his ward as he is of the dragons. As far as Stesha is concerned, he's the flare's Alpha, not Scourge, and Zenevieve was part of his flare as much as Minta was. A popular Beta girl usually has a generous number of lovers, and no one finds that unusual or improper, but I never saw her with a boy or a girl. The only ones Zenevieve was close to were Minta, Stesha, and Nilak.

Far above me and through heavy stone, I hear the cry of a dragon returning to the flare.

I know that dragon.

My glower deepens, and I wait, my arms folded tight.

A few minutes later, I hear rapid, heavy footsteps, and Stesha descends the stairs into the dungeon. His long, white hair is in wild tangles, his pale riding leathers are smudged with dirt and ash, and there's a feral expression in his blue eyes.

Anger blazes in my heart. "Where have you been?" Pride makes me swallow, *I needed you.*

Stesha snarls, "I don't answer to whelps who've had their knots for as long as a candle burns." He tries to push past me, but I step in front of him. "Move, Zabriel. I'm here to see my former ward. I assume she still lives? You haven't ordered her execution yet?"

On the one hand, it's good for me to have someone around who will call out my poor choices, and it would have been a devastating decision to order Zenevieve's execution without knowing why or how she betrayed us.

On the other hand, fuck Stesha.

I wish I were taller so I could look down on him instead of meeting him eye to eye. "The future queen was taken from us, and you flew away gods know where. I should throw you into one of these cells for deserting us."

"Gods know where? What do you mean, gods know where?" he demands. "Where do you think I was?"

"How should I know? I haven't seen you or Nilak for days."

Stesha stares past me, hungry to shove me aside and get to Zenevieve. "I thought there might be a way inside the barrier beneath the southern mountains. I searched the ravines, the caverns, every cave I could find, but the barrier is impenetrable from above and below."

"And if you did find a way in? Were you going to fight that imposter and his entire army single-handedly?"

Stesha's eyes flare with blue sparks. "*Yes.*"

Looking at the rage on his face, I believe him. "You would have been in for a surprise had you breached the barrier and come face to face with the so-called Shadow King. It's Emmeric."

Stesha's face slackens in shock. "Don't be idiotic. Emmeric is not the Shadow King."

"Isavelle spoke with him. Isavelle came back safely, by the way, if you care about the fate of the future queen."

"Of course she came back safely, otherwise, you wouldn't be here," Stesha replies impatiently. "Is Lady Isavelle *sure*?"

"She's sure. She saw Emmeric and Shar. He's severed his

bond with his dragon somehow, and his appearance has reverted to how he used to look, but it's him."

Stesha paces up and down the dank corridor. "I can't believe it. Emmeric, alive after all these years. And he was awake all this time? Not trapped like us?"

"It seems so. He's learned powerful magic these past centuries. He preyed on Isavelle's witch insight and pretended to be me before I bonded with Scourge, and he almost had her fooled."

"You always were as unsightly as each other," he mutters absentmindedly.

"I'd rather be unsightly than obnoxious." We exchange insults more out of habit than with any intent behind it, and it clears the tension in the air between us. "When Isavelle returned to me, she had Emmeric's scent on her. That isn't something I'd forget."

Stesha glances toward the corridor that leads to Zenevieve's cell, and his eyes are filled with anguish. "You're telling me that Emmeric had Zenevieve...he had her for five hundred..." He pushes both hands through his hair with a strangled moan. "I have to see her."

He tries to move past me, and though I wish dearly I didn't have to do it, I put up a hand to stop him. "Not right now. She's in and out of consciousness, and Isavelle is with her. The Temple Mothers will continue to watch over her."

"Zenevieve was put into my care, not yours."

"We must be sure that we can trust her."

"Zenevieve is innocent. Whatever she did, she was forced to do it by your brother."

"We don't know that."

His cold blue eyes narrow. "Did you feel relief when you

snatched Lady Isavelle back from that monster? Did all your pain suddenly cease when you held her in your arms? Emmeric had Mirelle for one hour, and he completely destroyed her. He's had Zenevieve for five *hundred* years. Do you even care what that girl has been through?"

Of course I care. I was vividly imagining him doing the same to Isavelle. "Zenevieve was passing on information about us to Emmeric. I have to know for certain that he has no influence over her before anyone can see her. Be patient, Stesha."

"How can I be patient when you were a breath away from ordering her execution?" Stesha shouts, reaching for his sword. His hand closes around the hilt.

I would be doing the same if someone was trying to keep me from Isavelle, but if Stesha draws steel on the king, I'll have no choice but to arrest him for treason. I seize Stesha's shoulders before he does something he'll regret. "I won't lay a finger on Zenevieve, nor order anyone to hurt her. She will be treated gently, no matter what she has done. No one wants her to be innocent more than I do. Zenevieve and I were friends, remember? If Zenevieve is still Emmeric's puppet, the less she sees and is told about us, the safer we'll all be."

"You don't trust me to not put us all in danger?" he snaps.

"The way you're behaving? No."

Stesha glares at me in silence, and I can feel his anger warring inside him. "Swear that you won't hurt her."

I put my hand on my heart. "I swear on my mother's memory that no one will harm Zenevieve, guilty or innocent."

Stesha steps back, wrenching himself from my grip and collapsing with his back against a crumbling wall. "Zenevieve has never hurt a soul. She wouldn't so much as startle a butterfly." He looks up and demands sharply, "Tell me you haven't forgotten that she is a kind, gentle, loyal person."

"I haven't forgotten who she was, but we don't know who she is now."

Despair overwhelms him. "I swore to her father that no harm would come to her. Now look what's happened."

"None of this is your fault."

"Yes, it is. I have made every mistake with that girl."

I don't know what he means by every mistake. I didn't pay Stesha and Zenevieve much attention in the last few years before Maledin fell, but I understand his anguish about his oath. An Alpha's word, his honor, is all that he has. Strength, speed, fighting prowess, bravery, they all mean nothing if an Alpha breaks an oath.

At least now I know that Stesha wasn't coveting my Omega when he touched her in the street and smelled her hair. My mate had just been down in the city with her friend "Odanna," and it would seem that she had some of Zenevieve's scent on her. Stesha clutched his head after our duel when I demanded he explain himself and said, *I think I'm losing my mind.*

What he should have said was, *I thought I scented Zenevieve,* and then we might have discovered the true identity of the young woman who'd befriended my mate, saving Isavelle a great deal of danger and heartache. Isavelle saw half her village slaughtered because of Zenevieve, including her mother and brother.

I assumed that Zenevieve and Minta were among the army of dragonriders, wingrunners, soldiers, and spellbreakers that flew with me to hunt Emmeric down, but she couldn't have been. "Why wasn't Zenevieve with us the day we were all sealed beneath the mountain?"

All the color drains from Stesha's face, and his eyes are hollow. He's silent for a long time, and then he pushes away from the wall and leaves the way he came without a word.

I frown as I watch him go, but a moment later, Isavelle emerges from Zenevieve's cell, and her expression is troubled.

"She doesn't remember me at all," Isavelle says. "The name Odanna means nothing to her. But she is a little calmer. I mentioned your name to Zenevieve, and she says she wants to see you. I pointed out that she already had and that she mistook you for Emmeric, but she doesn't remember that even though it only just happened. Her mind...it's broken."

I glance toward the cell. "I will try one more time, but if she's terrified of the sight of me, I'll come straight back. Wait for me here? I'll send the guards out."

Isavelle nods, and I head into the cells. Once the guards are in the corridor protecting my mate, I turn to Zenevieve.

"Do you know me, Zenevieve?" I ask softly, approaching her narrow bed.

"Zabriel." She reaches out and grabs my arm, her eyes wide and glassy. "I found him. I found your brother, and he's going to do something terrible. We have to stop him." Zenevieve stares blindly around the dark cell. "Where's Minta? I can't find my dragon. I can't sense her anywhere. Tell Stesha..." Her face crumples and she starts to sob. "Tell him I didn't mean it."

"Didn't mean what, Zenevieve?"

She lets go of me and falls back onto her pallet, weeping

and calling out for Minta and Stesha. A moment later her sobs quieten, and she falls unconscious.

I gaze down at Zenevieve with sorrow filling my heart. "Poor girl. What did my brother do to you?"

There are footsteps behind me, and when I look over my shoulder, I see that the Temple Crone has arrived. I move toward her and speak in a low voice. "What's happened to Zenevieve? She doesn't remember anything that she's done. It's like she thinks it's five hundred years ago."

The Temple Crone's solemn expression is tinged with grief. "I believe she's been in the grip of some powerful magic for all this time."

"As long as we were trapped beneath the mountains?"

She inclines her head. "I suspect so. Perhaps she was captured by Emmeric the day that he killed your mother and father. The dragonmaster should have more information about the last time he saw his former ward."

I feel a pulse of anger toward Stesha. I have no doubt he does, but he's not being forthcoming.

"*Ma'len*, I was always concerned by the unusual and close interest your brother took in Zenevieve. It was obsessive and malicious, and it worsened as they grew older."

My eyes widen in surprise. "Emmeric was obsessed with Zenevieve? I never noticed that. In fact, I barely remember ever seeing them together. Did he want to mate her?"

"No," she says sharply. "Not in an honorable way, at least. I don't believe that Emmeric was capable of tender feelings. It was not a natural, well-meaning kind of interest."

I turn back to the pallid, unconscious young woman. I have been hoping that Zenevieve recovers her memories, but maybe she's better off without them. Around us, slimy water drips down crumbling stone walls, and I feel heartless for putting Zenevieve in this place.

"Can you care for Zenevieve at the Flame Temple, Grandmother? The dungeons will only make Zenevieve sicken further, and perhaps the temple will soothe her torment."

She closes her eyes and inclines her head. "We would be honored, *Ma'len*." Her small smile tells me that not only does she think it's possible, but she thinks it's a good idea. "Is Zenevieve allowed visitors?"

I hesitate. She means Stesha. I want anything Zenevieve tells me to come from her own memories, not be something told to her by the dragonmaster. "Not yet. I will ask the dragonmaster to be patient."

"Patient? Very well, *Ma'len*," the Temple Crone says, but she raises her eyebrows and presses her lips together in an expression that says I may as well tell a dragon not to fly.

9

Isavelle

At Zabriel's suggestion, I spend the afternoon moving my scant personal items into his rooms. My nest stays where it is in the four-poster bed in its own room, and I fuss about with it, draping blankets and plumping cushions. I can't stop touching, folding, and diving in and out of the bed to check how it feels. I wonder if it means my next false heat is just around the corner, or even my true heat.

"You look as cozy as a kitten in a basket of laundry," Posette tells me with a smile. She's tall and skinny with her hair falling out of a plait, and until the invasion, she was a Veiled Virgin like me, in service to the Brethren. Now, she's one of my lady's maids.

I sit up, pretending I wasn't just imagining Zabriel's

glorious weight on my body as he kisses me. "Um, just testing it out for later," I say breathlessly and get out of bed.

As I shake out my skirts, Santha, another former Veiled Virgin with a round, ruddy face and sparkling brown eyes, joins Posette. They've both been helping me carry my things to Zabriel's rooms.

"You're right, Posette," Santha says with a sigh, examining me from head to toe. "This won't do."

I straighten up. "What won't do?"

Posette clears her throat. "As your lady's maids, Santha and I have decided that you must start dressing like a queen."

I glance down at myself. There's something wrong with my clothes? I'm wearing one of the homespun dresses that Captain Ashton procured for me the first night I was in the castle. I've worn this dress as I've cared for the refugees, tended the Temple Mothers' horses, worked in the kitchen gardens, and sadly, packed up my parents' cottage after Mother's death and Dad's absence. All my clothes are like this, though there's one very beautiful dress in my possession that was a present from Zabriel. He had it made for me, and I carried it almost reverentially to his rooms. It's delicate and pretty but hardly something to wear every day.

"What's wrong with what I'm wearing?" I ask.

"You're dressed like a village girl," Santha tells me.

"I am a village girl," I protest, and the two young women exchange exasperated glances. "All right, I won't pretend that nothing hasn't changed. After all, you've just helped me move my things into the king's bedchamber. But some things are going to stay the same. I intend to keep working as I did before. I haven't got the patience to sit around stitching poetry or whatever it is that queens and princesses do, and

I'm not going to wear a dozen petticoats. I'll feel ridiculous. This dress is just fine."

I don't want piles of silly, frilly dresses. They'll make me feel like those awful things Emmeric called me. Zabriel's brainless fucktoy. I shudder at the memory.

Instead of looking dismayed by my speech, Posette and Santha seem even more eager.

"Of course not, my lady. You're a dragonrider, and you should look like one," Posette proclaims.

I'm resettling some cushions in my nest, but I turn to her, my curiosity piqued. "I should look like a dragonrider?"

Dragonriders are ferocious and beautiful in their fitted clothing and billowing cloaks. Even off duty, they're remarkable in their tunics and long jackets, the men and the women. Nothing brainless or toylike about them.

"Yes, my lady," Santha says. "After all, you are a dragonrider, and that dress you're wearing isn't suitable for being up in the air and flying around."

No, it's not warm enough, and there's no protection for my legs. I can feel myself being persuaded as I ask, "What would those clothes look like?"

Santha hurries to a side table and collects a small stack of parchments. "I have been studying the dragonriders and what they wear, on and off duty. Before I was a Veiled Virgin, I used to work in the south at Arsters Manor, and I saw the fine ladies of that house nearly every day. I got to thinking, what if we combine a regal style with dragonriders' clothing, and make clothes that are just for you?"

Posette nods in agreement. "There's only one Queen of Maledin. You should have your own style."

They show me sketches that Santha has made of various

dresses, tunics, coats, cloaks, and even a jacket and tunic that resembles an outfit that I've seen Zabriel wear.

"These dresses and tunics could be in pale gold or a sandy color, and we could line these cloaks and jackets with teal and turquoise, but *this* dress would be in a bold red." Santha points to a long, formal dress with a bodice that looks like it's made from dragon scales.

I bite my lip, feeling uncertain. "I'm not sure. They're lovely, but don't you think these are too grand for me?"

"Your husband-to-be is a grand man," Posette points out.

True, Zabriel always looks like a king, whether it's in a ripped and dusty shirt, his intimidating black battle gear, or full gold armor regalia. "That's because of Zabriel, not his clothes."

"You are so smitten, my lady," Santha says with a laugh, and I realize I have a stupid grin on my face. "*Ma'len* is indeed regal. He has an excellent sense of style."

I sort through the drawings again, lingering over the designs that appeal to me. Maybe if I picked a few things, it would be a way to show Zabriel that I am committed to him, to Maledin, and to my dragon. I want to be able to move and work in my clothes, and many of these designs would allow that. I might even start feeling like the future queen. Everything about ruling beside him seems so daunting, but perhaps the right clothing can help me feel more comfortable in the role.

I think for a moment longer and then say, "There's a group of seamstresses in the castle. I met them once while they were sewing dragon banners for Zabriel's coronation. I don't know their names, but I can describe them. Will you please find them and bring them to me?"

Posette and Santha break into eager smiles and promise to be back as soon as they've found the seamstresses. Barely a quarter inch has burned from the candle before I hear them returning.

Three women in aprons greet me with brusque, bobbing curtsies and professionally severe glances at my attire.

A middle-aged woman with raven hair shakes her head, her lips pressed into a disapproving line. "Lady Isavelle is still dressing like this, is she? I can see why you need us, Santha. I'm Cranthel, my lady," she says to me.

"It's lovely to see you again, Cranthel. How is your husband? I hope he has recovered from his time spent in the dungeons." Cranthel's husband was imprisoned for two years by the Brethren for missing church to care for his sick mother. Zabriel released him along with other prisoners, which was the reason Cranthel was happy to sew the new king's coronation decorations.

The woman blinks in surprise. In a softer tone of voice, she says, "You remember what I told you about him, my lady? It's very kind of you to ask after him. He's doing very well, thank you, and he now works in the wyvern eyrie. He's enamored with those silver beasts."

"I'm very happy to hear it."

"I'm Nessy, my lady," says a red-headed woman in her thirties, then indicates a beaming young woman who looks around eighteen. "And this is Adnea. We all remember how you cared for the refugees when they were flooding into the capital."

"And we watched you fly through the skies on your dragon, pursued by that much, *much* bigger dragon and the king," Adnea gushes. "He must have been so happy to catch you."

"Adnea," Cranthel says sharply. "We don't comment on the private goings on between men and women."

"Sorry," Adnea squeaks, and blushes red to the roots of her hair.

"From what I've noticed, this new lot is very different to our prudish old masters," Nessy says, with a conspiratorial glance at me and a twinkle in her eye. "I think the king wanted us all to know he was about to capture his lady."

I laugh and blush along with Adnea. "Yes, he did want you all to know that."

"Now, where are these designs? I'm itching to see them," Nessy says, rubbing her hands together.

Santha passes them over, and the seamstresses cluster around the sketches and start going through them, all their heads bent together as they discuss the designs.

"This winter tunic is very handsome. And this riding habit."

"Such tight breeches on a young lady, hugging her bottom for all to see. Doesn't seem proper," Cranthel says.

"That's your old priest talking. We're not under the Brethren now. That big handsome king will love to see her bottom."

"So will everyone else. There'll be no hiding it," Cranthel replies.

Nessy grins. "Well, when he came into the Great Hall, we all saw his—"

"That's enough, Nessy. This capelet is elegant. And the high-collared dress. This one is very fine, and so is this one."

A short while later, Cranthel turns to me. "These clothes

are in a strange style to my eyes. I've never seen a queen dress like this before, but we've never had a queen who rides a dragon. If these are what you want, I believe you'll look very well in them. Hold out your arms, my lady." She takes a measuring tape out of a pocket and begins wrapping it around various parts of my body. She rattles off the numbers to Adnea who scribbles them down on a scrap of paper.

"You will use the best fabrics for Lady Isavelle's new clothes, won't you?" Santha asks them anxiously.

"Did you design these?" Cranthel asks, and Santha nods. "Then if your lady can spare you, we'd be grateful if you'd come with us to the city's haberdashers and choose the fabrics. I think you may have a good eye for colors."

Santha looks hopefully in my direction.

"Yes, of course you can go," I tell her. "I'm grateful you're all going to such an effort for me." Now that this project is underway, I find that I'm excited to see the results of all their hard work.

Just then, there's an almighty shriek from the dragongrounds. My room doesn't overlook that part of the castle, so I excuse myself and run back to Zabriel's rooms. Or rather, our rooms. As I stand on the balcony, I spy a commotion on the other side of the bridge. Nilak has thrown her wings upward as high as they can go, and she's filling the sky with her angry screams.

A black-haired man and a white-haired man stand nose to nose, and my heart sinks. Zabriel must have told Stesha that he may not see his former ward yet. Scourge is positioned protectively over Zabriel, jaws parted and baring his teeth at Nilak, making it clear that he will defend Zabriel if she tries to hurt him.

I hold my breath, wondering if this is the moment the last shred of friendship between Zabriel and Stesha snaps. A moment later, Stesha turns and places a hand on his shrieking dragon, and she settles, furling her wings and drawing in her neck. Zabriel lingers for a moment longer, and he seems to be speaking to Stesha, but Stesha ignores him.

I turn away and go inside, my heart heavy at the thought of the rift between the two men.

A FEW DAYS LATER, I remember Emmeric's crystal amulet that allowed me to pass through the magical barrier.

I left it in a small wooden box in Zabriel's rooms, and one snowy afternoon, I lift it out and sit at a table by the balcony, turning it over in my fingers. When Emmeric threw it to me, the crystal was lit up and warm. Now, the crystal is cool to the touch and dead-looking, and I suspect if I tried to use it to get back through the barrier, I'd be torn to pieces.

But I sense something within the crystal. I grip the stone tightly and close my eyes. If I'm a witch, then maybe there's magic that I can unlock and make this amulet usable again. Maybe Zabriel's army could pass through the barrier, or an assassin could sneak through and dispatch Emmeric. Perhaps the *Hratha'len* could use the crystal to destroy the barrier. Maybe I could help end everyone's suffering and find my missing family, along with all the other lost villagers.

There's a thread of power or connection within the crystal, but when I try to follow it in my mind, there's nothing there.

I sigh and open my eyes. I might be a witch, but I have no

idea what I'm doing. If I'm not careful, I could make things worse without meaning to or even find myself sucked through space and deposited at Emmeric's feet because I've played with magic that I don't understand.

I gaze out the window, watching the soft, fat flakes drifting down. Gunster. Joryan. Grimmond. Tilton. Falmere. Rosen. The names of towns and villages in western Maledin revolve through my mind as I wonder which one might suffer Amriste's fate, with all those of Maledinni blood impaled on spikes and left to die. If Emmeric makes good on his threat, he will murder the residents of five villages because I wouldn't name one.

If only I could see where the missing villagers are right at this moment. That would be a useful vision to have, but my visions arrive when they want to, not when I want them to. Even if I did see something, I wouldn't be able to tell if it was real or more of Emmeric's trickery.

There's only one thing to be done.

Slipping the amulet into my pocket, I go in search of Zabriel.

At this time of day, he's often at the barracks. On my way there, I pass through the kitchen gardens, wanting to check on the crop of rousta, one of the few late winter crops that grow in Maledin. It has a dull taste that needs a great deal of butter and salt to make palatable, neither of which we had much of at home—and never at the monasteries—but it is nourishing. Good food is good food at this time of year, especially after the upheaval of an invasion. Besides, there's plenty of butter and salt in the castle, so I've grown fond of the plain little vegetable. I kneel down in the snow and brush the flakes away from the thick, green stems. The starchy vegetable beneath has turned a creamy golden color. This rousta can be harvested the next time there's a thaw, which is hopefully just a few days away.

As I leave the kitchen garden, a rhythmic thumping sound reaches my ears, followed by grunts of pain. Curious, I follow the sound down a walkway and enter a small court-yard. It's deserted, except for a lone figure facing the wall, snow collecting on his white hair and broad back. As I watch, Stesha hits his head against the stones, hard enough that I'm amazed he hasn't knocked himself unconscious.

I hurry forward with a cry. "Stesha, don't. You're hurting yourself." I reach out to touch his sleeve, but I stop myself just in time. It's likely as inappropriate for an Omega to touch another Alpha as it was for Stesha to touch my hair.

The white-haired Alpha freezes. I can feel his desire for me to leave him alone emanating from his muscular frame. Still facing the wall, he speaks through clenched teeth. "Go away."

"Dragonmaster, please turn around."

He doesn't move, and so I step around him, and the sight of his face nearly makes me cry out again. There are lacera-tions on his forehead, and they're bleeding so much that his face is coated with blood. He stands with his forehead resting against the wall as if waiting for me to leave so he can continue beating himself.

As much as I don't like the man, a lump rises in my throat. "You can't blame yourself for what happened to Zenevieve. Haven't you punished yourself enough?"

Stesha glares at the stones as if he can bore through them with his eyes. "No."

My comfort is probably the last thing he wants, but I have

to try. "I hate to see anyone hurting as much as you are. Would, um, you like to talk about it?"

Predictably, he doesn't. Stesha turns and strides away without another word. I sigh and watch him disappear through the archway on the other side of the courtyard. Emmeric has already spread so much misery. I wonder how much more is to come.

I arrive at the barracks only to be told that the king left to go to the Great Hall just moments ago, and I follow him there.

Inside, the fire is roaring in the enormous stone fireplace and sending warmth and light throughout the cavernous room. Zabriel is seated at a trestle table with one of his dragonriders, who nods to him and departs as they see me approaching.

My mate spreads his arms and smiles at me, inviting me to perch in his lap, which I do. I nestle into his warm embrace, inhaling deeply and soaking in his warmth and strength.

"Can you smell my scent, little one?" he whispers in my ear.

I smile against his chest. Until recently, I couldn't catch my Alpha's scent. The Temple Crone gave me a special oil to spread on his skin, and his scent came vividly alive. Ever since then, I've been able to smell it on my own, very faintly, though it's getting stronger every day. "I can."

"What can you smell?"

"Cherries and spice. Freshly split firewood. And I can smell...victory. You won your sparring matches at the barracks?"

"How clever of you to know that, my sweet witch. I think

you must have especially keen senses. You smell of the gardens, and also a faint trace of...distress? What's the matter?"

"I don't think Stesha is coping with all that Zenevieve has suffered." I tell Zabriel about what Stesha was doing and our brief conversation.

Zabriel presses a kiss to my forehead. "You are kind-hearted to worry about the dragonmaster when he's always treated you as an annoyance."

I don't like Stesha, but his flinty, severe nature makes him a good soldier and dragonmaster, and he's always patient with the dragons. I first encountered him in a tug-of-war with Esmeral, but instead of ripping the scroll from her jaws or shouting at her, he merely held on and explained to her that she was too small to take messages to the barrier. He was kind to her.

Then he snapped his fingers in my face and told me what to do, I remember with a spurt of irritation.

"He has some good qualities, I suppose," I grumble. "Though he keeps them well hidden. But I didn't come to talk to you about Stesha." I wrap my arms around Zabriel's neck and nestle further into his lap. It always feels wonderful to sit here on his strong thigh, allowing his scent to wash over me. "I wanted to speak with you about Amriste. Is Mistress Hawthorne safe in the village? Will anyone arrest her if your soldiers pass through and discover she's a witch?"

"Arrest her?" Zabriel shakes his head as he slowly strokes my back. "Witches are protected under a Maledinni king. There's nothing illegal about witchcraft."

I look at Zabriel in surprise. "Oh? Then what has

happened to the witchfinders? Didn't they fight alongside the Brethren?"

During my time in Amriste and as a servant to the Brethren, I encountered dozens of witchfinders, all gloomy men dressed head to toe in black. They had special talents for uncovering witches, and orders from the Brethren to put them on trial and burn them at the stake. No one liked witches, but a collective shiver would go through our village whenever witchfinders rode in on their horses, swords at their hips, and their strangely perceptive eyes peering from beneath their broad-brimmed black hats.

"No, they didn't fight. None of them wished to face a horde of dragons, and they laid down their swords. As such, they have all been pardoned and are welcome to remain in Maledin if they wish, as long as they follow our laws."

"They were pardoned?" I exclaim.

Zabriel frowns at me. "Did I make the wrong decision? Should they not have been pardoned?"

"They rode about the countryside accusing people of being witches and burning them at the stake."

"That is true, but I was informed that the witchfinders were coerced into their duties as you were. Is that not true?"

I hesitate. It is true, but my hatred of witchfinders makes this very hard to talk about. "I sincerely hope your mercy isn't abused, and I'm grateful that Biddy and any other witches in Maledin are protected under the law. Witchcraft is what I wanted to talk to you about, actually."

"Oh?" he asks, pressing a kiss to my throat.

"I don't wish to be fooled by my visions ever again. I must learn to understand them."

Zabriel smiles and kisses me. "I thought you would want

that. Your powers are mysterious, and I wish to learn more about them as well. The *Hratha'len* will be able to..." He trails off as he sees me shake my head. "Not the *Hratha'len*?"

"This is human magic, not dragon magic. The only one who can help me is Biddy Hawthorne. The last time I departed my village, she told me to seek her out when I'm ready to become a witch as well as a queen."

Zabriel buries his face in my throat and breathes in deeply, and I wonder if he's trying to detect the scent of my oncoming heat. "Of course you must seek her out, but I wonder if now is the best time. Your heat will be upon you soon, and I selfishly want you all to myself."

"That could be weeks away. It could be months. There's no way for us to know, and my heart feels ready to face what happened with Emmeric. I feel like this is not only important, it's urgent."

I feel a throb of panic every time I remember Emmeric seizing my wrist and dragging me through a void to land helplessly at his feet. I want to know that the next time he comes for me, he'll be the one who falls in a heap.

Zabriel strokes the nape of my neck, and says softly, "You hope you can find the stolen villagers before Emmeric murders them."

"Maybe I'm the only one who can."

The past is out of my mind's reach, and so is the future, but the present could be mine to witness. After Emmeric intruded on my mind and made me see something that was false, I'll never be able to trust my visions until I've learned to understand them.

Zabriel thinks about this for a long time. "Fate has already declared our roles. I must be a merciful king and the strongest dragonrider for Maledin, and my bride must be a compassionate queen and a formidable witch. I will take you to Biddy Hawthorne, and we will ask her to return to Lenhale with us. I'm sure she will be comfortable in the castle or a house in the village."

I think about the cantankerous old woman with her weedy garden and flock of crows, dispensing foul-smelling but effective potions to villagers in need. Biddy Hawthorne likes muddy streets and meadows beneath her feet and the open sky above her head. Comfortable in Lenhale? I'm not sure she would agree, but perhaps we can persuade her to endure the cobbled streets and bustle of the city, for a time.

I draw Zabriel's silky hair through my fingers. "Thank you, Zabriel. As soon as you're ready to fly to Amriste, I would like to depart."

Zabriel smiles at me. "Then if the snow has stopped falling, how about we have your first riding lesson?"

THE SNOW LIES IN A THIN, fluffy layer over the dragongrounds. Fledglings, no bigger than large hunting dogs, cavort up and down, flinging showers of white up into the sky and snorting in surprise when it collects on their snouts.

Esmeral is bursting with happiness as we approach, her front legs stamping on the snow as if she senses that we're coming to her with purpose. She nuzzles my shoulder with her head and lightly nips at my fingers. Zabriel gets the same treatment, only she lays her head against his chest and gazes up at him with gold-flecked eyes.

"Such a beautiful girl," he murmurs with a smile, stroking her scales, and I can feel how much she loves his adoration.

The sky darkens, and suddenly Scourge's head descends, jaws open, and clamps his teeth around the base of Esmeral's skull in greeting.

"What a good idea, Scourge," Zabriel murmurs, his red eyes sparking as he shifts his attention to me. He tugs me to him, sweeps my hair aside, and grasps the nape of my neck with his teeth.

"Alpha," I whimper, my eyes closing as pleasure darts through me. My body goes limp in his arms, and I forget what we're doing here. I even forget where we are until he releases me, and I drag my eyes open.

I feel my nape. Esmeral and I both have teeth marks on the backs of our necks and our Alphas' eyes are smoldering.

"This is meant to be a riding lesson, and now I can't think straight," I say breathlessly.

Zabriel kisses me. "Scourge and I can't help it when we see you together. Our beautiful little dragons."

Scourge is watching me with a sly tilt of his handsome head. The first time I saw the massive black dragon, I was terrified. Now, with his scales rippling over his muscular frame and even with those teeth bared, I can see why Esmeral is completely smitten with him.

"He loves to watch me kiss you," Zabriel murmurs, slanting his mouth over mine once more and kissing me thoroughly.

"But he's a dragon," I say between losing myself in the strokes of his tongue.

"We're bonded. He feels what I feel, pleasure and pain. The stab wound in my side but also the sweet ache of wanting my mate." He gives me a final kiss, and then puts his hands on my shoulders and turns me toward Esmeral. "I will go on kissing you all day if I don't stop now. Would you like to ask your dragon a question?"

I reach out and stroke the soft scales beneath her jaw. "Esmeral, would you like to learn to fly with me?" I picture it as well as say it to her so that she can understand my question.

The dragon's eyes glow, and she shows me a picture of us in the skies with the smoke and tumult of a battle beneath us. I'm flooded with a sense of *yesness*.

"Esmeral would like that very much."

"Wonderful. Esmeral, I have seen you carry your rider beautifully. I know she'll be safe with you."

My dragon preens from the praise.

"Is that any way to speak to an inexperienced dragon?" The sharp voice cracks over us, and all four of us turn to look at the man striding toward us.

Stesha has washed his face clean and changed his clothes, but there are swollen gashes on his brow. Zabriel frowns but holds his tongue as the dragonmaster approaches my dragon.

"You wish to learn to fly with Lady Isavelle, Esmeral?"

"She told me that she does, dragonmaster," I reply, trying not to stare at the injuries on his forehead.

Stesha is still glaring at Esmeral. "To be the queen's dragon is to be a battle dragon. Not a silly dragon."

"Just because she's an Omega doesn't mean she can't be useful."

"Her designation has nothing to do with it. Dianthe had the makings of a fine battle dragon."

I glance at Zabriel with a question in my eyes.

"Mirelle's dragon," Zabriel replies. "An Omega."

"Oh." I never thought about what happened to Mirelle's dragon after the young woman flung herself from dragonback and died. I suppose Dianthe couldn't bear the pain and died with her.

"Dianthe was serene and obedient." Stesha narrows his eyes. "Listen to me, Esmeral. I'm watching you. Nilak is watching you." His white dragon has materialized silently by his side and is gazing down her snout at Esmeral. "Your Alpha is watching you and so is the king. All the dragons of the flare have their eyes on you. King Zabriel and Scourge will be the first ones to hear about it if Lady Isavelle gets so much as a saddle burn. Are you going to do anything dangerous to hurt your rider and anger all these Alphas?"

Esmeral can't understand the words Stesha is saying, but she recognizes his lecturing tone and feels the eyes of all the dragons. She raises her head and stares determinedly at the dragonmaster, the picture of an attentive and serious dragon.

Stesha looks at her for a long time. "You already know how to fly, but Lady Isavelle is going to make mistakes. New riders always do." Stesha glances at me. "Lady Isavelle will remain calm if she makes a mistake and will allow you to protect her."

I realize Stesha is waiting for me to answer his non-question when he arches an eyebrow at me. "Oh—yes, dragonmaster."

"Good. Because you are going to make mistakes. Lots of them." He turns to go, and I can't help but speak up about the injuries he's pretending aren't there.

"Are you sure you're all right, dragonmaster? I think your head must be hurting. May we help you in any way?"

Stesha keeps walking and sneers, "An Omega trying to shoulder an Alpha's concerns? Don't insult me, Lady Isavelle."

"An Alpha doesn't allow himself to feel insulted by compassion," Zabriel growls after him.

I glower at Stesha as he disappears, followed by Nilak. "If I didn't know that Stesha is acting this way because he cares about Zenevieve, I'd call him so many names right now."

Zabriel puts his fingers under my chin and tips my head up to look at him. "I'll deal with him. You and Esmeral should focus on each other."

I smile at Esmeral as she buffets her head against my hand. "A battle dragon. That sounds exciting, doesn't it? We Omegas are stronger than some people believe, aren't we?"

My dragon chirrups in agreement.

Zabriel smiles and then grows serious. "All right. Your riding lesson, *sha'len*. First of all, let's take a good look at your dragon."

Enamored by having our attention, Esmeral turns in an excited circle and poses with her wings spread and one foreleg raised.

"Yes, you are very beautiful, Omega," Zabriel tells her with a smile. "But we are assessing your battle capabilities." He turns to me. "You have a small, agile dragon. She's fast and brave. So far, she has carried you carefully from one place to another, but a battle flight is more demanding than traveling. The challenges you will face will be to stay on her back and remain focused as she makes fast maneuvers. She won't be able to intimidate her enemies and douse them in floods of dragonfire as a larger dragon can, but she can surprise them.

She can attack and be away again in the blink of an eye, almost as fast as a wingrunner."

The element of surprise. I like the sound of that. I also adore the sound of my Alpha speaking so authoritatively about battle dragons. It's sexy, and it makes me want to fly into battle by his side.

"Let's get you used to riding Esmeral while she makes fast maneuvers."

As I climb up onto Esmeral's back, Zabriel warns me, "You may struggle with feeling ill as you perform these drills."

I remember the lurching sensations that made me so unwell the first few times I rode on Scourge. As I've accepted who I am and Esmeral as my dragon, I haven't been nauseated while riding Scourge—and never on my own dragon.

"I think I will manage." I hope I will, anyway. "Can I fly low in case I fall?"

Zabriel climbs atop Scourge, who unfurls his massive black wings. "You must fly high so that if you fall, Scourge and I have time to catch you."

With that alarming thought, we formally begin my flying lessons.

The drills consist of performing the same flying patterns over and over, back and forth across the dragongrounds. First is an up-and-down pattern that makes me feel like I'm riding a bucking donkey. Then sideways wriggle that makes me think of a trout swimming up a fast-running river. At first, I grip the saddle tightly, terrified that I'm going to fly off into empty space.

"Move with her," Zabriel calls as he and Scourge fly past me. "Grip with your legs, not your hands."

I adjust my grip, and as my thighs hug the saddle, I cease feeling like I'm clinging on for dear life and start to meld to my dragon with my body as well as my mind. Esmeral's delight at being in the skies with her rider becomes my delight. My hands and shoulders relax, and I anticipate Esmeral's movements and move with them.

All of Lenhale is visible from up here. The turrets of the castle and the slate roofs of the town houses. The fields and rivers beyond. Below, many of the dragons are watching my riding lesson, and some of the fledglings are swooping back and forth, copying Esmeral's movements. I wonder who they'll choose to be their riders when the time comes.

I think of my brother Waylen with a pang of sadness. Though he was a nervous child, I think he would have loved to become a dragonrider. A dragon of his own might have brought him out of his shell and given him so much happiness, and I blink away tears as a fresh wave of loss hits me.

Sensing my distress, Esmeral spreads her wings and glides for a moment. I take a deep breath and gather my concentration.

"I'm all right. We can keep going."

Esmeral dips and rises in affirmation, and we continue the drills. A while later, Zabriel signals to me, and both our dragons head in to land.

I swing my leg over the saddle and slide the short distance to the ground. My legs are aching with fatigue. Now I know why my mate has such beautiful muscular thighs.

Zabriel swaggers toward me, a grin on his lips, and he pulls me into his arms. "*Sha'len*, you're a natural." He kisses me thoroughly, and with his free hand, he caresses Esmeral's scales.

Both my dragon and I attempt to take his praise like a fierce dragonrider and battle dragon, but we melt against his strong body. "You're an excellent instructor, and I could feel you keeping us safe."

Zabriel is still smiling, glancing between me and Esmeral. "Oh, look at that. How wonderful."

"What's wonderful?"

"Your eyes." He strokes my cheek with his thumb and smiles again. "I have noticed them changing gradually, and now it's happened all at once. Your eyes are the same color as Esmeral's. Turquoise, and flecked and rimmed with gold." He traces the backs of his fingers over my hair. "And look, your hair has turned a pale golden shade. The two of you have bonded."

I glance at Esmeral as if she's my mirror, which in a way she is. We gaze into each other's eyes.

"Look at you both," Zabriel murmurs huskily. "I'm so proud of my queens."

10

Isavelle

The crows greet us with cawing and flapping wings when Zabriel and I land our dragons on the outskirts of the deserted village. I nod to one of the blackbirds as I dismount Esmeral. "Good afternoon, Mistress Hawthorne."

"That could be an ordinary crow," Zabriel points out.

It could be, but I sense Biddy Hawthorne gazing at me through those glossy black eyes. I gaze from house to house, remembering the villagers who were impaled on spikes that grew out of the ground like monstrous black thorns. The spikes have all been destroyed, but the paving stones they disturbed are askew.

I'm not surprised when the old woman hobbles down the path toward us.

Zabriel remains beside Scourge but nods respectfully to Biddy. "Mistress Hawthorne."

She ignores him and clasps her hands together atop her walking stick. "Back so soon, girl? I thought there were too many handsome distractions in the capital."

I approach her with my hands folded in front of me and offer her a respectful nod. "Mistress, I have come to ask you to teach me witchcraft."

"Isavelle's handsome distraction will prepare a house for you in Lenhale, or even a room in the castle if you wish," Zabriel tells her.

Biddy Hawthorne watches me with milky blue eyes but addresses him. "Then you are easy in your heart that your mate is a witch?"

"My mate is many things, Grandmother," he replies. "A witch. A queen. A daughter. A dragonrider. Most of all, she's mine. I'm not threatened by any power that she possesses. If she becomes stronger, then Maledin will become stronger."

"And if she is forced to choose between being a witch and being the Queen of Maledin?"

"She won't ever have to—" Zabriel breaks off and laughs without humor. "You nearly had me tempting fate. I trust my mate to make wise decisions. She has a big enough heart for all the people in Maledin, including the witches."

There's a flap of wings out of the corner of my eye, and I can feel the stares of the dozen or so crows that have gathered around us. I wonder if Biddy is going blind and these birds are becoming her eyes.

"Why do you wish to learn witchcraft, girl?" Biddy asks me.

I think about my fears that I'll be manipulated by

Emmeric if I don't learn to control my powers. My doubts that I can be useful at all to Maledin as a witch or a queen. I can imagine how Biddy would scorn what she'd no doubt call my whining if I gave voice to these thoughts.

"Because I'm a witch," I tell her.

Biddy nods sharply. "That you are. Very well, I'll teach the first witch in five hundred years who needn't fear being burned at the stake. But I'll do so here. No mates. No dragons. Be off with you, *Ma'len*. You may post as many wyverns and their riders around the village as pleases you, but I can't teach a witch while she has a dragon nosing at her skirts all day."

Esmeral realizes that she's being talked about, and her turquoise and golden eyes widen and her nostrils flare with indignation. Behind her, Scourge lowers his massive head and utters a seething growl.

Zabriel's expression is thunderous. "My mate needs the protection of her dragon. Esmeral needs her rider. Dragons and riders can't be separated on the whims of one witch."

"The chit is free to do as she pleases. I have stated my conditions. I'm not teaching the Queen of Maledin witchcraft. I'm teaching Isavelle of Amriste." Biddy Hawthorne turns and makes her painstaking way back through the deserted village and up the narrow road to her cottage.

I stroke Esmeral's neck, as unhappy about this stipulation as I can feel my dragon is. "I've never heard of a witch in the city. I suppose I will have to do as she asks."

Zabriel's eyes are troubled. "You will go into heat soon, and I worry about you being in this isolated village in such a vulnerable state. Perhaps we should wait."

I take the amulet out of my pocket and show it to him. "This is the reason I don't think I can. Emmeric gave this to me. It's what allowed me to pass through the barrier and return to you."

Zabriel's eyes flare with red, and he makes a motion toward the amulet as if he wishes to grab it from me and fling it away from us but stops himself. "This is what did it? This belonged to Emmeric?"

"It was glowing when he gave it to me, and the glow lasted long enough for me to escape, but the light went out shortly after. Emmeric invaded my visions with something that isn't dragon magic. That barrier isn't dragon magic. I want to study this object with Mistress Hawthorne, and perhaps we can find a way to unlock the barrier."

Zabriel glares at the amulet for a long time. My mate is nearly twice my size and can speak in a voice that commands me to obey. If he tells me that I can't do this, there's nothing I'll be able to do to resist.

Zabriel wraps his arms around me and bows his head. "You say you have never heard of a witch in the city, Isavelle of Amriste. I think you will be the first, and you will have feet in both places. The streets and the fields. The walls and the meadows. The people and the forests. I suppose I will have to watch you fly away again and again." He presses his forehead against mine and closes his eyes. "But you must always come back to me."

ZABRIEL and I return to Lenhale together, and the following morning at the dragongrounds, I take Esmeral's head between my hands and press my forehead to her snout. "I will be gone all day. Take care of Zabriel and Scourge, and don't let their hearts grow too heavy without me."

Dawn light is creeping over the horizon, and the dragons are only just stirring, stretching their wings and yawning their massive, toothy jaws.

Esmeral twines her neck around me in a dragony hug and gives a soft trill. Then she cavorts over to Scourge. The black dragon has his eyes half closed and is lying as still as stone, and the only sign that he's felt his mate nestle against his side are twin streams of smoke suddenly issuing from his nostrils.

After I've said goodbye to the dragons, I meet my escort at the eyrie. Not the old one that burned down atop the cliffs because of me and Zabriel, but the new one on the eastern side of the castle. The wooden structure towers over me, and dozens of wyverns are emerging from the many arched windows, taking to the skies for their first flights of the day.

Captain Ashton steps forward, accompanied by five more wingrunners, and greets me with a short bow. "Lady Isavelle, we will be your escort and guard in Lenhale. My soldiers will always be within earshot, even if you can't see them or hear them. Wingrunners are quiet and discreet."

The young captain has always been so serious and difficult to read, but after the way he knew how to help Zabriel while he was sunk in pain and confusion during his rut, I have a newfound appreciation of the man. I give him a smile. "Thank you, Captain."

Fiala steps forward. "Would you like to fly with me, my lady?"

"Or you could fly with me," Dusan says, stepping in front of Fiala, who scowls at him.

They both look so hopeful, but I can't imagine why. "I

don't see why you're arguing over it. Having me on your wyvern will make you a target if we are attacked…" I trail off as both their eyes light up. I forgot that wingrunners find danger and peril to be the most wonderful things in the world. Fiala once impersonated me and was attacked by Brethren on all sides. I've never seen her happier.

"I would not like to tire your wyverns out too much," I tell them. "How about if I fly there with Fiala, and home with Dusan?"

My bodyguards seem pleased with the compromise.

"I hope I'm not taking you away from your duties," I say to Captain Ashton.

"This is our duty, and we are keen to execute it, Lady Isavelle," the captain tells me. "Shall we depart?"

Fiala directs me over to her mount. "Out of all the villages in Maledin, none have seen as much interesting enemy action as Amriste. We told the captain about the three mages who attacked you and Esmeral. We're delighted for the opportunity that we might shred such an enemy."

"Now that Emmeric has destroyed half of Amriste, I'm hoping that we'll be left in peace."

"Rotten pus-boil of a man," she mutters, and then proudly pats her wyvern. "This is Kagin, my lady. He's got a nasty temper, but he adores rousta leaves." She pulls some out of her pocket and holds them out to me. "Hold them flat on your palm and he'll eat them right up. Mind your fingers," she adds cheerfully.

As he scents his favorite treat, Kagin's head turns toward me as fast as a hawk turning its head. His black eyes sparkle dangerously. Wyverns are all skin and bones, their skulls clearly visible through their thin scales, and their teeth are more prominent than a dragon's. It would be rude to back away from my bodyguard's mount, but a cold sweat breaks out on my lower back. Even though Kagin is smaller than Esmeral, he's far more intimidating.

Trying not to tremble, I hold out the rousta leaves on my palm. "Are you, um, hung—" Kagin is indeed hungry. I can't help a tiny shriek as he lunges for the greenery and snaps it up, and it disappears down his gullet in a flash. Thankfully, I still have all my fingers.

Fiala beams and pats Kagin's flank. "Who's a friendly boy?"

She jumps up onto her mount, holds her hand down to me, and pulls me up behind her.

"I'm surprised he eats rousta leaves."

"Oh, wyverns eat anything."

Kagin turns his head and eyes me as if Omega women are his favorite treat.

Captain Ashton gives the signal to depart, and we shoot into the sky. I hold Fiala tight around the waist the whole way to Amriste. Wyverns fly quickly, and the journey takes half the time that it does on Scourge.

After the captain and his wingrunners have searched the village and its surroundings and determined that there are no Brethren lurking about, they disappear among the trees and houses, and all falls silent.

A crow is sitting on the edge of the well, sharpening its beak. I give the bird a respectful nod as I pass. "Good morning, Mistress Hawthorne."

I walk up the lane to her home and knock on the door. The cottage is as ramshackle as it always was, with dirty windows and straw falling from the thatched roof. The front garden is overgrown with weeds and strange-looking herbs.

Nothing happens, and I hear no reply. I'm about to knock again when a crow flutters down onto the overgrown path that leads around the back of the cottage, hops along the paving stones, and then glances back to see if I'm following.

Curious, I follow the crow around to the rear of the cottage. The morning is chilly, but thin sunshine pierces the clouds, and Biddy Hawthorne sits upon a wooden bench in her overgrown back garden, smoking her pipe. The crow flies away into the trees.

"I have come to you without my dragon or my mate. Will you teach me how to be a witch, Grandmother?"

The old woman eyes me for a moment, smoke slipping from her nostrils in a way that reminds me of Scourge. She points to an overgrown flower bed. "Fetch me a pungle plant. It has clusters of little mauve blooms in the spring, but you'll know them this time of year by their dull green leaves with purple veins. They have a twin root, so grasp it nice and firmly when you pull it up."

I hesitate for a moment. Is this a magical plant? Maybe this is a test to see if I really am a witch, and if I can't pull up a pungle plant, I'll have to go home.

There's a scrap of hessian sack laying by some garden implements. I kneel on the sack, grasp a pungle plant by the base of its stem, and pull. It comes up easily.

"Is it magical?" I ask, turning the plant over in my hands, hoping that something interesting is about to happen, or I'm about to learn about a powerful plant.

"They're an eyesore, and I can't stand them. Get rid of

them, stems, roots, and all, so I don't have to look at those ugly little flowers come spring."

"You want me to weed your garden?" I ask in astonishment.

"That's right. Proper apprentice witch work, this is."

Irritation sparks in my blood. I feel like I've been tricked. "And what will you do while I pull weeds?"

"Watch that you do it properly. Now, get on with it," she snaps. "You're not a queen in my garden."

I haven't lost the ability to labor over menial tasks hour after hour, but I have forgotten what it's like to be ordered around. People bow and curtsey to me at the castle. Zabriel showers me with so many pet names and coaxing words. *Please, sha'len, will you do this for me? It would make your Alpha so happy if you did that.* I would vehemently deny that any of that has gone to my head, but I'm bristling slightly.

As I pull up pungle plant after pungle plant, shaking the dirt from the roots and placing them in a basket, Biddy smokes her pipe and stares straight ahead. I wonder if she's off with her birds, flying over the village and feeling the wind whistling through feathered wings.

"What is being done about the witchfinders?" Biddy asks suddenly.

I wince, wondering how she's going to react when I tell her Zabriel pardoned them all. To give myself time to think, I reach for a large pungle plant, wrap my hands around the stems and leaves, and pull. Nothing happens. I pick up the trowel and use it to loosen the roots. Another arm-wrenching pull, and the pungle plant and all of its roots come out of the ground. Panting slightly, I shake off the soil and lay it in the basket. "What do you think should be done about the witchfinders?"

The old woman puffs on her pipe. "Why on the gods' stony earth are you asking me? You're the queen. I'm just a witch."

I sit back on my heels and brush the dirt from my fingers. "Mistress Hawthorne, it's because you're a witch that I'm asking you. It's witches who have suffered at the hands of the witchfinders."

"What I think doesn't matter farther than the end of this garden."

"Zabriel's advisors give him their opinion when he asks for it," I point out. "May I ask for a little advising?"

The old woman thumps her walking stick on the ground and snaps, "Advisor? Advisor? I'm your crone while I teach you, and don't you forget it, young witch."

Every conversation with Biddy feels like I can say nothing right. I know there must be a right answer to her question. I suspect Biddy wouldn't have asked me what was being done about the witchfinders unless she knew exactly what she wanted done about them. "Zabriel has pardoned everyone in Maledin who didn't take up arms for the Brethren. He believes that the people had no choice but to build their temples, sew their robes, care for their horses, or find their witches."

"We saw plenty of witchfinders in this village," Biddy says. "They were always around, hunting and torturing and burning."

I remember many of them passing through the village, sitting atop their horses and casting their hard, suspicious eyes around the village square. They seemed to sense there was a witch somewhere in their midst, but Biddy was clever enough or lucky enough not to be found.

"All those times they came here, and they never realized what you are."

There's a roguish grin on Biddy's lips. "Didn't look hard enough, did they? Did you ever meet with one, girl?"

I shake my head. "No, I must have been lucky because I never met a..." I break off. I was about to say I never met a witchfinder, but that's not true. I was able to keep out of their way when they passed through the village, but later I came face to face with one at Fliesch Monastery.

"I did meet a witchfinder. I forgot about that. He said something strange to me, but at the time I didn't realize how strange it was."

"Oh? What did he say?"

Mistress Hawthorne listens as I tell her the story. I was a Veiled Virgin in servitude to the Brethren at the Fliesch Monastery, and I'd caught the baneful eye of the High Priest. All the witchfinders reported to him, so I would often see the men dressed in black coming and going. Often I would be called to his office and given some horrible task for penance, and when I didn't do it correctly or fast enough for his liking, he would watch as one of his priests flogged me.

This particular day, the High Priest told me to go down to the dungeon and tend to a man chained in a cell. He mustn't die. If he died, I would be flogged twice as hard as usual.

I asked the priest escorting me down to the dungeon who the prisoner was.

"A witchfinder. He tried to flee over the border to Grendu, and he must be corrected before he's put back to work."

It surprised me that a witchfinder had been disobedient

because they all seemed to love their job. I'd heard they were given a substance called shackle, which helped them perform their duties and control their abilities. Not their magic. The High Priest was very clear that only witches use magic, and witchfinders use their *abilities.*

"This man has been whipped, and he's being starved of shackle until he repents," the priest told me. "Be careful, girl. Shackle starvation is violent and painful. It could kill him, and he's too valuable to lose. If he dies it will be your fault."

I didn't like the sound of my near-impossible task. The priest unlocked a cell and handed me a bag of healer's supplies and told me to get on with it.

There was very little light inside the cell. A thin shaft of sunlight from a grille high in the wall illuminated a figure on his knees in the center of the room, arms spread wide, and his wrists locked in manacles. He was one of the biggest men I'd ever seen, though I hadn't met Zabriel yet.

The man slowly raised his head and looked at me through a curtain of dirty blond hair. I don't know if it was the darkness of the cell, but his eyes looked black and lifeless as if he were already dead. Sweat was rolling down his bare chest and blood dripped from his back onto the wet stone floor. He watched me in silence through his locks of dirty hair. He looked mean. Or perhaps he was just in pain.

Keeping a tight hold of the healer's bag, I ducked under the chains and looked at the man's back. His shoulders were crisscrossed with dozens and dozens of bloody cuts. I was usually hit with a birch rod that left painful red welts and occasionally broke the skin. This man had been viciously whipped, every lash flaying a strip of skin from his back.

Sorting through the bag of salves, tinctures, and

bandages, I said, "They have beaten you so hard, and you've lost so much blood, I'm surprised you're still conscious, let alone alive."

"I regret I'm hard to kill," he muttered through his teeth.

Surely he didn't actually want to die. "What's your name?"

"Kane."

I hesitated. There was no reason for me to speak with this man, but I was starting to feel pity for him, and I didn't want to pity a witchfinder. I drew a healing salve out of the bag and opened the pot. "How many witches have you burned at the stake, Kane?"

For a moment there was silence, and then he laughed. A weak, wheezing laugh. "Why the fuck do you care?"

I opened my mouth to say, *Of course I care*, but then I remembered that I was wearing the robes of a Veiled Virgin. Good little Veiled Virgins love and adore their priests and hate witches.

"Or have you come to admire me?" Kane asked in a dark voice. "Do you wish to congratulate me? Are you hungry to know how many witches I've burned so you can lavish me with praise?"

I felt sick at the thought, and I swiped the salve across three cuts at once, and he hissed in pain.

When I finished tending to his wounds, I ducked back under his chained arm and headed for the door. There was a bucket of fresh water and a ladle, and I glanced back at the man. I doubted that anyone had given him a drink, and he was sweating so much.

When I held the ladle of fresh water to his lips, he tightened them and turned his face away.

Maybe he didn't like being a witchfinder after all. Maybe

he actually hated it. Still, it was my job to keep him alive. "You'll die if you don't drink something. I won't return until tomorrow."

Kane looked at me, then *really* looked at me. Those dark eyes seemed like they were trying to burn right through my soul. He opened his mouth to speak, and I tipped the water into his mouth. He half choked and spluttered a lot of the water all over me, but he swallowed the rest.

"That's a new way of thwarting me," he said between choking fits of laughter.

"Thwarting you from what?"

But Kane lowered his head, letting it hang, and let his suffering take him.

When I returned the following day, he was worse. His cuts were still bleeding and though his body was burning with fever, he couldn't stop shaking. I asked him if it was the shackle withdrawal, but he didn't seem to hear me.

I tended to his wounds and tried to coax him to drink water, but he wouldn't take any.

As I left the cell, the priest who'd brought me down there glanced in at Kane and shook his head. "I don't know why the High Priest is bothering to have you look after that witchfinder. That beating on top of the shackle withdrawal? He'll be dead in a day or two, and good riddance to him. He's an obstinate troublemaker who tried to run from his duty."

An obstinate troublemaker who tried to run from his duty. There weren't many in Maledin who were brave enough to try to thwart our oppressors.

I think it was the priest's words that made me do it. Later that day, as I cleaned the High Priest's office, I stole some shackle. It was kept in a locked box, but I'd spotted months ago where the High Priest kept the key.

The following day when I visited Kane, he was unconscious. I dissolved some of the brown powder in water and rubbed it on Kane's lips. It took some time for him to wake up and lick his lips, but when he did, his eyes sprang open. Half delirious, he drank a ladleful of the stuff, and then another. It was like watching a corpse come back to life. His wounds ceased to bleed and the color returned to his cheeks. I expected his flat black eyes to become a little more human, but they were as dead-looking as always.

Then they hardened in anger as he realized what I'd done. "What did you do that for? Your bastard fucking priests feed me shackle, and now you are too?"

"Keep your voice down, there's a priest outside your cell," I hissed. "You would have died if I'd not stolen that for you. Instead of cussing at me, why don't you think of a better way to escape next time?"

Kane glanced at the door and then back at me, a ghost of a smile on his lips. "Little heretic. You'll be whipped as well if they find out what you've done."

"Are you going to tell them?" I challenged him.

Kane laughed softly. "I spit at them. Every single one."

A wave of relief and satisfaction passed through me. Finally, here was someone who disliked the Brethren as much as I did.

"You must pretend to be sick and shaking for a while longer," I whispered. "Then I will tell the High Priest that you have sweated out the shackle and your wounds no longer endanger your life, and they'll let you out of this dungeon."

Over the following days, I privately reveled in my act of

defiance. I imagined Kane making it all the way to Grendu and finally freeing himself from the Brethren. If he could do it, maybe I could as well.

On the eighth day of Kane's incarceration, the wounds on his back finally closed.

I called out to the priest outside, "This man has healed and his life is not in danger. I'm no longer needed."

The priest came in and inspected Kane's back, and then unlocked his cuffs. Addressing Kane, he said, "You can sleep in the monastery tonight and see the High Priest in the morning for your shackle before you go back to your duties."

Kane's hands hit the ground as soon as he was unchained, and he groaned in pain. As the priest left the cell, I helped him to his feet.

"Next time, be sure to make it all the way to Grendu without being caught. Good luck."

Kane was rubbing his sore wrists and gazing at me through narrowed eyes. It was a strange, searching expression.

"What?" I asked, wondering if I had something on my face.

Kane whispered something. A word, or series of words, though I barely heard them and recognized none of them. They passed over me. Through me. I felt them like a physical thing, and they took my breath away. The cell was filled with light, but I had no idea where it was coming from.

I looked down at myself in panic and then up at Kane. "What did you just say? What did you do to me?"

Kane's dead eyes were suddenly burning with hatred and fury. He took a step toward me, and my heart leaped into my throat. Then he seemed to change his mind and he went back to rubbing his wrists.

"What was that about?" I asked shakily.

"I see fire in your future," he said in a dark voice.

The unfriendliness in his tone made my blood feel icy. Was he not going to thank me for saving his life? "Are you a fortune teller now?" I asked nervously.

A cold smile spread over his lips. "Maybe. Here's a prediction for you. When you see me coming for you...*run.*"

All the hair stood up on the back of my neck. The cell was too small. I was trapped in a cage with a wild animal. I turned on my heel and ran, and I didn't look back.

I saw Kane one more time the following morning, mounting his horse in front of the monastery. He was no longer dressed in rags but in the hateful black clothes and black hat of a witchfinder. As his spirited horse danced beneath him, Kane spied me, and I saw the flash of white teeth beneath the broad brim of his hat. He spurred his horse and galloped away, and nasty laughter trailed after him.

The reliving of that memory is so vivid that it takes a moment for it to fade and to realize I'm sitting in Biddy Hawthorne's garden.

Biddy has been listening to my tale in silence.

"I felt unnerved about the whole experience," I finish, rubbing my upper arms and trying to dispel the chill of that cell and the sick feeling in my stomach.

"And now?" Biddy asked.

"I shouldn't have helped that man. He was being beaten and punished by the priests, so I pitied him. I thwarted his suffering and made him better so he could ride away and kill more witches. I can't believe how stupid I was. I feel ashamed."

"Time will tell whether your pity was ill-founded. Now, how are you getting on with those pungle flowers?"

I look at the empty garden bed in front of me. "I pulled them all up while I was talking."

"Good. Nothing makes a witch feel more like a witch than dirt under her fingernails and an aching back."

I roll my fatigued shoulders. "I don't know about feeling like a witch, but I'm exhausted."

In a sharper tone of voice, Biddy asks, "Did you try looking at your hand?"

I study my hands, which are dirty but otherwise unremarkable. "What's wrong with my hands?"

"The day that the Maledinni of Amriste were killed, you were brought here by a false vision. While you were in the grip of it, did you try looking at your hand?"

I frown, thinking back to that moment. "I don't think so."

"If you had, it would have looked strange. Felt strange. If you'd tried to do something like button your dress or tie an apron, you would have found it difficult to do."

"Oh? Why's that?"

"Because it's not your hand, and it's not your vision. Next time you have a vision, raise your hand before your eyes. Give your fingers a task. If it's someone else's vision, if it's being forced upon you, you will feel clumsy. Your hands won't work like you want them to. If it's your vision, everything should seem easy. This is a small trick. A little detail. But an important one."

My heart races with excitement. I'm learning some real witchcraft. A way to protect myself and the people I care about. I raise my hands and look at them. "I should do something in my vision? Something like snapping my fingers?"

"Are you good at snapping your fingers?"

I snap the fingers of my right hand and then my left, and they make good, loud snaps.

Biddy nods. "Yes, just like that. You'll only be able to do it like that in your visions. You'll never be fooled again if you remember this."

The relief that pours over me makes me laugh out loud. I'll never be fooled again. Emmeric won't be able to trick me.

I pile all the pungle plants into the basket. When I get to my feet, I ask Biddy, "What kind of witch do you think I am, Mistress Hawthorne?"

I expect Biddy to say something vague, or to tell me that it's up to me to figure that out, but to my surprise, she answers the question.

"I believe you are a farseer, Isavelle. Yours is the gift to see. To know. To find. You're frustrated because you wish it would be clairvoyance, but seeing the future is seldom as useful as people think it will be. The future is clouded and uncertain. But the present? How things are at this very moment? That is a fine gift indeed."

I pick dirt out from beneath my fingernails. If it's a fine gift, I'd know where the missing villagers are. I'd be able to bring my father and sister home. They're out there somewhere and it hurts to know that they're likely scared and suffering.

"It is a fine gift," she said firmly, reading my downcast expression.

"You remember that I had a vision in your cottage the day I met Zabriel? I thought it was Zabriel I was seeing, but it was his brother, Emmeric. He's the Shadow King, and he wants Zabriel dead. He's the one who gave me the vision of my family returning home. He tricked me, and then he dragged me through some kind of portal and behind the barrier." I reach into my pocket and take out the amulet. "I was only able to return because of this. Emmeric gave me this and allowed me to return through the barrier, and then it seemed to lose all its power."

Biddy reaches for the amulet but hesitates and draws her hand back. She speaks more to herself than to me. "Something that belonged to the Shadow King and given willingly to you. He can't know what he has done…"

"Is it important that he gave it willingly? I thought the crystal was the important part, and we could figure out how it works."

"Don't give it to me, girl. This is the most important thing that has happened. Keep that crystal safe."

"But what if we find a way to unlock—"

Biddy Hawthorne heaves herself to her feet and turns away. "I will see you again tomorrow, girl. I'm tired. Be off with you."

She walks up the narrow path toward the back door of her cottage, goes inside, and shuts the door behind her.

There's a pile of garden waste at the far end of the flower beds, and I drop the pungle plants onto it before heading back to the village square to find Captain Ashton and the wingrunners to escort me home to Lenhale.

11

———

Zabriel

I feel the world shift the moment she walks into the courtyard. Slowly, I lower my sword and turn around, hunting among the soldiers and dragonriders for the sight of my perfect, peachy, blossoming Omega.

The barracks and practice grounds are crowded today. Godric is putting the newly recruited City Watch through their paces. Many of these men were soldiers under the Brethren, but others have never held a sword before, and none of the women have. None of them know how to fight alongside dragons and wyverns or protect civilians within the city walls. It astonishes me that the Brethren expected all women to stay at home, completely ignoring the fact that some women are far happier on a battlefield than in the domestic sphere.

As I drag a deep breath into my lungs, the sweet scent of

Isavelle's perfume breaks through me, overlaid with needy frustration. The sword falls from my hand with a clatter.

My mate is going into a false heat.

I march forward through the crowd, leaving my sparring partner behind with a confused expression on his face. I hunt left and right, stepping around groups of men and women testing their wooden practice swords for the first time. A group of soldiers part, and when I see her, I stop dead.

My Omega, flanked by her bodyguards. Seeing her is like the sun coming out, and she looks...*different*.

Her hair is so golden now that it glimmers as brightly as Esmeral's scales, and her turquoise eyes are luminous. There's a flush in her cheeks, and her fingers are tangled nervously in front of her. I don't recognize the clothes she's wearing. I've become accustomed to seeing Isavelle dressed the same as the palace maids, but today she's dressed as a dragonrider.

Isavelle looks unlike any dragonrider I've ever seen before. Her jacket is tan and embroidered with gold thread, and the charcoal breeches she wears are fitted to her hips and thighs. A cape swirls around her, and her long hair is in a single thick braid that rests on her shoulder. The wind teases tendrils of hair around her face, and she looks for me among the crowd as feverishly as I looked for her.

Dusan spots me, and relief washes over his expression, no doubt remembering that the last time Isavelle went into false heat, she hid in a hayloft beneath a pile of straw. He points me out to Isavelle, and a smile breaks over her face as she sees me.

As I approach, Isavelle speaks in a husky, flustered voice. "Zabriel. I needed to come find you, well, because..."

She doesn't need to tell me. I stroke the back of my finger over her cheek. "You're going into false heat."

The scent of Isavelle's false heat is flooding the courtyard, a space filled predominantly with men of mating age. Two Alphas and a dozen Beta males are all staring at my mate. Everyone becomes fascinated by an Omega in heat, especially one as luscious as Isavelle. I witnessed every head turn when my sister or mother walked into a room in this state. Right now, Isavelle could hypnotize the entirety of the Great Hall.

My possessive side ratchets up at the sight of so many curious and hungry eyes trained on my mate. I pull her into my arms and glare around the courtyard. Many soldiers remember themselves and hastily look away, though some of them have to be elbowed meaningfully by their companions.

The delicious softness of her breasts and rounded stomach are pressed against my body. I need to taste her mouth and remind us both that she's mine. She needs to be in a quiet, dark space so her Omega doesn't start to fret.

"Down here." I grasp Isavelle's hand and take her into a room filled with practice swords and battered helmets, then through heavy doors and down some steps. I collect a lantern as I go, and the sounds and light from the courtyard vanish behind us until we're very much alone. I turn into an antechamber and close the door behind us, balancing the lantern on a stack of shields. There are racks of polished swords and spears. It's a small room, and there's not a great deal of space for us, but that was the idea. Omegas need confined spaces when they're in heat. Open skies make them upset and anxious.

Isavelle doesn't seem to notice where we are. She moans

my name and pulls me down for a kiss, pressing herself against me so I can get my scent all over her. I stroke my tongue against hers, and she pulls away every now and then to breathe in deeply.

"You smell so good, Alpha," she gasps.

Meanwhile, her powerful perfume is making my head spin so much that I feel drunk. Sitting down on a trunk, I pull her against me so she's straddling one of my thighs.

"Where are we?" she asks breathlessly, gazing around.

"The armory," I murmur between kisses. "It's underground so it can be protected in case of a siege. I'll carry you to your nest in a moment. I just couldn't wait to..." Her beautiful face is upturned toward mine. My mouth descends onto hers. "Did you come looking for me? Do you need your Alpha, *sha'len*?" I whisper, running my tongue over her upper lip.

"I do. I was down at the dragongrounds with Esmeral and suddenly ten of the biggest dragons were all sniffing me. I was surrounded by massive scaly bodies, and then they started snapping and snarling and pushing one another out of the way. Scourge bellowed and bit and shoved them until they all moved back. I realized that the back of my neck and my belly had been aching since this morning, and suddenly I felt an overwhelming urge to run and hide."

I picture my tiny mate being jostled by Alpha dragons who are all excited by an Omega in heat, and then Scourge knocking them all out of the way to protect her. I feel a fierce throb of kinship for my dragon.

I notice the unusual textures of the fabrics beneath my fingers. "Omega, you're dressed differently."

She touches her embroidered jacket and breeches with

both hands and then looks hopefully up at me. "Do you like it? One of my companions showed me some ideas for clothing, and we had a few things made. This is for dragonriding. It's probably not what you're used to seeing a queen or a princess or a lady wear. I don't know what women in your time favored, but I want to be able to ride Esmeral and still feel like me, and..." My mate trails off, biting her lip. "I don't really know what I'm doing."

I press my forehead to hers and smile, whispering, "You look so beautiful, my bride."

Tears swim in her eyes. Sweet little dragon. She really is needy in her false heats.

"Really?" she asks hopefully.

"Truly. You look wonderful in whatever you're wearing, or even wearing nothing at all, but I love seeing you dressed for dragonriding."

I groan as the perfume of my pleased, horny Omega erupts around me. This is a world away from how she used to behave during her false heats. Isavelle would cry and push me away, hating that she felt so out of control. Even the delight of seeing Isavelle take me all the way to my knot can't compare to this moment. Isavelle is in a false heat and she came to find me.

I know just what my beautiful mate needs. I slide a hand into her hair at the nape of my neck, gather it into my fist, and squeeze, gently tugging on her sore mating gland. Isavelle's lips part with a gasp. Her relief is so intense that fresh tears well up in her eyes and run down her cheeks. I kiss the wet tracks and lick up her tears.

"You are a wonder, *sha'len*," I breathe. "I can't get enough of looking at you. Smelling you. Touching you. Watching you cycle through your heats. I would see Omegas flustered by false heats, torturing themselves and their Alphas, and hope that one day I'd have a beautiful little Omega wriggling in my lap, all hot and wet and frustrated."

Hearing me say *lap*, Isavelle burrows even further into me. Her arms clamp tightly around my neck, half strangling me. I laugh softly and turn my head to kiss her cheek.

"How long until this is the real thing?" she whispers.

"Are you anxious to get to the good part? Your true heat that will put your Alpha into a rut for days on end."

Isavelle moans in delight. "Yes. Rut me for days. Give me your knot."

I grin in the semi-dark as I recognize her Omega voice. She rarely lets it out, but I wonder if I'll hear it more often from now on.

I lick slowly up her neck, my teeth just grazing her throat. Torturing myself. Torturing both of us.

"Sink your teeth into me. Make me yours," she pleads.

The begging note in her voice makes me want to do anything she asks, but then I remember my last rut. How I was aching to fuck her but she wouldn't let me because of my stitches. She was taking care of her injured Alpha, but I haven't forgotten my promise to torment her back. Just a little, for fun.

"How much do you want me to make you mine?" I whisper in her ear.

"So much. *So much*," she gasps, gripping my shoulders urgently.

"Down here in the armory, surrounded by all these weapons?"

"Yes. *Yes*. I don't care where we are."

"Show me how much you want me."

She lifts her head, puzzled. "Show you, Alpha?"

Alpha. A wave of pleasure so strong passes through me that my eyelashes flutter. I nod at the cabinet opposite, which is just about the same height as her hips. "Just what I said. Show me your slick."

"You can feel it. I'm already slicking so much."

"Are you?" I murmur, squeezing her breasts and thighs. "How beautiful. Go over there and show me."

She's reluctant to peel herself away from my body but does what I ask. I settle back to watch her, my elbows propped on the shelves, drinking in the sight of my mate.

"How should I show you?" she asks shyly, looking over her shoulder.

My eyes run over her. "You know what your Alpha likes."

The flush in her cheeks is even deeper, but she's smiling as she takes off her clothes in the dim, cramped room. The air is warm, but her nipples tighten into points as she pulls off her jacket and shirt and then wiggles her breeches and underclothes down her legs. Tendrils of blonde hair fall around her face as she steps out of her clothes, and I see the soft gleam of her slick on her inner thighs. I want to jump up and stick my face in it, but I tighten my fists and make myself stay where I am.

Isavelle trails her fingers through her sex, and a powerful jolt of desire goes through me. "Alpha, you promised to... promised to..." She trails off with an anguished bite of her lip.

"You can say it. There's only you and me here."

She lifts her golden and turquoise gaze to mine, and I can see her gathering courage. A shy smile curves her lips. "You promised to...fuck me through my next false heat."

All the blood rushes to my knot hearing her use such words. "Is that what you want?"

"Please," she whimpers. "Can't you tell?"

I tilt my head to one side and smile at her. "How can I tell? Show me."

I want to look at her. Every intimate part of her.

"Well, I..." Isavelle begins and then realizes what I want. She turns around and leans over the cabinet, her hips raised, her breasts and cheek resting against the top. I groan low in the back of my throat as I appreciate her luscious body. The curve of her ass and thighs. Her swollen sex shiny with slick. My mouth waters and my cock stands to attention.

I push the heel of my hand against my shaft through my breeches, which is impatient to be taken out and shoved inside her. "By the gods, you're so beautiful, *sha'len*."

Isavelle moans and a fresh shimmer of slick coats her inner lips and drips down her thighs.

"How do you feel against your fingers?" I ask.

She reaches down between her legs, and I see her fingers play over her tender, slippery flesh. I take a shuddering breath and adjust my legs, the fabric of my breeches painfully tight against my cock.

With her cheek resting against the wood, she turns her head so she can see me, and still touching herself, she pants, "I feel so good. Do you like that, Alpha?"

My voice is husky with desire. "Oh yes, my beautiful dragon. You're so perfect."

"I like that you're watching me. Will you touch yourself as well?"

I unbutton and unlace my breeches and drag out my cock. With one hand around my shaft and the other around my knot, I squeeze and stroke myself, my eyes fastened onto her. She's breathing faster now as she rubs her clit. Droplets of her slick run down her inner thighs.

"Will you come over here, Alpha? I need you," she whimpers.

I grin at the needy sound in her voice. "But I like you right there."

"Please touch me, Alpha. *Please.*"

My instinct is to leap to my feet and ram my cock into her, but I stay in my seat. "You look so pretty while you're touching yourself. Don't stop, *sha'len.*"

"I need you, Alpha."

"What did I tell you during my rut? *When the time comes for your heat and you're begging me for relief, I'll torment you right back.*"

Her mouth falls open in surprise. "You meant that?"

"Yes," I say with relish, grinning so wide it bares my dragines.

Her little feet are pressing against the ground in frustration. She squirms with need. Isavelle was always too ashamed to show off her body to me, but not anymore.

"Alpha, you're not going to leave me like this for the whole of my false heat, are you?" she whimpers.

"Maybe I will. Why don't you come for me, and then I'll decide?" I sound calm, but I'm sweating with the effort not to leap to my feet and go over to her. Tormenting her? More like tormenting myself. I clench my teeth as I grip my cock and knot.

Isavelle goes on circling her clit with her fingertips, faster and faster. Her cries grow louder. Her skin flushes pink. When she climaxes, her slick gushes down her thighs.

I can't take it any longer. I leap to my feet, cross the room in one step, fall to my knees, and bury my tongue in her pussy, tasting as much of her as I can. She's so swollen against my tongue, and she tastes divine. I spread her wider with my fingers and plunge my tongue inside her.

"Omega. You're so perfect. You're so beautiful." I'm a starving man, desperate to have my fill of her. I get to my feet, dragging my cock up her thighs. Isavelle is sprawled over the cabinet with her braid tumbled to one side, the beautiful nape of her neck bared to me.

I plant a hand on the back of her neck, holding her down, and grasp my cock in my hand. "How much do you need me to fuck you, *sha'len*?"

12

Isavelle

"Please, please, _please_," I beg Zabriel. "Please fuck me, Alpha. I need you so much."

I lay panting over the cabinet with my legs spread. Alpha is here, holding me down. Protecting me. Wanting me. I'm aching with the need to feel him inside me.

He slides the head of his cock through my slick, and I moan his name. He's so close to giving me what I want, and I think I'm going to burst apart. A moment later, he shoves his cock inside me, parting my swollen, aching flesh and driving himself deep. Pleasure surges through me as I cry out.

Zabriel tortures me with slow, shallow thrusts. I know he can give me more. I reach behind me and feel several inches of his cock as well as his knot. I wriggle in frustration and brace against the cabinet. "Please. More. I want all of you."

"You want more, Omega?" he asks breathlessly, moving in and out of me with strong thrusts. "I've got plenty more."

"Yes. *Yes.*" My earlier false heats were stormy and uncontrollable. I thought I'd feel better having Zabriel with me, but I'm even more frantic.

I push against the cabinet so Zabriel can thrust deeper into me. He tries to gather me up in his arms, but I'm too desperate to let him.

"Let go, Omega. Come here." There's an authoritative growl in his voice, and all my willpower and thoughts vanish. I loosen my grip on the cabinet, and he pulls me into his strong arms, bent over me while I'm tight against his chest, his arms pinning mine down.

"Good girl," he groans in my ear, and he pulls me down on his cock at the same time he thrusts upward. All at once, I'm completely filled with his cock, and I cry out from relief and pleasure. In his Alpha growl, he says, "You're so sweet to fuck."

Every thought I have evaporates from my mind except for, *Alpha is pleased with me. I'm so sweet to fuck.*

Then a masculine voice that's not Zabriel's intrudes in my mind and sneers at me, *Brainless fucktoy Omega.*

I go rigid with a gasp and my eyes snap open. That was Emmeric's voice. Am I having a vision? Is he here?

Zabriel stops moving. "Isavelle?"

I'm still in the armory with Zabriel. It wasn't a vision, just a nasty memory intruding on my private moment with Zabriel.

"I'm—I'm fine. Don't stop."

Zabriel pulls out of me, puts gentle hands on my body, and turns me around to face him. One strong hand cups the nape of my neck and tilts my chin up so I'm looking at him. He's bent over me so that his shoulders and long hair keep me in darkness and warmth.

"Omega, I can smell it in your scent and hear it in your voice that you're distressed. What just happened?"

I open my mouth, but Emmeric's name sticks in my throat. "I don't want to say. I'll ruin this moment with you."

"You could never ruin anything. Tell me, Omega."

I take a shuddering breath. "Emmeric…"

Zabriel's eyes flare crimson, and his face tightens in anger. "Did you see him in a vision?"

I shake my head and gentle his fury with a hand on his chest. "No, I just remembered something he said to me. Let's forget about it." I try to kiss him, but I can't reach his mouth.

"I won't forget about it. Tell me what he said to you."

"He…called me names. Cruel words about what I am and what you and I do together. I was getting lost in that voice you use on me and then suddenly I remembered him."

Realization dawns, and Zabriel looks pained. "I said coarse things to you and it reminded you of him. I'm so sorry, Isavelle."

"No, no," I cry. "I love the things you say to me. You're nothing like him. You don't remind me of him."

Zabriel doesn't look like he believes me. I've never seen him look so devastated before.

"I should have asked before using that voice on you," he says hoarsely. "It's new to me as well. I can feel it coming in stronger and stronger lately. I'm so sorry, *sha'len*."

He looks so upset with himself that tears spring into my eyes and run down my cheeks. I throw my arms around his waist. "Please don't be sorry. Please don't not say them."

Zabriel takes my face gently in his hand and kisses each tear, licking the salt from his lips between each press of his mouth. He's so tender with me that it makes my heart ache.

"I'm sorry. I don't know why I'm crying," I tell him. "I promise you didn't do anything wrong."

His scent grows richer, and I feel it soothing me. That was something I was afraid of before, that he was controlling me somehow, but now all I feel is his care for me.

"You make yourself so vulnerable to me," he whispers. "I don't ever want to make you afraid of me."

I put my hands on his shoulders and gaze up at him. "You never could. Being this intimate with you is what I want. When we're together, everything is so intense, isn't it?"

Zabriel smiles. "It is, *sha'len*. I can barely think when I have you in my arms. I'm running on instinct to protect and adore you and make you mine."

"I can barely think, either. It makes me feel better knowing you're the same way." Zabriel doesn't think I'm brainless or his stupid little pet. Whatever Emmeric believes about Omegas is not my problem. "Please use that voice on me. I feel like it's something that will make our bond even deeper."

"But if it makes you feel terrible about yourself—"

I smile and shake my head. "It was an echo of a bad experience. You've just helped me understand us better."

Zabriel studies me for a moment. Holding me in his arms, he leans down and growls into my ear, "Who's Alpha's good girl?"

Oh, stars. Every thought that isn't Zabriel or his knot flees from my mind. I need him sinking into me. I want the powerful thrusts of his cock. "Me, Alpha."

My mate kisses me hungrily. His fingers seek my sex, and he thrusts two of them inside me. He works his fingers in and out of me while we kiss, his tongue caressing mine. His thumb swipes over my clit, and my cries spill into his mouth. I cling to his shoulders, feeling my climax build and build until I shatter around his fingers, squeezing him tight.

Zabriel turns me around, grasps his cock, and thrusts himself home.

My insides light up. I cry out with every thrust. I can't move. I'm completely in his power. The strength of his arms and body makes me feel safer than any nest.

After several long, delicious strokes that push deeper and deeper, I feel the mass of his knot thud against me. "Yes. *Yes.* Alpha, you feel so good."

"Omega, you should see what I see," Zabriel gasps, and I can tell he's looking down between us.

The wet slap of his knot hitting my sex fills the air around us, laced with my whimpers and his growls of pleasure. His fingers find my clit and rub me in circles as his cock slams in and out of me.

"Will you be a good girl and let Alpha knot you when the time comes?" he says.

"Ask me in that voice."

He repeats the question, growling it into my ear. I think I could climax just from the way his voice vibrates in my ears and on my clit.

"I wish I could take your knot now." There's space inside me that I need him to fill. I want to be stretched so tight around him as he locks himself inside me, but I won't be able to manage it until my first proper heat.

Zabriel groans and buries his face in my neck. "I wish you

could too. I want to thrust harder and harder until I force this swelling inside you and make you mine."

With each thrust, his knot stretches me wider, and the pleasurable burn has me screaming his name. He pumps into me faster and harder, and our sex is wild and out of control in the best possible way. His teeth fasten on the spot between my shoulder and my neck, and his dragines bite into my flesh. His hand lovingly grips my throat, and I surrender to the climax that explodes through me. His own orgasm takes hold of him, and his knot *thud, thud, thuds* against me. His arms and teeth hold me so tight, and then he slowly relaxes.

"You're so good to me, Alpha," I whimper. "You make me feel wonderful. You're all I want."

He grinds his still-hard cock into me, and lights and colors burst behind my eyes. I don't know if this false heat is stronger than the other or if it's because this is the first time we've had sex while I'm in this state, but I'm burning up with need for him. I wish he were in his rut so he could fuck me again right away.

Zabriel licks slowly across my neck and shoulder. "Such pretty marks in your flesh, *sha'len*. I can feel you wanting me again already. You're squeezing me so tight. Let's get you to your nest, all settled in and cozy, and I'll give you whatever you need."

"Mm, all cozy with you. That sounds wonderful," I tell him and try not to cry out in dismay as he draws his cock out of me.

Zabriel laughs softly. "I heard that little whimper. Does my Omega need me to be locked tight inside her?"

I feel drunk and unsteady as I turn around and entreat him. "Yes, *please*. I can't wait, Alpha. I hope it won't be long."

He does up his breeches with a grin and wraps me in his cloak. As he places my bundled-up clothes into my arms, he lifts me off my feet and against his chest.

"I'll carry you to your nest," he murmurs, kissing me. "Bury your face in my shoulder so the sunlight doesn't upset you."

When we emerge into the light, the sudden shock of it nearly makes me cry out. I clench my crumpled clothes even tighter to my face and burrow into his chest.

"It's all right, sweet girl. We're nearly there." He plants a kiss on the top of my head.

I hear voices around us. The courtyard is still crowded with people. Everyone knows that the Flame King is taking his Omega to her nest. We must reek of sex and desire for each other, and even though I'm encased in his cloak I'm very aware of my nakedness. People call out to Zabriel in greeting as we pass. I hear so many *Ma'len*s, and they're all smiling. I can hear it in their voices.

Zabriel whispers, "Don't worry, I'm walking quickly. But I do love to show you off and make sure everyone knows you're mine."

A moment later, we're in the coolness and quiet of the castle, and then he's shouldering through the door to my room and laying me down on the canopied bed that's been mine ever since I came to the castle.

His red eyes blaze in the darkness. "I'll get you some more blankets and light the fire. Make your nest perfect, Omega, and then I'm going to fuck you in it."

∿

TWO DAYS LATER, I emerge from my nest so relaxed that my bones feel as though they're made from water. Zabriel spent most of the two days with me, only leaving me occasionally to meet with his soldiers and read reports sent to him from the barrier and various defensive points around Maledin. When he returned, I tried to show an interest in what was happening, but in response to my panting questions about the country, he would thrust his fingers or his still-hard cock into me and tell me that I was what's important right now. It's hard to argue with a man whose scent makes me feel like I might explode if I don't feel the weight of his massive body on mine. Right now. *Urgently.*

Zabriel is with his soldiers now, but Dusan and Fiala are there when I emerge from my room, and they tell me the country is much as it was three days ago when I sank into a heat haze.

"You didn't miss anything," Dusan says with a shrug. "The barrier still stands. Emmeric is still a pile of wyvern shit."

"Will you return to Amriste today?" Fiala asks me. She's told me she enjoys protecting me in the village with her fellow wingrunners. There's always the exciting possibility that a group of enemies will show up and need a thumping.

I think about this for a moment. "I would like to see my crone, but my mind is on another crone this morning. Will you please take me to the Flame Temple? I would like to meditate and speak with Zenevieve. After that, I don't believe I'll need you for the rest of the day."

Both their faces fall when I tell them that.

"But I will want to return to Amriste tomorrow," I tell them, and they brighten once more. As we walk toward the temple, I tell them with a smile, "It's funny, I would have thought you'd seen enough peril and excitement recently without me putting you both in more danger."

"Never," Dusan asserts, thumping his chest with his fist. "Wingrunners thrive on danger."

One of the Temple Mothers who's been bringing me tea the past few days beams at me as I enter the Flame Temple. Her name is Mother Linnea. "It does me good to see an Omega with roses in her cheeks. Did you and *Ma'len* enjoy yourself in your nest, Lady Isavelle?"

I don't think I'll ever get used to people openly discussing my sex life with Zabriel, but I don't take offense. The women at the Flame Temple have my well-being in mind, and they have my gratitude for the way they've helped me bond with Zabriel and my dragon.

"We did, thank you," I say with a shy smile, running my fingers down my single thick braid and playing with the ends. "I'm feeling very close to my mate lately, and my dragon as well."

Mother Linnea nods and casts her eyes approvingly over me. "May I say how lovely you look in your new attire? You are a dragonrider, it is plain for all to see, but in these clothes, I see styles and decorations that I think must be human, and they suit you very well. The crisscross embroidery on your sleeves is charming."

I have worried that my fellow Maledinni would disapprove of their future queen wearing anything with a human design. A Temple Mother approving of the human elements of my clothes makes my heart lighten. I touch the stitches on my tunic and tell her, "One of my seamstresses is familiar with human customs from the part of Maledin that I'm from.

This decoration represents the maypole festival that is held there every spring."

But not this coming spring, I think sadly. The streets of my village are deserted, as are so many of the villages in the west.

"Do you wish to mediate before the Temple Flame, Lady Isavelle?" Mother Linnea asks me.

The center of the temple is dominated by a massive flaming font that keeps the cavernous space of black volcanic rock warm even though part of the ceiling is open to the sky. Once a week, Scourge replenishes the flames to prevent them from going out. I haven't yet seen his massive head block out the sky while liquid fire pours down, but I hope that I will.

"I shall, thank you, Mother. But first, I wanted to show you this." I dip my hand into a pocket of my jacket and draw out the amulet that allowed me to escape Emmeric. I hold it tentatively with both hands, hating the sight of it, but understanding that this object is important, and I must protect it. "I can't give it to you, but I want the Temple Crone to know about it. This amulet belonged to Emmeric, and it allowed me to pass through the barrier and return to Zabriel. I hoped that it might have been useful in disrupting the barrier, but my crone—that is, the witch who is teaching me human magic—believes it may be important in other ways."

Mother Linnea looks closely at the amulet and then nods. "Thank you, Lady Isavelle. I will mention the matter to the Temple Crone. If your crone believes it's important for you to hold on to, then you must do that. It likely isn't useful in our endeavors to bring the barrier down. We need a powerful counterspell for that, I'm afraid." For a moment, she looks exhausted and rubs her forehead, and I wonder if the strain of uncovering such a spell is keeping her awake at night. "I'll leave you to your meditations."

When I'm alone, I sit cross-legged on a rug before the Font of First Flames and close my eyes. My mind slowly quiets and drifts. I feel something lay down along my left thigh, and then another rests its head in my lap. I smile as I realize it's two hatchlings. Their mothers must have dropped them into the temple on their way to patrol the skies. I briefly imagine Esmeral doing the same one day, and I feel happy at the thought before letting it go.

With the amulet clutched tightly in my hands, I try not to hope for a vision of my missing father and sister and all the other villagers, but I'm still disappointed when nothing happens.

When I open my eyes, the hatchlings are basking in the warmth of the flames, their little bellies lifting and falling as they sleep. One is a pale lilac color, and the other is vivid orange. I wonder what Esmeral and Scourge's hatchlings will look like. They will be beautiful, dramatic colors, no doubt, and as feisty as their parents, especially if they take after Esmeral.

Carefully, I lift the head of the hatchling sleeping in my lap. Its soft spines prickle my palms, and I shuffle back before laying it carefully down on the rug. Neither of the hatchlings stir, and I leave them snoozing peacefully together.

A Temple Maiden points me in the direction where I can find Zenevieve. She's no longer a prisoner, but Zabriel wants her under the watchful gaze of the temple women.

Upstairs, there's a large room where half a dozen temple women are working at long tables, and I find Zenevieve in a nearby antechamber. It's surprisingly cozy for a room made of shiny black stone, with a narrow bed with plenty of soft blankets, a side table with books and a pitcher of water, and several lamps lighting the space with a soft yellow glow.

When I stop in the doorway, Zenevieve slowly sits up, puts aside the quill and paper she is holding, and places her feet on the floor. Gazing at her toes, she takes a deep breath and looks up. "Lady Isavelle."

"You know who I am?"

Zenevieve nods. "Yes, but if we have spoken recently, I'm sorry, I don't remember. I can recall my life before Maledin fell, but everything else is gone or hazy."

I point at a chair and ask if I can sit. She nods. "Do you remember being Odanna? Do you know why you were pretending to be Odanna?"

She hesitates and presses her lips together. "I'm not sure. I remember moments when I was conscious that I was deceiving you, but I couldn't stop myself from lying."

"Was anything you told me about yourself true?" I ask, though I wish I hadn't phrased that as accusatorily as it sounded to my ears.

"What did I tell you?" Her voice is sweetly husky and is pleasant to listen to. She's sitting hunched over and playing nervously with her sleeve. I can read her body language easily because I'm all too familiar with the emotion she's feeling.

Shame.

"You told me that your mother passed away several years ago, and your father was a Brethren priest."

"How strange that I said that. I must have based the story on the truth. My father was a dragonrider, and he fell in love with a Temple Maiden when she tended his wounds after a skirmish. There was no objection to the two of them sleeping together, of course, but they wished to marry, and it caused quite the scandal."

"You mean it wouldn't have been a scandal if they'd simply..." I trail off and make a vague motion with my hand.

Zenevieve's mouth twitches, and then she laughs. It's such an unexpectedly beautiful sound, and her whole face lights up. Even as pale and tense as she is, her loveliness can't help but shine through. "Would sleeping together have caused a scandal under the Brethren? How strange. The women of the Flame Temple never marry because it's believed that husbands get in the way of their sacred duties, though it's permitted for them to take a lover if they wish and to bear children. It's very hard to resist your designation or the desire to have children, and those desires are respected at the Flame Temple. My mother was a young Temple Maiden and already committed to this place when she met my father and wanted to marry him. She broke her oath, which is a far greater scandal than sleeping with a man."

"That's very different to how things were in Maledin until recently. I was a Veiled Virgin—a kind of Temple Maiden—and if I'd even smiled at a man, I would have been beaten black and blue. Ordinary women were punished for having a child outside marriage as well."

"Punished? How terrible. What strange people the Brethren were."

"What is it you're writing?" I ask, gesturing toward her paper and quill.

"Oh, not much," she sighs. "One of the Temple Mothers suggested writing might help unlock my memories, but so far it hasn't worked. Did I say anything else about myself when I was Odanna?"

I doubt this has anything to do with Emmeric, but I am curious to hear her answer. "You told me that you have always loved someone, but he never loved you back."

"Did I?" Zenevieve nibbles on her fingernail. When she speaks again, it's in a high, strained voice. "Will you please tell me something? Did the dragonmaster survive the war? Is he in Lenhale? He's very tall, an Alpha, and he has long white hair and blue—"

"Stesha is alive and well, and so is Nilak. They're both here in the capital."

Zenevieve drops her face into her hands, and she shudders in relief. Tears leak between her fingers. "I was so afraid to ask."

Well. No prizes for guessing who she loves but who doesn't love her back. I feel another spurt of annoyance toward Stesha. Zenevieve is one of the most beautiful women I've ever laid eyes on. She obviously adores Stesha, though the gods know why. She's twenty-one years old. She's not a child. From the sound of things, at some point in the past, he rejected her. Because he was her guardian for several years? Because he's too arrogant to love anyone but himself? Because he's holding out for an Omega at thirty-something years of age?

Idiot.

Zenevieve lifts her head and wipes tears from her cheeks. "You look angry. Have I done something wrong?"

"No, you haven't. I was just thinking how frustrating Alphas can be." Should I tell Zenevieve that Stesha is frantic over her well-being, even though he doesn't love her in the way that she wishes he loved her? "Stesha has been so worried about you. Do you remember him standing by your side in the Great Hall?"

Zenevieve takes a shaky breath. "He did? No doubt he was furious with me. I betrayed everyone."

"He wasn't angry. He asked to be punished in your place."

Zenevieve looks up sharply. Fresh tears well up in her eyes. "Please don't let him do any such thing. He's already been through enough because of me. When I think of how…" But what she was about to say is lost in a storm of crying.

I put a comforting hand on her arm. "Be easy. Stesha is not being punished, and neither are you."

After much mopping of her face and blowing her nose, Zenevieve asks thickly, "Are you saying King Aylard has decided I'm not to be executed?"

King Aylard? It didn't occur to me that she wouldn't know what happened to Zabriel's parents. "I'm sorry to be the one to tell you this, but King Aylard is dead. Emmeric murdered the former king and queen before trapping all the dragonriders beneath the mountain. Zabriel is the king now."

Sorrow fills her eyes. "I shall miss Queen Magritte. She was a kind and gentle woman." To herself, she wonders, "Did he tell me this? I can't remember." A shadow crosses her face, and a shudder racks her body. "Zabriel will be a better king than his father. And you are…his mate? His queen?"

"We're not yet mated, but he calls me his mate."

Zenevieve slips from the cot onto her knees before me and prostrates herself on the ground. "*Ma'len's* mate, I'm trying my best to remember anything about Emmeric so I may aid the people of Maledin in their fight against him. I'm trying as hard as I can."

I grasp Zenevieve's arms and pull her up to sit. "Please don't lie on the ground like that."

Zenevieve stares at her hands in her lap. "I wish I could remember." She opens her mouth, closes it again, and fresh tears run down her cheeks. "I know I spoke with Emmeric, and he told me things. I saw things. They are hovering at the edge of my memory and keep slipping away. I *will* remember them." She raises her eyes to mine, and they're filled with determination. "I'll tell you and *Ma'len* everything I know as soon as I can remember it. I want to help."

I take her by the hands and help her back into bed. "I believe you, and I'm grateful for whatever you will tell us. But for now, rest."

Zenevieve draws the blankets up around her and closes her eyes. She looks utterly exhausted by our conversation.

"Would you like me to pass on a message to Stesha?" I ask softly.

The young woman is silent for so long that I think she must have fallen asleep. Then she whispers, "The last time I saw the dragonmaster, I said something very cruel. He won't want any message from me."

13

Zabriel

A bolt of emerald lightning hits the tower in Joryan's town square. Splinters of wood and stone explode into the air and greenish-gray smoke belches into the sky. The smell is horrendous; a sharp, toxic scent that makes me cough and my eyes water. Flying overhead, I seek out the mage that cast the spell. My dragon dives toward the enemy, opens his jaws, and drowns him in liquid fire.

News reached Lenhale in the middle of the night that Brethren were converging in Joryan, and I gathered riders and wingrunners and immediately flew west. If we don't kill every last priest, this place could be filled with dead Maledinni on spikes by nightfall. I haven't the faintest idea where Emmeric has imprisoned the villagers or how he transports them here and impales them so cruelly, but this time, we have a chance to prevent it from happening.

Not one member of the Brethren Guard is in sight—the armored soldiers we fought during Maledin's liberation from the enemy. We're fighting robed priests, unarmed except for their wooden staffs, and wielding powerful spells unlike any that I've seen before. Granted, I'm no expert when it comes to these things. Even Maledinni magic is mysterious to me, though it's been all around me since the day I was born. Magic has never interested me. Dragons and sword fighting, that's where my interest lies.

Another bolt of greenish magic shoots toward me and Scourge, and we swerve away, but unfortunately, a wingrunner is not so lucky. He and his wyvern fly right into the path of the magic, and it hits him squarely in the chest. The rider tumbles from the saddle. Wyverns are trained to catch their falling rider, or at least to break their fall, and the silver creature dives desperately to save him. It's able to briefly catch the man with one of its powerful wings, slowing his descent, but the rider is unconscious. He tumbles onto the ground and lies there twitching, his skin a sickly greenish color. Then he throws up.

Scourge snatches up the robed mage who cast the spell in his jaws, and suddenly we're eye to eye. The man's hood flies back, revealing his face, which is a grayish color in the green firelight. His eyes are a strange color as well, clouded and unnatural. A jolt of recognition surges through me. Just weeks ago, Scourge carried an archer in his jaws who loosed a poisoned arrow that tore a wound in my dragon's flank. The poison ate away at Scourge's scales and flesh, and though the wound was treated quickly and has since healed, I haven't forgotten the man who hurt my dragon. This is the same man. His eyes and skin are a different, dead-looking color, and he's a mage instead of an archer, but it's him.

Yet it can't be because I killed him weeks ago. I threw my dagger, and it lodged in his chest. He fell to his death.

I'm too distracted by this revelation to ask my dragon to spare the mage so I can question him. Scourge snaps his jaws together, severing the man's torso and legs, and he flings the pieces over the roofs of the town.

There are wingrunners on the ground, racing up and down the cobbled streets on their mounts, searching for hidden mages. I land Scourge in the square and dismount, drawing my sword. Another unit of wingrunners arrives, these ones with foot soldiers riding pillion behind them. New recruits from the looks of them, men and woman born in New Maledin who have known only the Brethren their whole lives. Their faces aren't familiar to me, and they haven't yet learned how to dismount a wyvern with grace. This is probably the first mission outside Lenhale that any of them has been on. They fall into two lines, ready for their captain's orders.

I'm beginning to wonder if their first mission is going to be a short one. Joryan seems to be deserted, and all the mages have fled.

Scourge's head suddenly rears up, and he glances around, his head turning quickly in one direction and then the other. Then he stares at the ground between his forelegs.

A strange sensation pervades me. Not a sight. Not a sound. A feeling?

The ground beneath us trembles. I take a step back, gripping my sword. I've heard of distant lands where the ground quakes and steam and molten rock erupt, but that has never happened in Maledin before.

A pointed black thing bursts from the ground a few feet to my left. Then another and another, all around me. Shiny black thorn-like protrusions that grow and crack the earth open. Spikes that are thrusting skyward. Spikes that I recognize from Isavelle's village.

Spikes upon which the bodies are impaled.

It's a waking nightmare. A forest of black, barren thorns bearing people is growing up all around us. Some of the bodies are moving. They're not dead. They're dying. All of them, right in front of us. I reach for one of them, a woman bleeding from her nostrils and eye sockets and twitching in a way that turns my blood to ice, but as I touch her, she stops moving, and I know she's dead. All around me, lives are snuffed out while blood pools on the ground beneath black thorns.

My soldiers are screaming in terror. There's a clatter of weapons falling to the ground and the sound of running feet. The newest recruits are panicking. Wingrunners are shouting at them to hold their line and so is the captain of the foot soldiers, but only a handful of them listen to her.

I brace for the reappearance of the mages and for battle to resume, but nothing happens. The forest of spikes drips with blood, and the enemy mages have vanished.

Misery and failure wash over me. Despite our best efforts, the townsfolk of Joryan were still slaughtered. I can feel Emmeric laughing at me, and I wonder if he's pleased that I have personally witnessed how unstoppably cruel he is.

I can feel my soldiers and dragonriders looking at me,

wondering what is to be done. There is nothing to be done. No one can be saved.

The sun is rising, and the dawn light illuminates a blacksmith's shop. An assortment of farming tools is stacked in a corner. I go in and select an axe, return to the square, and swing the axe at the base of a bloodied root. The *chunk chunk* sound of the axe hitting hard wood fills the silence. These people need to be put to rest.

I hear orders being given for soldiers to find as many axes as they can, and soon the sound of chopping fills the air.

It's a grim task and seemingly never-ending. There are rows and rows of bodies wrapped in sheets in the square, and the sun is high in the sky when I look up from my work. The flutter of wings has distracted me. Half a dozen ravens swoop around me, cawing. I try to shoo them away, thinking that they've come to feast on the corpses, but as I watch them, I realize they're circling me, not the bodies. Biddy Hawthorne's birds? Then she'll know what's happened here. Right at this moment, Isavelle is with her crone in Amriste, less than ten miles from where I stand.

I hold out my arm, and one of the ravens lands on my gauntlet. "Tell your mistress I'm coming for my mate as soon as I can."

It fixes me with a gleaming black eye. I feel like I'm staring into the crone's own eyes, and I wouldn't be surprised if she heard me with her own ears just now. The bird launches into the air, and one by one, the glossy black birds swoop away.

When all the bodies of the townsfolk have been cut down and taken out into a field, they're given last rites. Dragon rites.

Flames and sparks fill the sky as the dragons beat their wings. All those burning bodies are a terrible sight.

I leave a dragonrider, a wingrunner, and the captain of the soldiers in charge of their units, and then Scourge and I fly to Amriste. When we land in a field next to the village, I've barely dismounted before I see Isavelle running down a footpath toward us. Her expression is distraught, and she reaches for me with both hands.

"I heard the roar of dragons this morning, and then smoke this afternoon. Mistress Hawthorne told me that her ravens saw black thorns in Joryan. They're all dead, aren't they? The Maledinni from Joryan."

I fold her in my arms and hold her tight, unable to speak the words.

"You smell like fire and blood," she whispers. "I'm so sorry, Zabriel."

I tell her what transpired in Joryan, leaving out the sickening details. She doesn't need to know how much suffering there was, and I pray she didn't see her mother and brother twitching and bleeding like that.

Isavelle blinks away tears. "Emmeric is too cruel."

There's a tight, angry feeling in my chest, and heated words spill from my lips. "His cruelty and spite are unfathomable. Who has he become? What caused his heart to blacken?"

Isavelle reaches up and touches my cheek, tears sparkling in her turquoise and gold eyes. Biddy Hawthorne is making her slow, painful way across the meadow and is panting and red in the face as she reaches us.

"Will you please spare me for the rest of the day, Mistress

Hawthorne?" Isavelle asks. "Emmeric has murdered all the Maledinni in Joryan, and I wish to be with my mate."

Biddy slows to a halt. "Joryan?" Her old face sags. "Help an old woman back to her cottage, and then be off to do your queening, girl."

Isavelle does so and settles the old witch into her threadbare armchair before walking with me back to Scourge.

I hold her close in my arms the whole flight home.

As we cross the bridge from the dragongrounds to the castle, a member of the City Guard approaches me. She's holding a rolled-up piece of parchment as wide as the length of my arm.

"*Ma'len*, while you were gone, this was posted at the eastern gate."

When I unroll it, it's as long as Isavelle is tall, and it's covered with prominent black lettering. I didn't think I had one emotion left inside me after my broken night's sleep, a battle, and then chopping down villagers impaled on spikes, but as I read the words on the parchment, anger races through me.

14

———

Zabriel

"What does it say?" Isavelle asks, placing her fingers on my wrist and standing on tiptoe to read the words.

I angle it away from her. I want to rip the poster to pieces. I want to watch it burn. I turn to the City Guardswoman and ask, "Have you checked the other gates for more of these?"

She shakes her head. "I don't believe—"

I crumple the poster in my fist, growling, "Then I'll do it myself."

"I'll come with you," Isavelle says, hurrying at my side as I stride along.

"You don't have to."

"I'm still coming with you."

She slips her fingers into mine, and after a moment, I hold hers tightly.

As we approach the western gate from the castle into the city, there are dozens of people gathered around, all peering at something posted to the outer wall, and my heart sinks. There are more of them.

One or two people notice us arriving and nudge their neighbors, and they all fall back as Isavelle and I walk into their midst. My bride looks up at the poster stuck to the castle walls, and a moment later, her mouth falls open. I turn to read the words.

HARKEN, *all true citizens of Maledin who love the sight of our winged protectors in the sky. Our country has been liberated from its oppressors! But for how much longer will peace last?*

There is evil in our midst! Evil magic is taking root in our capital! We have long understood the evils of witchcraft, but now they threaten our home and our king!

The future queen is...a witch!

A witch has no place on the illustrious throne of Maledin!

A witch will welcome the evil mage in the south!

A witch will slaughter the king and every dragon that protects us!

Our glorious King Zabriel was burned nearly to death while his so-called queen consorted with the evil mage in the south who would kill all good people in Maledin.

Something must be done before it is too late!

BELOW THE TEXT is a crude drawing of a woman who bears a resemblance to Isavelle being burned at the stake.

As I reread the identical poster, rage enflames me. All *true* citizens of Maledin. What is that supposed to mean? Humans and Maledinni alike are all true and welcome citizens, and that Isavelle could bring harm to me or any of the dragons is preposterous. I rip this poster down as well, breathing hard. My first instinct is to order the City Guard to search every home and warehouse in Lenhale until they find the people who printed this pamphlet, lock them away in the dungeons, and destroy their printing press. It's what my father would have done.

The crowd is at my back. These people want my bride to be burned at the stake. I can feel them wanting it, and I round on them with my teeth bared.

Isavelle places her fingers on my wrist and asks softly, "May I speak with them, Zabriel?"

I don't know how she's so calm right now when she's the one they want to burn, but I nod sharply, glaring at them.

Isavelle addresses the crowd. "I can see from your faces that you're afraid. You want Maledin to be free and safe and anything that's dangerous to be banished far, far away. You want the missing people of western Maledin to be returned to us. I want that as well. We've all been through so much. Things are better than they were under the Brethren, and we want them to keep getting better." She takes a pause for a breath. "I know you're curious about this poster and what it says. Yes, I am a witch. Right now, there's very little that I can do, but I'm learning. Sometimes I see things that are happening far away, but it's only happened twice. Before Maledin was liberated, I would have been burned at the stake for this ability. It was only a matter of time before they discovered what I am and dragged me to the pyre. I nearly was burned alive for another reason, but our brave king saved me from the flames."

Isavelle twines her fingers through two of mine, and I glance down in surprise at the sweet gesture. She's smiling at me. When I glance at the crowd, I see that many of their distrustful expressions have softened.

"King Zabriel has done so much for all of us, and I know he'll always protect us. I want to be safe by his side, always. I worry every time he flies into battle on his dragon."

One of the younger women is looking between us, and blurts out, "Did he really snatch you from a burning pyre, my lady? Just like in the stories that people are telling about you and *Ma'len*?"

Isavelle glances up at me, as if uncertain whether to talk about our private experiences, but I give her an encouraging smile. It won't hurt to share a little of what we've been through together.

"Yes, it did," Isavelle tells her. "And what a surprise it was. I was in peril from the Brethren when a handsome enemy commander swooped down on his black dragon and carried me away in his arms. At the time I was so shocked, and I asked him to let me go because I wanted to find my family. It took me a long time to understand the intense feeling between us, but finally I did. We're fated for each other."

Something magical happens while Isavelle is speaking with the residents of Lenhale. They forget all about the poster that was nailed to the wall. Even I forget about it, and it's crumpled in my fist. They ask her questions about us, and Isavelle answers them all. Her straightforward way of talking seems to be winning them all over, and their questions grow bolder and bolder.

When someone with eyes as round as saucers asks whether I bite her so hard that I leave scars, I tense up, because we must keep some things to ourselves. Isavelle squeezes my hand, reassuring me.

"That's something that happens between all Alpha and Omega pairs. If anyone feels as though their body has been changing since the liberation, the women at the Flame Temple are able to answer all of your questions. All are welcome there." She tells the gathered people how to reach the Flame Temple in the castle and that they may also speak with the women dressed in vivid red if they see them in the streets.

They ask her questions about designations for a while, and then someone asks if they can meet her dragon. The people grow even more excited and repeat the request.

Isavelle glances around. We're standing on a wide street, and there's enough room for a small dragon like Esmeral to land. She looks up at the sky, and there's a long moment of silence followed by the sound of beating wings. A gold and turquoise flash overhead. A friendly chirrup.

Esmeral flutters neatly down onto cobbles before us, sunshine glinting off her scales. Isavelle smiles as she steps forward and cups her dragon's face. Esmeral embraces her with her wings and nuzzles her throat.

My throat aches as I watch Isavelle and Esmeral together. They're the most beautiful sight I've ever seen. So fragile. So perfect. The only thing that would make them more beautiful would be to see Isavelle's belly swollen with my child and know that deep within a cave by the dragongrounds is a clutch of Esmeral's eggs, warmed by dragonfire. My son or daughter, and Scourge's hatchlings. When the time comes, we will be such proud fathers and overprotective mates. Esmeral and Isavelle will be more vulnerable than ever when Isavelle is carrying my child and Esmeral is guarding her eggs. I don't know how I'll ever let my pregnant mate out of my sight or control my temper if someone so much as looks at her the wrong way, let alone cope with posters that incite people to burn her to death in the street.

"Is she dangerous?" a man asks, looking at Esmeral's teeth.

"Of course," Isavelle replies, and there are several gasps as people draw back. "But only to people who wish me harm, so none of you are in danger." She smiles at the crowd, and I sense a ripple of relief go through them. Isavelle wants them to know they're already forgiven for believing that poster. In fact, she wasn't ever angry.

"You mustn't touch someone's dragon without permission, but if someone who is very brave wishes to touch her scales, you may ask her." She smiles at a young boy who is transfixed by the sight of the beautiful dragon. "How about you?"

"Oh, yes, please. May I touch her, miss?" the boy eagerly asks Isavelle. "I *love* dragons. My pa has been carving me wooden dragons ever since the coronation."

A woman who is likely the boy's mother puts her hands on his shoulders. "Are you sure she is safe to touch, my lady?"

Isavelle turns to Esmeral. "May this boy stroke your scales for a moment?"

Esmeral trills and lowers her head until it's only a foot from the ground. She offers her cheek with a friendly tilt of her head that disarms even the worried mother. As the boy strokes her cheek, Esmeral stretches her snout forward and closes her eyes, like a cat who is being tickled under the chin.

Isavelle watches them in silence, a wistful expression on her face. "You remind me of my brother, Waylen. I think he would have loved dragons, too."

The mother gives Isavelle a sad look. "We're so sorry for the loss of your brother and mother, my lady. Is...is the rest of your family missing with the other lost villagers?"

Isavelle nods. "We're searching for them. The mage to the south has them hidden somewhere. He's strong, but we will win." My mate is silent for a moment, and then she remembers where she is and smiles at the boy. "What do you think? Would you like to be a dragonrider one day?"

The boy is in awe of Esmeral. Her shining scales. Her teeth. Her talons. "How could anyone want to be anything that isn't a dragonrider?"

Suddenly, the sky overhead darkens and Scourge swoops over us. The crowd ducks and gasps in surprise as he flies by for a second pass, displaying his broad wings, his red eyes, and his gleaming black scales. He flutters onto a rocky outcrop above us, parts his jaws, and calls to Esmeral in a deep rumble. She chirrups back at him, and he furls his wings, content to watch over us now that he's assured himself that his mate is safe.

The boy turns to me excitedly. "Sir, um, *Ma'len*, does your dragon like to be petted as well?"

I grin at him and fold my arms. "No. But he loves chicken necks and flying by starlight, so I make sure he gets plenty of both."

While everyone is talking about dragons and their beautiful future queen, I give the torn posters to a guard and signal for him to get rid of them. Nobody cares about the posters anymore. My bride has just performed witchcraft without using a drop of magic.

Esmeral flies up to Scourge and they both head back to the dragongrounds, and Isavelle and I say goodbye to the crowd and walk hand in hand back up to the castle.

"That was incredible. They loved you," I tell her.

"They love Esmeral, and they love their king, and they're merely relieved that I'm not a wicked witch who wants to destroy the peace in Maledin."

"Don't underestimate yourself. Is it strange that watching you turned me on? All I can think about now..." I glance around. Well, why not? No one needs me right now, and I'm the king. The king is going to take his beautiful and clever bride to bed.

I pick Isavelle up in my arms and carry her up the stairs into the keep. Isavelle smiles and wraps her arms around my neck, holding on as I stride through the castle.

I lay her down on our bed and hurriedly yank at my breeches. My cock is straining, aching to be inside her. Isavelle pulls her skirts up and her underclothes down her legs and casts them aside.

Her slick is beading up on her sex and running over her inner lips to well in her tight channel, and the invitation is too much for me. I grasp my cock, and with a groan, I sink into her. Her grip on my shaft is insane, and she clutches my shoulders and cries out in pleasure.

"My bride. *My queen.*" I moan as I thrust into her.

"Nothing makes me feel more like a king than fucking my bride."

"It does?" she pants.

I squeeze her breasts and run my tongue over her nipples. "It's a king's duty to get his queen pregnant as soon as he can. I'll smell it when you're fertile. I will smell it when you're pregnant. I can't wait to tell you." I have no idea how her scent will change. I'll just know.

Isavelle smiles up at me. "Where I come from, the wives tell the husbands when they're pregnant, not the other way around."

"I'll tell you by sinking my cock into you and whispering in your ear that you're having my baby. Doesn't that sound better?"

She moans, and her sex clenches around me. Apparently, it does.

I start hammering her pussy faster. "Do you want my baby, *sha'len*? Does my Omega crave to be pregnant from her Alpha?"

"Oh, gods, yes," she pants, reaching down between her thighs to circle her clit. Her panting grows louder and louder until she cries out, flushing red with her climax from her cheeks to the tips of her breasts.

I gather her ass in my hands and lift her up, angling her body so that I can see the outline of my cock moving in and out of her.

"Fuck, that's sexy." I grasp her hand and place it over her lower belly. "Can you feel me? You're so full of me. Dragon's blood, I need to be even deeper. I need—I want —" I break off with a groan, and a spasm goes through my knot as I imagine being able to shove it deep inside her. My orgasm bursts through me, and I feel my cum pumping into her.

I drop my head onto her shoulder. We're both gasping hard and holding each other tight. "Are you going to give me beautiful sons and daughters who will be just as fierce and clever as their mother?"

"I want to give you everything, Zabriel," she whispers against my skin.

My heavy body is probably crushing her, so I roll off to one side and gather her against me.

"If I have a daughter first, can she be queen? Or will she have to step aside for a son?" Isavelle asks, stroking her fingers thoughtfully down my chest.

My heart clenches with longing. A daughter. I can see her already. She'll have dark hair, but Isavelle's rounded, beautiful features. As stubborn as her mother and as hotheaded as me. Will she be an Alpha, Beta, or an Omega?

"Our firstborn? If it's a girl, she will be the crown princess, and then she will be queen."

"Even if she's an Omega?" Isavelle asks with a worried crease between her brows.

I hesitate. It's happened in the past that an Omega crown princess has been forced to step aside and make way for a sibling with a so-called stronger designation. The records state that the Omega woman was always happy to step aside, but I've always wondered how much bullying went on until she felt she had no choice. I believe in my mate's ability to rule, so why wouldn't I believe in my daughter as well?

"Even if she's an Omega," I say firmly.

Isavelle wraps her arms tightly around me and buries her face in my neck. "I'm so happy to hear you say that." In a muffled voice, she whispers, "Emmeric called me so many disgusting names. If we have an Omega child, it would break my heart if they were called any of those things."

My arms tighten around her in anger as I hear Emmeric's hateful voice in my head. I can imagine what he called her. *Stupid Omega fucktoy. Brainless doll.* "I'm so sorry, *sha'len.* Unfortunately, in mine and Emmeric's time, such talk was common and rarely objected to."

With an Omega mother and sister, I didn't like those comments, but I didn't question why they were thrown around in the first place. We all believed that Omegas were precious and coveted and special, and yet people still talked about them with scorn, sometimes in the same breath.

"With an Omega queen as strong as you on the throne, you will shape what everyone believes about your designation. No one who saw you today could believe you're anything less than a queen."

She smiles and twines a lock of my hair around her finger. "Do you think there are other Omegas emerging in Maledin by now? I can't still be the only one."

I smile and kiss her. "I have no doubt that there's another Omega somewhere in Maledin. Maybe more than one."

Isavelle gazes out through the window at the sky. "I wonder who they are. I hope I get to meet them."

"*Ma'len*, what is to be done about the deserters?"

I'm in the War Room poring over reports from the barrier when Godric enters and addresses me. I throw the report aside with a grimace. The deserters. The new recruits who fled at the ghastly sight of villagers erupting from the ground impaled on spikes. "How far did they get?"

Godric's expression is severe. "They hid in stables and outhouses in a cowardly manner unbecoming of Maledinni soldiers, though none of them left the town itself."

Under Old Maledin law, they would have been punished severely. I remember my father once executing half a dozen men and women who ran from battle. I should give orders for the soldiers to be arrested and imprisoned at the very least, but I haven't got the heart. What happened in Joryan was a terrifying, sickening sight.

"What do you think I should do?" I ask Godric. I'm curious how bloodthirsty my closest advisor is in the wake of a tragedy.

"They have been taunted all day with stories of what happened to deserters under the former king, and I hear that none of them are expecting to live past morning. It was, however, exceptional circumstances. The deaths of so many of our kind." Regret fills his eyes.

I nod sharply. "I'm inclined to agree with you, and I've seen enough blood and misery today. Assign the soldiers to local patrol duties for a week, and they may visit the Flame Temple to unburden their hearts to the Temple Mothers. After that, they will return to western Maledin and guard the villages where there hasn't yet been any slaughter, and their captain will remind them that they're the lucky ones because they were not impaled on spikes."

Godric gives a short bow of assent. "Fitting duties for them, *Ma'len*. Your mercy does you credit."

He turns to go, but I call him back. "One more thing. The posters that slandered my bride and spoke of burning her at the stake. How were they able to be posted all over the city?"

Godric studies the floor for a moment. "The City Watch are all new recruits. Perhaps they didn't understand how inflammatory the posters were. Or perhaps they were in sympathy with them."

My temper flares. "Then they will soon be in sympathy with a dungeon cell."

"Yes, *Ma'len.*"

"My mercy has its limits, and it does not stretch to those who turn a blind eye to threats to my bride. Give these orders to the captain of the City Watch. He and his soldiers are to discreetly take down these posters if any more appear on the streets. No investigations. No punishments. No arresting anyone for putting them up. Just take them down. If I see one more of these posters, the City Watch will receive a personal visit from me, and they won't enjoy it."

"Yes, *Ma'len.*" He hesitates and then asks, "Are you worried about the consequences if the residents of Lenhale will not accept your queen?"

I step toward him, anger blazing in my chest. My fury must burn in my red eyes as he quickly steps back. "Not accept her? Who presumes to think they have a say in the woman I take as my queen?"

"I mean no offense, *Ma'len,* but a witch on the throne is something Maledin has never seen before, in your father's time or during the Brethren era. We must take pains so that such an adjustment is handled with consideration."

"Handled with consideration," I grumble. "You really are a king's advisor, speaking like that."

Godric manages a small smile, and after a moment, my

temper cools. I shouldn't bite his head off for doing his job. Protecting Isavelle is my first priority, and I'm grateful that he's thinking about her as well. "I'm not worried that Lenhale will reject my queen. Isavelle will prove that a queen who is a witch and a dragonrider is someone to be loved and admired."

He bows. "As you say, *Ma'len*."

15

———————

Zabriel

The following morning, Isavelle is dressing herself with the intention of returning to Amriste, and I'm mourning the sight of her plump ass, her soft stomach, and her legs with every garment she dons. I'm only half dressed myself. I've pulled some breeches on, but I haven't laced them up yet, and I'm still shirtless.

"Come back to bed, just for a little while," I say coaxingly, reaching for her. I'm getting hard just looking at her. The lacings on my breeches loosen even further.

Isavelle strokes her fingers over me and presses a kiss to my chest. "I can't. You know Mistress Hawthorne scolds me if I'm late."

"I'm the King of Maledin," I remind her severely. "What if I scold you?"

Isavelle gives me a cheeky smile. "She's scarier than you are."

"I'm seven feet tall with red eyes, and she's a rickety old woman," I splutter. "I ride a fire-breathing dragon, and I wield a sword that is longer than you are tall."

"Yes, but you think I'm adorable and sweet and you could never say a bad word to me," Isavelle replies. "If I'm late, Mistress Hawthorne will whip me with sharp words until my heart is raw."

My lips twitch. Isavelle's right, I could never even raise my voice to her. "What if I..." I lean down and speak directly into her ear using my Alpha growl, *"Tell you to do what I say."*

A pleased shiver goes through her. The fingers that were pressing against my chest a moment ago suddenly dig in. "What do you need, Alpha? I'll do anything."

Even more blood rushes to my cock. That's more like it. I lift my bride up in my arms so she can reach my lips, and she kisses me hungrily. I'll send her along to old Biddy with a message saying that it's my fault she's late. The future queen was needed for...urgent royal business. The old witch doesn't need to know the royal business was Isavelle being fucked senseless in the morning sunlight.

I have my hand beneath her skirts when there's a knock on our bedchamber door. I keep a hold of my bride and make sure my body is shielding hers as I call impatiently, "Come in." To Isavelle I whisper, "You want to be fucked hard, don't you?"

She whimpers and wriggles against me. The new arrival doesn't prevent me from drawing my tongue lovingly against hers before breaking the kiss and turning toward our visitor.

I was expecting one of the Temple Maidens with some tea

for Isavelle to drink, but instead, I see Godric standing in the doorway, and his expression is grim.

The smile fades from my lips. "What is it, Godric?"

Godric glances at Isavelle still held tightly in my arms, and his brows draw together. I sense that he wants my undivided attention. This is our bedchamber, but even if it wasn't, I can listen and hold my Omega at the same time.

"I said, what is it?"

Godric clears his throat and stares hard at the floor. "It has happened again, *Ma'len*. More Maledinni are dead, and the humans spared. This time in Falmere."

Isavelle gives a cry of dismay, and I hold her even tighter.

"He's really going to do it. Five villages, because I would not name one," Isavelle says in a choked voice.

"This is not your fault." To Godric, I say, "Prepare a unit of dragonriders and two units of wingrunners for immediate departure. I will dress and join the dragons immediately."

He nods sharply and leaves to carry out my orders.

I bury my face in Isavelle's throat and breathe in her scent deeply, knowing that holding her is the last good thing that will happen today.

"I will come as well," Isavelle says. "I can't go and learn witchcraft and pretend this isn't happening."

"You needn't see such horrors again. It will be a terrible reminder of what happened in Amriste."

"I want to," she insists. "I have to. I can't pretend it's not happening."

She's struggling to put a reason into words, but I understand because I feel the same way. I dread what I will see, but I must bear witness to what Emmeric has done, and so must she.

That afternoon, we send the Maledinni of Falmere into the sky. In darkness, we return to Lenhale, exhausted, grimy, our clothes and hair reeking of smoke and death.

Just after dawn the following morning, there's another knock on our bedroom door, and Godric informs us that, this time, the Maledinni of Grimmond have been slaughtered.

Isavelle bursts into tears, but she quickly wipes them away and gets dressed, insisting that she come with me again. I watch helplessly as she buttons her jacket with shaking fingers. I could forbid her from coming with me, but she won't thank me for my protection when it goes against her sense of duty. These are her people. She was born in the same lands, knew the same fields, trod the same roads.

It can't possibly happen a fourth day in a row. There's no mage powerful enough to burn through so much magic and cause so much death four days in a row. Yet on the fourth day, all the Maledinni of Rosen are discovered impaled on spikes. I don't think I'll ever get the stench of burning bodies out of my nose. Isavelle barely speaks a word all day.

On the fifth day, it's Gunster. Emmeric saved the worst for last.

When we reach what should be a bustling market town, we find a horror of blood and twisted bodies. I ask Isavelle if she can search the houses for sheets that we can use as shrouds to keep her away from the worst of it, and I quietly order Fiala and Dusan to keep a close eye on her and make her rest if she seems overwhelmed.

Esmeral shadows my mate wherever she goes, and I can tell from the way that Isavelle reaches out to touch Esmeral's scales that she's quietly drawing strength from her dragon throughout the day.

Every town has been horrific, but this is the worst because it's the biggest. There isn't enough space to lay out all the bodies in the main square, and so they must be stacked one on top of the other before being loaded into cart after cart and taken out into the fields to be burned.

When I lift one of the shrouded bodies onto my shoulder, I notice a sweet scent emanating from what was once a living, breathing young woman. The scent of an Omega. My heart gives a painful thump, and I have to take a deep breath and swallow down my howl of rage and despair. So innocent, so precious, and lost before she likely even knew what she was. Discovering her should have been a wonderful moment, but it's a reminder of how much I'm failing to protect my own people.

I look around for Isavelle and see her sewing a dead body into a shroud, her expression tight with grief. When she finishes, Dusan heaves the body onto his shoulder and lays it in a cart. Then they move on to the next. And the next. We work steady, and all this death lays heavy on us, suffocating us worse than smoke and flame. I saved my mate from the pyre and the Brethren and brought her to Lenhale, for what? More suffering? My chest aches at the site of my mate amid all this death. Every single body is a reminder of the mother and brother she has lost. As I take painful breath after painful breath, I'm conscious of how much she's suffering, and I can feel Emmeric laughing at me.

Several hours later, we're standing in a field while the dragons breathe liquid fire over the bodies and then fan the flames high with their wings.

"Five towns in five days," I mutter as ash swirls around us.

"How is he so powerful that he can do this to five towns in five days?"

Isavelle is standing by my side, both her fists clenched. She hasn't spoken a word all day, and her face is bloodless with anger. "I hate him. I hate him so much."

There are no tears in her eyes. My mate is beyond tears.

"I've had enough, Zabriel," she whispers fiercely. "We have to stop Emmeric. Everything we do from now on must be to make sure he never hurts anyone again. Death is too good for him. He needs to...he needs to..." She smothers a scream. "He needs to understand the pain he has caused. Hundreds and hundreds of years of pain. I want to make him *feel* it."

I reach out and take her hand. "We will put an end to the havoc he's been wreaking. I swear it."

"Do you think we can?"

The words *of course we can* materialize on my tongue, but they're not enough. I take Isavelle's face in my hands and tilt her chin up. "That man took my sister from me. My best friend. My mother. My country. I won't let him take more. I don't understand magic or the kind of power that Emmeric wields, but I have Scourge, and I have an army at my back, and he will not succeed in whatever foul plans he has brewing." I lower my head and press my forehead against hers. "And I have you. You were the one who woke me from my slumber, and it won't be for nothing."

Flecks of ash fall silently on Isavelle's plait, which is loosened from hard labor, and there are flyaway tendrils around her face. She holds me tightly, and all the while, the flames burn and burn.

THREE DAYS LATER, Isavelle finds me in the courtyard off the Great Hall, sitting on a stone bench and contemplating a bare patch of earth. The snow has thawed, and green shoots are just beginning to poke through the barren soil.

"Spring's coming," she says, sitting down next to me and taking my hand in hers.

I gather her against my body and kiss her temple. Her sweet scent envelops me, and I breathe in heart-soothing honeysuckle and crisp apple. Isavelle's words as she stood by the flames that consumed all the dead Maledinni of Gunster a few days ago come back to me.

Everything we do from now on must be to take away his power and make sure he never hurts anyone again.

She was speaking of breaking through that barrier and finishing off Emmeric, but there's something I can do in the meantime. Something I've been putting off. I don't want to face this. I don't want to *know*, but if my Omega can endure days of heartache and exhaustion giving the dead of western Maledin proper last rites while she's still carrying the weight of her own grief, then I should be able to face up to what I've been avoiding.

Isavelle places a hand on my chest and gazes up at me with concern in her eyes. "Why is it you look so sad today? Has something happened?"

"Nothing has happened, *sha'len*. I must do something that I have been putting off."

When my parents were killed, I wasn't in Lenhale. Scourge and I were on a training exercise through central Maledin with a large unit of dragonriders. I don't know if

Emmeric chose that moment on purpose because he believed that there would be fewer seasoned soldiers around to protect the king and queen, or if it was merely a coincidence.

When we returned to Lenhale, I was informed of their murders by my brother's hand. I saw my parents' bodies, all the blood that Emmeric had spilled, and I ran straight back to Scourge.

I don't remember much about the following two days. I was lost in a storm of grief and anger, and the frightening, crushing knowledge that I was no longer the relatively care-free crown prince, but the ruler of a country that had just been thrown into violent and bloody turmoil. My one goal was to find Emmeric and finish him. Every dragonrider, wingrunner, *Hratha'len*, and soldier who could be spared was sent to all corners of Maledin with orders to track him down. We'd been searching for him for years by then for the crime of raping our sister, but he'd always evaded us.

It was with shock and relief that I received news on the third day after the murder that Emmeric had been seen in the Bodan Mountains to the north. I should have suspected something then. My slippery brother had been found too easily, in too unlikely a place, but I wanted revenge for what he'd done to our family. I craved blood. I gave immediate orders for the army to march and fly to the north.

Emmeric was waiting for us. He was counting on his hotheaded older brother to do just that, and with some spell, some magic that's far beyond my comprehension, he sealed every last one of us beneath the mountains before we could shed one drop of his blood.

Thus, my very first act as the future ruler of Maledin was to lead my soldiers into five hundred years of captivity, and the people of Maledin into five hundred years of suffering under Brethren rule.

She presses soft kisses along my jaw. "If there is something you must do, then I'll do it with you."

I gaze at her slender fingers laced through mine. I can think of nothing more comforting than having my Omega in my arms, but I shake my head. "You may lean on me in times of need, but it's unbecoming of an Alpha to expect his Omega to shoulder any burdens for him."

"Who says so?" she asks.

"Everyone since forever, and your Alpha agrees. You've endured more than your fair share of ordeals these past few days."

"Everyone since forever is not a good enough reason. We're being an Alpha and Omega pair our own way. The New Maledin way."

"We are, but that doesn't mean I don't worry about my mate. You're exhausted. You might go into heat any day now, and you need your strength."

"I want to be there for you always," she says. "Because I love you."

I look at Isavelle in surprise. Her cheeks turn pink, and her hand in mine grows hot. I sense her absolute sincerity but also her vulnerability as she confesses such a thing.

I smile gently at her. "I have been curious about the human notion of love. I have heard it is something human mates say to affirm their commitment to each other. Is that right?"

She strokes her fingers across my jacket, right over my heart. "Yes, that's right, and we say *I love you* on all sorts of occasions. When we part ways, and when we are making up after a disagreement, but most of all, we say it when we feel so strongly for another person that there is nothing else we can say. Don't Maledinni ever say something like that to one another?"

There's little need to say anything when we can signal our commitment in other ways. Through scent, through deeds, through terms of endearment. I call Isavelle *Omega* when I want to remind both of us that we are made for each other and will never be parted. I call her *sha'len* because she's my little dragon and she always will be. I hold her in my lap or carry her in my arms through the castle because I want everyone to know how I feel about her.

"We don't," I reply, and her hopeful expression dims. "But that doesn't mean I can't say it to you."

"Really?" she asks, brightening again.

I pretend to think about it. "A Maledinni king speaking to his mate in such a human manner? Let's see." I pick her up and place her in my lap so she's sitting across my thighs and cuddle her close. "I love you, *sha'len*."

A beautiful smile breaks over Isavelle's face, and she traces my mouth with her forefinger. "I love you, Zabriel."

I tilt my mouth toward hers, asking for a kiss. She bestows me with her lips, and I kiss her for a long time while tangling my fingers in her hair.

"Your love is so precious to me and speaking like this only makes me want to protect you even more. Stay here, *sha'len*. I won't be gone long."

Isavelle's brow creases with worry. "Is it dangerous what you must do?"

"No, but it's painful." I take one of her hands and press it against my heart. "It would pain you as well."

Isavelle gazes at her hand on my chest. "When my father was unhappy or worried, he told my mother about it, and she would help him through whatever the problem was, and after, their love for one another was even stronger. I could see it in their eyes."

Envy swells in my chest. What must it have been like to have parents who so openly cared for each other? I never witnessed my parents comforting each other or even laughing with each other.

"Please let me come with you, Alpha. Please."

I groan and bury my face between her soft breasts. "When you beg me in that pretty voice, you know I crave to give you everything you want. All the Omegas who have ever lived are lining up behind you to tell you that you must let your Alpha bear this alone."

"I'm not them. I'm me."

I take a deep breath and let it out slowly. "I must speak with Captain Ashton. I have been putting this off because I haven't wished to hear the details. I wasn't there when my parents were killed, but he was."

"Then I must come. I wouldn't be anywhere but by your side while you learn about such things. You were by my side after my mother and brother were killed, and I will always be by yours."

I gaze at her and see that there are even more turquoise and golden flecks in her eyes. Her perfume is divine. Her being crackles with energy and power.

"Will you think your Alpha is a weak and cowardly man if he holds tight to your hand throughout?"

Isavelle gazes deep into my eyes. "I will think only how

proud I am of my mate for facing what is painful and allowing me to be at his side."

I wrap my arms around her waist and push my face between her breasts once more, and I stay like that, holding her. There's nothing I want to do without her. Nothing. The good things and the terrible things.

Finally, I lift my head. "Then if you're sure, let's go find the captain."

"I'm sure."

I look into her beautiful eyes a moment longer. "I love you, Omega."

She smiles again at hearing me speak the words of her people and mine together. "I love you, Alpha."

We find Captain Ashton at the wingrunner barracks, and he invites us into his private quarters. The room is scrupulously neat with a desk and chair, plain tapestries on the walls, and a rack of weapons. There's a bundle of scrolls on the desk that are likely reports on various wingrunner missions around Maledin.

Isavelle and I are invited to sit while Ashton moves around behind his desk and takes his own seat. I trace my finger along the inside of Isavelle's wrist, pretending to merely idle with her as an Alpha does with his Omega, but my heart is racing, and I must touch her to keep myself calm.

"Dusan hasn't been speaking nonsense to your mate again, has he, *Ma'len*?" Ashton asks. "There's plenty of wyvern dung for him to shovel if he has."

"Always, but I ignore him these days," I reply with a smile.

Ashton is a good-looking man and the highest ranked Beta in the country after Godric, but he isn't mated, which is unusual for a man over thirty. When Isavelle falls pregnant, perhaps it will encourage him to have many strong sons and daughters for Maledin.

I clear my throat. "I actually came to speak with you about before. Old Maledin. The day my parents were murdered."

The captain's expression is suddenly grave, and his gaze drops to his clasped hands. "Of course, *Ma'len*. I've been expecting that you would wish to ask me this, and I'll help you in any way I can."

"Can you tell me how it happened?"

Ashton takes a moment to cast his mind back five hundred years. "Your parents, the king and queen, were in the gardens together taking their usual evening walk. Your father didn't enjoy being disturbed at such a time, but one of my wingrunners had sighted your brother's dragon, and I went to inform the king. I knew where your parents would be at that hour, but of course, so did Prince Emmeric. As I approached the king and queen, so did the prince, dressed as a servant. I confess that I didn't recognize him right away. The king and queen did not raise the alarm as he spoke with them, so I didn't think anything was amiss. As I drew closer, I recognized the prince and saw sorrow on his face. He seemed to be begging them for forgiveness, your mother in particular. She was gripping the king's sleeve as if she was upset and your father appeared to be in shock."

I can see my mother's distraught expression in my mind's eye. I wonder if she was hopeful that Emmeric might feel remorse for what he'd done or if she felt only disgust and fear as she looked upon her son.

"Immediately, I was on my guard," Ashton continues. "I wanted to draw my weapon, but to draw on the king's son without a direct order..." He trails off and grips the arms of his chair. "A moment later, there was a dagger in Prince Emmeric's hand. He attacked the king, and your mother defended him. She fell first, and while your father watched her die, Emmeric took his life."

I saw their bodies. My mother had deep slashes on her arms. She must have raised them to defend herself and my father. She must have been screaming as he stabbed her through the heart. My father's throat was slit. There was blood everywhere.

Isavelle keeps her eyes on Ashton, but she squeezes my fingers. She wants me to know that she's here, but she doesn't wish to draw attention to the fact that she's comforting her Alpha.

Fuck it. I don't care. I take a tighter grasp of her hand.

"I'm so sorry, *Ma'len*." Ashton rubs a hand across his brow, and when he speaks again, his voice is agitated. "I should have trusted my instincts and drawn my sword. I shouldn't have been worrying about orders when the king's life was so clearly in danger. I could have struck him down and prevented it from happening. *All* of this from happening. Even if it had meant my execution, I should have done it."

"I don't place any blame at your feet," I assure Ashton. My father should have protected his mate, not allowed her to die protecting him. He should have known Emmeric didn't have one drop of sorrow in his heart after the things he'd done. "Can you tell me how Emmeric escaped?"

Ashton frowns. "He just...vanished. I've never seen anything like it. One moment, he was there, and then the next, he stepped away into nothing."

"That's how he managed to snatch me from the dragongrounds," Isavelle says. "He can travel vast distances in a moment. It's like he can make doors open and close wherever he wants them to, and he passes through some other place in a moment to travel so quickly. It's very powerful magic."

Ashton is silent for a long time. "The same kind of magic that he used to lock us away."

"How do you mean?" I ask. "We were beneath the Bodan Mountains."

"Were we, *Ma'len*? All of us and our dragons and wyverns?" He sits forward. "This is what's been puzzling me. We entered no caves when we were hunting for your brother. We didn't go underground. We didn't emerge from underground. What's the last thing that you remember that day?"

"Standing on the mountainside with Scourge and the other dragonriders."

"That's right. On the mountainside. There was blinding light, and then there was nothing for five hundred years until we were standing right back where we started."

"But I felt like we were beneath..." I trail off, feeling puzzled. I dreamed we were buried beneath immeasurable tons of stone for a long, long time. After the spell broke, we were right back in the same place on the mountainside.

"Perhaps we were inside the mountain, and yet not there," Ashton says. "Trapped in an in-between place with no way for anyone to reach us."

16

Isavelle

The apothecary's store is filled with an herbal, verdant scent emanating from the sacks of dried vegetation around the perimeter of the room and the bundles of plants drying on the walls. I take a deep breath, and I'm able to tease apart the different plants merely from scent. I think my nose is more sensitive lately.

"I would have thought the witch would have been able to brew her own medicines," Fiala says, toeing a sack of dried flowers while we wait for the apothecary to finish with another customer.

"Oh, yes she can," I tell her. "I've asked Mistress Hawthorne to teach me how to make medicinal potions, but her stock of dried herbs is depleted, so I'm purchasing what we need."

The village girls used to gather plants from the woods for Mistress Hawthorne, and traveling peddlers would supply the rest, but no peddlers have been coming through Amriste, and there's no one to go into the woods for her except me. Besides, little grows in winter and spring is only just beginning to arrive.

The apothecary finishes with his customer, tucks some copper coins into the pouch hanging from his belt, and turns to me.

I smile at the man. "Hello, I'd like to purchase medicinal stock for my crone. She gave me a list of the plants she requires." I hand over the piece of parchment.

His eyes widen at the word *crone*, and he stares at me and then Fiala and Dusan in their wingrunner uniforms. I spot the exact moment when he realizes who I am.

"Your, ah, crone has good knowledge of medicinal herbs, my lady," he says, studying the list. His polite smile seems forced as he measures out and packs up my order.

"Yes, she's a talented witch. May I ask, why is your store located in this alleyway? I thought an apothecary would be easier to find. Everyone needs your services."

"The Brethren priests gave me trouble when my store was more prominent," he explains. "It was burned down on several occasions when my herbcraft was accused of being witchcraft."

"I'm sorry to hear it, but you're safe now under a Maledinni king to move into a main square."

"If you say so, my lady." He doesn't look as if he believes me, and he avoids further conversation. He won't look me in the eye as I pay him.

I can guess why. As we leave the store, I ask my body-guards, "Have more posters about witches appeared around Lenhale lately?"

They exchange glances.

"One or two," Dusan concedes. "The City Guard takes them down almost as fast as they appear."

Is it my imagination, or do the eyes of strangers linger on me as we pass by, and not in a friendly manner? Two women with basketfuls of laundry stare at me, and I catch some of their loud whispering. "*...bewitched the king. He's obsessed with her, and it's not natural or healthy.*"

My stomach clenches, but I keep moving like I haven't overheard anything. I hoped that suspicion and hatred of witches would die out once the Brethren no longer controlled Lenhale.

We're halfway along the alley when a man staggers into our path. I move to one side to allow him to pass, but he follows me. Dusan and Fiala thrust out their arms, crossing the poles of their halberds protectively in front of me.

"That's close enough," Fiala says with a threatening scowl. "This is the king's mate. Move aside."

The man is middle-aged with a gaunt and weathered face. Sweat beads on his brow though the day is a crisp one. "I mean no harm," the stranger gasps in a quavering voice. "Queen Isavelle, will you speak with me a moment?" He bends at the waist in a shaky bow that threatens to topple him into the mud. "My name is Gaun of Lenhale, and I wish to offer my services to aid you in the fight against the Shadow King."

Gaun doesn't seem strong enough to fight against a stiff

breeze, let alone Emmeric. "Just Isavelle, please, or Lady Isavelle if you must. Are you unwell?"

He dabs at his sweating forehead with a handkerchief. "This is not illness, my lady. My body is starving for shackle, and the path to recovery is a long and difficult one."

Trepidation skitters down my spine. "You're a witchfinder?"

Here I am, a witch whose bag is stuffed full of suspicious plants bought for my crone, and I've just crossed paths with my natural enemy.

"I was, my lady. I mean you no harm, stopping you in the street like this. I wish to make reparations to you, former witchfinder to witch, and—and..." He stammers and clenches his hands. "On behalf of all the witchfinders in Maledin, we swear to help you and your, ah, husband? Mate? To help King Zabriel win this in any manner that we can."

Determination and guilt are writ large on his lined features, and he's shaking worse than ever. If this man doesn't sit down soon, he will fall down.

"You should have come to the castle and petition to speak with *Ma'len's* mate there," Dusan tells him. "Not accost her in the street."

"I have done terrible things..." He flashes a fearful look at the castle looming over the city, and I realize he must have been afraid that he would be arrested if he'd gone there, pardoned or not.

"So you lay in wait for her by the apothecary," Fiala accuses.

"I-I thought perhaps, as she is a witch..." Gaun stammers and looks sweatier than ever.

An offer of help from the former witchfinders of Maledin. It wouldn't hurt to listen to what he has to say. "There is a public house around the corner. Shall we go inside for refreshments?"

I lead Gaun in that direction with Fiala and Dusan following closely behind. We take our seats at a trestle table and order cups of mead. My bodyguards stand behind my chair, and I can feel them bristling with suspicion.

Gaun holds tight to his mead rather than drink it, and says in a scrupulously polite voice, "My lady, I was surprised when all the witchfinders were pardoned after the invasion, and even more so when I discovered that the King of Maledin will marry a witch. I thank you for not advising your future husband to prosecute us."

"King Zabriel pardoning you had nothing to do with me. My mate has no quarrel with the people of Maledin. Only with the Brethren and any who take up arms in their name. How many witchfinders were there under the Brethren?"

"Some two dozen, I believe. Ours is an uncommon gift. It was unacceptable to the Brethren for a woman to possess power of any kind, so warlocks were forced to hunt down witches."

"Warlocks?" I ask, having never heard the word before.

"The Brethren hated magic of all kinds. They called us witchfinders and claimed we had special skills, but we were really warlocks. Male witches skilled in sensing magic."

That sparks my interest. I've been carrying around the crystal that Emmeric gave me and meditating on it every chance I get. I feel it must be important and that I can unlock some kind of connection to Emmeric with it, but so far, I've been unsuccessful. I take it out of my pocket and show it to Gaun. "Can you sense any magic in this object?"

He studies it closely and lays two fingers on it. "There was magic in it. A great deal of magic, but it has dissipated."

"Did it belong to a witch?" I know it didn't belong to a witch, but I'm curious if Gaun can tell.

"It does not feel like a witch magicked this object. If I had to guess, I would say that the mage was male, but not human. Perhaps not even alive..." He concentrates for a moment longer and then shakes his head. "I'm afraid I can't tell."

"Not alive?" I ask in surprise.

"Many entities can wield magic, Lady Isavelle. Not all of them walk on two legs, breathe air, or imbibe food and drink. Some are quite formless, others unfathomable." He bows his head suddenly. "I wish to apologize to you and all the witches in Maledin, Lady Isavelle. The witchfinders were tormented by their work. Deep down, I think we all knew we were murdering our own kind, but between the shackle and the beatings, we were given no choice."

"You could have thrown yourselves onto the burning pyres instead of the witches," Fiala mutters.

Gaun's face fills with grief and regret. "Indeed we could have."

"What is it you're offering King Zabriel?" I ask.

His eyes brighten as he talks about his work. "For most of my life, I secretly collected literature on magic that was banned by the Brethren. They trusted me, and so they believed me when I told them the books, notes, and other papers I found had been destroyed. With help from two of my fellow warlocks—both former witchfinders—I am cataloguing the material in a building in the bookseller's quarter called Master Gaun's Magical Archive. This magical reference archive is the first of its kind in Maledin in five hundred years, or perhaps ever. If you or the king or any of your people have any use for this material, it is at your disposal."

In his impassioned words, I sense all his pain over the things he has done and his desire to make amends. "You are able to tell truly magical books and papers from superstitious scribblings?"

"Of course, my lady. I am a warlock, and I wish to wield my powers for good for the rest of my days."

"Then I think your archive is a wonderful idea. I will tell the king about it."

When I smile at him, he beams back at me. His smile is shaky, and he daubs his forehead with his handkerchief once more.

"Your shackle withdrawal still troubles you?" I ask.

Gaun takes a shuddering breath. "My lady, it is a living nightmare. Not only are there aches and fevers and stabbing pains, but the shackle starvation forces us to relive every terrible thing we have done. When I try to rest, all I see are visions of blood and fire...the faces of the women I tortured and murdered. If the Brethren wished to punish us, and they often did, all they needed to do was chain us in a cell and let shackle withdrawal turn us into shaking, screaming wrecks. All the shackle stores were destroyed when dragons attacked the Fliesch Monastery. Every former witchfinder in Maledin is suffering as I am."

Fiala mutters under her breath, "Good."

What he just told me about reminds me of the witchfinder I met, but something is puzzling me. "That's strange. I once met a witchfinder who was chained in a cell without shackle, and while he was sweating and uncomfortable, he was untroubled in his mind. We talked together as you and I are talking."

Gaun shakes his head. "Then you did not meet a witchfinder. Shackle deprivation would have driven him so mad that he would have been screaming and crying out for his mother."

"I'm certain that he was a witchfinder. The High Priest wished to punish the man for trying to escape, but he was too valuable to die. The priests had whipped him severely and chained him in the dungeons beneath the monastery. He bled and sweated, but he wasn't troubled by his conscience in the slightest."

Gaun frowns, his eyes growing troubled. "Can you describe this man? Do you know his name?"

"Yes, I remember him well. He was a tall young man with unkempt blond hair, and eyes so dark they appeared black. He told me his name was Kane."

Gaun's face slackens and he turns pale. The hand gripping his handkerchief starts to shake. "If Kane did not scream out in anguish over the things he has done, then I'm in no way surprised. I doubt he has ever been troubled by his conscience. I do not speak for Kane when I ask for forgiveness for the witchfinders. If you should ever cross paths with this man again, Lady Isavelle, keep your bodyguards close, and run."

HEAVY SLEET FALLS AS FIALA, Dusan, and I make our way back to the castle. The three of us are soaked to the bone and our teeth are chattering with cold as we pass through the gates.

"Let's stop by the Flame Temple," I tell my bodyguards. "I'd like to check in on Zenevieve."

"Good idea. We can get warm in front of the font," Dusan says, shaking slushy snow and droplets of water from his hair.

"The Temple Flame is for meditating in front of, not for warming your bony ass," Fiala replies.

"I can do both at once," he tells her with a grin.

When we arrive at the entrance to the Flame Temple, I see someone else who must have been caught in the sleet. Stesha is kneeling on the stone floor and staring into the temple. Water has pooled around him as the slushy snow has melted from his clothes.

Fiala, Dusan, and I all exchange glances and communicate silently.

Do we talk to him?

He'll probably yell at us.

You talk to him.

I'm not talking to him.

We all step carefully around Stesha and make our way inside. Half a dozen people are sitting before the flames, all of whom have been caught in the wet weather and their clothes are steaming as they dry. The three of us assemble as reverently as we can, our teeth still chattering.

The Temple Crone speaks behind us. "I have noticed that the need to meditate is great on wet winter days." There's a smile on her lips and a twinkle in her eyes that tells me we've caused no offense. "Thank you for joining us, *Ma'len's* mate, Fiala, Dusan."

I glance toward the entrance of the temple. "Did you notice the dragonmaster? I hope he's all right. It's freezing in that corridor, and he's soaked through."

Her smile dims. "Yes, I did. The dragonmaster has been out there for some time, but he doesn't wish to enter the temple."

"He'll make himself sick if he keeps this up. His lips are turning blue," Fiala mutters.

Zenevieve is here, and Stesha hasn't been given permission to see her. Zenevieve still hasn't recovered her memories, and meanwhile, the dragonmaster is freezing to death. "Perhaps we should let him see her for a moment. It might help them both."

The Temple Crone glances past me toward Stesha. "*Ma'len* has wondered the same thing to me. I don't believe *Ma'len* would be against it."

I leave the temple and carefully approach Stesha. "Dragonmaster, if you would like to see Zenevieve for a moment, the Temple Crone will take you to her."

I expect Stesha to leap to his feet and rush inside, but he doesn't move. He doesn't even look at me.

"You did hear me, didn't you? You may speak with Zenevieve. I am sure it will make her happy to see you."

Water drips steadily from his hair onto the flagstones. He's as still as a mountain. He doesn't even growl, *You may speak with Zenevieve, dragonmaster.*

I step directly in front of him, and his mouth tightens. He can hear me, but he's choosing to ignore me. "Zenevieve has been shedding tears over you. She needs to know that you forgive her for what happened." Whatever that is.

Stesha slowly gets to his feet, and I feel a flare of hope.

They're both so wretched over each other that I feel sure if they talk, they'll resolve whatever has broken between them.

"I..." he begins, his expression anguished.

Maybe my expression is too expectant, or he realizes who he was about to confide in. Stesha glares down at me, and then turns on his heel and strides away.

17

Zabriel

There's a loud, ominous thumping on the War Room door, the kind that makes me wonder, *What now?* I walk quickly forward and pull the door open.

Stesha is standing on the other side, bedraggled, blue from cold, and soaking wet. "What happened to you?"

He pushes past me into the room. "I went for a walk."

The dragonmaster paces up and down the room. I go to the terrace and look toward the dragongrounds. All seems fine down there. I spot Nilak within a cluster of Beta dragons, as regal as a queen. Scourge has Esmeral between his front legs while she plays with some fledglings.

"Zabriel, I need to show you this." Stesha reaches inside his jacket and pulls out a damp, squashed scroll. "This morning, I received this report from the wingrunners. They've spotted a wild flare in eastern Maledin."

Frowning, I take the scroll from him and read it. The report was written by Leibel, a battle-scarred wingrunner who occasionally escorts Isavelle to Amriste. The patrol spotted six wild dragons north of Bormont Valley. The wingrunners attempted to take a closer look but pulled back when an Alpha dragon aggressively displayed his wings and prepared to breathe fire. I read the description of the dragon. Golden with black flourishes and a size comparable to Scourge. It was a good idea they pulled back.

So there are still wild dragons in Maledin. If any of these wild dragons can be tamed, my army will be strengthened, and another rider will have a dragon.

If.

Wild dragons are notoriously hard to tame. They often attack anyone and anything that encroaches on their territory and have killed many experienced dragonriders and wingrunners.

I hand back the scroll. "It sounds like an Alpha protecting his flare."

Stesha tucks the scroll inside his sodden jacket. "Yellow with black flourishes. Do you realize the significance of a dragon of that description?"

A golden dragon of Scourge's size sounds vaguely familiar. "Remind me."

"There was an untamable golden Alpha in Old Maledin. My predecessor dubbed him Golden Terror and warned us to keep out of his way. Golden Terror had killed six of our dragons and riders. I believe this dragon could be his descendant."

The descendant of a notorious dragon-killer is loose in eastern Maledin. Brilliant. Fucking brilliant. If this wild flare decides it wants to be the only flare in Maledin, we could suffer losses that we can't afford right now. "Inform the dragonriders that they are to exercise extreme caution in eastern Maledin, and I'll make sure Captain Ashton speaks with the wingrunners—"

Stesha interrupts me. "That's not enough to keep our flare safe. I seek your permission to tame the golden dragon."

I stare at Stesha like he's sprouted two heads. "You want to what?"

"A dragon of that size and ferocity in our flare would be an asset, *Ma'len*." Stesha is suddenly addressing me as respectfully as he would have addressed my father.

"Out of the question."

Stesha glares at me. When he speaks, there's an edge to his voice, and he sounds more like the Stesha I know. "I'm trying to treat you as a king who deserves my respect. I sought your permission. I don't need it."

I fold my arms and glare at him. He's not trying very hard.

Attempting to tame a wild dragon is dangerous. A wild Omega could be tempted away by an experienced dragonrider, or one of the smaller Betas, but an Alpha? An Alpha protecting a flare? Suicide.

"You're already bonded to an Alpha. You and Nilak will be attacked the moment you approach this wild flare. You're our dragonmaster. I can't lose you."

Stesha's eyes flash. "If I'm not doing all I can for the sake of the flare, then I don't deserve to call myself the dragonmaster."

"You're trying to get yourself killed. You think I don't know the signs?"

Onderz behaved just like this in the days following

Mirelle's suicide. He completely shut down, and all he craved was a dragonrider's death. My best friend and his dragon died when they flew through an electrical storm. Suicide by wild dragon has been another way for an Alpha consumed by his own failure to leave this world.

"I must do my part for Maledin to help win the war, *Ma'len*."

"Shut up with the *Ma'len* bullshit," I shout. "You're not killing yourself and leaving the rest of us to fight back against Emmeric without you. I will lock you in the dungeons before I let you walk out of here."

"You don't order me around, Zabriel," Stesha snarls.

"I shall when you're self-destructing."

Stesha lunges at me and grabs hold of my jacket. I seize his shoulders, but he seems too overwhelmed with rage and despair to try to fight me. "I don't want to die. I want to *kill him*. I need vengeance for Zenevieve and everything he did to her. I can think of nothing else."

Stesha's scent reeks of anger and despair.

"I can't even face her," he says bitterly. "I want that golden dragon. I will tame him, and I will bring his flare to Lenhale, and we will be even stronger when the time comes to face Emmeric."

"That's impossible. If that golden dragon doesn't kill you and Nilak, he and Scourge will rip into each other the moment they lay eyes on each other. Neither will submit. A flare can't have two Alphas."

Stesha lets go of me. "Then I'll set up a new flare. An eastern flare, and I'll train new riders for all the dragons. This is something only I can do, Zabriel. I must do it."

"You may speak with Zenevieve. I was wrong to keep you from her. Go to her now in the Flame Temple."

He shakes his head. "I can't. She won't want to see me."

"If you quarreled, that was five hundred years ago—"

"I said I *can't*. Bring it up again, and I'll draw steel on you, Zabriel."

Dragon's blood, he's infuriating. This is how we're to part as he heads toward certain death, with him threatening to fight me? There's an old legend of a dragonrider called Yuric who abandoned his friends and family in their time of need. When he implored the gods to be forgiven, Ur, the King of the Dragons, told him he must perform six impossible feats before his honor could be restored, and he would be welcomed home. Stesha seems to be his own quest, and I don't even understand what he longs to be forgiven for.

"If you perish taming this golden dragon, I won't burn knotgrass in your memory. I will curse your name to hell and back for leaving me alone with this fucking mess."

Without a word, Stesha turns to go.

Maybe I'm being too hard on him. I don't want what are probably my last words to him to be in anger. "Wait. Don't go yet."

He hesitates and then turns back to me.

"I will protect Zenevieve in your absence. Emmeric will never hurt her again."

"Thank you." Stesha swallows hard. There's a long moment of silence, and then he asks, "Will you blade swear with me?"

To blade swear is to make a warrior's pact with the ally you most trust. You will have each other's backs in battle and protect the other man's beloved if he must be elsewhere.

He doesn't want to go, I realize. Being parted from her is torture.

"You know I will protect Zenevieve. Will you protect Isavelle if I'm not able to?"

"I will. I wouldn't ask you to blade swear otherwise."

Stesha has been by my side during every skirmish and battle I've flown into, first him leading me when I was Prince Zabriel, and then me leading him as Commander Zabriel and King Zabriel. He has followed my orders more scrupulously than I followed his.

I draw my sword then hold it out, the point facing down.

Stesha raises his hand and grips the pommel. "I will return. Seeing Emmeric perish is all I want. I will protect you and yours with my life. When you need me, my hand is on the blade with yours."

I cover Stesha's hand with mine. "My hand is on the blade with yours."

I throw my sword aside and pull Stesha into an embrace. He holds me back just as fiercely. He wants Emmeric dead just as much as I do, and I pray that his resolve won't get him killed.

I pull back and grip his shoulders with both hands. "Then go, but be sure you come home again."

Stesha straightens up with his hands by his sides and fixes me with a look of respect, one I've never seen in his eyes before. He puts his fist over his heart and nods sharply.

"Yes, *Ma'len.*"

18

———

Isavelle

It's been several weeks since the dragonmaster flew east with Nilak, and so far, there's been no word from him. I hope he still lives and that he and Nilak haven't been ripped to pieces by a dragon that sounds as dangerous as Scourge.

My heat is on my mind. My first true heat. I'm in an agony of waiting, holding my breath for something unpredictable. Whenever we're parted, Zabriel greets me upon my return by pressing his nose to the nape of my neck and kneading my ass with his big hands. The way he looks at me with those red eyes and a smile on his lips never fails to make me melt. I often wake up in the night, and he has his knot pressed between my thighs, and he sleepily whispers for me to squeeze it tight because he's aching. I do, and he groans and bites into my shoulder.

I feel restless and hollow from dawn to midnight. I woke this morning feeling snappish and irritated, which was soothed when Zabriel rolled on top of me, spread my thighs with his knees, and fucked me hard all the way to his knot. Lately, I've started begging for him to knot me, which only makes us both more frustrated because he physically can't, or at least he couldn't without being horribly cruel.

That night, as we have sex, I try to hold in the words, *Please knot me, Alpha,* because it's not fair to beg him for something he can't give me. It slips out anyway, and then I feel terrible because it probably reminds him of what his brother did to his sister.

I'm face down on the bed and crying into my pillow, "I'm so sorry. I said it again."

Zabriel presses kisses across my back and murmurs soothingly, "It's all right. I know you can't help it. Come and cry on my chest, sweet Omega." He gathers me up in his arms, and I cry out all my frustration and confusion.

The Temple Mothers tell me that a true heat will arrive in its own time, but I wonder if I'm being punished for all those times I pushed my mate away. Now all I can think is *knot. Baby. Zabriel's knot. Zabriel's baby.* Until I met Zabriel, it seemed impossible that I would ever have children because I was trapped in the monasteries. I remember the weight of my infant siblings in my arms, and suddenly, my breasts are aching, and the hollow feeling is so strong that, for a moment, I can't breathe.

My sleep that night is restless, and I wake so late that Zabriel is already gone. I put on my dragonriding clothes and go down to the dragongrounds. Esmeral races to greet me with chirrups and nips of my fingers, and the scent of frustrated Omega is rolling off her in waves.

"You as well?" I ask her as we walk together to join the flare. "The two biggest, strongest Alphas in the flare are our mates, and we're as needy as hell for them with no chance of relief. It's not fair."

Esmeral roars in agreement and sparks erupt from her throat.

Zabriel is standing beside Scourge, and I'm surprised to see him bare-chested with one arm lifted while Scourge noses at him. My mate's long hair spills down his muscular back, and he has one large hand splayed on his dragon's flank. I have no idea what he's doing, but he looks glorious smiling at Scourge.

Scourge sees me, and a moment later, Zabriel looks around, gazing at me with the same red eyes as his dragon.

"Your stab wound isn't paining you, I hope?" I ask, realizing that's what he's showing Scourge.

Zabriel glances at his scar and pats the healed arrow injury in Scourge's flank. "We were comparing battle wounds. I was checking on him, and he bit my clothes until I showed him mine. We're both healing nicely, don't you think?"

I reach up and run my fingers over the shiny red scar and the muscles by his ribs. Despite the crisp air of the day, Zabriel is roasting hot when I press my lips against his flesh. "Oh, yes. Beautiful."

Zabriel draws me into his arms for a kiss. He bends down so his mouth can reach mine, and then he wraps both arms around me and lifts me up against his chest. He has his back resting against Zabriel's side. Esmeral wraps her tail around Zabriel's legs and one of my ankles.

"We feel like a happy family, the four of us," I tell my mate with a smile.

"We are a happy family," Zabriel murmurs, pressing another kiss to my lips. "Soon we'll be an even bigger family because Scourge and I will have a dozen little ones to look after."

"I hope Esmeral will be responsible for eleven of those."

Zabriel gives me a mock-serious look. "I don't think so, Omega. I hope four or even five of them are mine. We should start with triplets. Girls, so I can spoil them like their mother. And then twin boys. They will all be riding real dragons by the time they're five."

I laugh and kiss him. "I don't think we'll get a say in the matter when it comes to children. We'll get what we're given."

"That's fine," he tells me with a charming smile. "What I'm given has worked out beautifully for me."

I feel a spurt of desire and love for this man. He has to survive this war. I won't be able to live without him.

"*Sha'len*, what's that expression in your eyes?" he asks, brushing his lips over mine.

I don't want to tell him I was thinking about losing him. "Esmeral still doesn't have a proper nest. You mentioned once that Omegas make their nests in caves?"

He tilts his chin toward the far end of the bluff. "Over there. One of the Alpha females should have shown her to the caves by now, but I don't think they have."

That's because Nilak doesn't like Esmeral. "How about we do it then?" When I show Esmeral a picture of Zabriel and me leading her over to the caves, she perks up. "She'd like that."

"Then let's go," Zabriel says and sets off down the dragongrounds with me in his arms.

"I can walk," I say with a laugh, as Esmeral walks at his side.

He presses his nose into the side of my neck and breathes in as he keeps walking. "You know I love to carry you. I want your scent all over me."

Over his shoulder, Scourge turns and starts to follow us. The cave mouth is enormous, and semi-darkness envelops us as Zabriel carries me inside.

Zabriel looks around in the darkness and breathes in deeply. "There are dragons in here with clutches of eggs. How wonderful."

Scattered around the cave are three Beta females and an Alpha female. Their bright eyes are glimmering in the darkness.

"They keep their eggs warm with dragonfire," Zabriel explains, holding me with his other hand on Esmeral's scales. "A special kind of dragonfire that burns low for many hours so they may go out and hunt, but they prefer to be in here where they can protect their clutch."

As we pass a tunnel, Esmeral sniffs the entrance before extending her long neck inside.

"What do you think, Esmeral?" I ask her. "Does that look like a good spot for your nest?"

Her lithe, glimmering body slips down the narrow passage. There's a rustling sound, and we can just glimpse her turning in a circle in the tight space. Then she settles down and rests her snout on a foreleg.

"She likes it," I tell Zabriel.

Scourge enters the cavern, and he hunts in the darkness

for his mate. He gives a soft grunt, and a moment later, Esmeral replies with a happy trill that echoes down the walls of the tunnel.

"It's a shame Scourge is too big to get into Esmeral's nest with her as you're able to get into mine."

Zabriel sits down on a smooth stone with me still in his arms. "I'm a lucky dragon in that respect."

His red eyes are bright in the darkness, and his flesh is suddenly burning even hotter. He shifts me on his lap until I can feel the bulge of his knot against my inner thigh. Ever so slightly, I rub against it, and, for a moment, his eyes close and he breathes deeply.

"What's it going to be like when I finally go into heat?"

Zabriel moans and kisses me. "It's going to be wonderful, *sha'len*. We'll be together. Completely together. I can't wait to be so deep inside you with your tight cunt around my knot and for your blood to burst in my mouth as I bite you." His teeth must ache because he sinks them into the spot between my neck and my shoulder. I used to be afraid of his teeth, and now every bite he gives me makes me slick myself. I beg for his bites during sex as often as I beg for his knot.

He runs his hot tongue over the fresh indentation. "I picture it so often, my teeth marks in your mating gland. My saliva will heal you, but my mark will remain, and with that taste of you, you'll finally be my bride."

I stroke my fingers across his chest, and my mouth waters. Taste. That's something I don't know about him. "What do you taste like?"

"*Sha'len*?"

I wriggle against his knot and smile. "Down here. I've

only put my mouth on you once, but you didn't finish in my mouth."

Zabriel glances around the cave to check that we're alone, a smile tugging the corner of his lips. There are dragons nearby, but no people. I don't mind about the dragons, and Zabriel doesn't either as I reach for his belt and unthread it before sinking down onto the soft earth between his knees.

With my hands on his strong thighs, I look up at him. "Can I find out?"

Zabriel spreads his knees as his breathing deepens. "I think I'll die from happiness if you do."

Together we pull his cock out of his breeches. I stroke my fingers along the length of his shaft, caressing the veins and then his rapidly swelling knot. Zabriel tips back his head and groans, and the muscles on either side of his throat flex. I love it when he does that. He does it again when I open my mouth and run my tongue up the underside of his shaft.

Feeling bolder, I suck on the tip, and he's deliciously hot and fleshy in my mouth.

"By the gods' aching balls," he growls, his voice vibrating powerfully in his chest. "Take me deeper."

I open my lips and suck more of him into my mouth. From this angle, I see the broad expanse of his bare chest and his silky hair spilling around his shoulders. His thighs are on either side of me, squeezing my body. My mouth is filled with a musky, slightly sweet taste.

When I take him all the way to the back of my throat, Zabriel's breathing hitches, and his hands reach for me. He grips my hair in his fist, and pleasure flashes through my mating gland. He thrusts rhythmically into my mouth, his hips moving against his seat on the rock. My nails scratch down his muscular stomach, and I can feel myself getting wetter and wetter between my thighs. His pleasure is making me ache for him.

Behind me, Scourge shifts restlessly. I can feel the dragon's red eyes on us, and he calls for Esmeral in a deep rumble.

Zabriel's tone is similarly urgent and deep. "That's my beautiful girl. That's my Omega. Oh, fuck. Oh, f—" He breaks off with a loud cry, and he clamps his hand around his knot over mine. His flesh rapidly swells, and I feel an answering clench between my legs. I want that part of him so much. My mouth floods with thick, salty fluid. It seeps from the corners of my mouth and spills over my lips. I swallow once, twice, but there's so much of it. When I pull away, Zabriel and I are still squeezing his knot and his cock is still releasing streams of cum.

Zabriel opens his eyes, and he pulls me up off the ground and into his arms.

"Careful. I'm covered in you."

"Good. I love you this way," he says, kissing me hungrily.

There's nothing for us to get cleaned up with, but Zabriel doesn't seem to care. He holds me in his arms, and I look around the cave. "I can see why the dragons like to nest here. It's very cozy."

As we're walking back across the dragongrounds, I realize how strange the flare looks without the large, bossy Nilak fussing over the Betas and preening their wings.

"Still no word from Stesha?" I ask Zabriel.

"Nothing. I've given orders that no riders are to approach the east while he's trying to connect with the flare. Another dragon or wyvern on the horizon could anger the Alpha and endanger Stesha and Nilak."

"They could already be hurt."

Zabriel thinks about this for a long time. "Stesha won't let anything happen to Nilak. If it all goes wrong, she'll return to the flare without him."

But will Nilak want to live without her rider? I don't know how I'd bear it if anything happened to Esmeral.

"Will you do something for me?" Zabriel asks.

"Anything," I whisper, pressing my cheek into his palm.

"I regret the way I've treated Zenevieve. I've known her since we were young, and she would never willingly betray Maledin. Will you..." He breaks off and closes his mouth. "Perhaps I shouldn't ask this of you after what she did."

"I don't blame her for the way she was used. I blame Emmeric. I will gladly be her friend and help her move on from what happened."

"Thank you, *sha'len*. While you have your bodyguards with you, will you consider asking Zenevieve to accompany you around the castle sometimes? The gardens. The drag-ongrounds. Those were some of her favorite places."

"Do you think that the familiarity will prompt her to remember the gaps in her memory?"

Zabriel takes a long look around at the dragongrounds and shakes his head. "I don't know. Maybe it's better for her that she never remembers what happened. I just want to make amends for the way I've treated her and for her to feel at home again."

"What do you think if I take her to Biddy Hawthorne? My crone is very wise and may be able to help her in ways the *Hratha'len* haven't thought of yet."

Zabriel considers this. "If she wishes to visit your crone, then she may go with you. First, bring Zenevieve down among the flare. Stesha taught her much of what he knows about dragons over the years. They will be good for her, and she will be good for them. The flare was there for her when her parents were killed. They will be there for her after…" He grimaces and rubs his eyes, like he hates even saying these words. "After whatever Emmeric did to her."

I wrap my fingers around two of his and squeeze them. "This is the right decision. I'm proud of my Alpha. You inspire me to be so much better than I am."

He raises his eyebrows in surprise. "Me? I have been stabbed in the ribs. I burned down an eyrie, threw Zenevieve into the dungeons, and nearly murdered Stesha. Worst of all, my Omega was kidnapped from my own castle. I must strive to be a better Alpha for the sake of my beautiful Omega."

I press my hand against his heart. "I can't wait to bear your mark. Your teeth in my flesh. My blood in your mouth."

Zabriel smiles. "My teeth in your flesh. Your blood in my mouth."

He says this with as much feeling as anyone ever said *I love you*. Then he kisses me, slanting his mouth over mine and tasting me with his tongue.

WHEN I ENTER Zenevieve's room in the Flame Temple, she resembles a wilted flower as she gazes wanly at the bedclothes with her head bowed. I was going to ask, coax, encourage Zenevieve to come outside with me, but I think the best thing to do is make this about something that isn't her.

"You must come with me," I tell her, injecting urgency in my voice.

Zenevieve looks up, startled. "I must? Why?"

"*Ma'len's* orders. Put these on." I hold out a cloak and a pair of boots. "The cloak is mine and will be a little short for you, but it's very warm, and I think these boots are your size. It's the dragons. They're restless without the dragonmaster."

"Stesha's gone? Where is he?" Zenevieve asks.

I motion for her to get dressed. "I'll tell you outside."

It works. Zenevieve's concern has her pulling on the boots and fastening the cloak around her shoulders. It touches the floor when I wear it, but on Zenevieve it dusts her calves. As we leave the temple with Fiala and Dusan following behind us, I tell her about Stesha's self-imposed mission to tame the wild flare to the east. I describe the flare's Alpha to her. "Apparently, the dragon is a descendent of one from your time."

Zenevieve gapes at me. "Stesha is attempting to tame one of Golden Terror's descendants? Has he lost his mind? He'll be killed, and so will Nilak."

"He hasn't lost his mind from what I understand," and then add under my breath, "though possibly he's been overcome by arrogance."

Zenevieve's expression is prim as she replies, "The dragonmaster isn't arrogant. He's very good at what he does."

"He thinks so as well."

A hint of a smile flickers over Zenevieve's lips. "Perhaps, but all Alphas are like that."

I think of Zabriel lounging on his throne or naked in our bed, looking every inch the king and pretty damn pleased with himself. Zenevieve's not wrong.

Zenevieve looks worriedly toward the east. "I hope that he and Nilak come back in one piece."

As we cross the bridge onto the dragongrounds, a huge black head rises up over the other dragons and fixes us with a bright red glare.

Zenevieve gazes up at him, her lips parted. "Scourge is even more magnificent than I remember."

He closes his eyes briefly and then turns away, his way of signaling that he's content for us to approach his flare. A turquoise and golden dragon launches into the sky with a shriek of delight and swoops over to us. Esmeral chitters excitedly at both of us, greeting Zenevieve like a friend.

Zenevieve gasps with pleasure. "It can't be. Is this Esmeral? You were a fledgling when I saw you last. You haven't grown much bigger, but your beautiful colors have come in." She studies me. "Oh, I see it. You and she are bonded. And are you both Omegas?"

I smile as Esmeral nuzzles my hand, and then to my surprise, she does the same to Zenevieve. I never see her act this way with anyone who isn't me or Zabriel. "We are. I'm so fortunate to have her."

Esmeral scampers over to Scourge and buffets against his flank, preening her head against his chest and forelegs, and she looks back at Zenevieve to make sure she's watching. I grin at my dragon. The little show-off.

Zenevieve understands right away. "The flare's Alpha is your mate? You are a lucky Omega."

Scourge rumbles approvingly in his chest as he gazes down at Esmeral.

We move among the flare, and Zenevieve names every

dragon and tells me about their history. How old they are, their riders, how many battles they've fought in.

A small white dragon with golden flourishes is fast asleep against a large female Beta. The Beta gets to her feet, extends her wings, and then takes to the skies. The smaller dragon yawns, and then slinks over to another resting dragon and falls right back into a doze.

Every time I've seen this dragon, it's been asleep. "That's the laziest dragon I ever saw."

Zenevieve smiles. "I like him. He's calming."

"How can you tell it's male?"

"Do you see how his snout is wide rather than narrow, and the spines of his crest point outward and then up?"

I compare the white dragon's appearance to Esmeral and see the differences. Noticing that I'm studying her, she races over and stretches her wings to the sky.

"We don't lie around being sleepy, do we? We like to be awake so we can make trouble for our Alphas."

Over my head, Scourge rumbles. Is it just my imagination, or is the dragon's red gaze full of disapproval?

"Don't tell Zabriel I said that," I tell him with a smile.

"It's strange to see the flare without Nilak. No Damla, either." Zenevieve lists off several more dragon names I don't recognize, and then says sadly, "I suppose they were killed in the recent fighting."

"I'm not sure about the others, but Damla was a strange case. Do you remember what I told you about seeing a vision of Damla and her rider, Tish?"

Zenevieve's sad expression fades away. She says slowly, "That's right, you did. Damla was cut open. Her *riesta* torn from her chest."

If Zenevieve can remember our conversation, maybe she'll remember further into the past. "I wondered if it was Emmeric who stole the *riesta*, but for what purpose?"

"Why would he do that?" There's genuine puzzlement on Zenevieve's face.

Disappointed, I shake my head. "I don't know. I wish I did." Changing the subject, I tell her, "I must fly to the west and spend the day with my crone tomorrow. Will you come with me?"

"A witch crone? I doubt she'll want me getting in the way of her time with you."

"Your grandmother was a witch. I'm sure she'd like to hear about her."

Zenevieve stares at me in confusion, and then she grimaces. "I remember now. Odanna told you that. My grandmother wasn't a witch. She was a Temple Mother."

"Oh. Right."

"Sorry about that," she says.

"No, it's not your fault. Please come tomorrow. I thought my crone might be able to help you recover your memories. It's possible she can try something the *Hratha'len* haven't thought of yet."

Zenevieve still hesitates. "I'd like to, but I'm not sure *Ma'len* would like me leaving the castle while I'm a prisoner."

"You're not a prisoner anymore. Come with me, I've got something to show you."

Up at the castle, I take Zenevieve to a bedchamber that's not far from mine. It's dusty and the furniture is in shambles, but we can fix that. "This is your new room."

Zenevieve's eyes are wide as she turns on the spot.

"Really? I'm to sleep here, and not in the Flame Temple where the *Hratha'len* can watch me?"

"This is your home now, if you'd like to stay."

She considers this, her lip caught between her teeth, and then she smiles. "Yes, please. I'd love to be close to the dragons."

With Santha and Posette's help, we sweep out the dust and cobwebs from the neglected room, throw out an old trunk and other rubbish, and polish the four-poster bed. Then we change the moldy old mattress for a fresh one, put sheets and blankets on the bed, and add curtains to the bed canopy. With a fire in the grate burning sweet-smelling herbs and applewood and decorative tapestries on the walls, the room feels cozy and smells a great deal better.

Zenevieve turns on the spot, admiring the room. "It's wonderful. I'm not sure I deserve the trust that you and *Ma'len* have placed in me, but I will strive to. Thank you."

In mine and Zabriel's room, I take out the amulet that Emmeric gave me and meditate on it, as I've been doing most days. Even though there isn't any magic in it, I still hope that it will show me something useful.

I sit cross-legged on the bed, the amulet in my hands, and close my eyes. The crystal feels cold and dead to the touch, but as my mind drifts, I think I feel something. A thread as thin as spider's silk. I try to follow it, but a moment later, it dissolves into nothing. Or maybe I imagined it, and it was never there to begin with.

～

ZENEVIEVE BORROWS some flying clothes from a fellow dragonrider, and the following morning, we arrive in Amriste with a unit of wingrunners. The sun is level with the tops of the trees behind the village, and there are several ravens watching us.

The wingrunners and wyverns disappear among the cottages, and I lead Zenevieve up the path to my crone's rickety front gate. She's already standing there, leaning on her cane.

Biddy fixes my companion with a beady look. The two of them met the day that "Odanna" came to Amriste, all the Maledinni villagers were killed, and I was attacked by Brethren mages. "I remember you, girl. I'm surprised that your head is still attached to your body."

"So am I, Grandmother," Zenevieve replies.

"Have you remembered anything about your time with Emmeric?" Biddy asks, and Zenevieve shakes her head. "Give me your hands, girl."

Zenevieve hesitates, then puts her fingers into Biddy's weathered, red-knuckle grip.

Biddy's severe expression fades as she closes her eyes. Then she opens her eyes and lets go. "There is poison in your body, child. You have been suffering for a long time."

"Poison? Am I going to die?"

"It has weakened you, but in what way, I can't tell."

"Do you think Emmeric poisoned me so I would forget everything that happened while he was the Shadow King?"

"Perhaps." Biddy's gaze flickers over her. I have the feeling Biddy knows or suspects more than she's letting on. "I can give you something to help work it out of your body. It may make you ill for several days. Even longer."

"Please. I would like that, Grandmother."

"Are you certain? You will have a grim time of it."

"I don't care. I just want to find out what happened to me," Zenevieve implores her.

"Go into the back garden with Isavelle and the two of you can do witchcraft while I make you up something to take back with you." The old woman shuffles inside the cottage and closes the door behind her.

Zenevieve's eyes are shining as we dig twisted, dead pumpkin vines out of a garden bed. When her thoughts finally catch up with what her hands are doing, she gazes at a vine she just dug up in confusion. "Wait. Is this witchcraft?"

I laugh and wipe my forehead with the back of my hand. "I'm told it is." I add in a whisper, "Usually, I have to work all day before Mistress Hawthorne helps me with anything, but she's in there working on something for you already."

Zenevieve looks pleased. "Well, we'd better pull up every single dead vine we can find."

Several hours later, Zenevieve and I are dirty and sweaty and sitting on the grass drinking tea, the garden thoroughly cleared of pumpkin vines. Biddy comes out, eases herself down onto a wooden stool, and passes Zenevieve a bag tied with string.

"When you're in your chambers tonight, make tea from this and drink it all at once. Keep the room warm, dark, and quiet. Your head will ache, you will feel ill, and you will sweat, so you must drink plenty of cool water."

Zenevieve tucks the bag into a pocket and covers it protectively. "Thank you, Grandmother. I will do as you say."

My crone frowns and watches her for a long time. "Be patient. Your memories will return when you are ready for them, and not before." She turns to me. "And you? Have you had a vision? Learned anything useful about that crystal?"

"No visions, and no I haven't," I tell her with a sigh. "I've been trying and trying. A witchfinder—or I should say, a warlock—examined the crystal briefly, but he couldn't tell me anything."

"A warlock? So that's how they're styling themselves now." Biddy gives a derisive snort. "As long as he doesn't go around creating messes for the rest of us to clean up. We don't need Maledin afflicted by plagues of toads or vanishing doorknobs."

"Master Gaun is setting up a magical reference archive."

"An archive? That sounds harmless. He should keep his hands busy fussing about with papers and leave the real magic to those of us who know what we're doing." There's a mischievous gleam in her eyes.

"You could visit the archive, Grandmother," I suggest, and a smile spreads over my face at the thought of the country's bossiest witch walking into premises that belong to a former witchfinder.

"Yes, Grandmother," Zenevieve adds with a grin. "Ask him why he never caught you."

Biddy Hawthorne cackles with laughter. "I may just do that, my girls. Oh, how I would enjoy the look on his face."

THAT EVENING, I sit at Zenevieve's bedside while she drinks the tea brewed from the herbs Biddy Hawthorne gave her. She gives me a nervous smile before swallowing it all down and passing the empty cup to Mother Linnea. The Temple

Crone gave Zenevieve her blessing on the matter, saying that there was no reason not to try human magic if she wished. However, I notice some disapproving glances among the other red-robed women of the Flame Temple. Nevertheless, the Temple Mothers agreed to take turns watching over Zenevieve as she rids herself of the poison in her body.

"How do you feel?" I ask Zenevieve as she settles back on the pillows.

The young woman takes a moment in self-reflection. "The same. There are no memories rushing back to me yet." Heat rises in her cheeks and her eyelids grow heavy. "But I do feel very tired all of a sudden. Perhaps after I wake up..."

Zenevieve dozes off, and I leave her under the watchful gaze of Mother Linnea.

In the morning, I visit Zenevieve first thing and find her awake but groggy and sweating profusely.

"Strange dreams..." she mutters, her eyes heavy-lidded. "The past. Dragons. Everything felt...strange."

"Were you dreaming of Emmeric? Of Shar?" I ask eagerly, before biting my lip. I shouldn't be prompting her. She needs to recover her memories on her own.

Zenevieve doesn't seem to hear me. She groans, rolls over, and falls back asleep.

Over the following days, I check on her morning, midday, and evening, but she's always the same. Hot, feverish, and exhausted. One afternoon, the Temple Mother in attendance gazes at Zenevieve sadly and says to me, "She calls out for Minta and the dragonmaster. She calls out for her parents, and she cries a great deal. Poor dear. There's so much sadness in her heart for one so young."

After six days of Zenevieve suffering like this, I tentatively ask Biddy Hawthorne if the tea could be too much for her.

"The tea is just tea," my crone says, a dangerously severe expression on her face. "What your friend has in her body is coming out, and it's about time it did from the sounds of it."

Not if it kills her, I want to reply, but my crone is in a bad temper today, and I wouldn't put it past her to order me to count pebbles in the woods if I talk back to her. One of Biddy's ravens, which is sitting on the garden fence by my elbow, clicks its beak warningly at me.

As soon as I return to the castle, I go into Zenevieve's room. She looks the same as she has for the past few days, only her cheeks are thinner and the circles beneath her eyes are a darker purple.

As I sit down at her bedside, a flowery scent washes over me. I glance around the room and say to myself, "It smells different in here."

"There were some soothing herbs burning on the fire," Zenevieve croaks and licks her parched lips.

I help her sit up and drink some water. "You're awake. I'm so sorry this is happening to you."

Zenevieve takes a few small swallows and lays back. "Please don't be sorry. I think it's working. I feel...different. Better. Lighter. Maybe my memories will return soon."

I'll settle for Zenevieve being well again and damn the memories.

Zabriel has suggested that I ask her gentle questions about the past, so I take a seat by her bedside. "If you don't mind me asking, what was Minta like?"

Zenevieve smiles tiredly. "Minta. My beautiful girl. I had her from a hatchling. I remember the day Stesha knocked on our front door carrying her in his arms. She was sitting with her forelegs on one of his shoulders, snuffling in his hair." Zenevieve trails off with a smile, seeming to enjoy that sweet memory. "He said to me in his serious way, 'Zenevieve, there's someone who wants to meet you.' I asked who it was, and as soon as she heard my voice, Minta scrambled down from his shoulder and scampered over to me. How beautiful she was. Perfect black scales, darker than night. Sharp little claws and sparkling emerald eyes. She was fast, too. She grew up quickly and we raced wingrunners for fun. It's unusual for a dragon to be that fast."

Stesha knew that Minta and Zenevieve belonged together, just as he guessed that Esmeral wanted me for her rider. "What made the dragonmaster bring Minta to you?"

"I don't know. He must have watched me playing with the hatchlings and he noticed something about the way Minta was around me. He senses these things, and usually he's right." Another smile spreads over her face. "That's what makes him the dragonmaster."

It's bizarre seeing someone smile so fondly while talking about Stesha.

I feel a spurt of anger. This man, this stubborn, cantankerous, idiotic man has refused to speak one word to Zenevieve since her return. I doubt I could be so kindhearted when I'm being ignored by a man who means so much to me. I think I'd break all of his things while screaming.

A chorus of roars can suddenly be heard from the dragongrounds, and I get up and lift the tapestry away from the window. It's late in the afternoon, and the sun is shining on the flare. Scourge is looking toward the east and his wings half unfurl. He doesn't take to the air to defend the flare, so whatever he sees probably isn't dangerous. I can't see anything myself, and then a pale speck appears in the sky. After a short while, it grows larger, and I can tell what it is. A white dragon.

"That's Nilak," I exclaim.

Zenevieve pushes herself up in bed. "Nilak? Did you say Nilak? Is she coming home?"

I study the white sliver in the sky as it approaches the castle. All the dragons are milling about the dragongrounds in excitement. "I think so. Yes, I'm sure it's Nilak."

"She has her rider, doesn't she? The dragonmaster is with her? He's alive?" Zenevieve doesn't give me time to answer before she pushes the bedclothes off her legs and staggers to the window. She's shivering and hunched over as she stands by my side, and her face is as sickly as death. I pull a blanket from the bed and wrap it around her shaking body. She doesn't seem to notice. All her attention is on the white dragon.

As Nilak circles into land, we glimpse a man on her back with white hair streaming behind him.

"He's there. I see him," Zenevieve cries, and her voice breaks. "I want to greet him. Help me downstairs."

I'm not certain that's a good idea, but Zenevieve is already hobbling across the room toward her boots. She's wearing only a nightgown and a blanket. Her long hair is in snarls down her back, and there's sweat on her brow.

"I should help you get dressed, and I could braid your hair."

Zenevieve brushes away my offer. "I don't care about any of that. Help me, please. I must see for myself that he's all right."

Once she has shoes on her feet, I wrap my arm around her painfully thin waist and help her along the corridor into the main part of the castle. Zenevieve looks like she's in pain from aching joints. Her limbs are trembling, and I'm angry all over again at Stesha. He doesn't deserve her suffering like this for his sake.

We're not the only ones who have gathered to witness the dragonmaster's return. The doors of the Great Hall have opened, and a crowd has spilled into the corridor that leads down to the dragongrounds.

A man with wind-whipped white hair and blood on his face climbs the stairs, and we see that it is indeed Stesha.

There's a hopeful smile on Zenevieve's lips, and then it dies. "He's hurt. He's been in a fight." A moment later, her face turns an even starker white, and she asks in a strangled voice, "Who's that with him?"

Stesha is carrying someone in his arms. It looks like a woman with red hair wrapped in Stesha's cloak, and though I can't see much of her face, I don't think I recognize her. The dragonmaster ignores the crowd, passes us by, and disappears down the corridor.

Zenevieve's face is stricken. "He's brought someone back with him? Who is she? You don't think—" Zenevieve sounds choked up and can't go on, but I guess what she was about to say. *You don't think that she's his mate, do you?*

There are drops of blood on the ground. Stesha's bleeding or the woman is hurt, which means he's gone to the Flame Temple.

"She's probably just someone he found injured on his way back to Lenhale." I don't sound very convincing. There was something fiercely protective in the way Stesha was holding that woman in his arms.

"I must see for myself," Zenevieve says, but she's shaking so violently that I worry she's going to collapse.

"No, I'll do it. You need to go back to bed." I spot Fiala and Dusan nearby and wave them over. "Please, will you take Zenevieve back to her room? Stoke the fire and make sure she gets warm." I give Fiala a meaningful look that says, *And keep her there before she makes herself any sicker.*

Fiala nods sharply. "Yes, Lady Isavelle. Come with us, Zenevieve."

Before my bodyguards can usher her away, Zenevieve grips my arm and whimpers, "Can you smell that sweet scent?"

A gust of wind blows along the corridor. I breathe in and catch the scent that Zenevieve is talking about. Sweetness like blackberries on the vine, but there's more to it than that. Melting brown sugar. The pleasing crunch of golden leaves beneath your feet.

I frown. "What *is* that? I've never smelled anything like it before. It's so..." Strong isn't the right word. The scent is vivid and complex and lingers in the air.

Fresh tears slide down Zenevieve's cheeks. "It's that woman. She's an Omega. Stesha has found his Omega."

19

Zabriel

Gossip flies around the castle faster than a wingrunner at full tilt. The whole place is buzzing with the news by the time it reaches me in the War Room. Stesha has returned from the east without any wild dragons but with an injured Omega woman.

An Omega. I take a deep breath and catch the scent of ripe blackberries and melting sugar. Definitely an Omega's scent, though of course, this stranger provokes in me none of the possessiveness and instincts to claim that Isavelle's scent does.

If Stesha has brought an injured Omega to the castle, he'll head straight to the Flame Temple, so that's where I go. Out in the corridor, the scent of blackberries is even stronger, and I smell blood as well.

I jog along the corridor and enter the temple. The infirmary is on one of the upper levels, and I take the black stone stairs two at a time. The Temple Mothers are clustered around a red-haired woman who is lying atop a wooden cot. Stesha's white cloak half covers her lifeless body, and Stesha himself stands over her as the mothers examine the Omega's limbs, head, and torso for injuries.

Meanwhile, blood is running down Stesha's face and arms and dripping onto the stone floor, something he doesn't seem to be aware of as his gaze is locked on the red-haired woman.

A Temple Mother approaches Stesha with a cloth to daub the blood on his face, but he fends the woman off. "I'm fine. Tend to Ravenna."

Ravenna. The country's second living Omega is called Ravenna, and Stesha is standing aggressively over her. So, he was right. He held out for his Omega all these years and now he's found her. His Omega was waiting for him at the end of a painful, centuries-long road.

"Stesha," I call out as I approach.

The dragonmaster looks around and sees me. There are cuts on his face and his usually pristine riding leathers have been torn open at the throat. He reeks of fury and violence.

"What happened to you? Did you fight the golden dragon with your bare hands?"

Stesha swipes blood from his chin and his expression darkens. "No. Another Alpha. Auryn's rider."

Who the hell is Auryn?

"It's not a wild flare," Stesha growls. "The golden dragon has already been tamed by a rider, and the woman was with them. He claims she's his," Stesha seethes. "But Zabriel, the way he was treating her. I never thought I'd see anything like it again. He's an *animal*."

"Is he dead?"

"No. I tried to kill him, but Nilak's and Ravenna's lives were in danger. Auryn was on a rampage."

Blood and wyvern piss. If two Alphas are fighting over this Omega, there will be scales shredded and blood spilled when the rider comes to take this woman back. "Where did you find her?"

"In the east. I was watching the flare from a distance, wondering how I might approach them. Then I spotted this other Alpha." Stesha's expression darkens, and he says through his teeth, "He was keeping this Omega prisoner. Hurting her. Abusing her."

Stesha suddenly whirls around and punches the solid stone wall. His fist cracks against it, and it must have hurt, but Stesha's too incensed to feel anything. "What the fuck is wrong with these Alphas? Don't they understand that they are doing the very thing they must not ever do? What warped his heart into something so *repulsive*?"

Stesha is shouting at the top of his lungs, and his words echo off the volcanic stone. Everyone turns to look as Stesha paces up and down, scattering drops of blood.

"You found her. We'll protect her. All of us," I assure him.

Stesha doesn't hear me. "That Alpha. I am going to kill that Alpha. If Ravenna wasn't so sickened from her false heat and from his abuse, I would have ripped his dragines from his mouth, severed his knot, and shoved it down his throat."

I realize what Stesha is saying. Like Emmeric did to Mirelle, this Alpha has been knotting an Omega who wasn't ready for it. "I understand how you're feeling. All the blood I shed after I saw how Isavelle was mistreated was never enough." His shouting isn't going to do his Omega any good. I put a hand on Stesha's shoulder and pull him back a few paces. "Over here."

"I don't want to go anywhere," he snarls, shrugging me off.

"You're shouting, and the woman needs her rest. Will you sit down for the Temple Mother? She's trying to help you."

Mother Linnea has approached us with a bowl of warm water, a tray of bandages, and a determined expression on her face.

"I don't need help."

"Stesha." I point at a nearby chair. "Sit."

His expression is thunderous, but Stesha sits in the chair and allows the Temple Mother to dab at his wounds. We watch as the women in red robes set up screens around Ravenna's bed, allowing her privacy as they treat her.

I put what I hope is a comforting hand on Stesha's shoulder. "It doesn't surprise me that you went hunting for dragons and found your mate among them. And an Omega. I thought you were crazy holding out for so long, but you were right."

Stesha frowns at me. "What?"

"Ravenna, she's your Omega. Isn't she?"

Revulsion is etched on his features. "Don't be fucking stupid."

"What?"

"Have you been clonked on the head in my absence?" he growls. "How could you possibly think such a ridiculous thing?"

"Well, you..." I gesture toward where Ravenna lies behind the screens. I was going to say, *But you fought for her. You're so angry she's hurt.* Of course he's angry. He's guilt-ridden over the abuse that Zenevieve might have suffered at Emmeric's hands, and before her, Mirelle. "Nothing. Never mind. Tell me about this flare."

Stesha glares at the Font of First Flames for some time, taking deep, furious breaths. "How is Zen?"

Zen? That's what he used to call her. "She hasn't recovered any memories."

"But how is she?" he demands, looking up at me while the Temple Mother dabs powder onto his split eyebrow to seal the wound.

"She's fine," I lie, knowing full well she's been lying in bed for days on end, too sick to leave it. I'll tell him after he's stopped bleeding in a dozen places. "She and my mate are becoming good friends. Again. She has her own bedchamber near Isavelle's nesting room, and she comes and goes as she pleases."

Stesha's shoulders unclench, and he pushes a bloody hand through his hair, leaving red streaks among the white strands. "All right. Good."

"How did this stranger tame the Alpha dragon of a wild flare?" I ask.

"Gods know how, but a newly emerged Alpha with no idea what his designation means and no knowledge of dragons shouldn't have been able to do it." He shakes his head. "I failed, Zabriel. I wasn't able to tame any dragons from the wild flare. When they attack, the fight will be deadly."

"You don't know they'll attack us."

Stesha is silent for a long time, his glittering eyes studying the screens around Ravenna's bed. Suddenly he shoots to his feet. "Yes, they will. He'll come after me. I must leave Lenhale now for everyone's safety."

"Don't be ridiculous. You didn't take any dragons from that flare, so that Alpha and Auryn have no reason to come after you. Sit down and be treated." I try to compel Stesha back into his seat, but he flings me off.

"Zabriel, don't you see? That rider will be out for my blood, and he won't stop until I'm dead. This Omega woman I rescued? She belongs to the Alpha I fought. They're fated. All of you are targets while I remain here."

20

Isavelle

I arrived at the Flame Temple in time to hear Stesha declare to Zabriel that the Omega he brought to the castle isn't his fated mate. Before I can feel any relief for Zenevieve, Stesha declares that he must leave.

"Dragonmaster, you can't go anywhere," I burst out. He can't leave again. Zabriel needs him here, and so does Zenevieve.

Stesha's brow tightens in annoyance. His face is cut and swollen from fighting, and there's blood on his clothes. "Who are you to give me orders, Lady Isavelle?"

I ran here, so I pause for a moment to catch my breath. "It's not an order. It's common sense. That Alpha will seek his Omega. If you leave and she stays, all that you'll accomplish is that there will be one less dragonrider to fight him off."

Zabriel turns to Stesha. "Isavelle is right. This Omega

must stay and be treated by the *Hratha'len*, and you must stay as well."

The air around Stesha crackles. He looks up at the sky through the open ceiling like he is wishing he were far away from here.

"Dragonmaster, why are you acting this way?" I ask. "The dragons need you. Zabriel needs you. Zenevieve needs you. Go and tell Zenevieve that this woman is not your Omega before she makes herself even sicker." If he's not in love with her then he's not in love with her, but to avoid her like this when they used to be so close is too cruel.

Stesha's eyes widen. "Zenevieve is sick?" He looks at Zabriel. "You didn't tell me she was sick."

I start to say, "Emmeric poisoned her, and my crone gave her some herbs to brew into a tea that is helping to—"

Still looking at Zabriel, he exclaims, "A witch's potion? You let your mate give Zenevieve a witch's potion? A Maledinni drank a nasty, hedge-brewed concoction filled with slugs, eyeballs, and gods know what else?"

Zabriel's eyes narrow. "Stesha, watch your tone and your words or I'll make you start bleeding again. Human magic has always been valuable to the Maledinni."

"Not to me, it hasn't," Stesha retorts. "We have the *Hratha'len* to tend to us. Humans may prescribe each other any swill that they want, but how dare your mate force it on Zenevieve."

My stomach drops. This is the first time anyone's spoken so angrily against witchcraft to my face. Is this how everyone feels but they're too polite to say it to me?

I step into Stesha's line of sight. "Dragonmaster, would

you please stop addressing Zabriel when I'm the one talking to you? I can speak for myself."

Stesha looks down his long nose at me from his great height. "It is Maledinni custom to address an Omega's Alpha."

"It's not my custom. Zabriel doesn't mind if you talk to me, as long as you don't touch my hair."

Stesha's face turns red, and he roars, "I'm not going to touch—"

A cool voice cuts across our argument. The Temple Crone has approached us. "*Ma'len*, dragonmaster, please. We are attending to a sick Omega who needs peace and serenity. Your loud voices and angry scents are frightening her."

"We apologize, Grandmother," Zabriel tells her with a respectful nod. "We'll take this outside."

As we leave the Flame Temple, Stesha attempts to stride away from us.

Zabriel catches his arm and holds on tight. "No. Listen to my mate."

Stesha's jaw clenches, and he fixes his eyes on a spot over my head. "Continue, if you must."

I want to prompt, *Continue, if you must, Lady Isavelle*, but for Zenevieve's sake, I don't. "No one forced Zenevieve to take any 'witch's potion.' Mistress Hawthorne sensed poison in Zenevieve's body and gave her some herbs. We consulted the *Hratha'len* about them, and then Zenevieve made the tea and drank it. It's helping to cleanse the poison from her body. It could be the poison that is blocking her memories from returning."

Stesha is silent but his throat is working. Finally, he asks, "Is it working?"

"Zenevieve has been sweaty and shaky since she drank the tea, but she has been talking to me about Minta," I say softly. "She spoke fondly of the day you gave Zenevieve her dragon."

Stesha presses the heels of his hands into his eyes. Speaking more to himself than to us, he mutters, "You've never seen a rider and a dragon more perfect for one another. Minta was a hatchling, and Zen was just fourteen, but I knew. Minta and Shar—" But he breaks off with a groan.

"Minta and Shar were brother and sister," Zabriel tells me quietly. "The two dragons were always together at the dragongrounds."

Emmeric's dragon, Shar. The dragon that may still be alive, trapped beneath Emmeric's tower.

"Poison," Stesha says shakily. "On top of whatever else he did to her, Zen was being poisoned. Now you and your crone have made things even worse." His angry gaze is directed at me. "Leave Zenevieve alone from now on."

His words sting, and I answer back with my own anger. "Like you leave her alone? As in completely ignore her?"

"You presume a great deal," he snarls.

Zabriel steps in front of Stesha so they are nose to nose. "Watch your temper and your accusations around my mate. You will discover all the assurance you need about Zenevieve's health if you speak with her yourself."

Stesha's nostrils flare, and he says in an icy voice, "Excuse me, *Ma'len*. I must prepare the dragonriders for an attack from a wild flare."

We watch him stride away. Zabriel gathers me into his arms and presses a kiss to the top of my head. "You and

Zenevieve have done nothing wrong. Stesha is being overprotective and unreasonable."

I'm tired of talking about Stesha, so I say to Zabriel, "Another Omega in Maledin at last. Her scent is the blackberries that I can smell?"

"That's right. Her name is Ravenna."

I reach up and touch his cheek. "You'll protect her even though it puts the castle and the flare at risk?"

"I can't say I'm delighted that we may be attacked by a furious Alpha with a feral dragon, but as king and an Alpha, it's my duty to protect those who are suffering. No one is going to mistreat an Omega and get away with it while I'm on the throne."

I wrap my arms around his waist and press my face against his chest. "Thank you," I whisper. "For protecting Ravenna, and for allowing me to be the one to speak to Stesha, though I don't know how much he listened."

"Don't worry, he doesn't listen to me either."

"What did Ravenna say? Have you spoken with her?"

"Not yet. She's exhausted from a false heat, and whatever else this Alpha has been torturing her with. Stesha said..." Zabriel rubs a hand over his pinched brow. "It sounds like this Alpha has been knotting her before her designation has emerged."

My stomach clenches at the thought. What a terrible experience this woman has had. I have a kind Alpha who was patient with me as my designation emerged and the *Hratha'len* to explain what my body was doing. Ravenna's had no one.

"Will you speak with this Omega when she awakens?" Zabriel asks me.

"Me? Surely you or the temple women will be the best ones to talk with her."

He gently brushes his knuckles over my cheek. "When you first came to the castle, what I longed for the most was to give you an Omega to speak with."

"I believe what you longed for the most was a kiss."

He bends down and does just that. My lips part, and he caresses my tongue with his. "You are right. First I wanted to give you a kiss, and then another and another. Then I wished that you had another Omega to speak with." He glances into the temple. "Ravenna is going to be frightened and confused. She'll take comfort from talking with another Omega and understanding that she's safe here."

"Then I will talk with Ravenna as soon as she's awake."

RAVENNA SLEEPS all day and night and through the following morning as well. The *Hratha'len* move her to a canopied bed in a warm, darkened room, and fill it with blankets and cushions to soothe her distress.

In the afternoon, I take her a steaming cup of mereed tea and call softly through her bed curtains. "Ravenna, I've brought you something to drink."

There's a slight rustling sound from within but no reply.

"My name's Isavelle. I'm an Omega as well." I hold my breath in hope that she will open the bed curtains. The silence goes on and on. Finally, I add, "I'm so happy to meet another Omega. As far as I know, you and I are the only ones."

An exhausted voice answers, "If you're happy to be an Omega, why do I feel so terrible?"

"Good question. Do you mind if I open the curtains and speak with you a little while?"

There's a short silence and then a sigh. "If you like."

The room is only lit by the fire in the grate, but Ravenna still winces as I pull back the curtains. She has a pretty face with wide-spaced hazel eyes and masses of curly red hair, and she's pressed herself into the far corner of the bed under a mountain of blankets. I'm relieved to see that there are no bruises or cuts on her face, though there are scrape marks around her neck like an Alpha has been dragging his teeth over her flesh.

I place the steaming cup on the bedside table. "This is some special tea I drink around my false heats."

She glances mistrustingly at the cup. "You say the same strange things that he does."

"What strange things?"

"Omega. Heats. I thought he was making it up."

"The man who called himself your Alpha? No, he wasn't making them up."

Ravenna's face falls. "Oh."

"You're safe here. I promise no one is going to hurt you. You must have so many questions about what's been happening to you."

"Is that poison?" she asks, peering at the cup. Before I can answer she picks it up and gives it a sniff. "Mereed. That's unusual. I've never had tea made from the mereed plant." She takes a tentative sip.

"You know your herbs," I observe, and for some reason that makes her flinch.

"Is what's happening to me got something to do with the dragons? Suddenly there are dragons everywhere."

"You mean, the reason your body is changing? Yes, it's because of the dragons. Do you know the story, 'The Mountain Prisoner'?"

"The one the Brethren hated us telling each other? Yes, I know it."

"It wasn't really a story. There really was a dragonriding king asleep under the Bodan Mountains for five hundred years, and he woke up and took Maledin back from the Brethren and the Shadow King. The dragons awoke a dormant part of you. Your Omega part."

Ravenna frowns into her tea as if I've just made everything ten times more complicated than it already was. I probably did. "Is everyone happy about the invasion except for me?"

The invasion. That's not a good sign, calling it the invasion. I ask carefully, "Do you miss the Brethren?"

Ravenna laughs without mirth. Once she starts, she can't seem to stop until there are tears running down her face and her laughter turns into a sob. "You must be joking, but I ask myself why I must be thrust from one hell into another."

"I'm so sorry for what has happened to you. That Alpha who had you, the others aren't like that. They hate Alphas like that."

Ravenna's whole body tenses in fear, and she glances toward the door. "There are more of them?"

"Good ones, I promise."

"How many?"

"Some. Not many. The man who brought you to the

capital is an Alpha. My mate is an Alpha as well. He found me just after the dragons returned to Maledin."

A look of fear passes over Ravenna's beautiful face. "Did he hurt you? Did he pull you up onto his dragon and fly away with you against your will?"

Oh, boy. How do I explain to this terrified young woman that I endured the good kind of kidnapping? "I promise that you have no need to fear the Alphas in Lenhale. They will not hurt you. No one in this castle, or this city, will so much as lay a finger on you. Zabriel, who is my mate, and Stesha, the white-haired man, are good men who will protect you. I know this because they have both protected me on many occasions." It sticks in my throat to say kind words about Stesha, but I'll put my personal quarrel with him aside for Ravenna's sake. He's an ass, but he did take a beating and save Ravenna's life.

She's silent for a moment, and then she asks, "How did they protect you?"

"They both risked their lives to save me when I was a starving, beaten, Veiled Virgin. Mostly it was Zabriel. He's the king, and my mate."

"So they won't come in here and start doing and saying crazy things?" she asks nervously.

"They won't. They understand the terrible things that were happening to you, and they won't let them happen ever again."

"But you're the queen," Ravenna says quietly, gazing at the cup in her hands. "Of course they will fight for you. I'm no one. I'm less than no one."

"They will fight for you," I say firmly. "You're safe, and you're not no one."

Ravenna sips her tea. I feel like she wants to believe me, but her trust has been battered. "I knew the Alpha who took me before the invasion. He was cruel and sadistic then, and he's cruel and sadistic now."

"How did you know him?"

She hesitates and then says carefully, "He pursued me."

"He was hoping to marry you?"

Ravenna shakes her head. "He wished to kill me. Now, things have become very strange between us. When I run from him, he commands me to stop, and I find it impossible to resist. My body reacts to his in strange ways. His scent is…" She struggles for a way to describe it. "*Bewitching*, but it isn't witchcraft. I seem to be the only woman who is affected by him." Her eyes harden. "Go on, judge me if you want to for talking about a terrible man in such a way. I promise you that I am in no way infatuated with him. He is the very last man I would choose for myself."

"You are describing the way an Omega reacts to her Alpha. I have experienced it myself. You can't control it."

Her eyes widen. "Really?"

"Truly."

The empty cup slips from her fingers. She wraps her arms around her knees and drops her forehead on them. "I thought I was losing my mind," she gasps, lifting her head. "I'm not mad?"

"Not in the slightest. You have no doubt been enduring periods of restlessness and aching followed by bouts of feverishness in which you wanted to hide away in the dark. This is what's happening to you right now, and it's why you feel so out of control and vulnerable."

"Yes, that is exactly how I feel. You have been through the

same as me? Does your neck ache too?" She winces and passes her hand over the back of her neck.

Now I understand why Zabriel wanted me to be the first one to speak with Ravenna. There's a vast difference between someone telling you that what you're feeling is normal, and someone saying, *This happened to me as well.*

"It does. It took me many weeks to accept what I was, and I kicked up such a fuss about it every step of the way."

"And your Alpha? How have you learned to trust a man you didn't choose yourself?"

"It wasn't easy, but he was patient with me. He waited for me to be ready for him." I lower my eyes. "I'm sorry. That must hurt you to hear after what you've been through."

She shakes her head. "I'm happy for you. I honestly am. I told him to his face he was a monster, and I was right. He blamed me, saying I wasn't behaving as I should. Whatever bond there is between us, I presume there is a way to sever it?"

"I...don't know. Perhaps."

Her face falls. "There's no way to sever this bond, is there?"

I bite my lip. "I really don't know, but I don't think so. From what I've heard, this is a unique bond that only happens once in a lifetime, and to very few people. Fated matches are very rare, and they're forever."

Ravenna passes a shaking hand over her face. "Then the gods are crueler than I ever believed, for they have chosen for me a man who I must hate, and who wishes me nothing but suffering."

"Why does he want you to suffer?"

"Because he is a witchfinder, and I am a witch."

My mouth falls open in shock.

Ravenna sighs and her shoulders slump. "Call the guards and have me burned at the stake if you wish. I'm too tired to fight any more. You can have my confession, and I'll sign it, but torturing me is pointless. I can't give you any names. All the witches I knew were burned a long time ago."

I sit up excitedly in my chair. "You don't understand. I'm a witch too."

A smile spreads across Ravenna's face. "Are you truly? Well met, sister. How is it the king hasn't had you killed? Is it because he's in love with you?"

"Zabriel doesn't persecute witches. They are free and protected in Maledin."

"And the witchfinders? Have they all been arrested?" she asks eagerly.

My smile fades. "Well, no. I spoke with a former witchfinder not long ago, and he explained to me how they were controlled by the Brethren, and they are all delighted they no longer have to torture and murder women. The witchfinders have been pardoned and will be allowed to remain free as long as they abide by the laws of this land."

"All of them? All of them are delighted that they no longer have to torture and murder women?" Ravenna laughs and shakes her head helplessly.

Cold trepidation skitters down my spine. "The man who stole you. The man with the yellow dragon. Can I ask his name?"

"Of course you can. It's Kane."

21

Zabriel

I gather up Isavelle's golden hair in my fist, lower my nose, and breathe in deeply. With a groan, I pull her into my arms and kiss her hungrily. "Is it wrong to revel in how wonderful you feel in my arms when everywhere there is so much unhappiness?"

Isavelle goes up on tiptoe with her hands pressed against my chest. "There is, isn't there? But I must kiss you in private or else I'll die."

I slant my mouth over hers once more. It's been four days since Stesha returned to Lenhale with Ravenna, and Zenevieve is still unwell after drinking the herbal tea that Biddy Hawthorne prepared for her. The Temple Mothers assure me that Zenevieve isn't in any danger, but I hope that she begins to recover soon.

I back my mate up against a wall, kissing her all the while, and lifting her up in my arms. I tell her of the sweet ache in my heart and soul in the Maledinni way, and then the human way. "My knot aches for you, Omega. My blood sings for you. I love you." The more ways that I can tell her I'm hers, the happier I am.

Isavelle's eyes grow hazy, and she sucks her lower lip into her mouth. "I'll be thinking about you all afternoon. Please, will you use your lips and tongue on me when we are in bed tonight?"

Hearing my formerly shy mate request that I lick her pussy until she comes has me grinning so wide that I reveal my dragines. "Anything you want, *sha'len*. As much as you need."

I kiss her again, our mouths open, our tongues dancing together. The air reeks of lust by the time we reluctantly part and go about our duties.

I find Stesha out at the training grounds, working through his anger and frustration on a couple of unlucky Betas. Three of them are attacking him at once, and he's raining down heavy blows on them with a practice sword.

"Would you like to spar, dragonmaster?" I call.

Stesha lowers his sword and thinks about it. The Betas' expressions are hopeful. "Fine. I'll happily knock you into the dust."

The Betas scurry away before Stesha can change his mind.

"Who knocked who into the dust the last time we crossed swords?" I remind him. The two of us fought when Stesha smelled my mate's hair, and I won.

"That didn't count. I was distracted by the scent of a girl I thought had been dead for five hundred years."

"We wouldn't have had to fight if you'd just told me that."

Stesha glares at me. "Are we going to fight or are you going to fuss about with words like a dragon with her eggs?"

I throw my cloak aside and grab a practice sword. Stesha is gazing at me with his head on one side while his fingers flex on his sword's grip.

"Why are you looking at me like that?" I ask.

"I'm finding my motivation. I'm trying to decide whether to imagine that you're Emmeric or that witchfinder prick."

My eyes widen. "Please don't imagine it too vividly. I like my head attached to my body."

"Scared, boy?"

He really is an ass sometimes.

I lunge for Stesha, and the fight begins. Our swords clash, and we fight fiercely. I leave him an opening by mistake when he feints to the left. Stesha rams his elbow so hard into my solar plexus that I see stars, and then he sweeps my feet out from under me. I land flat on my back in a cloud of dust.

The dragonmaster never gloats, but he smirks for a mite too long before reaching down and helping me to my feet. "Order has been restored."

"We're going again," I grumble, rubbing my chest.

"I'll knock you into the dirt as many times as you wish, *Ma'len*. Just like old times."

We go for another bout, and this time, it's Stesha who ends up in the dirt. I hold out my hand, but he ignores it and gets to his feet by himself.

"Is the flare prepared to fight Kane and Auryn?" I ask.

Stesha twirls his sword in his hand. "I've been thinking about that, and maybe we won't have to. Kane is weak. I proved that when I stole his mate from him. A dragon like

Auryn won't want a weak rider and has probably killed him by now."

"Let's hope so. It would be one less problem to worry about."

A dozen castle maids have gathered at the edges of the courtyard, giggling behind their hands and staring at us.

Well, not *us*.

"What are they looking at?" Stesha mutters, glancing around at our unusual audience. Usually, only soldiers observe us sparring.

I push my hair out of my eyes and laugh. "Like you don't know."

"I wouldn't ask if I knew."

"They're looking at you, idiot."

"What? Why?"

I've never seen a man so annoyed by being admired. "The unmated dragonmaster cut quite the dashing figure as he rescued a damsel Omega. Everyone's talking about it."

Stesha shoots a lethal glare at the maids, and they scatter in all directions while giggling madly. He turns back to me and raises his sword. "Again."

"Why are you still unmated, Stesha? Take a Beta as your mate. Take an Alpha. Your Alpha dragon adores you, so why wouldn't one of our strongest women?"

Stesha glances toward the castle like he's thinking about someone inside. A red-haired someone, perhaps.

"Ravenna won't be happy with another Alpha, no matter how poorly her mate treated her," I tell him. "Even if you kill him. You know how this works."

The dragonmaster points his sword at me. "You have

spoken nothing but dragon shit since we began sparring. Shut up and fight me."

I lift my blade, and the sound of clashing metal fills the courtyards.

When we step back from each other sometime later, we're both sweating and filthy from being knocked into the dirt. The outcome is a draw, and we're both annoyed by this.

Stesha examines the nicks on his practice sword. "I heard..." He trails off into silence.

I wait for Stesha to continue. "You heard?"

"I heard you spoke with Captain Ashton about the day the king and queen were murdered. If you're interested, I have something to add to that conversation."

"You know more about that day?"

Stesha shakes his head. "Not about that day. I saw other things. If you're wondering how it is that Emmeric has a heart full of hate and spite, I know how." He goes over to a stone bench and sits down.

My stomach lurches, but I sit beside him, stretching out my legs. "So, tell me."

Stesha glares across the sparring grounds, lost in thought. "I was very fond of your mother. Queen Magritte went out of her way to be kind to me after my parents were killed, and I was apprenticed to the former dragonmaster. She treated me almost like a son. For years—" Stesha abruptly breaks off.

I wait as patiently as I can for him to continue.

"Do you remember when Queen Magritte fell from her dragon and broke her wrist?"

"Yes, I remember."

There are angry sparks in Stesha's eyes. "She didn't fall. She displeased her Alpha, and he pushed her down some steps. I saw it happen. The king knew I saw it. He liked that I saw it and couldn't do anything. If I had, he would have had me beheaded." His fists clench tightly. "For years, *years*, I watched your father hurt her."

I lean forward, my forearms braced against my knees. I saw my mother's injuries. The black eyes. The bloody lips. She told me again and again that it wasn't Father. That she fell down. That she walked into something. Always, she denied that he hurt her.

"He was hurting Emmeric as well. Did you know about that?"

I glance up at the dragonmaster. "What?"

"The king also did that in front of me, and Emmeric hated that I knew. Emmeric was belittled, criticized, humiliated, punished even more than the queen. It was the king's favorite pastime, from what I could tell," he says bitterly.

I was always so uninterested in finding out why Emmeric and my father hated each other so much. Family fights were something to escape from. Guilt slices through me as I remember how I would leave and go ride my dragon whenever trouble started brewing. "I never saw it, and Emmeric never said anything to me. Why did Father hide this from me and not from you?"

"Deep down, I think kings fear their eldest sons. You were a walking reminder that someday he would die. Anger you, and that day might have come sooner than he wished."

Only when the time came, the blade wasn't in my hand. It was in Emmeric's. So that's why he killed our parents. My father I can understand wanting to kill, but our mother? That was cruel and spiteful.

But Stesha isn't finished with his revelations. "The way your father was with the queen, Emmeric was with Mirelle."

Pain flashes through my heart. "No, not Mirelle. She would have told me if he was hurting her. She would have told Onderz."

"Since when did Omegas ever speak up about being poorly treated?"

I push my hands through my hair and groan. I told Isavelle that Omegas weren't listened to or respected in Old Maledin, but it seems I didn't know half of how bad it was inside my own family.

"I should have done more," Stesha muttered. "I fantasized so many times about killing the king that when I heard Emmeric had slit his throat, I was glad. But I couldn't be happy about what happened to your mother. She deserved kindness and protection, and she never had either. I'm sorry for burdening you with all this. I just thought you should know."

"You did the right thing. I need to understand Emmeric to be able to stop him. Thank you, Stesha."

As we're leaving the sparring grounds, I spot a tall, thin figure in red robes watching us from an archway. The Temple Crone.

"Grandmother," I say with a respectful nod, and Stesha echoes my greeting.

"*Ma'len*. Dragonmaster. Excellent sparring today. May I speak with you, Zabriel?"

Stesha heads for the dragongrounds, and I walk by the Temple Crone's side. "How is the new Omega?"

"She's resting and healing. I actually wish to speak with

you about your Omega. Shall we go in search of her? I understand she's in the castle today."

I nod, wondering what the Temple Crone can have to say about Isavelle. We find my mate at the dragongrounds practicing flying drills with Esmeral.

"Her flying has greatly improved," the crone observes as they pass overhead.

"Yes, it has," I agree, feeling proud as I watch the Omega pair flutter gracefully to the ground.

Esmeral dashes back to her mate, and Isavelle approaches us with a breathless smile, her cheeks flushed with exertion. She goes up on her toes to give me a kiss, which I lean down and receive, and then she turns to the crone.

"Hello, Grandmother. I don't see you down at the dragongrounds very often."

"I should come more often to visit the dragons. They are such a restoring sight." She gazes appreciatively at the enormous creatures for a moment, then she turns to us. "Will you please both come with me? There's a proposal I wish for you both to hear."

As we follow the Temple Crone, Isavelle shoots me a puzzled look, but I shake my head, telling her I don't know what this is about either.

Once we're seated opposite her on some garden benches in a walled courtyard, the Temple Crone says, "*Ma'len's* mate, you are approaching your first heat. What a happy time this is for you and your mate and all of us in Maledin. Omegas are such a joy."

I must look pained because the crone asks me, "*Ma'len*, is something wrong?"

"I was thinking of the past, and how we must do better for our Omegas."

I was expecting her to ignore my words or to brush them off, but she says, "Yes, we must. I am happy we agree, *Ma'len*. This is something I've been thinking about a great deal. By King Aylard's time, perceptions of Omegas had become negative. They were looked down upon. Now we have a chance to start fresh. To celebrate Omegas as they were meant to be celebrated."

"That will be challenging seeing as most people have very little idea of what an Omega is," Isavelle says.

"Just so, Lady Isavelle." The crone's eyes brighten even more. It seems she's pleased how much we're all in agreement. "We must find a way to educate the people about their designations." She hesitates for a moment and then says to me, "*Ma'len*, I would like to propose we bring back the Ritual of the First Heat."

My mood, which had already bottomed out after my talk with Stesha, plummets even further. I've heard about this ritual, but I never witnessed it in my time. It amounts to a royal Omega being locked away by the *Hratha'len* to endure their first heat alone. The idea is to demonstrate to all in Maledin that he or she is a strong, worthy Omega who can rise above the storm of emotion, passion, and instincts of a heat. To project an aura of serenity and poise to the people.

In reality, they spent five miserable, pointless days weeping behind closed doors. The Maledin that I grew up in had its fault, but at least we recognized that tormenting an Omega and their Alpha like this served no purpose whatsoever.

The words are out of my mouth before I can think twice.

"Out of the question. That ritual is outdated and barbaric, and it's not the way I intend to welcome my bride into this marriage or onto the throne. Isavelle will not suffer like that."

The Temple Crone hesitates. "If I may think out loud for a moment, *Ma'len*?"

"If you must," I growl.

"You are right that it is outdated, and in our time it would have served no purpose. I have no wish to return to the rigid, ceremonial ways of our ancestors. I thought only of the ritual as an event that would bring the people together and get them talking. A way for us to spread the word about what you and the future queen are. The ritual will demystify the ways of Alphas and Omegas. There are designations emerging all over Maledin, and all of them will feel as lost inside their own bodies as Lady Isavelle felt in those first weeks."

"They can come ask you if they want to know about their designation. That is what the Flame Temple is for."

The Temple Crone inclines her head serenely. "Of course, *Ma'len*. My apologies for suggesting it."

Isavelle glances between us with a frown. "What's the Ritual of the First Heat?"

The Temple Crone glances at me for permission to speak, and I grudgingly nod my head.

"Up until about a century before King Aylard was on the throne, it was the custom that a royal Omega, or an Omega fated to a royal, would spend their first heat away from their mate. It was lonely and distressing for them, and something which I would not ask anyone to endure lightly. When the Omega emerged after their heat and the pair were reunited, a feast day was declared throughout Maledin, and the people would celebrate. The ritual declared to all in the land that the royal line was a strong one."

"Why did the practice end?" Isavelle asks.

"Times changed. The Maledinni put aside many unpleasant and demanding rituals and our society progressed. They placed a great deal of stress on the bodies of the Omegas and their Alphas."

Isavelle's scent is suddenly filled with distress. "But you want to bring the ritual back? You want me to spend my first heat apart from Zabriel?"

"You will not," I growl, seizing her hand and glaring at the Temple Crone. What the hell has come over this woman? "Isavelle doesn't need to prove anything to anyone."

The Temple Crone glances at me, probably checking how close I am to losing my temper, and she decides to speak quickly. "I would only wish to see it return if the two of you see merit in it. The ritual is a significant event. Talk of Alphas and Omegas would be on everyone's lips. They would understand that while our instincts to mate are strong, our hearts, minds, and bodies are even stronger. *Ma'len's* mate, there are many people in Maledin who do not understand themselves. Newly emerging Alphas and Omegas are living in silent and potentially dangerous confusion."

Isavelle's eyes are filled with anguish. "I understand what you're saying. Ravenna's designation emerged, and she had no idea what was happening to her, and she suffered because of it. There could be more like her right at this moment. Dozens more."

"Precisely. The Alpha, Kane, didn't understand his instincts and duties either. If he overheard a garbled version of what Alphas and Omegas are, or if he learned about mating from watching the wild flare, it's possible that he did not understand just how cruel he was being to his Omega."

Isavelle's voice rises in anger. "You think Kane was confused? He *wanted* to hurt her. He hates her. His heart is black and he's beyond help."

"Indeed, *Ma'len's* mate." The Crone inclines her head in that infuriatingly serene manner that means she's heard you, but she's not agreeing with you.

"If Zabriel and I take part in this ritual, you believe that Alphas and Omegas all over Maledin will better understand themselves?" Isavelle asks.

"That is my hope, but the decision is yours and *Ma'len's*," the Crone replies. "You remember how hard your own designation was for you to come to terms with. We've never had to educate a whole country of people about their designations before."

Isavelle squeezes my hand, conflicting emotions flickering over her face. "Would Zabriel at least be able to take me to the ritual chamber himself?"

"No, I wouldn't," I snarl, my gaze fixed on the crone. "The location of the ritual is a secret because too many Alphas were driven mad by the separation and broke down the doors to take back their Omegas." I don't blame them. My heart is pumping hard at just the thought of being separated from Isavelle. "We don't need to do this. I'll send criers to every town and village. Print posters and books about Alphas, Betas, and Omegas. The Temple Mothers can ride out and set up tents where curious people can ask all the questions they want about their designations. Word will spread on its own. We don't need the ritual."

The Temple Crone nods and gets to her feet. "Thank you

for listening to me, *Ma'len*. I hope that I haven't caused you any offence."

When we're alone, I pull Isavelle into my arms and hold her tight, needing to feel her body against mine. Isavelle wraps her arms around my waist and clings to me. Just hearing someone speak of separating us makes fury heat my blood, and my Omega's scent is filled with unhappiness.

"Spending my first heat with you is the one happy thought I have to cling to right now. I don't want to be taken away from you," Isavelle whispers.

"No one's going to take you from me," I growl, bowing my head so her face is pressed against my throat and the possessive scents emanating from my mating gland. "No one. Not my enemies, and especially not my own people."

22

Isavelle

For a woman who endured a terrifying time among a wild flare, Ravenna shows surprisingly little fear as we enter the dragongrounds. Her false heat has ended, and she walks with a straight back, revealing no sign of weakness or injury. I'm proud of my fellow witch, though I don't know her well enough yet to feel like I can comment on it except to tell her that I'm happy to see her looking so well.

Ravenna's large, hazel-colored eyes move over the dragons, who are eyeing us with interest, and remarks, "This group of dragons is so much bigger than the others. What did you call it? A flare? And they're so calm around people."

I introduce her to Esmeral first, who is by far the least threatening dragon in the flare. "She will get her nose all over you because you're an Omega," I warn Ravenna as Esmeral crosses the open ground toward us. "All the dragons will. Maledinni and dragons alike are all fascinated by Omegas."

Esmeral heeds my silent request not to come too close just yet, and she blinks her beautiful eyes at Ravenna. My fellow witch nervously holds out her hand like you would to a cat you're trying to make friends with. Esmeral takes this as an invitation to bound right past Ravenna's fingers and shove her snout into Ravenna's armpit.

I gasp in dismay, but Ravenna bursts out laughing as Esmeral snuffles her way up to her neck.

Omega! I can feel Esmeral thinking excitedly. *Omega. Like us!*

"She tickles. Isn't she sweet. May I stroke her scales?"

Esmeral emits a strong feeling of *yesness*.

"She would love that," I tell her, and now I'm smiling as well. This is going better than I expected.

While Ravenna and Esmeral get to know each other, I see Nilak striding up and down the flare, snapping at overeager dragons who are attempting to approach us. It seems like the huge white dragon is protective of the newest Omega. When I was first among the flare, Scourge was the one who kept me from being overwhelmed by dozens of curious dragons.

A small, sleepy dragon slips past Nilak, yawning luxuriously and showing off rows and rows of shiny white teeth. I recognize him as the lazy dragon that Zenevieve took a liking to. When he closes his jaws and opens his eyes, he seems surprised to find that he's no longer among the flare. Catching a fresh scent on the wind, he makes his languorous way toward Ravenna, blinking beautiful golden eyes.

The dragonmaster has emerged from among the dragons and is watching us with folded arms and a fierce scowl.

Ravenna notices him and withdraws her hand slowly from Esmeral's scales. Trepidation flashes through her eyes at the sight of an Alpha, and I can feel how much she wants to run, but then she takes a steady breath and steps toward him.

"We haven't properly met. I wanted to thank you for bringing me here."

Stesha gives her a sharp nod but doesn't reply.

"Were you badly injured in the fight with Kane?"

"No," he says with an edge to his voice.

I could tell Ravenna that Alphas, or at least Stesha, detests being on the receiving end of an Omega's concern, but I think he's being stupid, so I don't.

The sleepy dragon rubs his snout against my side. "Who is this, dragonmaster? I've encountered him once or twice, but he's always been asleep."

"This is Calyx." There's a long pause as Stesha gazes at the dragon, and then he says slowly as if only just realizing himself, "He's an Omega."

Calyx moves over to Ravenna, and she caresses his scales. He closes his golden eyes and his shiny gold claws dig pleasurably into the earth. The two of them look so beautiful together, her red hair burnished by the sunlight and his white and pale gold scales, that I'm struck by a glorious vision of Ravenna mounted on Calyx and me astride Esmeral as we fly through the skies. I want that so much my chest aches.

"Do you think he might be Ravenna's dragon?" I ask Stesha excitedly.

"Are witches to ride all our dragons?" he snaps, eyes blazing.

He turns away, and I watch him go, fuming silently.

"Ignore him," I tell Ravenna, turning back to fuss over the

two Omega dragons. "I'm grateful that Stesha rescued you, but he can be such an ass."

A few at a time, with much biting and hissing to keep them in line, Nilak allows the bigger dragons to greet Ravenna. Scourge waits until last, and the others clear out of his way as he approaches like a moving mountain.

Ravenna visibly swallows as we're cast in his massive shadow. "He's... He's as large as Auryn."

"This is Zabriel's dragon, the flare's Alpha and Esmeral's mate," I tell her proudly. "His name is Scourge. He doesn't enjoy being stroked, but he seems to like it when I press my palm against his chest, like this." I move forward and touch his warm scales. His eyes close briefly, and then he turns to look at Ravenna. I know him well enough now to understand it's an invitation for her to do the same.

Fear flashes through Ravenna's eyes. "Are you certain that's safe? Auryn hated to be touched. If one of the other dragons even brushed against him, he would roar so loud that the ground trembled. Kane could barely control him."

How pleasing to hear. What threat can Auryn be to us if his rider doesn't know what he's doing? "Scourge has never hurt anyone who didn't deserve it, and he always warns you when he's angry. You will hear dragonfire rumbling in his chest, and he bares his teeth when he's on the verge of attacking. Do you see how calm he is right now? He's still and silent and his jaws are closed."

After a tense moment, Ravenna steps forward and brushes her fingertips over one of his scales.

"He's beautiful," she whispers, gazing at her hand touching his scales. "So strong and regal. The man with black hair and red eyes. The big Alpha who looks like this dragon. That's your mate?"

I can't help the smile that spreads over my face as I think of Zabriel. "Yes."

"And does he treat you well?"

The skepticism in her voice makes my heart ache. "Always. Since the moment I met him. He's always been so patient and loving."

Ravenna catches her lip between her teeth and gazes at her hand pressed against Scourge's scales. Finally, she drops her hand and moves away, her eyes filled with confusion. "That white-haired Alpha was compassionate, and your mate welcomed me with a soft word. You're a witch who rides a dragon, and you're so friendly to me. Everyone here is being kind. I never expected it. I'm overwhelmed. Being a witch has always been so..." She gives me a sad smile. "Terrifying and lonely."

Wind gusts across the dragongrounds and guilt slices through me. "Ravenna, there's something I must confess to you. It's about Kane. I knew him before we were liberated from the Brethren. I've long been ashamed of this, and I wish dearly that I hadn't, but I once saved his life."

Ravenna's eyes widen in astonishment. "A witch saved a witchfinder's life? How could such a strange thing happen? Didn't he try to kill you? Interrogate you?"

"I didn't know I was a witch back then. I was a Veiled Virgin in service to the Brethren, and the High Priest ordered me to tend to his wounds after they whipped him for trying to escape. He was chained up in the monastery dungeons. I knew what he was. I could have so easily killed him, but I pitied him instead. I'm so sorry."

Ravenna is silent for a long time. Then she says quietly, "You have a kind heart."

My body burns with shame. "I wasn't kind. I was stupid."

I won't look at her, so she touches my wrist. "I always mean what I say, or I say nothing at all."

She can't possibly be telling the truth, but when I glance up, her gaze is clear and honest. "I don't deserve you saying that when he hurt you so badly. I'm so sorry."

Ravenna smiles at me. "You never know. Maybe he's alive for a reason. I'm here in Lenhale because of him, and I've met a fellow witch."

I sigh and slump against Esmeral. "We could have met another way. Why couldn't my visions have shown me you?"

"You have visions?" she asks with interest.

"Not very useful ones, and very rarely. I haven't had one in weeks."

"Visions *are* rare. You're lucky to have even one. I would love to hear about them, so let's never speak of Kane again. I prefer to put him out of my mind for good."

We walk among the dragons for a while, and I tell her of the things I've seen and what they have meant, and how my connection to Zabriel broke the spell holding him and his people captive beneath the mountain.

Finally, Ravenna turns to me with a smile. "My heart is light today. It's occurring to me that I have a future to look forward to. I never expected to live for very long, being what I am, but with a queen who is a witch and a man like your Alpha on the throne, I believe it might be safe at last for me to feel hopeful."

Hearing Ravenna say that makes me feel choked up with

emotion. "Would you like to come with me to meet my crone tomorrow?"

She brushes a red curl from her face, her eyes glowing with warmth. "There's nothing I'd like better."

When I tell Zabriel the plan later that evening, he's less enthusiastic about it, and he reminds me that Kane may be searching for Ravenna. "You may go, but I'm sending dragons with you. Wingrunners won't be enough if Auryn is in the skies." His red eyes flash. "If Biddy doesn't like it, then she can tell it to the ravens. I don't give a damn."

First thing the following morning, Ravenna and I meet my usual unit of wingrunners at the dragongrounds instead of at the eyrie. Stesha and Nilak are to escort us, as well as Sundra and her dragon Merrex, and Calliope on Verdun. Three Alpha riders and three Alpha dragons to escort us. Zabriel is taking no chances.

Nilak's frosty blue eyes are trained on the skies like she's dying to take a bite out of Auryn.

Captain Ashton approaches us, gazing at Ravenna with soft brown eyes like he's never seen anyone more beautiful in his life. She does look particularly lovely this morning in an olive-green cloak with her long red hair in a braid over her shoulder. There's color in her cheeks and she's smiling.

"My lady," he murmurs, looking shyly at her from beneath thick lashes. "We are your escort to Amriste." I imagine that courtly tales of dragonriders and wingrunners pressing kisses to a lady's hair and wearing their ribbons into battle are flooding his mind. I don't know if Maledinni have such tales, but if they do, Ashton looks like he's dying to enact every single one of them.

"Lady?" Ravenna asks in confusion. "I'm not a lady. I'm just a village witch."

Ashton glances uncertainly at me and then back to Ravenna. "Um, forgive me. We have always addressed Lady Isavelle this way, and—well—"

"Just Ravenna, please. Or Miss if you prefer."

"Yes, Miss Ravenna. Let me introduce you to the rest of your escort. Would you like to ride with me? This is my wyvern, Sovern. He looks formidable, but I promise you have nothing to fear."

Seeing as we have a dragon escort anyway, I decide to fly on Esmeral. A short while later, I'm mounted on my dragon and Ravenna is sitting behind Ashton with her arms around his strong torso. I've never seen the captain sit up so straight and look so pleased.

Biddy Hawthorne isn't pleased when we all land in Amriste. I can tell so immediately from the raucous caws of her ravens.

"We shan't get a thing done with all this dragon magic spilling over everywhere," she grumbles when we arrive at her cottage gate. She snaps at Ravenna, "Who are you?"

"This is Ravenna, Mistress Hawthorne," I tell her. "She's an Omega, and she's a witch."

"It's an honor to meet you, Grandmother," Ravenna says with a polite bow of her head.

Biddy's temper is somewhat mollified. "Hm. Well met, girl. Tell me what you can do."

"Very little, really," Ravenna says with an apologetic note in her voice, and then describes several marvelous and powerful things. "Summoning and protection spells, wards, and I'm rather good at poisons. And…" Ravenna trails off, her expression suddenly tense. "…I see ghosts. Sometimes."

"Ghosts?" I exclaim. "That must be frightening."

She gives me a quick smile. "You would think so, but they really just want to talk more than anything. Many ghosts I've known since I was a child. Only, lately, they haven't been speaking to me." Ravenna's expression is glum.

"Make yourself useful, girl," Biddy tells her. "Put a protective circle around this cottage and ward off all the dragon magic. It's making my head ache. Isavelle, go with her and see what you can learn."

Ravenna accepts a bag of something from Biddy, and when the old woman shuffles inside, she explains what she knows about protective circles.

"Salt is excellent, but you can use dried herbs, or sand if it's an emergency and you know the witchfinder is coming, or anything else, really. Once I was so desperate that I used flour. The protection comes from your magic, and what you use for the circle can strengthen or alter how it works. Let's see what your crone has given us." She reaches into the bag and fine, smoky-scented powder slips through her fingers. "Fireplace ash. That's different. I wonder if it's good for blocking dragon magic. Would you like to try it?" She holds out the bag to me.

"Oh, no. I couldn't. I don't know what I'm doing."

"I'll help you," she tells me with an encouraging smile. "This will be easy for you, I promise. Here's what you do."

Under Ravenna's instruction, I walk three times around the cottage, sprinkling ash as I go, concentrating on blocking out the dragon magic. When it's complete, I gasp in surprise as the circle glows for a moment, and then all the ash disappears.

"Perfect," Ravenna tells me with a smile. "We're protected from interfering magic, and the circle has vanished so that no one knows you cast it, which can be very important if you don't want people to know it's there." As we head inside, she tells me, "Concealment doesn't matter so much anymore, and I'm glad about it. I look forward to marking out magical circles with candles, bundles of herbs, pretty stones. A proper witchy circle. I love clutter."

When we go inside, Biddy's scowl has cleared. "Much better. Now I can think."

The three of us spend what turns out to be a happy afternoon discussing witchcraft and encounters with incompetent witchfinders over the years. Both Biddy and Ravenna had several near misses, and their stories have me biting my nails and then laughing in relief. Thankfully Kane isn't mentioned, and Ravenna and I are both smiling when we leave.

Later that night, I'm walking along the corridor to the room I share with Zabriel when I round a corner and run into someone. I'm in the middle of apologizing when I realize that it's Zenevieve. I've not seen her out of bed since the day Stesha returned to Lenhale. There are still dark circles beneath her eyes, but I'm delighted to see her up and walking about.

"Zenevieve, are you feeling better?"

"I am, thank you," she says with a breathless smile. She's wearing a nightgown and a blanket wrapped around her shoulders like a shawl. There's nothing unremarkable about her appearance until I notice that there's something bundled up beneath the blanket and she's holding it tight to her chest.

"What's that you've got?" I ask because it doesn't occur to me that if she is hiding something, she'd hide it from me.

Her cheeks turn bright pink. "Nothing," she squeaks and hurries along the corridor to her room.

I watch her go. How strange. I wonder what that was about.

23

———

Zabriel

I haven't spent this many hours on my dragon since we retook Lenhale from the Brethren. Every day, I join the other riders in patrolling the skies, keeping an eye out for wild dragons approaching the capital. Scourge and I approach the east, skirting the edge of the wild flare's territory. Stesha was able to point it out on the large map in the War Room for all the riders. We don't enter that area, but I scout it, hungry to know what Auryn and Kane are up to just out of sight.

That afternoon, Scourge and I are circling into land at the dragongrounds when an ear-splitting roar rends the air. I look up into the sun's glare to see something massive diving at us, talons first.

Shock and alarm rebound back and forth between me and my dragon, and we both think as one, *Dive!* Scourge plummets toward the ground as massive black claws rake the sky above our heads. Then my dragon is shooting upward again, dragonfire bubbling up his throat. He opens his jaws and unleashes an arc of it, and the attacking dragon has no choice but to careen away, back toward the east and away from the flare.

I get a good look at the dragon and am angry but not surprised to see that his wings and scales are vivid yellow, his talons are black, and there's a dark ridge along his spine. He carries a man on his back.

Auryn, and his rider, Kane.

There are no other wild dragons in the sky that I can see. Kane is an arrogant fool to come here, one man and one dragon against a whole flare.

Scourge pursues the pair, and triumph pounds through my blood knowing we have them on the run. Auryn banks to the right, attempting to maneuver so his jaws are facing in our direction. His throat is glowing red. I urge Scourge to pull to the left, as close as we can to the wild dragon, and as we pass by, Scourge's talons shred several scales from the yellow dragon's flank. A warning, and he had better heed it.

The golden dragon roars in anger, and there's something wild and unhinged about that roar. Surely no rider is able to control such a dragon. I look over my shoulder, hoping to see Kane tumble from dragonback. If Auryn can shake his rider loose, I feel certain he'll return to his flare in the east and he won't have to die.

But Kane is still astride his dragon, and Auryn finds fresh strength in his wings to fly almost directly upward into the sun again. His scales meld with the piercing yellow light and scatter it in all directions, and I lose him in the glare. Now I understand why riders in Old Maledin would tell tales of Golden Terror, the biggest dragon you ever saw, suddenly appearing out of nowhere and ripping their dragons apart.

There's shouting below. Riders are running over the bridge to the dragongrounds. Suddenly, Auryn is flying low and swiftly straight at the flare. Scourge and I are going in the wrong direction completely.

Panic ignites my belly. My dragon turns and gives chase, but we're trailing behind. No other rider has had the chance to mount their dragon, and the flare is in disarray. Dragons are shrieking and roaring. A cluster of four or five very young fledglings break away from the flare and run toward the cliffs, fleeing toward the safety of the nesting caves where they lived as hatchlings. Small, vulnerable dragons who have barely had the chance in life to stretch their wings.

Auryn's jaws part in menacing delight. Sparks stream behind him as he prepares to breathe fire.

"No," I shout, urging Scourge to fly faster, but I know it's too late. We're going to watch the little creatures be incinerated. Fully grown dragons are hardened to fire, but so much dragonfire at such a young and vulnerable age will be deadly.

Auryn skims over the dragongrounds, straight at the shrieking, terrified fledglings.

There's a turquoise and golden flash. A blur of long neck and vivid wings erupts skyward with a defiant, furious shriek. There's a petite woman on Esmeral's back, her golden hair flying like a banner. As Auryn passes over them, Esmeral latches onto one of the golden dragon's leathery wings with her sharp teeth.

The wing rips. The massive dragon roars in pain and fury. Auryn's thrown off-balance, his wings flailing wildly as he attempts to stay in the air, but he's moving too fast. He topples to one side and crash-lands hard against the base of the cliffs, sending clouds of dust into the air.

The fledglings race back to the flare, panicking but safe.

Within the clouds of dust, Auryn's tail and one wing are thrust awkwardly into the air. While he still flies, I hold a strap and move down Scourge's flank. As dirt skims past my feet, I jump from my dragon, tuck myself into a ball, and roll. I'm up again as Scourge wheels away back into the sky. If Auryn attempts to fly away, Scourge will be ready to attack, but right now, I don't think the golden dragon is going anywhere.

I raise my forearm before my nose and mouth as I stride forward through the dust. Isavelle. Esmeral. Where are they? How dare this idiot attack my flare?

Over the furious blood roaring in my ears, I hear hissing and spitting. Esmeral has Kane backed against the cliff, her teeth bared and sparks erupting from her throat. He's bleeding from a cut on his brow, and he's glaring at the little dragon with eyes filled with hate.

Not far away, a crumpled figure is lying motionless on the ground.

"Isavelle," I shout, breaking into a run. Hearing me, she slowly sits up. She's covered with dust and coughing her lungs out.

I skid the last few feet to her on my knees and pull her into my arms. "Isavelle. *Sha'len*. Where are you hurt?" I feel her ribs and limbs, hunting for broken bones. Her sleeves are ripped open, and her palms and elbows are bleeding.

Isavelle throws her arms around my neck. "Alpha, you're all right. I was so scared for you up there."

The strength of her arms around my neck assures me that she's not badly hurt, and I squeeze her tight. I push my nose into the side of her neck, breathing in her sweet scent to calm my thundering heart. She and Esmeral saved the fledglings. A pair of Omegas fought a wild Alpha dragon and they survived.

Over her shoulder, Kane is glaring at us. I get to my feet slowly, taking Isavelle with me.

"Stay behind me," I say, shielding her with my body as I face the enemy rider.

An ominous rumbling sound fills the air. Auryn's head rises above us, a white-hot glow at his throat. I feel a dozen riders and their dragons at my back, closing in around us.

"It's over," I call to Kane, who is still backed against the rocks by my mate's furious dragon. "Call off your dragon, or you will both die."

"Fuck you," Kane seethes. His long black coat and high black boots are covered in dust. Stringy blond hair hangs in his eyes.

Auryn is looking right at me, and his jaws part. I suffered through weeks of pain when my hand was burned by dragonfire. Other riders have been splashed in battle and survived. Will I survive a torrent of dragonfire pouring down on my head? Doubtful.

I turn to push Isavelle away from me and prepare to use my Alpha's growl to order her to run, but something fluttering and red steps past us.

The Temple Crone.

She's walking calmly toward Auryn, her spine straight in her bright crimson robes. The yellow dragon's head rears up and back as it focuses on a new target. He opens his jaws. Kane gives a nasty laugh.

Heloise and Elysant, the spellbreakers, appear on either side of me. Far from being afraid for their crone, their expressions are bright with anticipation.

The crone is so small and frail in the shadow of the malevolent yellow dragon. Flames lick around Auryn's teeth. Just as the glow of dragonfire reaches the top of his throat, the crone lifts her hand. Her red robe falls back, revealing a skinny arm with loose skin and a knobby elbow. The massive dragon blinks, and then closes his jaws and meekly lowers his head.

The Temple Crone turns around and walks back the way she came. "Your captive, *Ma'len*," she says with a demure nod of her head. The spellbreakers have proud smiles on their lips.

As if she's been told she can stand down, Esmeral gives Kane one final, angry hiss, then returns to Isavelle's side to nuzzle her rider.

Kane takes several angry steps toward the crone, his fists bunched at his sides and his face suffused with rage. "What did you do to my dragon, you hag?"

The spellbreakers scream in outrage at the insult. Both of them lift their hands, which fill with swirling magic.

Beside me, Temple Crone keeps her eyes fixed on Kane, but she raises a placating hand and her spellbreakers slowly lower their arms. "You already have our attention. I thought it wise to prevent you from hurting anyone else before you have the chance to request your audience with the king. That is why you're here, isn't it?"

"I'll rip you to pieces," he snarls.

The Temple Crone smiles at Kane, and then with a flick of her fingers, every dragon surrounding us unfurls their wings with a snap.

Kane's mouth falls open as he takes in the sight of dozens of raised dragon wings and the lethal dragons attached to them. Even I'm impressed. I had no idea the crone possessed such a deep connection to the flare.

"That is a very fine dragon you have there, young man," the crone continues conversationally, in the tone you might use with a small child who's picked up a stick and declared he will fight a whole army. "We are able to mend his wing if you wish. My Temple Mothers are healers, and our dragonmaster is highly skilled. I believe the two of you have met."

Kane is still staring at the dragons, his eyes narrowed. "How did you do that?"

"I asked them. They trust me," the crone replies.

"Liar," he snaps. "You used magic on them. I know a witch when I see one. So it's true what they say about Lenhale being infested with hags."

The crone's expression turns chilly. "I am a *Hratha'len* priestess, as are my spellbreakers, Temple Mothers, and Maids. We are privileged to have two resident witches in the castle. There are no *hags* here."

Kane doesn't seem to know what to do with this statement. "Mess with my dragon again, you sour-faced bitch, and I'll—"

I've had enough, and I call out to him with my hand gripping my sword's hilt, hoping Kane gets the message without me having to draw my weapon. "I'm King Zabriel, and this is my home and my people you're threatening. Speak your purpose here."

Kane rakes me from head to toe. There's dislike in his eyes, but also curiosity as he sizes me up. "You're like me, aren't you? An Alpha. There aren't many like us."

I regard him in cold silence. I'm nothing like him.

The sky darkens, and with a beating of wings, Scourge swoops in to land, the other dragons parting to give him space by my side. He levels his massive head at Kane and parts his jaws.

Kane glances from Scourge's red eyes to mine. "This is your dragon?"

"I'm waiting for you to tell me your purpose here."

Kane snorts in disgust and shifts his weight, his manner haughty as he gazes around at the gathered riders, *Hratha'len*, and dragons. Though he's massively outnumbered, he's reveling in the spectacle he's making. "You're treating me like dirt when I have something you need."

"You have nothing but a few dragons that you can't control," I tell him. "If you don't speak, I will lose my patience and kill you."

Kane gives me a nasty smile. "You won't kill me. Give me the red-haired witch, and I'll end this war for you. I'm not leaving without her."

24

———

Isavelle

I'm pressed tight against Zabriel's side as Kane makes his horrible demands. He wants Ravenna? Every dragon in Lenhale will rip Kane to pieces before we hand a vulnerable Omega over to such a monster.

Esmeral glares at Kane, showing him her pointed white teeth. Heat radiates from her chest, and dragonfire rumbles within her soul core. I'm so proud of her. Our first chance to defend Lenhale from our enemies, and together we were able to down a massive dragon and his deranged rider and save a group of panicking fledglings.

Kane glances at Esmeral with a curled lip. His eyes graze over me and move on.

Then his attention snaps back to me.

A nasty smile spreads over his face. "Well, well, well. I knew we would meet again one day, witch." He says *witch* like it's a curse word. He strolls toward us, his cold, black eyes fixed on me. "Didn't I tell you that the next time I saw you, you'd better be running?"

Zabriel draws his sword. "Threaten my bride again, and I'll gut you where you stand."

Kane stops in his tracks and glares at Zabriel. He puts his hand on his own sword's hilt, his jaw grit in frustration. Anger is rolling off him in sickening waves. He wants to hurt me. He believes it's his gods-given right. "Your bride? The Brethren were fools, but at least they didn't put vermin on the throne."

Zabriel's scent is bursting with anger. "Whatever you're offering, I don't care. You have nothing but a punchable face and a short lifespan. Take your dragon and fuck off."

"Do you keep your brains in your knot?" Kane asks with a derisive laugh. "If you don't hear what I have to offer, then you're as stupid as the Brethren, and that's saying something."

Someone is approaching from behind us with long strides. A man stops on Zabriel's other side, his long, white hair dancing in the breeze. Stesha holds his sword, a lethal expression in his wintry eyes.

Kane glances at the newcomer, and then his self-control snaps. His face transforms in hatred, and he draws his sword. "You took my mate from me. Did you touch her? Did you fuck her? I'll *kill* you."

Kane runs at Stesha with his sword raised and brings it down in a vicious swing, one which Stesha parries easily. While Kane is off-balance, his sword arm flung out to one side, Stesha plants his foot against the man's chest and sends him sprawling into the dirt.

"You want to do this again?" Stesha asks him, striding

forward. "I'll do this again. I'm not as much fun as hurting unarmed women, am I?"

Kane glowers up at him. "Fuck you. Kill me, then. You two witches. Use your magic on me. Blast me into nothing. Give it your best shot."

"We are not witches," Heloise seethes, red fire flickering around her fingertips. "We are sacred wielders of dragon magic."

"You're a witch who deserves to burn," Kane snarls.

Both women raise their hands, balls of red magic forming between their fingertips, and they hurl them at Kane. Everyone flings themselves backward by several paces.

Kane shouts a word into the sky. "*Nah-vahneh.*" Both balls of magic collide with an invisible force, shatter into a thousand pieces, and dissipate into nothing. The shout echoes across the dragongrounds, growing louder and louder until finally fading away.

Kane gets to his feet, a gleeful expression on his face. "You see what I can do? Do you understand now?"

Zabriel's frowning, and I can tell he doesn't understand. I touch his arm and whisper, "Witchfinders are warlocks trained by the Brethren to wield words of power."

"No matter," Zabriel seethes. "If he can't be killed with dragon magic, I'll run him through with my sword."

A sick sensation spreads through my stomach. *You're treating me like dirt when I have something you need.*

I'll end this war for you.

"Zabriel, there's something we need to consider first," I tell him. There's a bitter taste on my tongue.

He turns to me in surprise, one dark brow raised.

Kane tips back his head, laughing at the top of his lungs.

"The witch has figured it out. The witch has more brains than the king. Give me what's mine, and I'll do what a thousand witches and ten thousand dragon whores can't do."

My throat aches with despair. "Ravenna doesn't want you. You don't deserve any woman, let alone someone as good and kind as her. You can't even say her name."

"What makes you think we will hand her over like she's goods to trade?" Zabriel asks.

Kane swings his sword playfully back and forth with a huge grin on his face. "You tell him, witch. Tell your king what he's too stupid to figure out on his own."

I narrow my eyes, hating Kane from the top of his head right down to the toes of his boots. To Zabriel, I say, "Witchfinders are trained in special kinds of magic. Revelation. Disruption. Destruction. They can find hidden witches and they know when someone is lying to them. They can dispel magic, and they're especially good at breaking through magical wards. I think he believes he can destroy the barrier to the south."

"I *can* destroy the barrier to the south," Kane says. "I can bring it down with one word."

Zabriel folds his arms, unimpressed by his insistence. "If my spellbreakers can't do it, what makes you think you can?"

"I'm the *only* one who can. Give me my mate, and I'll shatter that barrier in a second. You can slaughter the shadow bastard with my blessing. Good riddance to that piece of shit."

"Is there any chance he's able to do this?" Zabriel asks me.

No chance, and I can prove it. "I have an idea, but there's someone I will have to talk to. May I address Kane?"

Zabriel is glaring at Kane but pushes his fingers into my

hair and rubs them against the nape of my neck. "Of course, Omega. My bride always has my protection and trust."

My heart swells hearing Zabriel say that. Kane's lip curls in disgust.

"Allow your dragon's wing to be mended and then leave," I tell Kane. "Return tomorrow and you will have our answer. If you hurt anyone in Maledin, you will be arrested. You may have a dragon, but we have an army."

"Why should I go anywhere?" Kane snarls and jerks his chin at the spellbreakers. "Those pathetic hags couldn't punch through wet paper, let alone the southern barrier. I can do it. I know I can."

This man was able to fool and manipulate me once, but it's not happening a second time. "Do you want healing for your dragon or not?"

Muttering under his breath, Kane sheaths his sword and steps aside. He scours every face on the dragongrounds and then stares at the castle with so much intensity. I know he's hunting for Ravenna.

The Temple Crone, three Temple Mothers, and Stesha move forward to examine Auryn's torn wing. The enormous dragon snaps and growls but the Temple Crone is able to quiet him with a few murmurs.

"A little Omega dragon did this?" Mother Linnea asks in tones of surprise as she examines Auryn's ripped wing.

"Esmeral has always been a handful," Stesha mutters.

I'm smiling to myself as I kiss Zabriel's cheek and walk away. He stays behind to make sure Kane behaves.

I cross the stone bridge back to the castle and find Ravenna sheltering in a doorway. Her face is pale and her nails are cutting into her palms. "I saw everything that happened. Kane has come here for me, hasn't he?"

"He has, but he's not taking you. He's trying to bargain for you, but what he's offering is worthless." I explain about his words of power and the claim about the barrier.

Ravenna nibbles on her lower lip as she watches Kane and Auryn in the distance, her hazel eyes huge with worry. Her red hair whips around her face in the wind. "Kane's quite powerful. He might be able to do it."

"Break through a barrier of that strength and size? He has no chance, and I can prove it. Would you like to come with me?"

THE STREETS ARE wet from early spring showers as Ravenna and I arrive at a building and knock on the rain-darkened door. Overhead, a sign swinging in the breeze reads, *Master Gaun's Magical Archive.*

Master Gaun himself answers and welcomes us inside, and he introduces us to his two assistants. "This is Master Simpkin and Master Artor."

The two men greet me with friendly murmurs and handshakes, but they turn pale as they gaze upon my companion.

Ravenna's lips twitch and her eyes sparkle. "Master Simpkin. Master Artor. I hope you have both recovered after the last time we met."

"Ah, quite well, thank you," Artor mumbles, staring at his shoes.

"The injuries have faded but the memories have not,"

Simpkin says with a pained smile. There's a brief silence, and then he bursts out, "We deeply apologize that we—"

Ravenna shakes her head. "You had no choice but to hunt me, as I had no choice but to defend myself. Shall we call it even? We meet as equals now. Brothers and sisters. Lady Isavelle tells me that you all call yourselves by your proper title now, which is warlock."

The two men bow to Ravenna, hastily uttering words of thanks for her generosity and understanding. I get the impression that they're more than a little in awe of her.

Master Gaun serves tea, and the five of us sit before the fire while he tells us of the progress they're making cataloging the great many books and artifacts in the archive.

"But I don't imagine you came here to talk about our work," Master Gaun says. "May we help you with something?"

"Yes, I think you can," I tell them. "The former witchfinder Kane has come to the capital."

"And now he has a dragon," Ravenna tells them.

A chilly wind seems to whip around the cozy room. Master Simpkin's mouth falls open in horror. Master Artor's teacup rattles on its saucer.

Master Gaun looks fearfully at the door as if the man we're speaking of might stride through it. "H-he's not coming here, is he?"

"I doubt it, and he's not been given permission to explore the city."

All three men breathe sighs of relief.

"I wish to ask you about his abilities," I say. "Kane claims that he's able to use a word of power to break the southern barrier and allow the dragon army through. I don't believe that Kane is strong enough."

The three men glance at each other. Master Gaun says thoughtfully, "There is such a word. A common one. We often spoke it against protective wards set up around witches' cottages."

"Miss Ravenna has heard it several times," Master Simpkin tells me, wincing an apology. "The lady makes exceedingly strong protective wards that we were never able to break. Has Kane broken your wards?"

Annoyance flashes over her face. "He has."

"Did Kane ever use a word of power on you?" Master Gaun asks me. "Perhaps the word of revelation?"

I'm about to say that he hasn't when I think back to the last day in the dungeon with him. "I think perhaps he did. He mouthed a word, and though I didn't hear it, something happened. Suddenly there was blinding light all around me, and after that, his manner toward me altered entirely. He looked like he wanted to kill me."

"You were standing right in front of him, but you didn't hear him, and yet he was able to reveal what you are," Master Gaun muses. He gets to his feet and motions the others to join him. "Allow us to give you a demonstration, my lady."

The three men line up, and as one they shout at the top of their lungs, "*Rrus-nahl.*"

Ravenna and I glow faintly here and there. At the tips of our fingers and noses. The curve of Ravenna's chin. The glow is far weaker than when Kane used the word on me, and then it fades away.

"That is the first word a witchfinder learns," Gaun says, resuming his seat. "We three must shout it together to make it work at all, but Kane merely needs to form the word with his lips. If he shouted, I daresay every witch in Lenhale would glow as bright as the sun on a summer's day. When it comes to breaking or disrupting the barrier, I would not like to say that he couldn't do it, Lady Isavelle."

Ravenna and I are silent as we leave the archive. The rain has started falling again, and my mood is as gray and sodden as the sky. I felt so sure that the former witchfinders would laugh off Kane's claims and tell us he's too arrogant for his own good.

"I don't care what Kane is offering. We're not going to hand you over to that monster. We will find another way to bring the barrier down."

When we reach the castle, Ravenna hunts among the clouds as if searching for a golden dragon. "Tomorrow, when Kane returns to the castle, I would like to speak with him alone."

THE FOLLOWING MORNING, Kane enters the Great Hall where Ravenna is waiting for him. Zabriel stands by my side, holding tight to my hand. I feel sick with worry. I felt sick all night and my eyes are burning from lack of sleep. I don't know what Ravenna wishes to speak with Kane about, but there's a hard lump of apprehension in my belly.

Sometime later, the door to the Great Hall opens, and Kane strides out. He completely ignores us, but there's a triumphant smile curving his lips as he heads back to the dragongrounds.

Ravenna emerges a moment later, looking pale and defeated.

"Ravenna, no," I cry, running forward to take hold of her hands. "You didn't promise that you would go with him, did you?"

She squeezes my fingers. "I'm all right. Everything will be okay." She turns to Zabriel. "When you are ready to breach the southern barrier, send word to Kane in the east. He will bring the barrier down and keep it down long enough for your army to pass through."

Zabriel regards her with a solemn expression. "You don't have to do this. You owe us nothing, and we may yet find another way to breach the barrier."

Ravenna gazes resolutely up at him. "*Ma'len*. That's what I should call you, isn't it? *Ma'len*, I owe you a great deal. All witches do. I want to repay you and help end this war. There are no doubts in my mind that I should do this."

"But Kane—" I say.

"He has promised that he won't hurt me."

"Do his promises count for anything?"

Ravenna's eyes cut away from me, and my heart feels crushed. When I turn to entreat Zabriel, his lips press together, and he gives a tiny shake of his head. He won't stop her from doing this.

I hunt desperately for a way to change Ravenna's mind. "Remember Mistress Hawthorne, my crone? You can go to her. Hide there. You can set up wards, and she will make them stronger. I can visit. We can all be together."

I see it so vividly in my mind's eye. Ravenna and I sitting on the grass in Biddy Hawthorne's garden with a basket of woodland herbs between us, talking and laughing while we bundle them up for drying. Happy and carefree. The old witch is sitting on the garden bench smoking her pipe, asking us questions, telling stories, or chiding us to work harder.

Three witches, together. The three of us, safe and happy in Maledin for the first time ever, with no witchfinders to threaten and hurt us.

I want that so badly I can barely breathe.

Ravenna keeps her eyes fixed on the ground. "I can't express how wonderful that sounds, but now is not the time. I must go, and you all have work to do here."

Kane is going to hurt her. She'll be all alone with him, and he'll make her suffer because he hates what she is. "What if I decide it's my duty as the future Queen of Maledin to protect a fellow Omega from a brutal Alpha?"

Ravenna gazes at me with reproach in her eyes. "A witch would remember that it's my decision. None of us are free from the Brethren until the Shadow King has been defeated."

I swipe tears from my cheeks. This can't be happening.

"I'm not the one who needs saving," Ravenna reminds me. "There are others that the Shadow King is holding prisoner who need your help. Remember them and forget about me."

She pulls away from me, walks down the corridor toward the dragongrounds, and my last hope dies.

Zabriel reaches for me and cups my face. "I'm so sorry, *sha'len.*"

Why couldn't the gods have granted Ravenna an Alpha like Zabriel? I wrap my arms around him and squeeze him tight.

As we follow Ravenna, I wipe tears from my cheeks. I

wonder if Emmeric knows that another Omega is suffering because of him. If he did, he'd probably laugh.

When we reach the dragongrounds, Zabriel puts his hand on the hilt of his sword. The dragons have pulled back. Scourge is perched atop the cliffs, wings spread and red eyes glowing.

Auryn dominates the dragongrounds, his jaws parted as he surveys the other dragons. His wing has been mended, and the tear is a scar in the leathery membrane.

Kane has his arms folded, and he's drumming his fingers on his biceps. At the sight of Ravenna crossing the bridge toward him, Kane goes completely still, and all expression drops from his face. He's completely transfixed, drinking in the sight of her.

Ravenna's walking in the manner of someone being led to the gallows, but it's not too late for some final words. I hurry forward and whisper, "Once the barrier is down and the Shadow King is dead, take your chance. Alphas are weakest just after their ruts. You say you know your poisons."

Ravenna raises an eyebrow. "Lady Isavelle, that's murder."

"If we were Alphas, we could duel with Kane and kill him, and no one would charge us with a crime. Because we don't have size and muscle on our side, we can't defend ourselves? We are witches. No one pushes us around."

Ravenna smiles and squeezes my fingers. "Your courage gives me strength. What a sight you and your dragon were as you attacked Auryn yesterday."

"Killing Kane isn't the only option," I continue, with single-minded purpose. "If you don't wish to break the law, then we can use the law. The City Guard will arrest Kane and put him on trial for abusing you. You only need to speak up, and we will all be on your side."

Ravenna listens carefully to what I have to say, and then she puts gentle arms around me and holds me close.

"Blessing be upon you," she whispers and then slips out of my arms.

Kane watches her walk toward him in his evil black clothes with a gloating smirk on his lips.

He's won. He's got everything he wants, and my throat burns with the unfairness of it all.

Esmeral appears at my side, clicking and spitting angrily in Kane's direction. As soon as Ravenna reaches Kane, he lifts her up in his arms and carries her atop Auryn, just how Zabriel has carried me and climbed one-handed many times before. He wraps an arm around Ravenna's waist while she keeps her expressionless face averted from him. Kane's smile is filled with malice as he speaks into Ravenna's ear. He pushes his fingers into her hair just above her nape, makes a fist, and pulls her hair tight.

Ravenna's lips part. In relief? In fear? That's something Zabriel has done for me as well, to soothe the ache in my mating gland, but the ferocious grip he has on her hair looks cruel.

Zabriel takes me in his arms and presses a soft kiss to my forehead. "I hate this as well, *sha'len*. I'm so sorry. Ravenna is doing the people of Maledin a great kindness. With her help, we can end this war and bring the villagers of western Maledin home."

I turn to Zabriel, place my hands on his chest, and implore him. "After the barrier is down, can we make this right? Can Ravenna come back to Lenhale, and can we make Kane pay for his crimes?"

"If Ravenna wishes it, after the war, I will send dragonriders after Kane."

Auryn spreads his wings and launches into the sky. The golden dragon circles over us, taunting us, and then flies swiftly toward the east and out of sight.

25

Zabriel

The following week, there are blossoms on the nectar plum trees in my mother's favorite garden. Spring is in the air, and its fresh, sweet scent reminds me so much of my mate.

The Temple Crone enters the garden just as I'm about to leave it, and I greet her with a smile. "You have hidden talents, Grandmother. We should send you out to tame the wild dragons of the eastern flare."

Now that we have a way through the barrier, we can start planning an attack, and we'll be able to bring Isavelle's family and the missing villagers of western Maledin home.

"With these old knees?" she asks with a laugh. "I'll leave the adventuring to you young riders." Despite her smile, there's a somber expression in her eyes, and I wait for her to speak. "I wish to bring up the matter of the Ritual of the First

Heat with you again, *Ma'len*. Since we spoke about it, several others have approached me, asking whether we should bring it back."

"Have they," I growl, my good mood crumbling away.

"Yes, *Ma'len*. My spellbreakers. Mother Linnea. Godric. Captain Ashton. Please don't think too harshly of them. They are aware that they are suggesting something potentially distressing for both you and your Omega, but they are concerned about the safety of the people in the kingdom."

All Betas, who have no idea how much they're asking Isavelle to suffer if she takes part in this ritual. "They need to keep their noses out of mine and my mate's private affairs. Every other Alpha and Omega pair is allowed to conduct their mating in peace."

"Just so, *Ma'len*."

By Scourge's aching balls, I hate the way she says *just so*. "Is this because of Ravenna?"

"Yes, *Ma'len*. I believe it is."

"My heart hurts for Ravenna, but I fail to see how the Ritual of the First Heat would have changed anything. The man who has her is pure evil."

"Very true, *Ma'len*, but Ravenna won't be the only Omega emerging at this time."

Fists clenched, I look across the garden at the swaying nectar plum blossoms. What would my mother tell me if she were still alive? I remember her sweet, patient, long-suffering smile. No doubt she would have made any sacrifice that was asked of her.

"If the people you named have so much to say, then we will meet with them and they can say it to my face." People are brave around the *Hratha'len*, but we shall see how much they want to interfere with my Omega when I'm glaring at them with Scourge's angry red eyes.

The following morning, Isavelle and I stand hand in hand in the War Room. At the table with us are the Temple Crone, Mother Linnea, Godric, Leibel the wingrunner, Captain Ashton, Stesha, and the spellbreakers, Heloise and Elysant.

I'm annoyed that Stesha is here. If he had a mate, he would pound me into the dirt if I presumed to tell him what to do with her. Isavelle was able to shed some light on Ashton's motivations when I spoke with her last night. Apparently, the Beta fell for Ravenna the moment he saw her. I glare at the captain. Making Isavelle suffer isn't going to bring Ravenna back to us. The spellbreakers love *Hratha'len* rituals, Mother Linnea has a soft heart and is probably fretting for the kingdom's Omegas, and Leibel? I have no idea what Leibel is doing here.

The Temple Crone addresses us all. "I believe the quickest way to resolve this issue would be for everyone to explain why they believe the Ritual of the First Heat should go ahead. Perhaps my *Hratha'len* would like to go first?"

Mother Linnea and the spellbreakers speak of the sacredness of such a ritual and how much the people stand to learn about Maledinni culture, while Isavelle stares straight ahead. My mate has been unnervingly quiet this morning, and I don't believe she slept well the night before, and neither has she declared that she won't do this ritual, as I have several times.

"It is a fine ritual," Heloise says firmly. "Nothing is more admirable than an Omega who can hold her head high in the eye of the storm. Omegas all around the kingdom will aspire to be just like *Ma'len's* mate."

Mother Linnea wrings her hands, her brow creased with anguish. "I don't believe the ritual should become a permanent custom, but I have thought and thought about the quickest way to encourage the kingdom's Omegas to come forward and make themselves known to the Flame Temple, and this ritual seems to be the answer. I wouldn't ask this of *Ma'len's* mate if I didn't believe that she was strong enough. She has already made us so proud as she defends our dragons and stands by *Ma'len's* side, and I believe Isavelle will succeed at this as well."

Godric clears his throat. "We have all seen how Lady Isavelle asserts her human side through her witchcraft. The whole kingdom is aware that the woman destined for the throne is a witch, but do they know she's a dragonrider? Do they understand that she has Maledinni blood? We must bring this fact to everyone's attention. After all, it's a Maledinni throne, not a human one."

Captain Ashton's expression is troubled. "In Old Maledin we understood Omegas, but they were still not treated with honor and respect. If we don't do something to make the people understand that an Omega is strong and precious, not weak and stupid, then they will be pushed around even more than they were before." He glances at my mate. "Forgive me, Lady Isavelle."

"There's nothing to forgive, Captain," she whispers.

Then the only person left to speak is Stesha, and he's wearing a sour expression.

"What are you even doing here?" I snap.

"It wasn't my idea. The Temple Crone thought there should be another Alpha's voice in the matter."

"So voice it. Would you agree to this?"

Stesha glares from one person in the room to the next. "No, I wouldn't."

My fists clench with vindication. Only another Alpha can understand how barbaric this is.

"But I'm not the king, and the people aren't relying on me," Stesha continues. "You all speak of an Omega's duties, an Omega's sacrifice. But what about the Alphas? Maledin's newest Alphas need to understand that their duty is to lead and protect. They can't do whatever the fuck they like to Omegas. This ritual is about an Alpha's self-control as much as his Omega's strength of will. Can *Ma'len* exercise discipline along with his Omega? Will Alphas be inspired to keep level heads and their knots to themselves if they hear the king can?"

Stesha's cold blue eyes bore into mine.

I don't think I've ever been angrier with Stesha, and he once touched my mate's hair. Everyone around the table is nodding along with him. Even through my fury, I can feel how persuasive his argument is.

"I won't say I agree with bringing back the ritual, but I can see the merits. You decide what's best for your Omega, Zabriel." Stesha flashes a look at Isavelle and mutters, "With Lady Isavelle's opinion, which I have no doubt that she will freely give you."

Silence reigns. I've never felt so outnumbered.

Isavelle takes a shaky breath. "You have all made your feelings plain. It seems as if we have no choice but to—"

My stomach lurches. "All of you, get out. I want to speak with Isavelle."

When everyone has filed out of the room, I pick Isavelle up in my arms and sit down with her, holding her tight against my chest. I feel like I'll lose my sanity when one of us has to leave Lenhale for a matter of hours. The thought of being parted for days while she suffers through her first true heat makes me want to break things.

"No one would speak for us," I seethe. "Stesha wasn't on our side. Not even Ashton. I thought the man had a heart."

Isavelle strokes my cheek, her turquoise and golden eyes huge with worry.

I close my eyes and press my forehead against hers. My heart is pounding. "I thought you and I were past all the suffering. The separation. It nearly broke me hearing you cry and whimper through your false heats. True heats rage harder than the highest fevers. Exhaustion, dehydration. Not all Omegas survive. There are risks. I need to be there to protect you."

"I won't be alone. The *Hratha'len* won't let anything happen to me."

I grip her shoulders. "You want to do this? Are you punishing yourself because you feel like you failed Ravenna? She's one of the bravest people I've ever met. I commend her. You don't need to suffer."

"What does your heart tell you we should do?"

My heart wants my Omega. I stand up with her in my arms and carry her to our room, shedding her clothes as soon as the door is closed. I'm desperate to be inside her, and I make love to her so fiercely that it's like I'm trying to convince her not to do this through the force of my thrusts.

After, she lies in my arms, stroking her fingers through my hair.

"Emmeric took you from me, and I swore I'd never let you

go again," I tell her. "What kind of Alpha would I be if I willingly allow you to suffer?"

"Perhaps our love will be all the stronger for it."

I rub my fingers across my forehead. We put the idea of the ritual behind us, and now my good-hearted mate has been bullied into a corner. "I wanted to leave everything that's cruel and barbaric in the past and focus on the future with you."

Isavelle presses her hand to my heart. "Our sons and daughters will be born into a Maledin where people understand their designations. But first, we have to make sure that there is understanding."

"You want to do this?" I ask her. "Really?"

Her expression is conflicted. "I don't feel like we have a choice, do you?"

I'm the fucking king, I want to shout. But I don't because it feels like something my father would have done.

I press a kiss to her forehead and hold her close until she falls asleep in my arms.

Even before I open my eyes in the morning, I know. I feel it when I pull her into my arms. I smell it in the air around us. Her scent has grown even richer and sweeter. My dragines ache. Blood pulses through my knot.

Isavelle presses a hot cheek against my chest and moans, "Zabriel. Everything hurts."

Her first true heat is starting, and my rut has answered her call.

⁓

ISAVELLE IS pale and shivering as we stand side by side at the wyvern eyrie. *Hratha'len* women and six wingrunners are waiting to escort my bride to the ritual, a secret place that will be hidden from me and everyone who is close to us.

"What a happy occasion this is," the *Hratha'len* Crone says, but there's nothing happy about her somber face and tone. "Our future queen's first heat. *Ma'len's* mate will be taken to a secret place where dragons can't reach her and then returned to his side after her heat for a great celebration. A feast day will be declared all throughout Maledin."

There's an indignant trill, and Esmeral flutters out of the sky and lands next to Isavelle. My mate places her hand on her dragon's neck. "Can Esmeral come with me? Can my bodyguards?"

Heloise shakes her head. "No, *Ma'len's* mate. Because of your distress, your dragon will alert Scourge to your where-abouts, and the people closest to you may betray your loca-tion to *Ma'len* unwittingly."

Isavelle's *distress*. I glare at Heloise, who is wearing a cold expression. Isavelle looks crestfallen. She won't have one friend by her side this whole ordeal.

"Everyone move back. I want to speak with my Omega."

All the *Hratha'len* and wingrunners step back a few paces, and I gather Isavelle into my arms. Her body against my aching one makes me moan under my breath, and I inhale her perfume deep into my lungs.

"We've made the right choice, haven't we?" she whispers.

If you can call being pressured and browbeaten by my advisors, soldiers, and the *Hratha'len* a choice. If anyone tells me that Omegas are weak, stupid little playthings after what

Isavelle and Ravenna are sacrificing for Maledin, I will punch them in the face.

"You can change your mind at any moment—" I begin.

Isavelle puts her fingers over my lips. "Don't, or the moment I get into my nest, I'll jump right out and run all the way back to you."

"I mean it, Omega," I say urgently. "Call the ritual off if it all becomes too much for you." I lift my eyes to the *Hratha'len* women. "You will bring Isavelle back to me if she asks?"

All the women bow their heads in assent.

"Of course, *Ma'len*," Heloise and Elysant reply. As the most senior members of the *Hratha'len* after the Temple Crone, the two spellbreakers have been put in charge of the ritual. Mother Linnea will be attending to Isavelle as well, which I'm glad about. She has a kind nature and Isavelle likes her.

"I can do this," Isavelle whispers fiercely. "For the Omegas in Maledin who don't understand what they are. For Ravenna. If she can be brave, so can I."

I pull my cloak from around my shoulders, fold it up, and place it in her arms. "I've been wearing it for days, and I've been scenting it as much as I can." Comforting scents, the kind that soothed her when we first met.

Isavelle presses her face into the cloth and breathes in deeply. "Will you suffer as well?"

I'll be in agony until she's back in my arms, and I'll resent everyone and everything for separating us. "I have endured every rut of my life alone. My concerns are all for you."

She reaches up and strokes the hair back from my face. Taking her time about it, touching me as much as she can. "When I'm back, we will tell the people that the king and his bride are back in each other's arms. His Omega ran as fast as she could back to his side, craving his good heart and his strong arms, and she won't be parted from him ever again."

Parted. My heart aches. Even the word is unbearable.

"We will be together for my next heat," Isavelle promises. "We've waited this long. We can wait a little longer."

My teeth throb in my mouth. I want to draw my sword and tell everyone to get the hell out of my sight and never speak of this ritual again. Only Isavelle's sweet hand cupping my cheek and her turquoise and golden eyes holding so much bravery make me swallow my fury and say instead, "I am holding you close in my heart."

"Will you say it in your dragon's growl?" she asks.

I put my lips against her ear, take a deep breath, and say as convincingly as I can through all the pain I'm feeling, "Alpha's with you, *sha'len*. My Omega is the bravest Omega in the world."

Isavelle gives a choked moan and presses a kiss to my lips. "I love you."

I physically can't let go of her. She has to pull herself out of my embrace with tears in her eyes as the *Hratha'len* women grip my shoulders while my arms still reach for her.

Esmeral tries to follow her rider as she approaches the wyverns, but the Temple Crone gestures for her to stay back. "*Ma'len*, will you please see to your mate's dragon?"

I put my hand on Esmeral's scales, drawing her close to me and soothing her with my scent, as I wish I were soothing my mate right at this moment. Instead, I'm watching her climb up onto the wyvern behind a wingrunner, her cheeks flushed with her heat and her eyes huge and troubled. She has my cloak clenched in her arms. Her eyes meet mine.

My heart feels like it's going to shatter as the wyverns launch into the air. Esmeral cries out. A pained sound escapes my lips.

With a sense of unreality, like this can't actually be happening, I stare after the wingrunners as they fly south. No doubt they will change direction as soon as they're out of sight of the castle. I watch with an aching chest until they disappear over the horizon.

Esmeral shoots into the sky with a scream of despair and flies away.

I stare around at the wyverns, the off-duty wingrunners, the eyrie. What the fuck just happened? I walk without looking where I'm going, my boots clattering on the wet cobbles. Suddenly there are people around me. I'm on the crowded city streets, and people scramble to get out of my way. My hands are curled into fists with rage.

They took my Omega from me.

I want to shout my agony into the sky. They *took* her.

And I let them.

In one of the main squares, people are gathered around a poster, and I ignore it until a word catches my eye, and I lurch toward it. *Queen.*

It's another poster decrying my mate as an evil witch who must be burned at the stake. I rip the poster down and shred it with my fists. How dare they. *How dare they.* People in this country want my mate dead. Emmeric and the Brethren want her dead, and now my own people want the same. I press my fists to the sides of my head and howl in agony and rage.

They want her dead, and I let her out of my sight.

26

Isavelle

"**D**rink this, my lady."

With a shaking hand, I reach out and take the steaming cup from Heloise and swallow down a mouthful. I've been here for two days, and after the first few hours, Heloise has been the only other person I've seen. The tea tastes strange, and with a grimace, I ask, "What is it?"

She places a cooling cloth on my sweaty brow. "Mereed tea, as usual. Your heat must be affecting your sense of taste and smell. That happens sometimes."

That's never happened before. I glance past her at the mostly empty room. I'm tucked into a curtained bed. There's a small table with a water pitcher and nothing else. This building looks like it was built not long ago from split logs. Built to last but with very little adornment.

"What is this place?" I ask.

"A retreat for the *Hratha'len*. We come here to meditate. Please drink all your tea, *Ma'len's* mate. It is my duty to care for you."

I wish Mother Linnea were here instead of Heloise. I've never been fond of the stern, flinty-eyed spellbreakers. In awe of them certainly, though they possess little patience or warmth. Still, I wouldn't want Zabriel to be angry with Heloise if I returned to him unwell and dehydrated, so I obediently drink my tea.

As soon as the cup is empty, Heloise plucks it from my fingers and the cool cloth from my brow and turns away.

"Could you sit and talk with me for a little while?" I call after Heloise. Hearing her stories about Old Maledin and how she became a spellbreaker might distract me from my aching body.

Heloise closes the door behind her as if she hasn't heard me.

Oh, well. She probably isn't very good at telling stories anyway.

I close the bed curtains, lay back down in my nest of blankets, and try to sleep.

It's just a few days. I can be uncomfortable, shivery, and lonely for a few days for the sake of all the Omegas in Maledin. When word spreads among the populace about the ritual, they'll understand that Omegas aren't *stupid little fuck-toys* at the mercy of their heats and mating instincts, and they should be treated with respect. Maybe Ravenna will hear of this wherever she is and feel inspired to protect herself from Kane.

Or maybe he'll just pin her down and call her disgusting names while he does cruel things to her.

My eyes fill with tears. Every emotion is so much more potent right now, and it was a mistake to think about Ravenna. I curl into a ball, sobbing, and once I start, I can't stop. I cry so hard that my body shakes and my throat spasms. To ease my heart, I picture soaring through the skies with Esmeral. Yes, a crisp, sunny day with my dragon, the wind in my hair and not a care in the world. Such a day could happen. It might be our reality if we manage to defeat—

No, no, no, don't think about him. I quickly recoil from that thorny path and picture Zabriel instead.

I miss you so much, Alpha.

I need you.

My fingers push between my wet thighs, and I make myself come while thinking about Zabriel's handsome face and strong, comforting body. I've lost count of how many times I've climaxed since I arrived. It's never enough, and it's over too quickly. I shove my fingers inside myself, but they do nothing for me. Panting and frustrated, I bury my face in Zabriel's cloak and breathe in deeply.

I fall asleep, and the next time I open my eyes, the light beyond my bed curtains has changed. My mouth is dry, and my stomach rumbles with hunger. Normally, my false heat would be passing off by now, but my body still burns with fever, and my core aches more than ever.

There are footsteps outside my bed, and the curtains open. Heloise again. She's working so much harder than the others.

"May I have some more tea please?" I croak.

"Yes, in a moment. May I have *Ma'len's* cloak, *Ma'len's* mate?"

My body is curled around Zabriel's cloak. There's so much fog in my head that I can't think. "His cloak?"

Heloise holds out her hand. "I need it for the ritual. I'll bring it right back."

Confused, I reach into my nest and draw it out, and Heloise yanks it from my fingers. With a wooden expression, she gathers up all the blankets and takes the bed curtains down. Light pierces my eyes, and I squint and hold my hand up before my face. With everything in her arms, she heads for the door.

"What are you doing? I need those." I sit up and try to stop her, but I'm too late.

"I'll bring them right back." She closes the door behind her, and a moment later I hear a click.

I lay back down on the bed, shivering and confused. There's nothing warm and soft to cover myself with. My nest is bare and exposed. What is Heloise doing? The *Hratha'len* women have attended to me in my heats before, and they brought me tea but left my nest alone.

The empty room feels cavernous, and I press myself into a corner of the bed, struggling to breathe normally. Panic makes my heart race, and a sense of foreboding is steadily creeping over me.

"Hello?" I call. "Heloise?"

No answer.

"Elysant? Mother Linnea?"

Silence.

"Is this part of the ritual?"

Am I being punished for something?

"Heloise? Elysant? Mother Linnea? I don't like this. I want to stop the ritual." None of the *Hratha'len* answer me, so I try one of the wingrunners. "Leibel, are you there?"

I walk to the door on wobbly legs, but it's locked. That was the click I heard. I alternate between hammering on it, calling out, and pressing my ear to the wood. Heloise doesn't come back. No one comes. The silence is complete, like I've been locked in here and left to die.

With my arms wrapped around my shaking body, I take stock of the room. There are no windows to escape through, only narrow gaps up near the ceiling to let in light and cold air. No other doors. The bare bed. The small table and pitcher of water.

I go to the pitcher so I can at least quench my unbearable thirst, but I discover that it's bone dry. I stare in shock at the empty pitcher. This isn't a mistake or a test. This is wrong. Someone wants to hurt me.

Someone wants me to die.

The hugeness of the room is too much for me, and I crawl on my hands and knees over to the bed, and then under it. It's dusty and uncomfortable under here, but at least it's a small space. I tuck myself into a ball and wait. Someone will come. Zabriel will find me. Scourge will find me. My mate's dragon has always found me when I've been in danger.

I fall in and out of dozes. My dreams are dark and frightening, and then I'm awoken by terrible cramping in my core that makes me writhe about in pain. My only sense of time passing is the light changing in the room. I'm shocked awake again and again, in pain and covered in sweat. The room is light, and then it's dark again. I feel more alone than I ever have in my life. More even than my days locked in the dungeons beneath the monastery. At least back then I could hear the weeping of the other prisoners, and a priest would occasionally come by to give me dirty water to drink or kick a moldy piece of bread in my direction.

I dream that I've died and been forgotten. I hear Zabriel and Scourge in the room, and when I call out to them, they just laugh. My thirst is raging. My insides ache. The *Hratha'len* must have decided I'm not good enough to be Zabriel's mate, and they've left me to die.

For the first time in what feels like a hundred years, there are footsteps outside my door. I lift my head hopefully, wondering if it's Zabriel coming to take me away from here.

"Who's there?" My voice is weak and raspy.

Whoever it is unlocks the door, but then there's the sound of footsteps hastily receding as if the person has broken into a run.

Whoever it was unlocked the door.

I drag myself out from beneath the bed and pull myself to my feet using the bedposts. Black spots swarm in front of my eyes, and I have to blink hard to clear them. There's a woman's scream somewhere outside in the glade. A blood-soaked, gurgling cry.

I limp over to the door and open it. I see the wooded glade and the little stream that I glimpsed when we arrived to begin the ritual. The place is completely deserted. Did I hallucinate the scream?

Just thirty feet away, the stream burbles and gurgles enticingly.

My heart thumps painfully at the thought of moving out into the open, but my thirst is stronger than my fear. Gasping and shivering, I hurry across the grass and collapse onto my knees. Dipping my hand into the cool water, I scoop it again and again into my mouth, swallowing down every last drop.

I press my wet hands over my face. My eyes feel sunken. My lips are cracked and flaky, and my hair is crusted with perspiration. It's a bizarre thought given my predicament, but I can't help but panic as I wonder what Zabriel will think if he sees me like this, dirty, bedraggled, and half dead. I pull off my nightgown, scoop water over myself, and rinse my hair and body clean. I want Alpha to adore me, not recoil in disgust.

Shivering, naked, and cold, I glance around the glade. All the light and space clash against my nerves. Everyone is gone. No *Hratha'len*. No wingrunners.

"Zabriel," I cry, calling for him even though I know he's not here. "Alpha, please. Where are you?"

I picture Scourge filling the sky with his vast black wings. His proud head. His blazing red eyes. I'd give anything to hear his furious roar. There's only vast, aching space and silence that batters my skull. My flesh crawls from exposure. I don't want to go back into the room where Heloise locked me up and left me to die, but maybe I can find my blankets and hide somewhere else. Maybe there's a hole I can crawl into until Alpha finds me.

Footsteps move through the grass. My head snaps up, and I see a tall, robed figure, familiar in the way a recurring nightmare is familiar. The man pulls his cowl back, revealing flinty gray eyes and a salt-and-pepper beard. He leers at me, revealing yellow teeth.

The High Priest reaches for the belt of his robes. "You smell like you're dying for something, girl. I've got just what you need."

27

———

Zabriel

I've always met the confusion, rage, and irritability of a lone rut head-on. It's unbecoming of an Alpha not to be able to handle such a time with at least a spoonful of dignity and self-control, but what I thought of as a rut before was laughable. A light inconvenience. A distraction.

I feel like I'm losing my mind.

My rut has sunk its dragon's teeth deep into me, and it's gnawing on me night and day. I can't sleep, I have no appetite, and my whole body is racked with fever and aches. My insides feel too big for my skin. Everything is painfully stretched tight and swollen, and there's nowhere for my frustration to go except to be channeled into restless anger.

I let Isavelle go. I held her in my arms and smelled the perfume of her heat, and *I let her go.* The first day of her absence is agony. The second day is all the worst days of my life occurring simultaneously and over and over. On the third day, I'm shaking and sweating so badly that I can't even find the Flame Temple. I'm lost in my own castle, the home where I've lived for twenty-three years. I'm raving like a madman as I blunder around, and people are fleeing out of my way.

Someone steers me in the right direction, and the next thing I know, I'm face to face with the dancing flames of the font at the center of the temple.

The Temple Crone speaks behind me. "*Ma'len*, what an excellent idea to come and mediate before the Temple Flame."

I swing around to face her. "Where is Isavelle? Something's wrong. We have to bring her home."

The crone's face swims before my eyes. I think she's trying to look sympathetic. "Your rut is unusually strong this time, *Ma'len*. I have heard that the ritual can affect an Alpha this way, but your Omega is safe in her nest, and all is proceeding as it should."

I clutch my head and shake it. My skull feels like it's full of angry bees. "No. Something's *wrong*, I can feel it. Isavelle needs me."

"An Omega's first true heat can last an unpredictable length of time, but there is some good news already, *Ma'len*. News of the ritual has spread all over Maledin, and people are learning for the first time what their designations mean."

"Don't speak to me of other people when all I want is my bride," I roar.

There's a moment of chilly silence. "Just so, *Ma'len*."

"Shut up with your *just sos*," I seethe. "Tell me where you've taken her. I want Isavelle back."

"*Ma'len*, the ritual forbids me from—"

"Fuck your fucking ritual!" My Alpha's growl fills the cavernous temple and reverberates off the walls. I hear an answering bellow from the dragongrounds. "Something's gone wrong. Isavelle needs me."

"The *Hratha'len* will protect *Ma'len's* mate no matter—"

"They don't protect my mate. *I* protect my mate, and I say my Omega needs me. Where. Is. She?"

The Temple Crone fixes me with a stern expression. "I can see why it was stressed in the records that the Alpha must not know the whereabouts of their Omega during the ritual. I believed you had more self-control, *Ma'len*. I will make some tea."

Fuck her fucking tea. Fuck everyone who's conspiring to keep my Omega from me. I'm snarling as I breathe in and out, and my teeth are bared. "Then I'll find her myself. I'll search the whole of Maledin."

Down at the dragongrounds, I climb up onto Scourge. He's found Isavelle before when she's been in danger, and this time will be no different. Esmeral emerges from the caves, still in her heat, but from the looks of her blazing eyes and the lash of her tail, her anger matches mine, and she's coming with us.

"We shouldn't have been separated from Isavelle for one second, and we're going to get her back, aren't we?" I ask the little dragon.

Esmeral screams in agreement, sparks flying around her teeth. That's the spirit.

As we soar into the sky, the torment of the past few days drops away like the ground below us. I finally feel like I'm doing the right thing. I should have gone in search of her days ago. *I should never have let her out of my fucking sight.*

We fly south, and I consider all the likely places for a secret *Hratha'len* temple. Not in the east where the wild dragons are. Not at the southern border. Perhaps somewhere in central Maledin where there are rolling hills and thick forests.

We fly back and forth in a zigzag fashion all day and much of the night, resting occasionally. Dawn creeps up on the horizon. Scourge and Esmeral have shown no signs that Isavelle is calling to them.

Scourge is hungry, and he hunts for fish in a nearby lake, and he and Esmeral eat. My dragon noses some raw white flesh toward me, but I have no appetite for anything that isn't Isavelle.

I mount up, and we keep flying. We make it all the way to the south and the hateful magical barrier. I curse my brother under my breath and then turn back. We fly over the western part of Maledin, along the border of Grendu, and then over the deserted villages.

The sky darkens into night, and we land again. It's starting to feel like Isavelle has completely vanished.

"She can call out to you," I remind Scourge and Esmeral. "Both of you. Isavelle has done it before when she's been in danger, and she hasn't even realized she's doing it."

Scourge bows his head. Esmeral gives a soft, sad trill.

Perhaps Isavelle is so weakened that she can't call.

Perhaps she's already dead.

Esmeral shelters under Scourge's wing for a short rest. I pace around for a while and then sit down. I'm not tired, but as I lean against Scourge's body, I suddenly pass out.

I'm shocked awake by mad chittering in my ear and something yanking on my leg. It's still dark, but the stars and moon have moved across the sky. Esmeral has awoken us by butting her head against Scourge's side and tugging on my breeches.

"What's wrong? Can you hear Isavelle?"

Scourge grunts in surprise. *Mate. Omega.*

"She's found her? Esmeral, do you know where Isavelle is?"

Esmeral is screeching at me to hurry up and move, but I'm already climbing up onto Scourge's back. We launch into the sky, and Scourge and I follow the gold and turquoise streak. Esmeral is flying east, back toward central Maledin, a place we've already searched, but maybe Isavelle was passed out while we were nearby. Maybe she wasn't in danger and didn't need to call out for help, but I feel instinctively in my heart that something is wrong.

The small dragon leads us to a craggy, wooded area with streams running through narrow valleys, and she arrows toward the ground. The sun has risen, and she's heading for what looks like a sheer rock face. She lands and disappears among the trees. Scourge alights in a clearing, and I proceed on foot over mossy rocks.

When I come upon her, Esmeral claws madly at a gap in the rocks with a stream flowing out of it. The space is too narrow for a dragon, even one as small as her, but I can squeeze through.

"I'll go get her. I'll bring her out to you, Esmeral," I tell the dragon, and shoulder my way through the space. I breathe in deeply, hunting for any trace of Isavelle's scent.

The narrow crevice opens into a shady glade, lush with plants, moss, and dappled sunlight. A wooden temple stands at the center, built in a style I recognize as *Hratha'len*. A sense of peace pervades the place, but the scents in the glade are anything but peaceful.

Fear, panic, and violence fill the air.

Isavelle is naked in the grass by the stream. A tall man in robes is standing over her. She inches away from him, moving backward on her hands. He looms over her, moving like a predator who's cornered his prey. Their scents wash over me. Isavelle's sickly fear. The man's—the Alpha's—hatred and lust. I've smelled his scent before when he stabbed me at the barrier, and one word throbs through my soul.

Kill.

Before he can realize I'm there, I run forward, grab hold of him with both hands, and hurl him across the clearing. He hits a tree and slides down it with a groan. I recognize his face this time, as I should have the last time we met at the barrier. The Brethren High Priest who nearly burned Isavelle alive.

"Get the fuck away from my Omega," I snarl.

Behind me, Isavelle gasps in shock. "Zabriel?" she calls in a choked-up voice. Like she can't believe it's really me.

I hunker down and touch her cheek, so full of rage and relief that I can't speak.

It's me.

I'm here.

I'm so sorry.

She glances past my shoulder, and my beautiful little queen's face hardens in anger. "Will you kill him for me, Alpha?"

I press a kiss to her lush, beautiful mouth and breathe, "It will be my honor, *sha'len.*"

I stand up and unsheathe my sword. The High Priest gets

to his feet, and he draws two short swords. They glimmer and flicker with magic. My Alpha wants me to charge in and run him through, but I force myself to hold my ground. If I die because I'm overconfident and impatient, if I can't protect Isavelle, she will be the one who suffers.

Those swords he's holding. They're nothing like I've ever seen before, and there is no doubt the magic they possess gives the priest some advantage.

The priest's silvery gaze flicks from me to Isavelle. "Give her to me. She's mine."

Rage burns in my chest. "You always snatch at what isn't yours, priest. My woman. My people. My country. Did you steal those swords from Emmeric? Did you betray your master to hunt down my bride?"

"Your brother owes me a great deal more than what I've been given for my service," he snarls, his expression petulant.

"I don't have a brother, and you're a fool if you thought that Emmeric wouldn't use you and throw you aside once you served your purpose." He takes a step toward my mate, and I slash at the air to make him pull back. "Don't even look at her."

The priest's hands clench on his swords in frustration. "But I must have her. I'm like you, aren't I? I've got these..." He prods at his gums with his tongue. "*Teeth*. The world is full of entrancing scents. My appendage has the strangest bulge. It bothers me day and night. It *aches*." His attention snaps to Isavelle and sharpens with hunger. "I can smell her. She needs to be rutted like an animal. I've heard that's what she's for. I always knew there was a reason she was my constant irritation. You take her first if you want to. I can wait. I'd like to watch you break her."

I lift my sword with a roar and bring it down in an arc straight at his head. I will silence his disgusting words. The High Priest crosses his blades and parries my blow. I should have knocked him to the ground or at the very least broken his grip on his weapons, but energy crackles and sparks, and the magical swords knock me back several feet. I swing my blade again and again, but each time, the swords repel my strikes.

"What are you doing, you fool?" the High Priest cries out, shocked and disgusted that I've attacked him. "You might be king, but you don't know how to control the vast masses that are the people of Maledin. Your brother needed me to do that, and now you need me too. I've changed and become like you. It's a sign that we're meant to work together."

I slowly lower my sword. "Maybe you're right."

The High Priest stares at me. "You agree?"

"No, you fucking idiot, I'm going to kill you," I snarl.

The High Priest gets his swords up just in time as I bring another crashing blow down on his head.

Out of the corner of my eye, I see that Isavelle has pulled herself to her feet and is watching the fight. He'll hurt her if I don't kill him. He'll make her suffer for the rest of her life.

No matter how hard I swing, I can't break the priest's hold on those magical swords.

I'm covered in sweat and breathing hard. My arms are tiring, and my wrists are aching from the shock of striking what feels like a solid wall. Meanwhile, the High Priest shows no sign of exertion or strain.

"*Nah-vahneh,*" Isavelle shouts, and her voice rings out across the clearing.

It's the word of power that Kane used against the spellbreakers. The result isn't as dramatic as it was then, but for a moment, the swords' green magic flickers like a candle about to go out. The High Priest frowns at his weapons. I'm so surprised that I nearly miss my chance. I grip my sword with both hands and swing downward, and this time, I knock the blades out of the priest's hands. I follow up with a kick to his chest and send the man sprawling.

The swords hit the ground, and I step over them to get to the priest.

The man raises a panicked hand, trying to fend me off. "I can be useful to you. I know so many things about Maledin. The people. Spare my—"

With a roar, I flip the sword in my hand and thrust it through the priest's chest. His eyes go wide, and blood gurgles from his throat. All the misery he's sown in my lands and the hurt he's caused my woman, and he thinks I will spare his life and ally with him. I pull the sword out, and his body goes limp with death.

I lift my eyes to my Omega. She's trembling with cold, and her eyes are filled with anguish that's slowly bleeding into relief as she realizes the man who's tormented her for so long is dead.

"It—it worked. That word was all I could think of to help you." She lifts her turquoise and golden eyes to mine. "You killed him."

I drop my sword, cross the clearing in two strides, and scoop her into my arms. My inner Alpha roars with victory as I slam my mouth over hers. There's so much I want to say. So much I want to know about what the fuck has been going on here, but I can't make myself stop. We end up on the ground, and I plant kiss after kiss on her mouth, her throat, her chest.

"Alpha, I'm so sorry I couldn't make you a nest," Isavelle sobs. "I'm sorry this isn't what you wanted."

I shake my head, trying to tell her it doesn't matter. I don't care about nests. I just want her.

"Get...you inside," I manage between frantic swipes of my tongue. "Dark. Safe."

"Please, I need you now. I can't bear it any longer. Please, Alpha. Here. Don't make me wait any longer."

A growl travels up from my knot and out between my gritted teeth. My hungry gaze devours her lush beauty. She grabs hold of my jacket and fumbles with the fastenings. Transfixed by the sight of her flushed breasts and swollen sex, I'm useless in my efforts to undress myself. She pushes my jacket and shirt from my shoulders and unlaces my breeches. I feel them loosen around my straining knot and push them down my legs.

Isavelle takes one look at my cock, makes a strangled sound, and then rolls onto her belly and lifts her ass in the air. Her sex is swollen and dripping with her slick. I fall forward over her, planting a hand by her head. Her mating gland on the back of her neck is pink and raised with her heat, a double heart-shaped mark covering her nape, like the wings of a butterfly. So delicate and perfect.

I grasp my cock and notch it into her sex. Isavelle is panting and crying out.

"Please, Alpha. Please, please, pl—*ah.*" She shrieks as I slam into her.

The heat and tightness of her pussy is overwhelming. The sensation of being inside her is so exquisite that it's like the very first time with her. Bright colors burst in my mind, my chest, my knot. Instinct and desire rage through me, and I pull back and thrust again, harder. And then again. There's growling in my ears, and I realize it's mine.

Isavelle cries out my name. *My* name. The name just for her.

"Alpha. More. Please, I can take it."

It's nothing like the sex we've had in the past. A man who is dying of thirst doesn't drink. He gulps and consumes because his life depends on it. My cock is glistening with Isavelle's slick as I draw most of it out of her and then ram it home again. This time she takes me all the way up to my knot and cries out. I fuck her fast and deep, more greedily than I ever have before, but it's still not enough. There's more space inside her that I need to fill. With my cock. With my knot. With my cum. With my baby.

I drag my teeth over her mating gland, and she shrieks with pleasure, her inner muscles rippling along my length.

"Bite me, Alpha. Please bite me. Please knot me."

I wanted everything to be perfect the first time I knotted her and drove my teeth into her flesh. This is a wreck of a first heat, filled with terror and pain and the blood of our enemies. Isavelle doesn't even have a nest. I should wait until I have her safely back at the castle to claim her. I should, but I don't want to. I have my Omega beneath me now, and we're both so deep in the grip of this mating.

"Bite me, Alpha, please. Make me yours."

My purpose crystallizes. Triumph surges through my dragines. My perfect mate.

Mine.

28

Isavelle

Zabriel's breath is hot on the back of my neck. His knot is slamming against me with every stroke. My Alpha has always been so careful when we have sex, but now he's wild and unrestrained. I can feel my body ready to give around him so he can thrust that thick swelling deep inside me. I want it so much I don't know how I'll go on living without it. My climax rushes up to greater heights than it ever has, and I scream his name, but then it's over, and I still want more. I feel like I'm cursed only to need but never be satisfied.

"Alpha, please, *please*—"

Zabriel snarls and grips the back of my neck with his hand, pinching his fingers into my flesh and forcing me to the ground. His cock hammers into me. His knot feels impossibly large, but it's all I want. If he splits me open, I don't care. I'll die happy.

"Good little Omega," Zabriel snarls through his teeth, sounding more like he's threatening me than praising me. "You want my knot, don't you? I'm going to knot you so fucking hard that you'll see stars. You won't be able to leave me. I'll have you. Locked tight to me forever."

His blunt nails scrape across my mating gland, and I wail in pleasure. His hand moves to wrap around my throat. His lips move against my nape. "Good. Fucking. *Omega*." The last syllable is drawn out with a groan as he starts to climax. One thrust and I feel his knot push inside me, but not far enough. My eyes go wide as pleasure-pain flashes through me. A second, ferocious thrust and Zabriel's snarl reverberates through my ears as his massive swelling suddenly breeches my entrance, and he shoves it deep inside me. At the same time, Zabriel opens his mouth and bites down brutally on the back of my neck. I feel his dragines penetrate deep into my flesh.

Everything turns white behind my eyes. I can't breathe. I can't move. Zabriel can't thrust, but he can push into me, working his knot deeper as it expands and floods me with his cum. My belly feels swollen. The knot is rubbing rhythmically on a spot deep inside me, and I feel a climax stronger than I've ever felt before rise up and break over me. I've moved beyond existence. I could stay in this moment forever. Zabriel clenches me ruthlessly tight in his arms, his knot deep inside me. His teeth in my mating gland.

Slowly, Zabriel unclenches his teeth and lifts his head. Just about the whole weight of his massive body is on top of me, but right now, it feels amazing to be pressed down into the grass and moss.

"Omega," Zabriel groans huskily. "Mine. Finally." He

seems dazed and drunken. I barely remember how we came to be here in the grass. I don't know how Zabriel found me, but he did. After so many days of pain, he's here.

He eases onto his side, taking me with him. I twist the top half of my body around so I can look at him. There's blood on his lips and coating his teeth, spicing his beauty with violence. I kiss his panting mouth and taste myself.

He wraps his thick arms around me and keeps me tight against him. "I've got you, Omega. You're safe." He says it over and over again. "I'm not letting you out of my sight."

We lay like that for a long time, soaking in the scent and feel of each other.

His knot inside me feels like it has grown roots, and I don't know how we'll ever get it out, but I don't care. I'm exhausted and lay in his arms.

"Omega. Why were you by this stream?"

"I was thirsty," I confess in a whisper. "The *Hratha'len* locked me up without any water."

Rage ripples through Zabriel. I feel it moving beneath his skin and through his cock. "*Hratha'len*," he bellows. "Where are you?"

"I think they're all gone. I haven't seen anyone but Heloise since the first day, and then just before you came, I heard her scream. It sounded like she was being murdered." I lick my parched lips and try to swallow, but my mouth is dry.

"By the High Priest, I suppose," Zabriel mutters. He eases us closer to the stream and then dips his hand down, scoops up a palmful of water, and holds it to my lips. "Drink, *sha'len*. I'll take care of you now."

The cool water flows past my lips and into my mouth, and

I swallow it down. Zabriel scoops up more, and then a third time.

"More, please," I gasp.

"Not too much all at once. You'll be sick." He uses his wet fingers to gently wipe sweat from my brow and cool my burning flesh.

"How could they let you suffer like this? I can see that the *Hratha'len* haven't been taking care of you."

I shake my head. "I don't know."

Zabriel twists up my hair and examines the back of my neck. "You're bleeding from my bite. Mm." He gives a little hum of appreciation before running his tongue over the ridges of my torn flesh. "This is the scar you'll bear for me always that shows everyone that you're mine. Whenever I see it, I'll remember how perfect this moment was with you."

I touch my nape with a smile, feeling the indentations and ridges. His tongue has soothed the marks and stopped the bleeding.

Zabriel gives an experimental tug with his knot, and we feel it coming loose. He sits up. "I want to see this."

We're both looking down between my legs as he slowly drags his knot out of me. His cock is glistening with my slick, and as soon as his swollen, veiny knot pulls free, it's followed by a gush of cum. Alarming quantities of cum, actually. No wonder my belly felt so full.

"Stars, Zabriel. You must be thirsty as well."

"I'm fine," he says, and I can hear the grin in his voice. "Would you like some more water?"

"Yes, please."

He lets me sip from his palm again, and his lips move against my throat as I swallow. Life feels like it's returning to my body and strength to my hands. He supports my body with his strong arms, and I take a deep inhale of his rutting scent. I moan in pleasure. "I never felt so wonderful before."

I was dangerously close to death not long ago, but Zabriel has brought me back to life. His mouth seeks mine, and a sweet kiss soon becomes a heated one. I roll onto my back and pull him on top of me, his swelling cock protruding between us, the head an urgent shade of purple.

"You want me again? You're not sore or exhausted?" he asks through gritted teeth, ready to let me go and get up if I show the slightest hint of hesitation.

I'm not going to let our enemies ruin this time for us. This is his rut. It's my true heat. This is what we're supposed to be doing.

"Please, Alpha, please," I beg him, making my voice as needy as I can to shred his self-control. He's so beautiful when he lets go.

Zabriel groans and thrusts into me so hard and fast that my insides light up. There's a tiny pinch of pain, but it's soon smothered by pleasure as my Alpha ruts me hard.

His red eyes are gleaming as he gazes down at me. "That's my good Omega. You're so fucking pretty stuffed full of me. Are you going to watch yourself get knotted?"

I moan and place my hands against his hips, feeling him moving, watching his cock as he pumps into me. My fingers drift farther down, and every now and then, I stroke his swelling knot, making Zabriel gasp and swear through his teeth. There's a deep, growling purr in his chest as he gets closer and closer to his climax.

"Want to fuck you constantly," he snarls. "Omega's sweet pussy is mine. Say it. *Say it.*"

"I'm all yours, Alpha."

"Yes. *Yes.*" His thrusting quickens, and his knot swells to alarming proportions. I think I might have panicked if I were watching this the first time. It's going to get even bigger once he shoves it inside me. I watch in pent-up fascination as it slams against me, once, twice, three—

Zabriel snarls a curse word in Maledinni, gives an almighty thrust, and his knot pushes into me. I scream at the sudden, intense intrusion, and then again as Zabriel falls forward over me and buries his dragines into the spot between my neck and my shoulder. His pulsating knot works against the spot behind my clit, and I climax hard, my core clenching around him even though I'm stretched impossibly tight.

"Fuck, yes, come on my knot, Omega." He licks the bite marks left in my flesh and then sinks his teeth into me again. Zabriel keeps thrusting into me, and though he's barely moving, the pressure of his knot makes my orgasm go on and on.

He lets go of me with his teeth and covers my throat with kisses. "You feel how deep your Alpha is inside you? Are you going to have my baby, Omega? You're so full of my cum. Stretched tight around me while I'm locked in tight. I'm making you pregnant right now, I can feel it." His feet find purchase on the ground, and he shoves himself deeper, while I continue to climax and wail, my arms wrapped tight around his neck. He won't stop talking in that way or pushing his knot into me, and I can't stop coming.

"Alpha's good fucking Omega," he says and sinks his teeth into my neck. His teeth are all I need. I can't believe I was ever afraid of them.

My core finally stops clenching around him, and I collapse bonelessly against the ground, my arms above my head and my legs limp. How was the second time even more intense than the first?

Zabriel runs his tongue over my many bite marks. "You're so well fucked, *sha'len*. Just look at you." He strokes his finger down my nose, over my lips, and between my breasts. "That should hold you for a little while once I get my knot out of you."

"How long's a little while?" I pant.

"You see that precipice up there?" he asks, pointing to the cliff overhead. It stands twice as tall as Scourge. "If someone dropped a feather from there and it floated down, you would want me again by the time it settled on the ground."

I laugh, pushing my hair out of my eyes. "I believe you."

His face grows serious. "I want to lie here with you until the swelling in my knot goes down and that feather falls so I can rut you again, but this is not a safe place for us to be."

Together we look at the High Priest's dead body on the ground a short distance away, a grisly reminder that this place belongs to our enemies.

Zabriel is giving an experimental tug on his knot to see if it might pull loose when we hear a muffled noise. Someone calling out, and then a thump.

Both our gazes land on Zabriel's sword, which is lying in the grass several body lengths away from us out of his reach.

"Fuck," he mutters, and pulls sharply on his knot. I feel it tug inside me, but it doesn't move. "Wrap your arms around my neck, *sha'len*."

I do as he asks. Pushing an arm beneath me, he gathers me against his chest and knee-walks us over to his sword so he can grasp the hilt. As he sits up, his knot shifts to a new angle inside me, and I moan in pleasure. A smile tugs on Zabriel's lips as he stares around the glade, sword brandished in his hand.

"*Sha'len*, your little moans are so beautiful."

I look down between my legs. "Doesn't imminent danger and peril make this thing go down?"

Zabriel laughs. "It's too happy where it is. Knots don't give a damn about danger and peril. Knots get Alphas into trouble all the time."

There's another muffled noise, and this time we can clearly tell it's coming from the temple.

Zabriel lowers his sword. "That doesn't sound like someone dangerous. We'll go inside and see who it is as soon as I can stand up." He lays his weapon beside my head and braces himself over me, drinking in the sight of me on my back in the grass. "Did you enjoy your first knottings, Omega?"

I arch my back and stretch my arms over my head. "Dragon's teeth, I did."

Heat and desire flash through his red eyes. "I can't wait to get you into your nest and rut you until we pass out." There's an answering pulse in his knot, and it feels like it's getting bigger again.

"Stop that. We're supposed to be trying to make it go down."

He grins wider, showing his dragines.

It takes a long time for Zabriel's knot to shrink back to a size that means he's able to pull it out of me, probably because the man attached to it insists on sucking on my nipples and whispering dirty things in my ear.

When we're able to stand up and get dressed, Zabriel in his breeches and me in his shirt, my mate holds tight to my hand with his sword held protectively in front of him. We circle the temple first and find Heloise's body lying in the dirt, her throat slit and her eyes wide and glassy.

"The High Priest must have killed her," I tell him.

"She's lucky he got to her before I did," Zabriel growls. "The betrayal. I don't understand it."

We enter the temple, and I point out the room in which I was being held. Inside, the scent of my misery hangs in the air.

"This is what they did to you?" Zabriel asks, his voice trembling with rage. "This isn't a nesting place for a royal Omega. This isn't a nesting place for any Omega. No blankets. No bedclothes. No *nothing*."

"Heloise took them all away from me."

He whirls to face me. "And my cloak? Did she take that from you as well?" I nod. "What did you do for days on end? Where did you hide?"

I point to the dark, dusty place under the bed.

The muscles on Zabriel's forearm bulge as he grips his sword, and his fury banishes even my cloying scent from the room. "I trusted the *Hratha'len* to take care of you as I would take care of you. They'll pay dearly for this so-called ritual."

We explore the rest of the temple, which doesn't take long as there are only a handful of rooms. One door is locked, and Zabriel breaks it down by ramming his shoulder into it. As the door splinters and springs open on its hinges, we discover where the remaining *Hratha'len* have been since the beginning of the ritual. Bound and gagged on the floor of this room.

Zabriel slices through the bonds holding Mother Linnea's wrists behind her back.

"What the fuck has been going on?" he demands.

The Temple Mother sits up, moving slowly as her body is stiff from lying prostrate for so long. She pulls the gag from between her teeth. "*Ma'len*, it was Heloise. She—she seemed to lose her mind after the ritual started. She overpowered us and threw us in here. I was the first to be taken, and I watched as everyone else followed me, one by one, bound and gagged."

Mother Linnea crawls over to Elysant and a Temple Maiden and unties them.

"I was the last to be taken, *Ma'len*," Elysant says tearfully. "My sister spellbreaker tricked me."

Zabriel is breathing hard through his nose, his chest lifting and falling as anger boils through him. "None of you could stop Heloise? None of you, when you all swore to protect Isavelle? Your ritual nearly cost my Omega her life."

The Temple Maiden is staring at the sword gripped in his hand, and she bursts into tears. "*Ma'len*, we're so sorry. We didn't know what Heloise was doing. We were so fright—"

"*Shut. Up,*" Zabriel shouts, and she falls silent. "Wrap up Heloise's body and the priest's body. Take them back to Lenhale and wait for me in the Flame Temple." As they get to their feet, he adds, "Stay away from my mate. If I see one *Hratha'len* priestess before my rut is over, you'll all pay dearly."

Zabriel picks me up with one hand and holds me against his chest. I wrap my arms around his neck as he strides from the room and out into the fresh air. For some time, he paces up and down by the stream, inhaling my scent and struggling to get his temper under control. I stroke the back of his neck and press kisses to his throat.

Finally, he stops pacing and presses a kiss to my lips, and his eyes are no longer burning like dragonfire.

"Where does my Omega wish to be? I'll take you anywhere. Give you anything that I can."

I think about it for a moment. "Take me to my nest in the castle. I want to be there with you."

"Then that's where we shall go." He carries me out of the glade to where Scourge and Esmeral are waiting for us. Esmeral greets me with loud, relieved cries and much spreading and flapping of her wings.

Zabriel carries me up onto Scourge, and we all head for home. I don't want to think about the fact that the *Hratha'len* are all there, or that I might have even more enemies within the castle. I huddle deep inside my Alpha's cloak and press myself against his chest. As long as I'm with Zabriel, I'm safe.

29

———

Zabriel

Isavelle falls asleep in my arms after just a few minutes in the air. I draw my cloak around her as we fly, protecting her from the frigid wind. My poor, exhausted, half-starved mate.

I carry my sleeping Omega into the castle. I would prefer it if everyone left us alone, but it seems as though word has spread that the king flew off in a rage on his dragon to bring his Omega home. Dozens of people arrive in the corridor from the Great Hall, the courtyard, the kitchens, and the Flame Temple.

One of Isavelle's former Veiled Virgin friends who is now her lady's maid picks up her skirts and runs toward me. Santha, that's her name.

"Oh, poor Lady Isavelle." Santha reaches for my mate. "What happened to her, *Ma'len*?"

"Don't touch her," I snarl, and she flinches back. I distrust everyone, and I will continue to distrust everyone until my rut passes and I can figure out what the hell has been going on.

"No one approaches my mate on pain of death," I announce to everyone in the corridor. My growl reverberates off stone. "Now *move*."

Everyone draws back against the walls, leaving a path for me.

I take Isavelle into her nesting room, place her on the bed, and heap blankets on top of her. The room is cold, but at least it's dark and silent. I'll make it perfect for her. I'll erase the memory of that horrible bare room where my mate shivered and cried for days on end. She must have felt like the world had forgotten about her and everyone hated her. My heart aches at the thought.

Isavelle's eyes open, and she looks around. "My nest." Her gaze lands on me. "Zabriel, you brought me home," she breathes, then draws her face down to mine. I kiss her, tucking the blankets even more tightly around her.

"You're safe now. Close your eyes. I'm going to light a fire, and then I have to leave you alone for a very short while, but I'll lock the door behind me. Rest now."

She whimpers and holds tight to my hand, reluctant to let me go, but soon her exhaustion overwhelms her, and lulled by the cozy blankets and darkness, she drifts off to sleep.

Once the fire is lit and the flames are dancing, I step out into the corridor and lock the door behind me, slipping the key into my pocket. When I turn around, I see Stesha leaning against the wall with his arms folded, staring straight again.

"What do you want?" I growl.

"Me? Nothing."

"Then what are you doing here?"

"I thought you might need me."

"I don't need anyone."

For once, Stesha doesn't snap and snarl. "You need things if you're going to stay in that room until your rut passes. Go get them, and I'll wait here." He nods at the locked door. "I blade swore with you. You protect mine. I protect yours."

Right now, I don't want anyone near my mate. I wish I could barricade her into a room with tons of stone, but I can't, and Stesha's right. I need food and water for Isavelle. He guessed that leaving her unprotected even for a short while is making me tense.

When I don't answer, Stesha's jaw flexes, and he moves to leave. "It's fine. I understand that you can't trust me."

"Wait."

Stesha hesitates. My mind is an angry snarl, but I have to trust someone. "That ritual was torture for my mate from beginning to end. She nearly died. I don't know what the fuck is going on, but the *Hratha'len* are not allowed anywhere near Isavelle."

Stesha nods sharply and settles back with his shoulders against the wall.

I go to the kitchens and gather food onto a tray myself, as it's the only way I can be sure it's safe for Isavelle to eat and drink. I ignore everyone around me, and they have the good sense to pretend I'm not there either.

I hurry back to Isavelle, and I'm relieved to see that the door is still closed and Stesha hasn't moved from his position. As I reach into my pocket for the key, he peels away from the wall and turns.

"Stesha. Thank you," I call after him.

"Don't thank me. I should have said what I really wanted to say at that meeting, which was that everyone should fuck off and leave you and your Omega alone."

I watch him stride away down the corridor. If he had, it probably wouldn't have made any difference. The Temple Crone was adamant that it was the only way to help Omegas like Ravenna, and Isavelle took that deeply to heart.

The fire has made Isavelle's room warm and cozy. I peek through the bed-curtains and see my mate sleeping restlessly with pink cheeks and a small line between her brows.

I place the tray of fruit, cold meats, and bread on the bedside table, strip off all my clothes, and get into the nest with Isavelle. She inhales and awakens immediately.

"Alpha. You feel so good, Alpha." Her hand slides down and grips my knot, and my eyelashes flutter. I want to fuck her, but in a moment. She needs to eat. I fumble through the bed-curtains and pick up a bowl full of nectar plums in syrup and a spoon.

"Eat this," I tell her, holding the spoon to her lips. "It's a preserved nectar plum. Sweet and cold."

She opens her mouth, and as I feed her a bite, the juice stains her dry lips. I smother a groan and lick it off, remembering how I licked her sex in this way.

"Would you like another? Some water?" She shakes her head, not wanting either, but I pick up the cup of water and hold it to her lips. "Just drink a little, for me."

She takes a sip and then lifts her thigh over me to climb astride my thighs. Her slick coats my shaft. I barely have time to put everything back on the bedside table before she sinks down my length.

I throw my head back in pleasure "Gods, you feel incredible."

I hold her breasts as she works herself up and down my shaft, moaning every time her sex hits my knot. She seems to be trying to work it inside herself, but she hasn't got the strength, and I'm deliberately not helping her. It's wonderful seeing her moving like this. I love when my Omega is this hungry for me.

"I can't do it. Help me," she begs breathlessly.

I take pity on her, grasp hold of her waist, and begin to thrust up into her. "Is this what you want?"

"Yes, Alpha, yes." She grips my wrists with both hands, her eyes closed, her lips parted as I thrust harder and harder. The blankets are heaped up around us and the canopied bed is filled with both of our scents. This is the heat that I wanted to give her. Safe and warm and cozy while I knot her over and over.

I push my heels into the mattress and thrust up into her with a shout while I pull her tightly down on my knot. Isavelle cries out sharply as I'm forced inside of her, and I draw her down into my arms so I can sink my aching teeth into her shoulder.

She relaxes and melts against my chest, my knot deep inside her. Safe at last, she finally falls into a doze.

I'm still knotting her and making her drink water several sunsets and sunrises later. She's still slicking and perfuming and feverish with her heat. "It's been seven days. Your heat should have ended after three days. Five at the most."

Isavelle grinds the heel of her hand into her eye and irritably pushes her hair back. "Heloise gave me tea to drink. She insisted that it was the same tea as always, but it tasted strange. Perhaps it was something to make my heat more intense instead of soothing it."

"That would make sense," I growl through my teeth. That vile bitch. A stronger heat while my Omega was exposed, dehydrated, and starving. It would have finished her off faster. "I wish I could bring you some of your usual tea to drink, but I don't trust the *Hratha'len* right now."

"I don't need them. I feel fine apart from needing you so, so much." She supplicates me with her eyes. "I'm sorry, Alpha."

I sit up in outrage. "You think I can't fuck you? You think The Flame King would leave his Omega wanting?" My rut might be over, but the scent of my Omega's heat is all it takes to make me hard. I can battle in full armor for days on end. Fly to the limits of my country and back without rest. Intimidate my enemies until they run away screaming. If my Omega needs to be fucked for a ten-day, by the gods, I can do that too.

I'M LIMPING as I leave Isavelle's nesting room four days later. I'm chafed in places that I wouldn't like to admit, and my thighs ache from fatigue. Isavelle's heat lasted thirteen days, and she needed me constantly for every single one that I spent with her. Her temperature has returned to normal, and she's finally, mercifully, sleeping soundly. For her sake. Merciful for her sake. I was absolutely fine, of course. I could have lasted another ten days. Twenty, if anyone asks.

I rest my palm against the door, shove my hand down the

front of my breeches, and push the fabric away from my poor aching knot. I groan in relief.

"She finally let you up for air, *Ma'len*?"

Dusan grins at me. Fiala is by his side, her eyes trained resignedly on the ceiling. Both of them are dressed in their wingrunner uniforms and holding their halberds.

I yank my hand out of my pants. "Yes, Lady Isavelle's heat has ended. She's sleeping peacefully. I need to speak with the Temple Crone."

"May we stand guard by this door and guard Lady Isavelle in your absence, *Ma'len*?" Fiala asks, and the stout, dour woman is suddenly fighting back tears. "We thought we'd never see her again."

I hesitate, looking at the key to Isavelle's door in my hand. I lock it and pass the key to Fiala. "No one but me, and I mean *no one*, is to unlock this door and pass over this threshold. Not the two of you. Not even Lady Isavelle."

"No one, *Ma'len*," Fiala swears fiercely. "We will guard her with our lives."

Fiala and Dusan would have stopped Heloise if they'd been allowed to protect Isavelle during the ritual. My mate was completely friendless.

I turn and head down the corridor but then turn back to them. "I shouldn't have separated the three of you. You would never have allowed my mate to suffer as she did. I regret it. I will always regret it."

Fiala shakes her head. "You were trying to do your best for Maledin, *Ma'len*. We see everything you do. How hard you work. How much you care."

"That's why we're devoted to you," Dusan adds, and for once, there's not a trace of irony or joking on his face.

A strange, warm sensation twines around my heart. They're devoted to me? I've inspired their devotion, despite making mistakes both foolish and disastrous? Despite the fact that our enemy is my own brother, and I've so far failed to defeat him?

"That's... You're both..." I scrub my hand over my face, words failing me. It's been the most exhausting rut of my life. "Thank you."

When I enter the Flame Temple, all the Temple Maidens and Mothers bow their heads, but not in respect or greeting. They keep their heads bowed from shame.

As they fucking should.

The Temple Crone makes her way across the enormous black stone floor toward me. The lines on her face are etched deeper than usual, and somehow, her spirit visibly sags. It seems as though she hasn't been sleeping well. With her head bent, she says, "We failed *Ma'len's* mate. There is endless sorrow in our hearts."

"I don't want your sorrow. I want you to explain yourselves."

The Temple Crone beckons Elysant forward. The spellbreaker's eyes are swollen with crying, and her cheeks are thin. "Spellbreaker Elysant, tell *Ma'len* what you have told me."

The spellbreaker relates the same events that Isavelle has told me. "After we arrived at the temple and *Ma'len's* mate entered the chamber, Heloise ceased calling her *Ma'len's* mate and referred to her as *the witch*. She overpowered us one by one and tied us up."

My brows draw together in a hard frown. "She called

Isavelle the witch? Why? Does Heloise have a hatred of witches?"

Elysant bites her lip. "I think she must have, but I had no idea. She never said so, and now she's... Now she's...dead." Her face creases as she sobs, and her shoulders quake.

I watch her without a shred of sympathy in my heart. She cries for a traitor. Elysant should have realized how Heloise felt about Isavelle and spoke with the Temple Crone, or at least stopped Heloise when she went mad and tried to kill my mate.

"*Ma'len*," the Temple Crone says softly. "We have kept Heloise's body, and that of the Brethren priest who killed her. Do you wish to see them, or may they be laid to rest?"

Elysant looks up hopefully. "May we give Heloise dragon rites so that she may beg the gods' forgiveness for what she has done?"

"No," I say coldly. "She may not have that privilege. Take their bodies into the Bodan Mountains and let their bones be picked over by carrion."

The spellbreaker turns away, nodding tearfully. "Yes, *Ma'len*."

One of the Temple Maidens approaches me with a tray bearing a pot of tea and a cup. She trembles as I glare at her. "To soothe your mate, *Ma'len*."

I stare at the pot and cup. I don't want it near my mate. I don't want any of them near my mate. I have always honored the *Hratha'len*, and I believed they would honor my mate. Something here is rotten, and I don't know if it was just Heloise or if there's more to this that I cannot yet see.

"Throw it out." I turn on my heel and leave the temple.

30

Isavelle

While I'm in heat, there's blessedly little to think about. My thoughts are consumed by Zabriel. My hunger for him. Zabriel. The fresh teeth marks in the nape of my neck. Zabriel. The blissful sensation of fullness every time he knots me. Zabriel.

Zabriel.

Zabriel.

I suspect I'm close to wearing him out by being so demanding, but my Alpha will swallow hot coals before he leaves his Omega unsatisfied. I lose track of time. My heat lasts so long that I can't remember not being gripped by the desire to wrap my arms and legs around my mate and cling to him while he fucks me through an orgasm. When the sight of my Alpha didn't make me instantly roll onto my belly and present myself to him.

Slowly, after many days, I fall into longer and longer dozes. I can form a coherent thought every now and then. I can say sentences that aren't, *Please, Alpha, please, please, please.*

Finally, I awaken one afternoon and haven't slicked myself in my sleep. Zabriel's not in my nest, but I don't immediately want to wail because he isn't here. The dark, hot, coziness of my nest feels stifling rather than safe. I sit up and push open the bed curtains, blinking in the dim light, but the desire to dive back beneath my many dozens of blankets doesn't overwhelm me, so I sit up.

I gaze for a long time at my bare feet on the rug, my head sluggish, attempting to recount all that has happened. The Ritual of the First Heat. What the hell was that? That wasn't the ritual that the *Hratha'len* Temple Crone described to Zabriel and me. It seemed more like Heloise was trying to kill me. She very nearly did kill me. She might have been coming to finish me off when the High Priest found her and killed her.

I squeeze my eyes shut as the memory of him standing over me blazes to life in my mind, reaching to undo his robes with a manic gleam in his eyes. The terror was paralyzing. I couldn't make myself move. All my strength and will to fight had been sapped by days and days of miserable heat. I never imagined I'd ever again feel so powerless while cowering before him. The *Hratha'len* were trying to kill me, and he was going to finish the job.

Then Zabriel was there. Wonderfully, improbably there, and I still don't know how.

I lift my gaze and look at the door. Zabriel has spoken with the *Hratha'len*, and while he's no closer to understanding what happened or forgiving them, he's had extra guards posted around the castle and given my bodyguards instructions that I'm never to be alone.

I can go out there if I wish. Zabriel has finally given me the key to the room.

I should probably go out there.

Yet I'm still sitting here wishing for Zabriel's strong arms around me and his deep voice purring in my ear. That kind of craving is just fine when I'm in heat, but it's over now, and I have to stand on my own two legs.

Holding on to the bedpost, I pull myself to my feet. My legs are shaky. Zabriel coaxed me to eat and drink between knotting and biting me, but I had no appetite at all during my heat. There's a platter of food on a side table, and I eat fruit, cheese, and bread until my stomach stops rumbling.

Fiala and Dusan are outside my door when I unlock and open it, and the sight of them makes a smile break over my face. I embrace them both, hugging them as hard as I can, and my heart swells with gratitude.

"I don't ever want to be without either of you," I whisper.

"We will never let anyone hurt you again," Fiala says fiercely. "Neither will *Ma'len*. I'm so sorry, Lady Isavelle."

"We'll take you anywhere you want to go," Dusan says eagerly. "Amriste, the dragongrounds, into the city, you name it."

There are many places I should go, but there's only one place that's calling to me right now. I dreamed about the lost villagers while I was in my nest. Not a vision, but it has reminded me that I need to focus on them. There's nothing else that feels more important right now.

"Actually, can you take me to my chamber? I promise I

will want to go somewhere more interesting soon," I add quickly as Dusan's face falls.

"Of course, Lady Isavelle. Anywhere you need to go," Fiala assures me.

As we pass Zenevieve's door, I knock on it, but there's no answer. "How's Zenevieve?"

"Much improved, my lady," Dusan tells me. "We've seen her meditating in the temple and down at the dragongrounds."

"There is color in her cheeks again, and I have even seen her smiling," Fiala adds.

"That is good news. I'm happy to hear it."

I bid goodbye to my bodyguards at the bedroom door. When I go inside, I head straight for the box where I keep Emmeric's amulet.

With the crystal in my hands, I lay back on the bed with my eyes closed.

"Send me a vision," I whisper, to no one and nothing in particular. "Show me where my father and sister are. Show me the missing villagers. Give me something."

In my exhaustion, I feel that spider's silk thread of consciousness brush against mine. Instead of grabbing hold of it as I have the other times, I gently drift toward it, and instead of dissipating, I sense it thickening and growing stronger. I feel my heartbeat quicken but coax myself to lie very still in my body and my mind. The thread is a little bird I mustn't startle with any sudden movements.

I lay there for a long time, my body present in the room but my mind drifting further and further away. I don't follow the thread. I meander in its general direction, inching closer in slow increments. In the distance, from whence the thread originates, I hear a voice, indistinct as if it's underwater.

"...aster...ree...it...unish..."

As I draw closer, I can see nothing in the void but the soft glisten of the thread, but the voice grows louder. It sounds like someone or something muttering angrily to himself.

"The brazen little destroyer and her mate. We made them hurt. We made them suffer. Now they are dead. *Dead.*" There's a brief cackle of laughter before the angry ranting starts up again. "The brazen little destroyer. Her mate. The black prince. The white master. The green-eyed bitch. They must be punished. They must *all* die."

The person seems to be reciting a list of enemies, and their rasping voice is familiar. I've heard it once before, but I can't remember when. I wonder if this is a vision I'm having, or if it's something else. I lift my hand before my eyes to see if I can snap my fingers as Biddy Hawthorne told me to do, only it's too dark here, or I don't have a hand.

"The green-eyed bitch lost her mind, and she should have lost her head. You promised he would kill her. You *lied.*"

I strain for a reply. This person seems to be talking to someone, but no one is answering.

"Failures. Too many failures. You said they would never come back."

It's not Emmeric's voice, but I heard it at his tower. Frustration and curiosity make me mentally dart toward it, but it's a mistake.

Green fire expands in the darkness. Green fire in the shape of eyes. "Who's there?"

I gasp in surprise and sit up. As my heart thunders in my ears, I realize I'm in my bedroom, still clutching the crystal to my chest. My connection to whoever was speaking is broken. I lie back down and close my eyes, trying to find that thread once more, but it's gone.

Was it real, or was it a trick? I can't tell if what I heard was real or something sent to manipulate me, but I don't feel manipulated. I feel confused.

I swing my legs out of bed, push the amulet into my pocket, and go in search of Zabriel, escorted by Fiala and Dusan.

I find my mate in the semi-deserted Great Hall, in the company of Mother Linnea. He's glowering at her from his immense height, and she has her hands tucked into her sleeves with her head bowed. Zabriel is half turned away from her in the manner of someone who doesn't want to speak to her and is waiting impatiently for her to finish what she came to say. His sparking red eyes land on me.

"I understand all that, Mother," he tells her, his tone curt. "But you must see why I do not trust my mate with you. Any of you. Excuse me."

Leaving the Temple Mother behind, Zabriel takes two long steps toward me and sweeps me into his arms. His scent cascades over me as his lips descend toward mine, and he covers my mouth with a searing kiss. It occurs to me that his kisses might feel lackluster after the intensity of my heat, but that split-second thought is banished by the heavenly feel of his tongue running against mine and the possessive bite of his teeth in my lower lip.

"What did Mother Linnea want?" I ask, gasping slightly. My bodyguards have melted into the background to give us our private moments, as they always do when I'm with Zabriel.

"She was bleating the same things as the rest of them," he mutters, taking my hand and walking me out into the fresh air. "That the *Hratha'len* are still loyal to me, and they love us both. Heloise was acting on her own interests, not theirs." He pinches between his eyes with a growl. "It's not that I disbelieve her, but my anger is too raw, and I have no satisfactory explanation why Heloise would turn on you. Until I do, they must keep their distance or suffer my fury." Zabriel's angry gaze softens as it lands on me, and a smile touches his lips. "It is good to see you out of your nest and walking around. Not that I don't love to see my Omega cozy in her nest, but I was starting to worry."

"I feared I was beginning to wear you out."

"Absolutely not. I could have gone on for a year." Zabriel tries to look stern, but his lips twist into a smile. "Better a feast than a famine. After craving you for so long, after hoping for my Omega for a decade of my life, I shan't utter one word of complaint when my Omega begs for my knot over and over." He slides his fingers beneath my hair and across the nape of my neck, and a dreamy expression comes into his eyes. "I love my teeth marks in you. Do you know that? I haven't said it nearly enough."

Beneath my hands, his muscles flex as he gathers me closer to him. "Say it again," I whisper.

Zabriel's eyes blaze red. "My teeth belong in your flesh," he growls, and then he gives me another kiss that's spiced with his teeth.

"What happens next?" I ask between presses of his mouth. "With us, I mean. Officially."

"Officially? You're my bride, and we will celebrate our union in the not-very-distant future. Maledinni weddings are days-long affairs, especially when they're royal weddings. After the wedding, you will have your own coronation, and I'll finally get to see my beautiful queen wearing her crown." His lips curve into a smile and he cups my belly. "And you'll get pregnant, hopefully soon. Dragon's blood, the sight of you wearing a crown and sitting on a throne with a swollen belly—" He breaks off with a groan and kisses me again.

I can see that in my mind's eye, and it does look beautiful, but another image replaces it. "What I'm imagining and anticipating is a little more private and intimate. You and me in bed, and you're deep inside me while my belly's swollen."

Zabriel moans in longing and swipes his tongue across the side of my throat and my still-tender mating gland. "Perfect," he breathes. "Wonderful. Absolutely beautiful."

What did I come to speak with Zabriel about? Suddenly I can't remember. Something hard is pressing against my thigh. His knot, but something else as well.

"Oh!" I cry, dipping my hand into the pocket of my dress and drawing out the amulet. "This is what I came to speak with you about."

Zabriel shoots the object an irritated look. "Tell me more about us in bed while your belly is swollen with my baby. I want to talk about how sweetly I'll fuck my pregnant queen."

"So sweetly," I say, pressing my lips to his. "You'll hold me so beautifully in my arms and make me feel so safe and loved. But, Zabriel—"

"So safe. So protected. All mine." Zabriel's pupils are blown, and now they're more black than red.

"I was saying..."

But Zabriel's too far gone in this fantasy, and he doesn't

hear a word I say. He lifts me up in his arms, carries me inside the castle, and turns down a deserted corridor.

"Someone might walk along here and see us," I whisper, but I'm unfastening the front of my dress so he can suck on my nipples. Suddenly I'm aching for him.

"They won't. Your bodyguards," Zabriel mutters, too busy laving my breasts with his tongue to speak in full sentences. He pushes up my skirt and unlaces and yanks down his breeches. The head of his cock slides through my slick sex, and I feel a blaze of need for him. He buries the shaft of his cock inside me with a groan. After just a handful of thrusts, I feel his knot slamming against me.

"Do you want my knot?"

"But I'm not in heat."

Zabriel drags his teeth over my throat, making me see stars. "Doesn't matter. You can take it whenever you want to now."

My eyes widen in surprise. "I can?"

His tongue flicks my lips, and he repeats, "If you want to."

I want to.

I feel that ache inside me that tells me I want more of him. Not as fiercely as I feel it during heat, but it's there, and I want him to fill it.

"Please, Alpha."

"Anything for you, Omega."

Gravity pulls me down on him as he thrusts upward. Zabriel drives me higher and higher until my climax breaks over me. My Alpha groans and squeezes me tight in his arms, the hammering of his cock growing more urgent until, with one mighty thrust, I feel his knot push into me and expand. It's even more intense than when I'm in heat.

I cry out loudly before remembering where we are and stuffing his shirt into my mouth. I go on wailing around the fabric while Zabriel pushes my hair aside and bites the nape of my neck.

Zabriel grips me tightly with his dragines, his hot breath on my skin. Slowly he releases me.

As I raise my head, I realize we're in a corridor, and we're locked tight together. His knot isn't going anywhere, which means we aren't either. "Oh, no. What are we going to do now?"

Zabriel laughs softly, turns around so his back is against the wall, and slides down until his long legs are splayed out in front of him and I'm sitting in his lap. "We'll wait here together."

It's so warm and cozy in his arms, and I settle with my cheek against his chest. My eyes are just beginning to close when I remember why I sought my mate out in the first place. I sit up and draw the amulet out of my pocket.

"I was meditating on this crystal, and I heard something. Can you tell me if these words mean anything to you? *The brazen little destroyer. Her mate. The black prince. The white master. The green-eyed bitch. They must die.*"

Zabriel is falling into a doze, but he opens his eyes, and his brows draw together in puzzlement. "Who must die? Who said that to you?"

"I don't know. I overheard it, somehow, like the person was talking to himself. I thought the black prince might mean you, and the white master could be referring to Stesha, but I have no clue who the other people might be."

Zabriel gazes at the amulet. "I never heard anyone call me the black prince, and Stesha has always been *dragonmaster.*"

"I thought it was Emmeric speaking, but it didn't sound like him. Once, he spoke that way when I was in his castle, and for a moment, he didn't look like Emmeric either. It was like something took him over. When he grabbed hold of me, his hands were cold."

Zabriel rests his head back against the wall as he thinks. "The green-eyed bitch. A woman with green eyes. That could be you, but the brazen little destroyer and her mate? I have no idea."

"Why call you the black prince and not the black king? And if it was Emmeric I heard, why not call you by your name?"

"The white master and the green-eyed bitch," Zabriel murmurs. "Maybe that's referring to Stesha and Zenevieve. Her eyes were once green. Perhaps...wait, what do you mean, something took him over?"

I recall that moment in Emmeric's tower. "It was very strange. Emmeric's face changed and his voice changed. His eyes glowed green. He said something about his enemies. He called you a boy with the black dragon and mentioned the girl who has lost her mind. That you were his vilest enemies."

"Me and Zenevieve, his vilest enemies? I can understand Emmeric's hatred of me, but Zenevieve never did a thing to..." Zabriel's face goes blank with shock. "You said Emmeric felt cold?"

"Ice cold."

Zabriel seizes my upper arms. "The brazen little destroyer and her mate, is that what he said? The black prince. The white master. The green-eyed bitch. The five of us who were mentioned? You're certain it was just the five of us?"

"Yes, completely certain. He repeated it several times. What does it mean?"

Zabriel pushes his hand through his hair, his expression bewildered. When he speaks, it's to himself more than to me. "This magic he possesses isn't like dragon magic. It's someone, something else's magic. He could have flown back there on Shar after we all returned to Lenhale. He was so curious. So captivated by power, and we never checked if there was a body. *Stupid.*"

Now Zabriel's completely lost me.

Zabriel pulls back his sleeve and shows me his right forearm. "Do you see these scars on my arm? You may not have noticed them as they're very faint. How strange that I was thinking of that day not so long ago."

As he turns his arm back and forth, very faint silvery lines catch the light, and I stroke my fingers over them. "I never noticed before. How did you get them?"

"Once, when I was young and stupid, I stuck my arm into the air while Scourge was breathing fire. We were on a mission in the mountains to destroy a lich's phylactery."

I frown in confusion. "A what's what?"

He explains that a lich is an undead sorcerer that keeps a piece of its soul tethered to this plane inside an object, and if its body is destroyed, it can use the extra piece of its soul to resurrect itself.

"Six of us went into the mountains on our dragons. Mirelle and her mate, Onderz. Me. Stesha. Zenevieve." His gaze darkens. "And Emmeric. Mirelle and her dragon Dianthe destroyed the phylactery. *The brazen little destroyer.* Scourge and I killed the lich, or we thought we did. I was burned, and I spent weeks in the

Flame Temple recovering and forgot all about that day. But what if the lich didn't die? What if it was only injured or hiding? What if Emmeric flew back to the lich's lair, and he encountered it and it possessed him? It's possible, isn't it? Tell me I'm not crazy."

"I don't know if it's possible, but it's compelling. Emmeric wields strange and powerful magic that he must have learned somewhere. His nasty, rasping voice and cold, dead-feeling fingers didn't seem human. If he's undead, it explains why he's survived this long. If you all destroyed the lich's phylactery, I can believe it wants revenge. Mirelle and Onderz are dead. You lost your parents and your country. Zenevieve has been through gods know what, and Stesha has been beating his head bloody and going on suicide missions. If you're right, it's even more urgent that we stop him before he manages to kill you all."

I wriggle in Zabriel's lap, and I'm able to ease myself off his knot.

Zabriel laces up his breeches, gathers me into his arms, and stands up. "If Emmeric is a lich, then we have to find his new phylactery, destroy it along with Emmeric, and make sure the lich's soul really is banished this time."

I consider this. "I have been wondering about the *riestas*. He ripped out Damla's soul core, but it must have been for a reason. I wonder if he's harnessing the power of dragon magic somehow. Maybe he's done this to other dragons over the years. Minta, or perhaps from wild dragons."

Zabriel nods as he carries me outside. "Something has been keeping my brother alive for all these centuries, and he wanted you far away from Shar as soon as possible. You could be right, *sha'len*."

As we emerge into the sunshine, Zabriel takes a deep breath and gazes around. Then he turns to me.

"We must plan what comes next. Our wedding and your coronation, or sending word to Kane and blasting a hole in that barrier for my army to pass through?"

I want to be wedded to Zabriel. I want to be his queen, but how can I greet the people with a crown on my head while so many people from western Maledin are missing, including my father and sister? "I want us to defeat Emmeric first. I want the country to be whole and my family home before I celebrate our wedding."

I hunt Zabriel's expression for any sign of misgiving or disappointment, but he cups my cheek and kisses me.

"I love that, *sha'len*. Let's bring them home."

31

Isavelle

A lich. What if Emmeric is a lich?

In matters of magic, I feel hopelessly clueless, but I've been making new and unlikely friends who can help me understand. On a crispy and sunny morning, Zenevieve and I walk side by side through the city, with Fiala and Dusan following behind us.

"What a beautiful morning. I always enjoyed springtime in Lenhale." Zenevieve smiles at bulbs spearing through the ground wherever there is a patch of earth. All the ice and snow has melted, and blossoms are budding on the trees. A few more sunny days, and spring will burst forth.

I tiredly rub my eyes, trying to appreciate the sight as much as my friend. I didn't sleep much the previous night. After deciding with Zabriel to focus on defeating Emmeric and bringing home the missing villagers, I tried harder and harder to uncover where he hid them. My fear is that if we kill Emmeric before finding them, they could all be lost forever, which means poor Ravenna is trapped with Kane until the villagers are home.

Hour after hour I sat cross-legged, gripping the amulet, but nothing came to me. Even the silk-like thread that connected the amulet to Emmeric seems to have vanished. I wonder if he finally realized the object was being used to spy on him and severed the connection.

"You're feeling better?" I ask.

"I feel like I am myself for the first time in my life." Zenevieve takes a long, appreciative look around at the city streets as if she's seeing them with new eyes. "Everything looks new. Smells fresh. Tastes interesting. I seem to be on the cusp of something. It's like I might get my memories back at any moment." Her smile dims. "Which is terrifying, when I stop to think about it."

It's strange to wish for something that you fear. In the back of my mind, I worry that if I see a vision of my father and sister and the missing villagers, they'll all be dead.

"How do you think Ravenna is?" Zenevieve asks.

I glance eastward at the empty skies. I wish I knew anything that's happening in the east, but no one is permitted to travel there. "Ravenna survived all these years as a witch. I have to believe she can hold on a little longer."

Zenevieve's expression grows rueful. "The moment I laid eyes on her, I wished she'd never come. I feel terrible about that. Kane seems like an animal."

"Worse than an animal. A monster." I can't comprehend what it must be like to be hated by the man you call Alpha.

"Can I ask how people in the capital felt about witches in your time?"

Zenevieve muses on this for a moment. "Honestly? We didn't think about them all that much. There weren't any witches in the capital. They lived out there among the hedges and fields."

"But if the dragonriders were asked what they thought about witchcraft, what might they say?"

"A dragonrider would probably say that the only magic worth anything was dragon magic. But I don't believe that anymore. I'm grateful to the *Hratha'len* for taking such good care of me these past few weeks, but your crone is the one who has healed me." Zenevieve clasps her hands to her chest and gazes down as if marveling at herself. "Something's... gone, and I don't miss it. I'm full of new possibilities."

I almost say, *Please tell Stesha because he hates that my crone helped you*, but Zenevieve is in such a good mood that I don't want to spoil it by bringing him up. "Do all dragonriders feel that way? Zabriel is a dragonrider, and he always addressed my crone respectfully as *grandmother*, even before she was my crone. He's believed my visions when I've had them and has never spoken against me learning witchcraft."

"Zabriel is a tolerant man with a good heart. Not all are made the same. Also, it helps that he adores you with every breath he takes."

I smile to myself. He does, as I adore him.

As we walk, I keep an eye out for more of those posters railing against me and demanding that I be burned at the stake, but thankfully there are none in sight.

"Do you think I can win over the people in Maledin who still distrust witches?" I ask.

"I honestly don't know. After the ritual of your first heat, there's a great deal of talk about you. You might be a witch, but you're a Maledinni first, and what does a Maledinni do?"

"Tell me."

Zenevieve smiles. "Survive. Prevail. Five hundred years of being locked away can't keep us down, so neither will a few superstitions."

I can only hope that I catch some of Zenevieve's optimism.

"Is there anything in particular you wish to speak with the magical archivists about?" she asks me.

"There is, actually." When I bumped into Zenevieve on my way out of the castle, I told her where I was going but not why. I relate to her my conversation with Zabriel, and our theory that Emmeric is a lich. "Zabriel told me of a day when a group of you went into the mountains to hunt down a lich. You were in the party. Do you remember?"

She nods, her expression troubled. "I remember it well because it was one of my first proper missions as a trainee dragonrider. I was so proud and excited when Stesha asked me if I'd like to accompany him and the other Alphas. Mirelle came with us as well, and the poor thing was terrified by the thought of a lich, of getting in the way of the dragonmaster's temper, that she would mess up and Emmeric would laugh at her. But she and Dianthe did well. Zabriel believes that the lich survived, and Emmeric went back alone and became possessed?" She pauses, searching her memory, and then sighs in frustration. "I wish I could remember anything from my time with Emmeric that might help you confirm or refute this idea."

While we're talking, a boy of seventeen or eighteen

approaches us and calls me by name. "Lady Isavelle? Is it Lady Isavelle herself?"

His expression is hopeful until Fiala and Dusan step in front of me and brandish their weapons in his face. The boy isn't armed that I can see, and his manner is sweet and puppyish. I place a hand on Fiala's shoulder, and they lower their weapons but don't draw back just yet.

"Yes, I'm Isavelle. You're not from Lenhale, are you?"

The boy's shoes are muddy and worn as if he's traveled a great distance, and his clothes are woven from a cloth I've never seen before and cut in an unusual style.

"I'm not, Lady Isavelle," the boy says, a hesitant smile spreading over his face once more. "I hoped that I would meet you, and here you are passing me in the street not a day after I've arrived. There's something I wanted to ask you." He takes a breath as if steeling his nerves, and then asks, "Can—can boys be Omegas as well?"

"I believe so. Yes, I'm sure they can. Not long ago I met a dragon who is a boy and he..." The sweet scent of honey cakes, cut grass, and orange blossoms washes over me. It's coming from the boy. I seize his hands with a cry of delight. "You are an Omega! How wonderful." I take a deep breath, and I'm certain of it. This is the third Maledinni Omega in the country.

The boy's grin is huge now, and his blond curls bounce as he talks. "I didn't know what was happening to me. My body was behaving so strangely, and I couldn't speak with anyone about it, and I was so ashamed and confused. Then I heard about heats and um, knots." He whispers the word and blushes. "Alphas and Omegas. Your mate, the king and his dragines. The ritual has been all anyone can talk about."

My throat feels thick with emotion. "Really? People have been talking about the ritual? From how far have you come?"

"I hail from Tenelva, my lady. A small village in the hills above Bister where we dye thread and weave fabric. It's a remote part of the country, but three times a week, traders come to buy our goods, and with them comes news from the capital. Your ritual was on everyone's lips. I couldn't get enough of hearing about it, and then word came that something went wrong. The king was hunting for you. I left that day to travel here, and all along my route, the only things I heard were about you and *Ma'len*. We were all afraid for you and hoped that *Ma'len* would find you safe and sound." He smiles at me, uncertain but sweet. "And here you are, my lady. I am graced to see you with my own eyes, looking so well."

Every time I think of the ritual, my heart shrivels, and my mood turns black. I've felt nothing but anger and regret, anger at the *Hratha'len* for the suffering they caused me and my mate, and regret that Zabriel and I let anyone separate us. "It means so much to me that you are standing before me, and that you speak such kind and hopeful words. I started to believe that the ritual was all for nothing."

He shakes his head urgently. "No, my lady. Don't think that even for a moment. Because of you, I felt courage enough to tell a dozen of my fellow travelers why I was journeying to the capital, and I wrote letters home to my family to tell them the truth about why I left so suddenly. No one treated me with disdain. Far from it. They were full of curiosity about my designation, and I even spoke with others who believed they were developing their own designations."

Some of the anxiety and anger I've been carrying around loosens in my chest. "Will you tell me your name?"

"Onri, my lady." He glances nervously at the castle. "I did set out with the intention of meeting with the *Hratha'len*, but I have been told that they turned the ritual into a disaster. Perhaps now I have seen you, I had better just go home."

Onri has come all this way, and he has no one to talk to about being an Omega. I want to sit down with him for several hours and answer all his questions, but I must see the archivists about Emmeric as soon as possible.

A flash of red catches my eye. Mother Linnea is standing on the other side of the square, her hands in her sleeves and a forlorn expression on her face. I haven't spoken with her or laid eyes on her since the ritual.

I turn to my bodyguards. "Fiala, would you please ask Mother Linnea to come and speak with me?"

"Of course, my lady."

I watch the wingrunner cross the square and speak with the Temple Mother, and then the two women return to my side.

"You have been keeping your distance from me, Mother Linnea," I say.

"I have been forbidden to speak with you, my lady."

There's so much sadness in her face. Sadness that's echoed in my heart. I miss speaking with her. I miss the Flame Temple. The solitude and silence. Sitting with the young dragons. Hearing the soft voices of the Temple Maidens as they work. Before the ritual, the *Hratha'len* were kind and patient with me. It's because of them that I had people to speak to about my designation and was finally able to bond with Zabriel through his scent. I have bad dreams about Heloise, but I have many more happy memories because of the rest of the *Hratha'len*.

But can I trust them? Can I send vulnerable Omegas to the Flame Temple after the way they treated me?

"I am so thankful that you are a witch, Lady Isavelle," Mother Linnea suddenly says. "I tell the gods so every day when I kneel before the font."

I blink in surprise. "You are?"

"If you were not a witch, you could not have protected yourself and *Ma'len* from Emmeric's priest. I hear that man possessed magical swords that *Ma'len* was unable to overcome on his own. Our king is alive because of you."

"Heloise was not filled with gratitude," I point out.

Mother Linnea's eyes fill with pain and she lowers them to the ground. "I don't understand why she did what she did. I can't swear that there are no other traitors in the *Hratha'len*, but I am loyal to you and *Ma'len*, always. That much I can promise, for what it's worth." She bows her head respectfully and turns away.

"Wait," I call to her, then turn to the boy at my side. "Onri, this is Mother Linnea, one of the *Hratha'len*. The Flame Temple is open to you if you wish to visit, or you may feel safer speaking with Mother Linnea here in the city. Or you may wish to go home. I'll leave the decision up to you."

"You forgive the *Hratha'len* after what they did to you?" Dusan asks in a low voice.

It's too soon for forgiveness. My feelings are too raw.

I say to Onri, "You are not a witch, are you?" He shakes his head. "Then I trust that Mother Linnea will welcome and protect the newest Omega in Maledin. Omegas are valued, even if witches are not."

Mother Linnea looks pained by my response, but she turns to Onri. "Welcome to Lenhale, Omega. How wonderful to meet you. I will be happy to introduce you to the Temple Crone, or share a meal with you in the city, or merely see that you have enough provisions for your onward journey if that's what you wish."

Onri looks up at the castle. A dragon is circling one of the turrets, a sight that seems to capture the boy's interest. "I've heard I am like this because of the dragons. I would very much like to see them a little closer, if that is possible."

A smile breaks over Mother Linnea's face. "There is nothing I would like better than to show you the dragongrounds, and there may even be hatchlings in the Flame Temple for you to meet."

Onri's face lights up. He bows to me and wishes me health and happiness. "It was an honor to meet you, Lady Isavelle. I hope that I may speak with you again one day."

My bodyguards, Zenevieve, and I watch as he and Mother Linnea walk side by side up to the castle.

Fiala's somber expression is conflicted. "I get so angry whenever I remember the ritual or see one of the *Hratha'len*, but I think you made the right decision for Onri, Lady Isavelle."

"Onri will be safe with Mother Linnea, but I still don't trust the *Hratha'len* enough to feel easy about Lady Isavelle stepping foot within the temple," Dusan says.

"No," Fiala agrees. "Neither do I."

The four of us carry on our way through the town until we reach the sign on the large wooden house proclaiming Master Gaun's Magical Archive. When I knock, Master Simpkin opens the door.

"What a pleasure it is to see you again, Lady Isavelle," he

says with a smile, bowing us inside. "And who is your lovely friend? Another witch?"

I introduce Zenevieve to the former witchfinders. "Zenevieve is not a witch, but a dragonrider."

"Former dragonrider," Zenevieve adds with a pained expression. "I don't believe my dragon survived the war."

"You don't believe?" Master Artor asks, his brow creasing with confusion.

"I was the Shadow King's captive after he killed the former king and queen, but I have no memory of my time with him. I can't remember it, or he made me forget. I don't know which."

Master Artor looks thoughtful. "How interesting. I am in the middle of compiling a section on memory. Would you like to examine it with me?"

The two of them peruse a section of shelving while Master Gaun and Master Simpkin offer me a seat at their worktable, which is heaped even higher with papers and books than last time. There are more shelves and cabinets lining the walls and standing in rows. The archive gives off an aura of barely organized chaos.

"I hope Miss Ravenna is well," Master Gaun asks me, sitting down. He and Simpkin still carry the frailty of sickness, though they're perspiring less and their eyes are brighter.

"I don't know, I'm afraid. Kane came for Ravenna and took her back to the wild flare in the east. It was the price of Kane's help to bring the barrier down."

Both their faces fall.

"We are very sorry to hear it," Simpkin says, and I realize he means it. "Such a lively and spirited young woman. How strange fate is to have promised them to each other."

I have a few choice words I'd like to say about Kane and where I'd like to stick his fate, but if I'm to help my fellow witch, I must focus on why I'm here. "I have a theory about what Emmeric—the Shadow King—is and how he has survived for so long. Have you ever heard of a lich?"

I relate everything that I saw in my vision and what Zabriel remembers from that day on the mountain, and I tell them about coming face to face with the man who used to be Zabriel's brother.

Master Gaun frowns for a moment and then says, "An undead mage. How very interesting. I have read that hundreds of years ago, there were a great many liches in Grendu. Come with me, Master Simpkin."

The two men head toward the back of the room and rummage among crates of books. I watch as they consult a tome, turning pages back and forth while deep in discussion. They take what they have found over to Master Artor, who exclaims in excitement before they all hurry over to where I'm sitting.

"There are signs that you are correct, Lady Isavelle," Master Gaun tells me and shows me an illustrated page. A tall, skeletal figure with bony fingers and glowing eyes clutches what looks like a lantern.

Zenevieve approaches and points to what the lich is holding. "That's the phylactery that Zabriel's sister destroyed."

"If the lich was able to cling to life until Emmeric returned, he may well have struck a deal with the young prince."

"Is there any way that we can know for sure?" I ask.

"We might be able to if we saw Emmeric in the flesh," Master Artor says.

"But we would certainly be killed the next instant," Master Simpkin finishes with a grimace.

Master Gaun turns to Zenevieve. "What do you remember of the Shadow King? Were you close?"

"When he was just ordinary Prince Emmeric? Not particularly. When I first arrived in the capital, he was awkward around me. He seemed to want to be my friend but didn't know how. I told him to be kinder to his dragon, but he didn't seem to understand, and so I avoided him. Later, he became downright cruel and gloating. He once declared that I would always be unhappy and that I deserved it. It was after that day in the mountains."

It's similar to what Zabriel said, that Emmeric became crueler over time, but that doesn't make him a lich.

"Can't we tell from his magic what he is?" I ask desperately, looking between the archivists. "The things he has done? Could a Maledinni possessed by a lich lock a dragon army away for five hundred years, cause spikes to grow from the ground, and slaughter whole villages of people?"

What follows is a great deal of rummaging through bookshelves, crates, and stacks of papers—by the archivists, that is. Zenevieve and I watch on, as we're scolded each time we move a book out of its "order."

"I can't see any order, can you?" Zenevieve whispers.

I smile and shake my head.

"Ah!" Master Simpkin cries, thrusting a finger into the air, avidly scanning the page he's reading. "I have it. Liches are experts at manipulating planes of existence."

Master Gaun slaps his forehead and gasps, "Of course.

Manipulating the planes of existence explains everything." He hurries forward to read over Simpkin's shoulder.

Zenevieve and I exchange questioning looks. It does?

Master Gaun notices our baffled faces and explains, "There is the material plane, which is the one we are standing in now. Then there are the elemental planes of fire, wind, earth, and water. There is the chaos plane. Finally, there are the two transitive planes, called the ethereal plane and the astral plane."

"The astral plane is one you are familiar with, Lady Isavelle," Master Artor tells me, spreading out a scroll that shows a complicated diagram of overlapping spheres, covered in spidery writing.

"I am?" I ask, tilting my head from side to side but still unable to make sense of the illustration.

"You described listening in on Emmeric's conversation from within a dark place. You sent your mind across the astral plane to his."

"Could Emmeric drag me through the astral plane from the dragongrounds to beyond the barrier?"

Gaun shakes his head. "The physical form cannot traverse the astral plane, but he could traverse the ethereal plane. A powerful lich can use the ethereal plane as a corridor with a thousand doors opening anywhere he chooses, or he can hide people and objects away, holding them in suspension."

I grip his arm. "You mean like keeping a dragon army captive for five hundred years, or whole villages of people?"

He inclines his head with a small smile, pleased that I've caught on. "Just so, Lady Isavelle."

"Then all we have to do is enter the ethereal plane and bring everyone home."

"I doubt it will be as simple as that."

"I broke Emmeric's spell once before and freed the dragon army. I can break it again."

"Do you know how you broke the spell?" he asks.

I frown, thinking hard. "No, but I know I did it. I wanted my mate so badly that I woke him up. I want the villagers home just as much."

"The bond between you and *Ma'len* is a special one. A powerful one. It might not be a circumstance that's easily replicated."

"You are saying that I will never be able to find my family or bring them home? They're gone forever?"

"There is a spell…" Master Simpkin murmurs, leafing through a stack of papers. "Here it is."

He hands me a sheet of crinkled, yellowing paper, and I read, *The Intraplanar Spell*.

"Gold dust," I say, reading the first item on the list of ingredients. This is definitely not witchcraft, which requires little that can't be easily dug up, cut down, picked, or foraged from the forest. The instructions are vague as well, something about scattering gold dust, drawing on a source of power, and then elevating one's mind. A witch would be precise. A witch would tell you to inscribe a circle of protection, turn around three times, and then thrust a dagger through an apple. Good, clear instructions. Still, if elevating my mind will bring the villagers home, then I will elevate it to the moon and back.

"I wonder where I can get gold dust," I wonder aloud.

"Lady Isavelle," Master Gaun says tentatively. "You're not actually thinking of—"

I lift my gaze and glower at him. "I am. Why?"

He reaches for the paper, but I hold it away from him.

"Because it is *dangerous*," he says. "This is not the same as healing a broken bone or meditating on a strange voice. You are tearing holes in the fabric of reality."

"What makes a lich so special? Why can Emmeric perform this spell and not me?"

Gaun puffs his cheeks out, thinking. "Innate ability. Vast reserves of power. Years of study."

"What if I find vast reserves of power? What if I study? I have innate abilities too."

"You do, but..."

"I could do it. Zabriel and I are incredibly powerful together."

Zenevieve nods eagerly, backing me up. "They are. I watched the two of them bring down a wild Alpha dragon."

"Highly commendable." The archivist gives me a weak smile. "I know little about the Maledinni except that you are all wonderfully determined. You are a dragonrider and a witch, which is a rare thing indeed. Possibly you are the only one of your kind who has ever existed. But I would urge you to be cautious. This is a powerful spell, and you and your mate could get hurt. Emmeric may return these people to you eventually. After all, they are human."

"Emmeric has no particular hatred of humans, but that doesn't mean he cares if they live or die. Those are my villagers and all that's left of my family. I have to bring them home."

Zenevieve gives me an encouraging nod. "You should at least speak with Zabriel about it. He values your abilities."

"May I borrow this spell?" I ask the archivists. "I promise

to take good care of it and return it to the archive when I'm finished."

Gaun opens and closes his mouth, and then deflates with a sigh. "Who am I to say no to the woman who freed us all from the Brethren and brought the dragons back to Maledin? Of course, Lady Isavelle. I trust we will all still be here tomorrow, and you won't have torn a gaping hole in the fabric of time and space?" He gives me a stern look as he takes the spell from me, rolls it up, wraps it in a protective cloth, and hands it back.

I accept the scroll. "I'll do my very best. I've grown fond of this new Maledin, and I don't want to see it ripped apart, by me or anyone else."

32

Zabriel

I rest my knuckles on the tabletop, gazing at the wooden pieces representing dragons, wyverns, and foot soldiers arranged on the map of Maledin. Right now they're clustered around the castle, but at some point in the near future, they'll be sent south to the barrier.

"It's a formidable army, *Ma'len*," Godric tells me.

But will it be enough? I learned a hard lesson the last time I pursued Emmeric. Too large a portion of our army went after him, and the capital was vulnerable. This time our force will be smaller, and Emmeric is even more powerful than he used to be.

"We won't have surprise on our side," I mutter. "Once Kane breaks through the barrier, Emmeric will know he's about to be surrounded by dragonriders. He'll fight like he's got nothing to lose. It will be his last stand." I raise my eyes to Godric. "I worry about how many of our people will die."

Godric says firmly, "We are all prepared to die for our country. Emmeric will not lock us away a second time."

Few of us have faced a lich before. They're unpredictable and difficult to kill, and I lay awake last night wondering what kind of gruesome magic he's going to inflict on us.

"First things first," I say, straightening up. "We bring the missing villagers home. The gods forfend that Emmeric use them as some kind of human shield during the fight. Isavelle is working on this right now."

I hear footsteps outside in the corridor, and a moment later, someone knocks softly on the door to the War Room. As it swings open, Isavelle appears, and her eyes are alight in a way that tells me she has news to impart.

I cross the room in two long strides and pull her into my arms for a kiss. All news can wait until I've had my fill of tasting my Omega and breathing in her scent.

There's a pointed cough behind me. "I'll leave you now, *Ma'len*."

Isavelle goes up on tiptoe and wraps her arms around my neck, parting her lips for me so I can kiss her even deeper.

"Hmm? Oh, speak soon, Godric." But I'm talking to an empty room.

I lift Isavelle up in my arms, perch her on the edge of the big wooden table, and slide a leg between her thighs. She's my mate at last. I am still coming to terms with the fact that this Omega is all mine, officially and forever, and she will always bear my teeth marks on her neck. I dreamed of this moment for years and years.

"What's that smile for?" Isavelle asks, tracing my lips.

I smile even wider and kiss her again. "You. Always you." There's a crinkle of paper by my ear, and I realize my mate is holding something. "What's that?"

Isavelle withdraws her arms from around my neck and unrolls a piece of parchment. "It's a spell that I am hoping will show me where the missing villagers are." She explains what she learned about the planes of existence.

"When I pardoned them, I never thought I'd hear from the witchfinders ever again. Who could have imagined?"

Isavelle raises her hand to my cheek. "I doubted your mercy, and now I see that your instincts were right."

I hold tightly to her wrist and then turn my head and kiss her palm. "I have learned what it means to be king my way. Mercy for my people, but they will never separate us again. *Ever*." I swear this harder than I swore my coronation vows, and I seal the words with a press of my lips to Isavelle's.

"This spell is nothing like the little witchcraft I've learned. Master Gaun warned me that it's dangerous, and I don't know if I'm able, but there isn't anyone else. I woke you up and brought the dragons back to Maledin. There's witchcraft inside me. There's dragon magic inside me. With both, maybe I can do this. But I'll need your help to cast the spell."

"Me?" I exclaim. "I don't know what use I'll be. I don't know the first thing about magic."

"I think I can do the casting if you assist me. I need a source of power."

I rub my jaw with my hand and smile. "Well, I've got plenty of that, *sha'len*, but it's not the magical kind."

Her lips twitch in amusement. "Your ego is as healthy as ever. I do think you have a magical kind of power as well. We have a great deal of energy crackling between us, don't you think?" She traces her fingers down my chest.

I watch the path she tracks over my skin and feel my body flush with heat. "I didn't know fucking could cast a spell."

Isavelle smiles. "I don't know if it can, but I feel like you and I can do all manner of incredible things together. Would you like to try?"

"Absolutely." If it doesn't work, at least I'll have made my mate come today. "What do you need for the spell?"

Isavelle glances around. "Some space on this floor. Gold dust. You. Oh, and some candles. The spell doesn't ask for candles, but if I don't set something out in a circle around us, I won't feel like I'm doing proper magic."

"I'll get what we need," I tell her, moving toward the door. "Artists have been decorating your throne with gold dust. I'll ask them for some."

"I have a throne?" she asks in surprise. "Decorated with gold?"

"Only the best for my bride." I shoot her a smile as I leave the room.

It doesn't take long to gather the things Isavelle has asked for, and I return to the room. My mate is holding the crystal amulet, though she's explained that the connection to Emmeric vanished after he seemed to catch her eavesdropping.

"I thought we might need this. I don't know why. It's a gut feeling."

"Trust your instincts, *sha'len*. They have given me life and breath, so I'll never doubt them." The smile she gives me is soft and beautiful. "How do we do this?"

She thinks for a moment. "I believe skin-to-skin contact is

the best way. If you lie down naked, I'll set up the spell and join you."

I take off my clothes and drape them over the back of a chair. I lie down on my back and watch as Isavelle moves around me, lighting candles in a circle and scattering gold dust, which shimmers all around me.

As I watch her undress, I murmur, "This is what all those posters have been warning me about. My mate is getting her claws into me for her witchy purposes."

Isavelle smiles and shakes her long, loose golden hair with her fingers. It brushes against her naked back. "You sound delighted about it." She gives my erection a pointed look. "You look delighted as well."

"I am," I purr, taking my cock in my hand and squeezing my length and my knot.

Isavelle places the amulet and a piece of thread by my side. When she steps toward me, I reach for her, and she straddles my hips, her sex pressed against my shaft.

Isavelle takes both my hands in hers and closes her eyes. She remains still for a long time, her lips barely moving as she speaks under her breath. I just make out her words. "Ethereal plane. Part the veil. Tell me your secrets. Show me what I seek. Ethereal plane. Part the veil."

Her body atop mine grows hot. With her breasts thrust forward and her slick slowly coating my knot, I can't help the small groan of desire that escapes my lips. Isavelle's lips don't stop moving, and her eyes remain closed, but she shifts her hips until the head of my cock spears into her tight channel.

My head rears up, and I bite down on an exclamation of desire. Our hands grip each other's as Isavelle moves ever so slightly back and forth on my length.

I feel our connection through the spell as well as through my cock. Is this witchcraft? I love witchcraft. I should practice more witchcraft.

Isavelle stops whispering. Her eyes stay closed, but her eyebrows rise as if she's witnessing something surprising. "I see them, Zabriel. Hundreds of them, all in their houses. They think they're home. They don't know they're adrift in the ethereal plane. Every village is full of the missing. Joryan. Gunster. Amriste too. They're whole. They're alive."

I want to ask her what she's seeing, but I'm afraid I'll break her concentration.

"This plane is different to ours," she whispers. "My magic doesn't belong here. I can sense that *thing* everywhere."

That thing must be the lich possessing Emmeric.

"It's a spider's web. The tendrils are everywhere, but they're weak. He hasn't been here in some time. He's neglected this place. His plans are focused elsewhere."

Suddenly, Isavelle gasps and her eyes fly open. She snatches up the amulet and the thread and quickly winds the thread around the crystal.

She presses her hands against my chest, panting, her turquoise and golden eyes wide as they stare into mine. "I think I've done it. Bound all the threads of Emmeric's magic in the ethereal plane to this world so that we may enter and rescue the villagers. But it will have to be done soon. I don't know how long that seal will hold or how long it will take Emmeric to notice what I've done."

Tears suddenly crowd her lashes. "I found them, Zabriel. Everyone who's missing. We can bring them home."

33

Isavelle

"*Sha'len*, you saw them?" Zabriel whispers, cupping my cheek and smoothing my tears away with his thumb. He half sits up and kisses my throat. "How wonderful you are."

I wrap my arms around his strong body and hold him close. "I couldn't have done it without you." My mouth seeks his, and as we kiss, he falls back, sending gold dust shimmering into the air.

Zabriel holds me close and turns us so that I'm beneath him, and he sinks the rest of his shaft into me. He groans in pleasure and his eyelashes flutter. "I'll cast spells with you any time you want, my sweet little witch."

The circle of candlelight bathes us with a warm glow. We're both covered in gold powder and our bodies glisten as he fucks me. Zabriel's knot slams into me, and he lifts his eyes to mine, a question burning in their red depths.

"Please, Zabriel," I whisper breathlessly. "Please knot me."

Maybe we shouldn't get into the habit of him knotting me when we're not in the privacy of our room or my nest, but it feels so good to cast caution aside.

He's the king, this is his castle, and I want his knot.

"Sweet little Omega," he murmurs, taking hold of my hips in his strong hands. Gathering my thighs around his hips. Moving my body into the best position to take his knot. "Fuck, I want you so bad. I want you. *I want you.*"

With a groan and a mighty thrust, he forces his knot deep inside me, pushing us both over the edge into our climaxes. I cling to him, and as I cry out, all the magic that had gathered within us suddenly and violently dissipates. All the candles around us gutter, sending shadows dancing over our bodies.

Zabriel traces his fingers over my gold-dusted breasts. "Look at you, my little dragon. Covered in gold."

I open my eyes and enjoy the sight of my mate's skin shimmering and glittering.

Zabriel picks up the amulet bound with thread and examines it. "Emmeric won't be able to use magic to protect himself in the ethereal plane?"

"I don't believe so."

"Then if he follows us, I'll run him through with my sword. Swords work everywhere."

There's the sound of running feet in the corridor growing louder and louder. Several pairs of running feet. Perhaps we should have cast this spell in our bedroom and not a room that anyone can enter.

Zabriel reaches out and snatches his cloak from the back

of a chair and wraps it around my naked body just moments before Mother Linnea, Elysant, and Godric burst inside.

"*Ma'len*, are you safe? What is going on in here?" Godric cries out, taking in the sight of us naked, shimmering with gold dust, and within a ring of candles.

"As you can see, I'm perfectly well, and so is my bride," Zabriel drawls, his hands braced on either side of my head. With our legs tangled together, it's plain to see what we were just doing. Zabriel's bare ass must be coated with gold dust.

"I felt a strange discharge of magic," Elysant says, her hands clutching each other anxiously. "I was afraid something terrible had happened."

Zabriel and I exchange sheepish glances. That discharge of magic will have been both of us climaxing and the spell's magic dispersing.

"Good news," I tell our three bewildered onlookers, hoping that they'll leave us once they understand what we were doing. "I've found the missing villagers, and I know how we can rescue them."

"You have?" Mother Linnea exclaims, a smile breaking over her face. "How did you do that?"

I draw Zabriel's cloak farther up my body to hide my blushing cheeks. I wasn't expecting any follow-up questions.

Zabriel notices my embarrassment with an amused twitch of his lips. "We will happily tell you everything, but you're going to have to give us a moment."

"*Ma'len*, are you unwell?" Godric asks anxiously. "Was it the spell? Do you feel weak?"

Elysant's eyes widen with alarm. "*Ma'len*, you should not have participated in your mate's witchcraft. What if the spell has drained you to the point of illness?"

"There's nothing magical about my inability to stand up. The consequences I'm suffering are purely Maledinni."

The spellbreaker's brow creases in confusion. "*Ma'len*?"

Zabriel smiles as his tongue plays over one of his dragines. "I'm stuck."

AT DAWN THE FOLLOWING MORNING, in an empty field in western Maledin, I stand facing the dragon army, the wingrunners, ranks of foot soldiers, and a dozen Temple Maidens and Mothers.

Even with Zabriel at my side, how intimidating it is to face them like this, all the battle-proven warriors who drove the Brethren from Maledin, and all the brave men and women who protect the capital. I've seen Zabriel address them in his authoritative voice from his great height. He was born to be king. He feels in his bones that he's worthy and he commands respect. I feel very small standing by his side. It was easier facing Kane and his enormous dragon.

I take a deep breath and prepare to address the dragon army for the first time. To make my first request of them as their future queen. "I was there with many of you as we cut down dead bodies that lined the streets of western Maledin. I helped you wrap the bodies and watched with you as we sent them as sparks and smoke up into the sky. They were terrible, never-ending days. Now I ask to work with you all again, but this time, we have a hopeful day ahead of us. We can bring the lost villagers back to Maledin, as many of you were returned to Maledin after such a long period of being locked away.

"In a moment, I will open doorways into a place very much like the world we live in, only it's a shadow world. A place not meant for us. My sister and father are there. Many other people's families are there. Humans. Maledinni. All that remains of the lifeblood of western Maledin. The people Emmeric stole from us.

"I'm able to cast the spell, but it requires powerful magic, and I can't do this alone. I would like to draw upon the magic within all your dragons to cast this spell."

Esmeral bounds forward, followed by Scourge at a more sedate pace. A smile breaks over my face as the massive black dragon lowers his head and consents to me briefly stroking his jaw.

Merrex and Verdun move forward, and slowly dragon after dragon form a semicircle around me, just as they did for the Temple Crone the day that Kane attacked the flare. The sight of so many enormous creatures silently gazing down at me is breathtaking.

Stesha is standing back with Nilak, his eyes narrowed and his arms folded. He glances at his dragon as if they're communicating silently. Nilak looks at Esmeral and all the other dragons who are waiting patiently to help with my witchcraft. Her nostrils flare, and then she moves forward to join them. I think it would have hurt Nilak's Alpha pride too much to seem afraid of a ritual that even a little Omega like Esmeral is participating in. Stesha looks annoyed. But then, Stesha always looks annoyed.

"Will that be enough dragons for you, my lady?" a woman calls with a good-natured grin when there are fifteen dragons gathered around me.

I recognize her as Sundra, an Alpha who rides the silvery Merrex. "I think that will be plenty, thank you."

"We're glad to help, both of us," Sundra says, drawing her fingers over Merrex's scales. "You and your little dragon saved two of Merrex's hatchlings from that golden monster."

Esmeral nuzzles my shoulder, and there's a lump in my throat as I whisper to her, "Did you hear that? We did that. You and me. Are you ready for this?"

My dragon chirrups softly. Esmeral is always ready for anything.

I take a bag of gold dust from my pocket and begin walking in a circle, scattering it as I go. I whisper the words of the spell, concentrating on opening doorways into the ethereal plane, not merely looking into it like last time. Instead of drawing on Zabriel's power, I gather the energy that's emanating from the dragons all around me. They give it willingly, and I catch glimpses of myself as the dragons see me. Small, vulnerable. No flame or teeth to protect me. No wings to escape from danger. But one of the flare just the same. Without them lending me their magic, I could never hope to open doorways into another world.

In my mind, I see them. Nine portals.

There are several gasps around me. Opening my eyes, I see one of them shimmering before me. An enormous flat surface towering over us, bending light and scattering it this way and that.

I call, "There are doorways just like these in every village where people are missing, and they are lit up so brightly that you will see them through the gloom. Search every cottage, stable, workroom, and tavern for the missing, and then escort them back home. I've opened portals all over western

Maledin. Once you are inside, you will see them for miles around, marked by great shafts of light. Tell the people you find to run to them and escape. Escort those who need your help. We mustn't leave anyone behind."

Everyone is listening closely to my instructions, and there are several nods when I've finished speaking.

At my side, Zabriel reaches for my hand and squeezes it. My eyes are suddenly misty with emotion. "I am so grateful to each and every one of you. We're bringing them all home."

Godric approaches my mate and speaks in a low voice, but I hear every word. "*Ma'len*, you mustn't enter the plane yourself. You are too important to risk your life in such a place."

"I won't ask my people to do anything that I won't do myself." Zabriel glances at me. "And for certain I won't stand idle out here while my mate and your future queen puts herself at risk because I know Isavelle is going in there."

"Then allow me to remain by your side, *Ma'len*," Godric continues. "Your mate has her bodyguards to protect her."

Zabriel smiles in amusement. "You think I need protecting, Beta?"

Godric returns his smile, but his eyes remain worried. "It is a privilege and an honor to fight at your side."

"I am anticipating no fighting today, but your help and support are always welcome." Zabriel turns and addresses the dragon army, raising his voice for all to hear. "If you find yourself lost in there, remain calm. You're still in Maledin, and the landmarks are the same. Anyone who isn't familiar with this part of the country, stay with those who know it well. Give your names to Santha as you pass through this portal. Give the names of your dragons and wyverns as well. We will leave no one stranded."

My mate turns to me and wraps his arms around me. Lowering his head, he buries his face in the back of my neck and breathes me in. "You smell wonderful today. Different. Hopeful."

Lifting his head, he smiles at me, and I stroke his cheek. By his side, I can't help but feel we have a chance.

As if he can't help himself, Zabriel pulls me into his arms once more and breathes in. "Gods, I can't get enough of you."

I hug him fiercely, until we finally draw apart. Together with our dragons, we walk toward the shimmering portal.

Santha is standing by with a quill in one hand and an open book in the other. She gives me a quick smile and begins to scribble down names as dragons, riders, wyverns, and wingrunners file through the portal and vanish.

34

———————

Zabriel

As I pass through the portal, all the hairs on the back of my neck stand up.

I don't remember much about what it was like to be locked away beneath the Bodan Mountains, but echoes of that place wash over me as I move through the misty landscape. There's not a breath of wind in the ethereal plane, and everything is in ghostly shades of gray. Up on the hill, trees are stirring, but there is no rustling of leaves. My footsteps are strangely muted. I feel Scourge's uneasiness as he paces beside me. This is not a place for the living.

Isavelle slips her hand into mine, and I lean down to hear her voice. "Our group has come through the portal. Are you ready to fly to Amriste?"

We arranged the army into parties to search all the deserted villages, gather the missing, and lead them out of the ethereal plane. As I watch, groups of dragons, wyverns, and their riders depart in all directions. Far in the distance, I see the light from Isavelle's portals rising into the sky. Beacons that will guide everyone home.

"I'm ready. Lead the way, *sha'len.*"

Amriste is a small village, so there's just me on Scourge, Isavelle on Esmeral, her bodyguards, and four more wingrunners. We navigate to Amriste just as we would in the material plane, by landmarks and our dragons' innate sense of direction, but it's strange flying here. There's almost no wind, and the landmarks are dead-looking.

We land just outside the village near the portal that Isavelle created. The wingrunners hurry toward the cottages and search for residents. As soon as I dismount, Scourge takes off once more, and he patrols back and forth between the portal and the village, a dark shape in the opaque sky, keeping us all safe.

Isavelle grips my hand, and we hurry into the village square, Esmeral, Fiala, and Dusan following just behind us.

There are half a dozen people by the well, standing in a strange tableau. Waiting for water that's never drawn and exchanging pleasantries in words that are never spoken.

Isavelle approaches a woman and gently tugs the bucket from her fingers. "Mrs. Ackworth, it's Isavelle Harrow. Can you hear me? We're going for a short walk. It's not far."

Mrs. Ackworth blinks like she's waking up, but her eyes are still dreamy. "What's that, dear?"

"Esmeral, will you carry these people to that portal and then return to us?" Isavelle asks her dragon.

The turquoise and golden dragon stands patiently while we help six people climb up onto her back, and then she walks them out of the village toward the portal, a wingrunner jogging alongside and encouraging everyone to hold on tight. The villagers sit astride her in the manner of slightly dazed children riding a donkey at a summer fair.

Isavelle turns fearfully to the cottage that she used to call home. "What if they're not there?"

I put my hands on her shoulders and squeeze them gently. "Would you like me to come in with you?"

Isavelle shakes her head. "I'll be all right with Fiala and Dusan. You help the others."

I'll do no such thing. I have an ominous feeling that Emmeric will appear at any moment riding Shar. It doesn't seem possible given how Isavelle described the wretched state of Emmeric's dragon, but I want to watch the skies. I squeeze her hand, resolving to wait right where I am. "Go get your family, and we'll take them home."

Isavelle and her bodyguards disappear inside the cottage while I stand in the square, keeping an eye on the skies and watching my soldiers half walking, half carrying dazed people out of the village. I can see their footsteps and their mouths moving as they talk, but no sound reaches me. It's unnerving.

Slowly, the place empties out. I fold my arms and shift on my feet. I didn't think I'd miss them, but Amriste without Biddy's swirling, cawing crows is strange.

"You shouldn't be here."

I turn quickly and see a figure standing in the shadows. My heart thuds in my chest. I didn't hear him approaching, and his seething, rasping voice travels unnervingly through the air.

My brother wears long, dark robes, high at the neck with

fitted sleeves. The attire is strange, but his looks are just as I remember. Long, brown hair. Gray eyes. A face that so closely resembles my own, only with finer features and thinner brows. In his fifteenth year, his coloring changed to match Shar, his hair darkening to black and his eyes turning midnight blue with a golden ring around his irises. Even though we were never close, I feel a sharp tug on my heart. I don't miss him, but I miss my shattered family. I miss knowing I belong to people.

Emmeric flicks his eyes up and down my body, his expression disgusted. "Look at you. Walking around in my domain. Touching my things."

I draw my sword, keeping the blade low, but ready. If Isavelle comes out now, she'll be in danger. Raising my voice in the hope that she'll hear me and stay hidden, I say, "What are you doing here, Emmeric?"

Scourge. Where are you?

There's a roar in the sky. I can't tell if he's close by or far away.

Greenish light flickers in Emmeric's eyes and strange expressions twitch across his face. This thing is wearing my brother's skin. It's grotesque. "Tell your dragon to stay back or I will slaughter every villager in the ethereal plane."

I hesitate. Isavelle bound his magic. Can't he tell, or did it not work?

Stay back for now, I tell Scourge.

I feel my dragon circling overhead, filled with anger and desperate to sink his teeth into Emmeric.

"What do you want, Emmeric?" I ask. "Can I even call you Emmeric? Is there anything left in there of the man I once called my brother, or are you a walking corpse possessing a handful of memories that belonged to a man who was once a prince?"

"*You* figured it out?" the creature sneers with Emmeric's voice and Emmeric's lips. "You did?" For a moment he's shocked into silence, and then he bursts out laughing. "Of course you didn't. It was the witch."

He says *witch* with as much disgust as Kane.

"Who are you? What are you?"

Emmeric's cruel smile widens. "Ah, Zabriel. There's no need for all this confusion. Dragonrider or immortal mage, I always hated you."

The patronizing, sneering tone is pure Emmeric. He loved to tell me I was all brawn and no brains. That I was a stumble-headed, clumsy-minded oaf, but his insults were nothing to me. I was the crown prince. I was a dragonrider. I had friends, I had talent, and I threw myself into whatever task was before me and ignored my brother until the day he forced me to see him. I found Mirelle beaten and bloodied and crying hysterically, and suddenly Emmeric had all my attention.

"You raped our sister and broke her mate's heart. You killed our parents. You did gods know what to Zenevieve. And for what? Revenge for that thing that gives you power? Does it make you feel special, wielding something else's magic?"

"Is he suffering, that white-haired bastard?" Emmeric asks with relish, ignoring my questions. "It must hurt him every time he looks at her. Zenevieve never liked me, even before I was a lich. I saw it happening, and I stopped it. I'm more powerful and clever than any of you. Me. *Emmeric.* Not the lich." His voice grows shrill and vindictive.

"Saw what? Stopped what?"

"They don't deserve to be happy, and they never will be," he shrieks. "None of you do. I'll make you hurt like he does, only your suffering will be worse by a hundredfold. Your people don't like witches. Your people don't trust humans who have power after what I put them through. They want the dragons to rule. How I will laugh when they burn her."

I narrow my eyes. The posters in the city. The superstitious whispers about Isavelle. Was that Emmeric? "You've been stirring up hatred against my mate. How did you do it?"

"Everyone is so terrified these days that I barely had to do a thing. I hear your own people nearly killed her during her first heat." He laughs like it's the funniest thing he's ever heard.

"Why did you go back, Emmeric? That day in the mountains when we burned the lich's phylactery. Was it to finish the lich off, or were you hoping to find a powerful ally? Did it force you to submit, or did you welcome it with open arms? Who raped our sister? Emmeric, or that thing?"

"It was all me, dear brother. I welcomed the lich. He needed me, unlike any of you. He wants revenge against all of you who nearly destroyed him, and in exchange, I receive all his power." His smirk is dark and menacing. "We started with Mirelle because she's the one who burned the phylactery. You should have heard her crying for Onderz. So pitiful, and he wasn't able to save her. Do you think that's why he killed himself? Because of the guilt?"

I grip my sword harder, my chest aching as heartless words spill from my brother's lips.

Emmeric continues, "You'll be buried alive once more very soon, make no mistake, and this time, I'll make sure you're so deep that the mountains will crush the life out of you, and your brainless whore will be gone forever."

"That will never happen," I seethe. "Now that I know what you are, I can finish what we started and destroy both of you."

"How ambitious. If you're going to become a nuisance, I'll just kill you now." He raises his hand in the manner of a mage casting a spell.

Nothing happens.

Emmeric stares at his hand in utter incomprehension. He seems to be struggling with unseen forces. "What did you do to me?"

Pride throbs through me. Isavelle did it. The threads that Isavelle wrapped around the crystal amulet have bound his magic.

He looks up at me, panting, his face contorted with rage. "That little bitch did this to me. She was spying on me as well. How *dare* she. Once I've killed you, she's next."

I raise my sword and attack. Emmeric closes his eyes. For a fraction of a moment, I wonder if he's going to stand there and let me run him through.

At the very last second, Emmeric's eyes open, and they flare with green magic. He's broken Isavelle's spell, and I'm hit with a discharge of magic that's so strong I'm blasted off my feet and into the sky. My sword flies out of my hand. I sail through the air, and I can't tell which way is up or down. Everything is gray, and the world is tumbling around me.

I land hard on my back, my armor clanking and something in my body going *crack*. All the air has been forced from my lungs, and I stare blindly at the sky, my body shuddering as I starve for breath. I force myself to sit up, and by the time

I'm on my feet, I'm able to draw a little air into my lungs. My head is throbbing, and my ribs feel like they're on fire. I feel like I've broken six of them.

I haven't got time to be distracted by broken bones. I need to get back to Isavelle. The landscape around me has changed. Where's Amriste? I turn on the spot, hunting for a familiar landmark. I've landed within a thicket of trees, and I can't even see Isavelle's portal.

Emmeric suddenly blinks into existence at my side. I'm alone with an undead mage, and I let go of my sword. I can't believe I lost my fucking sword. I feel Scourge in the sky, fast approaching, talons extended and hungry to rip Emmeric in two.

The thing that was once my brother glances at the sky, and I can tell he's wondering how soon Scourge will reach us.

"Who are you looking for? What are you so anxious to find?" Emmeric's eyes are narrowed in suspicion.

He noticed me turning on the spot and looking for Isavelle. "My dragon."

"Do you think I've forgotten everything I learned as a dragonrider? You don't need to look for Scourge with your eyes when you can see him with your mind." A smile splits his face. "You're looking for your foul little witch. Did you bring her into my domain and then lose her, idiot?" He laughs. "Don't worry. I'll find her for you."

In a blink, Emmeric vanishes. A massive shape blackens the sky. Ten razor-sharp talons swipe at the empty space Emmeric was just occupying. Scourge roars in fury and frustration as broken twigs and shredded bark rain down around me.

35

———

Isavelle

I push my creaky front door open and blink in the darkness. My home was always gloomy on overcast days, but there are no cheery lamps or firelight to brighten the interior now. It's cold, and a shiver goes through me.

Fiala, Dusan, and I are standing in a vestibule where we used to leave our muddy boots and wet coats and cloaks. I move forward into the darkness and see two shadowy figures in the tiled kitchen.

Dad's sitting in his big chair by the unlit fire. Anise is standing by the table, bent over like she's cutting a loaf of bread or preparing a pie, only the table is empty, and she's not moving. They are gray, colorless, and resemble posed corpses.

"Dad? Anise?" I call in a choked-up voice.

Dad turns slowly to look at me. Anise raises her head and stares. Both of their expressions are totally blank.

This is all wrong. This is frightening. Is this how Zabriel suffered for five hundred years, alone in the gloom and forgotten?

"Isavelle, you're home," Dad says in a slow, flat voice. "Your ma's out at the baker. She'll return in just a moment, and then we'll all have tea. Come warm yourself by the fire." His arm gradually extends to indicate the empty fireplace.

I feel a warm hand on my shoulder, and Dusan gives me an encouraging nod.

"This isn't home," I tell them both. "You have to come with me."

"Don't talk foolishness," Dad says. "Have you brought friends? Anise, call your brother in for tea."

I watch helplessly as Dad reaches for his pipe that isn't there and fills it with nothing. Anise dusts her hands on an invisible apron.

"Please, Anise. We have to get out of here."

"Where have you been, Isavelle?" Anise asks and then frowns in puzzlement. "Weren't you with the Brethren? Did they let you go?"

"We have orders from the Brethren," Fiala says suddenly. "Important orders for all in Amriste."

Anise frowns at her. "Oh?"

I catch on to what Fiala is saying. "Yes. We all have to gather at the monastery to pray. It's very urgent that we go right away."

"Well, if that's what they want," Dad says, and even in this dreamlike state, I can hear the grumble in his voice. He always disliked the Brethren, but he knew it wasn't wise to disobey them.

My sister is still reluctant to move. "Don't forget Ma and Waylen. Are they in the bedroom or outside? I haven't seen them in..." Anise trails off with a frown.

"They are gone. I'm so sorry." I don't know what else to say.

"Gone where?"

Dad looks around, his brows drawing together. "They were here. I thought...I sensed..."

I wonder if he felt it when his wife and son were ripped from this place and killed. I hope he didn't. "Quickly, let's go."

As we reach the door, all the dishes on the sideboard rattle, and there's a muted blasting sound. An ominous feeling washes over me, and I hurry forward and yank the door open. The square is completely deserted. No villagers. No wingrunners. No Zabriel. He wouldn't leave without me. Something must have happened.

Esmeral, I call.

She's somewhere nearby. I can feel her, but I can't find her.

In the distance, the portal beams its white light up into the sky. I'll take my family there and get them out. Esmeral will find me, and then we'll find Zabriel.

"Quickly, this way," I urge the others, and the five of us walk down the path and out of the village. Fiala, Dusan, and I hustle Dad and Anise as calmly and firmly as we can. Dad is so weak that Dusan slings one of my father's arms over his shoulders and bears his weight. I keep a tight hold of my sister's hand.

We're halfway across a deserted field when I hear a nasty voice behind me.

"Going somewhere?"

I turn around and face Emmeric, pushing Anise behind me. Out of the corner of my eye, Fiala and Dusan take their halberds from their backs and grip them with both hands.

"Be careful. He's got his magic back," I warn them. The binding spell breaking must have been what caused that blast.

"Yes, I have," Emmeric seethes. "I must be more careful with my things in the future. You've been having fun with my useless crystal and learning all my secrets, haven't you? Now I understand why everyone hates witches. They meddle. They *interfere*. Hags, the lot of you."

"Do you want to know how I did all this?" I ask, saying the first thing that comes to mind.

Esmeral, where are you?

Fear rises in me, but I'm able to control it before it overwhelms me. He's a mage, but I'm a witch. This is my village we're standing in. My home, ethereal plane or not.

"I don't care," Emmeric says, but his eyes glimmer with interest. Power, that's what he cares about, and I've been the first person in five hundred years to threaten his.

"Yes, you do," I counter. "You don't understand witchcraft. No one does because everyone hates us so much. That's why we'll always get the better of people like you and the Brethren." I'm edging away as I talk, trying to sound calm but feeling panic rising in my chest. How far away was the portal? Too far. Emmeric is going to kill Dad, Anise, Fiala, and Dusan, and it will be all my fault.

"Do you feel understood by my idiotic brother?" Emmeric mocks. "Do you feel seen? That fool understands nothing but how to swing a sword. I pity you, witch. Bound to a man by his scent without having a choice in the matter."

The fact that Zabriel is King of Maledin and he is not seems to be driving Emmeric mad. I would love to tell Emmeric how Zabriel helped me cast the spell that opened all these portals and bound his magic, at least for a while, but I've just thought of a better way to distract him—with anger.

I sweep my hair aside and trail my fingers over the teeth marks in my neck. "You understand nothing. I fell for Zabriel before I even caught his scent. I would choose him again and again and again."

Emmeric raises his hands, and in his flaring green eyes, I see the intent to kill.

I close my eyes and visualize a portal right next to us. Even with my eyes closed, I see a sudden flare of light.

Fiala and Dusan exclaim in surprise, and then Fiala yelps, "Sir, Anise, this way."

I open my eyes and grab ahold of my family. My bodyguards are holding them. They reach for me, and the five of us fall through the portal together.

The moment we're through, I let go of the others and whirl around with a gasp of panic to see Emmeric attempting to follow us, eyes flashing, teeth grit and bared in anger. Just before he steps through, I shout *close* with my mind, and it snaps shut in his face.

Everything falls silent.

"Where are we?" Fiala asks, gazing around.

Cold wind rushes through my hair. It smells like we're

home because the air is earthy and damp. It even feels like our Maledin. There's wet grass beneath my feet.

The low cloud of this morning must have descended over the land. We've stumbled from fog into even more fog.

36

____

Zabriel

I push the door to Isavelle's cottage open with a groan of pain and clamp one arm around my chest to support my broken ribs.

"Isavelle," I shout raggedly, sweat pouring down my brow. It hurts to breathe, let alone speak, but I shout her name over and over as I stride haphazardly through the rooms. I refuse to limp around because of Emmeric. I'm uneven, that's all. Momentarily off-balance.

I crash into the sideboard, sending a shower of plates and cups to the floor. The crockery smashes silently as I grit my teeth in a scream of pain.

The cottage is abandoned. Isavelle's not here, and neither is her family.

Stumbling against a chair, I head outside once more. If Isavelle's not here, I know where she's gone. As soon as my mate found her father and sister, she would have headed straight for a portal and guided them out of the ethereal plane. All I need to do is get to the Amriste portal that lies across the fields, and I'll probably run right into her coming back in here to find me.

Encouraged by this thought, I make my way as quickly as I can out of the village and back to Scourge. I was able to struggle up onto his back so we could fly back to Amriste, but I fell badly while I was dismounting, and the pain in my chest is growing steadily worse.

I grasp the leather strap on Scourge's flank so I can pull myself up my dragon's side, and paralyzing pain blazes through my body. If I can't mount my dragon, what kind of fucking rider am I? I try again and make it partway up to the saddle before everything goes white behind my eyes and the world disappears. For a few moments, there's no pain, only unconscious bliss.

I land on my back, and my chest seems to burst open with agony. I lie there staring up at the sky, feeling like my insides have turned to dragonfire. I'm a soldier. Injuries are a given when you go into battle. This is *nothing*.

As I level myself to my feet, there's a wet, gurgling sound in my throat. When I take another breath, something goes awry, and I start to cough. I cough so long and hard that I can't breathe. My eyes are streaming, and every racking movement nearly makes me pass out again.

When I open my eyes and look down at the hand I've been coughing into, my gauntlet is covered in blood.

Oh, fuck.

That's not good.

My broken ribs must have punctured a lung.

I wipe my mouth and raise my head. "Go to the portal," I tell Scourge. "Find Isavelle. She's the one Emmeric is looking for, not me."

Scourge growls in defiance and drags his talons across the ground.

"I'm *fine*. I'll follow. You can reach her faster than I can, and she needs us now."

He hesitates for a moment longer, and then, with a flap of his wings, he's off, flying toward the portal. At least one of us has to be there to protect Isavelle. Trying my hardest not to breathe too deeply and set off another coughing fit, I make my slow, painful way toward the portal.

It's still far off in the distance when I see two figures come through, one dressed in red robes and the other wearing the black and silver of a wingrunner. They see me and break into a run.

I recognize the pair as they reach me. Elysant, the spell-breaker, and Leibel, the scarred wingrunner. Their expressions are filled with shock as they take in my injuries.

"*Ma'len*, what happened to you?"

"Emmeric," I say through tightly gritted teeth. "Did you see him?"

"We've not," Leibel replies. "Allow us to help you."

"Where's Isavelle? Did you see my mate?"

"No, *Ma'len*. We did not," Elysant says, focused on the light she's conjured into her hands.

The indifferent way she speaks of my missing mate gets on my nerves. I feel something pass around my chest and arms. Leibel is binding up my wounds, and Elysant is helping him. I'm used to haphazard field medicine, and I don't take much notice. It's only when the rope is cinched around my wrists and pulled tight, binding my hands behind me, and causing a fresh shock of pain in my chest that I realize something isn't right.

"That was easier than I thought it would be," Leibel grunts in surprise. "We didn't even need the potion you prepared."

"It was not luck," Elysant tells him. "The gods are on our side."

"What the—" I wrench myself away from them and fight against the ropes. They're not ordinary ropes. They glimmer with red magic. Dragon magic. "Elysant. Get these off me right now."

She respectfully bows her head. "As soon as the deed is done, *Ma'len*."

I look from one to the other, trying to fathom why this is happening. "What deed? Do you intend to murder me? Have I shamed you, slighted you, angered you? Tell me what it is I have done as man or king to make you turn against me like this."

Both of them drop to one knee and bow their heads. "We mean you no harm, *Ma'len*. We are your most loyal subjects."

"I am not feeling your loyalty," I growl and turn to the portal. I'll get to Isavelle, ropes or not. As I try to leave, Leibel gets to his feet and shoves me off-balance, and I topple to the ground. "For what purpose am I bound like this? I demand you release me."

"We are acting for the good of Maledin, *Ma'len*," Leibel tells me, grabbing hold of the ropes and pulling me into a sitting position.

"I need to get to Isavelle. She's in danger."

Leibel and Elysant exchange glances but say nothing.

"Do you not care about the fate of the future queen?" I ask.

"Oh, yes. We care very much about the witch's fate." There's a sinister note in Elysant's voice.

I look from spellbreaker to wingrunner. This isn't about me.

"Where is my mate?" I ask quietly.

Neither of them answers.

"I said, where's my fucking mate?" I shout. I don't care about the pain in my ribs. The pain is nothing. I try to get to my feet, but Elysant holds out her hands and the rope glows. Her magic forces me down.

I struggle for several minutes and then give up, panting. "Isavelle is innocent. You can't hurt her. This is unforgivable."

Leibel stands still as stone, his face like granite, while Elysant concentrates on her spell.

"The Ritual of the First Heat. It wasn't only Heloise who wanted Isavelle to die. You two wanted it as well."

Elysant inclines her head, eyes filled with sadness. "Yes, *Ma'len*. It was our plan, and Heloise was going to take the blame, but in the end, she died for nothing. My grief has been unlike anything I have known. I must put things right for her, and for Maledin."

"It would have been easier if the lady had died then," Leibel says dispassionately. "Simpler."

I can't believe what I'm hearing. They're going to murder my mate. "Have you been working for Emmeric this whole time? Did you reveal the location of the ritual so the High Priest could attack Isavelle?"

Elysant's face transforms in disgust. "Work for Emmeric? Never, *Ma'len*. The High Priest must have followed the witch's scent and murdered Heloise to get to her. We are loyal to the Maledinni, more loyal than anyone. We seek to preserve the sanctity of the Maledinni throne for the rightful rulers of this land."

"There are other women," Leibel tells me.

"There are no other women. There is only Isavelle," I seethe.

The two of them exchange grim looks.

"I knew that he would feel this way. *Ma'len* is an Alpha," Elysant says. "You Betas never understand."

"If there can be no other women, then there can be another king," Leibel replies. "We did provide for this inevitability."

"Who is it that covets my throne?" I seethe through my teeth.

Scourge will save Isavelle. He and Esmeral will find my mate and kill anyone who threatens her. They will never forsake their riders. Dragons possess the most loyal of hearts.

"A good and honest man who puts Maledin first," Leibel tells me. Why did I never notice before how cold his eyes are? "A man who feels the correct way about witches. Purge them from this country and end our five-hundred-year persecution by humans once and for all."

"We were not persecuted by witches," I exclaim. "We were defeated by a prince of Maledin and an undead mage."

"We were locked away beneath a mountain so that humans could overrun Maledin. There are more of them here than ever. We are outnumbered, *Ma'len*. While a witch sits on the throne, we must always fear that they will rise up and overthrow us. They have tasted power. They will crave to steal it back, and she will aid them."

"You are raving. Isavelle is not a threat. Her strength is that she is both dragonrider and witch. Have you seen what she has done today? All the people we have been able to rescue because of her."

"More humans," Leibel mutters. "It is convenient that she could not cast this spell while there were still Maledinni to save."

"She did not know how to cast this spell until now," I snarl. "Her own mother and brother were murdered."

"Your mate no doubt allowed them to die along with the rest of the Maledinni. Humans are vermin." Leibel spits on the ground.

"Do not behave so disrespectfully toward *Ma'len*," Elysant chides him. "He's still our king."

"We're right to act now," he mutters. "Any brats that woman bears have the chance of being human."

An echo of Isavelle's scent floats across my mind. Just before she stepped through the portal, I breathed her in, and there was a sweet note of hope blooming from her mating gland. I thought I was smelling her optimism that we would bring her family home, but I suddenly realize what it really was.

The hope in her scent is our first child. The tiny life nestled deep within her. Isavelle is pregnant.

"Let me go," I shout, thrashing from side to side. The ropes bite cruelly into me. I try to inject my voice with my Alpha growl and impel them to do what I say but I can't draw breath into my lungs. "Let me go, right fucking now."

"I know it will be hard for him, but I know *Ma'len* will choose us over that witch once he's finally free of her clutches."

Leibel takes a long look at me. "We will bring you her body and a knife. What you do next is up to you."

"Please stay with us, *Ma'len*," Elysant implores me. "As much as you will wish to follow your mate into death, we need you. You have been a good king, except for choosing her."

My shallow breaths are painful and black spots start to dance before my eyes. Every time I exhale, I feel the bubbling of blood in my throat. I'm trapped. There's no way for me to reach Isavelle. I'm going to lose her and our baby.

"He will kill her quickly, though she does not deserve a quick death," Leibel says, triumph burning in his eyes. "When we approached him with our plan, he asked to be the one who wields the blade. He never liked her from the start. Never trusted her. He spoke so strongly to convince you and Isavelle to take part in the ritual, and she was supposed to die then. You could have mourned her and moved on by now. Or not," he adds with a shrug.

Elysant entreats me with her eyes to understand this madness. "You must see that we have no choice but to do this, *Ma'len*. It would have never worked having Lady Isavelle as queen. Nobody trusts a witch."

37

Isavelle

The fog swirls around us. Shapes are indistinct. A tree here. A narrow path there. There's not enough detail for me to get my bearings.

Anise's face slowly loses its dreamlike expression. "What's going on? Where are we?"

Dad breathes in sharply and looks around. "That's strange. Weren't we in the cottage a moment ago?"

"You're back in Maledin," Dusan tells him.

Dad frowns. "I apologize for my bluntness, soldier, but who are you?"

"We're Lady Isavelle's bodyguards."

"Lady Isavelle?" Anise exclaims and turns to me. "Since when are you Lady Isavelle? I don't recognize these soldiers' uniforms. Was there an invasion or something?"

Anise is joking, and the glimmer of a smile on her lips

fades as I say, "Yes, there was. I'll explain everything later. We have to go."

"We can't go yet," my sister says. "Where's Ma and Waylen? I haven't seen them for so long. Did they already go to the monastery? Will we meet them there?"

"Oh, Anise," I manage before tears spill down my cheeks. "I'm so sorry. They're dead."

I didn't mean to say it like that. I wanted to soften the blow somehow. They don't argue with me, and I wonder if somehow in that dreamlike place, they suspected that something had happened to Ma and Waylen. I look from my sister's panicked face to my father's stricken one. Anise throws her arms around my neck and bursts into tears.

"I couldn't find them in time," I sob, holding on to Anise and looking at Dad. "I didn't know how to save them."

Dad's whole body has stiffened, and what little color there was drains from his cheeks. Fumbling for his daughters, he folds us into his chest and covers his face with his other hand. They both cry against me, Anise's wet, noisy tears, and Dad's dry shuddering.

"I'll tell you everything back at the castle," I promise. "We must move."

"Who was that man chasing us?" Anise asks, pulling away and wiping her tears.

"He's the one who killed Ma and Waylen. He's dangerous and very powerful."

"Is he Brethren?" Dad asks.

I shake my head. "The Brethren are all gone. They were nothing compared to Emmeric and what he can do."

I search the sky overhead for wings. *Esmeral. Where are you?*

No response from my dragon. She must be in the ethereal plane, and I wonder if she went back to find me when I didn't return through the Amriste portal.

Please don't let her cross paths with Emmeric.

"We must reach the others. We need dragons or wyverns so we can get you safely back to the capital. Can anyone see the light from the Amriste portal in the sky?"

"Dragons and wyverns," Dad marvels under his breath. "What a strange land I've returned to."

We all turn on the spot, trying to get our bearings.

"Isavelle, who's that?" Anise asks, and we all turn to look where she's pointing.

"I don't—" But before I finish speaking, a strange sensation rips through me.

I'm suddenly torn away from my family and bodyguards.

I'm looking through the fog, only now I'm all alone. I glimpse five people a short distance away. Two soldiers with halberds. Two villagers. And...

Me?

We're all standing together, just as I left them a moment ago. Anise is still pointing into the fog. I shout for them, but they can't hear me.

I'm in two places at once. This must be a vision.

In the murk, someone or something is moving, and it's not what Anise is pointing at. It's something else.

I don't know how I know it, but whatever it is, it means me harm. They carry a blade. They crave to shed my blood. A shiver goes through me. I wonder if I'm about to watch myself be murdered.

That is if this is even real. Mistress Hawthorne told me how to tell a true vision from a false one. I lift my hand before my eyes and click my fingers. There's a loud, sharp snap. I click the fingers of my other hand with the same result.

This is real. Someone's trying to kill me. Emmeric? But why do I need a vision to know that? It's very obvious that Emmeric is trying to kill me. Frustration flashes through me. Why must my visions always be so—

With a lurch, I'm back in my own body.

"Isavelle? *Isavelle.* Are you all right?" Dad asks me. His hands are gripping my upper arms. "We were calling your name but you wouldn't respond."

I brush his hands away and peer through the fog, hunting for that shadowy figure. "I had a vision. I thought I saw..."

"A vision?" Fiala asks. "What did you see, my lady?"

The shape that Anise was pointing to comes out of the fog. He strides closer and closer and stops five paces from me. His hollow, ravaged expression is so unlike the collected man I've known.

I move protectively in front of Anise. "Is there something you need, Captain Ashton?"

Fiala and Dusan move up beside me, gripping their weapons. This is their captain, but they're protecting me.

"I wanted to ask you something," Ashton says, taking a shuddering breath. His hand clenches on the hilt of his sword, and he fists his hair in the manner of a man despairing. "Why couldn't you save Ravenna? Why still has nothing been done to save her?"

I feel a pang of guilt and sadness. "I want her back more than anything. You and I can talk about it back at the castle, but for now, have you seen Zabriel? Where is he, and where is Scourge?"

There's a frantic shout in the distance and the sound of running feet. "Lady Isavelle!"

I half turn toward the voice. A man is running at full tilt toward us like his life depends on it. I peer through the mist. Is that Godric?

This is all too strange. Something's not right, and I need to get my sister and father back to the safety of the castle immediately. I hunt the skies for Scourge and Esmeral. I wonder if they made it out or if I should make another portal and go back in there.

Before I can do anything, Godric reaches us, panting hard and holding out his hand to me. "Lady Isavelle, you're in great danger. Come with me, quickly. You can't trust him."

I glance at the whey-faced wingrunner, who seems too swamped by misery to be any danger to me. "I can't trust Captain Ashton?"

Godric's eyes flare in alarm. "Not Ashton. Behind you."

The back of my neck prickles, and I feel a looming presence. There's the *schhk* of a sword being unsheathed. Anise screams.

A deep voice growls, "I thought I'd killed you with the ritual, but back you came. Now you have me drawing steel. You have been a thorn in my side from the moment we met."

"Please, Stesha. You don't have to do this."

There's a long silence. Hope flickers in my heart, but then it dies.

"I have no choice. I gave my word."

Thank you for reading The Flame King's Bride. If you enjoyed this book, please consider leaving a review on Amazon and Goodreads.

ACKNOWLEDGMENTS

This book would not have been possible without the love and support of many people. Thank you to Mr. Vincent for always being so proud and encouraging. Thank you to my beta readers Darlene, Edresa, Evva, and Liz Booker, who gave me the motivation to keep going with all their excitement and encouragement. Thank you to my amazing proofreader Rumi Khan. This time I didn't add anything in after you read it, Rumi, I promise! Thank you to my editor Heather Fox. This wouldn't be half as much fun and my books wouldn't be half as good without you.

BOOKS BY LILITH VINCENT

Chloe Chastaine is the alter ego of Lilith Vincent, who writes steamy mafia romance with dark themes, bad men, sweet heroines, and breeding. Please always read the trigger warnings.

Steamy Reverse Harem

THE PROMISED IN BLOOD SERIES (complete)

First Comes Blood

Second Comes War

Third Comes Vengeance

THE PAGEANT DUET (complete)

Pageant

Crowned

Steamy MF Romance

THE BRUTAL HEARTS SERIES (ongoing)

Brutal Intentions

Brutal Conquest

Fear Me, Love Me

ABOUT THE AUTHOR

Chloe Chastaine is the fantasy-loving alter ego of Lilith Vincent and an author of lush novels with OTT obsessed heroes and the strong but sweet heroines who bring them to their knees.